GEORGE ELIOT: AN INTELLECTUAL LIFE

George Eliot:
An Intellectual Life

Valerie A. Dodd

MACMILLAN

First published 1990

Published by
THE MACMILLAN PRESS LTD
Houndmills, Basingstoke, Hampshire RG21 2XS
and London
Companies and representatives
throughout the world

Printed in Hong Kong

British Library Cataloguing in Publication Data
Dodd, Valerie A. 1944–
George Eliot: an intellectual life.
1. Fiction in English. Eliot, George–
Critical studies
I. Title
823'.8
ISBN 0–333–31094–2

For
Peggy Cattell and Juliet McLauchlan
teachers and friends

Contents

Acknowledgements

This book started life as an Oxford thesis and I would like to thank my Oxford supervisors, Rachel Trickett and John Jones, for their help. I also owe a debt of gratitude to the late Catherine Ing.

I have received much help from the staff of the Bodleian Library, as well as those of the English faculty, St Anne's College and the Philosophy faculty. The efforts of the cheerful and efficient staff of Buckinghamshire County Libraries, and especially of the staff of the reference section in Aylesbury, have been much appreciated. I would like to thank Ellen Busby and Margaret Blaine at the Brill branch and Katy Dent in Haddenham. Mr S. H. Barlow, FLA, formerly of Nuneaton library, has been helpful in answering my questions.

Friends and family have helped in many ways too numerous to mention in full. The late Dr Rosemary L. Eakins stimulated my thoughts by discussing with me her work on the Higher Criticism and the Dissenting Academies. Bernadette Swanwick assisted me in the translation of Strauss' Latin preface to *Das Leben Jesu* and Virginia Rushton, who typed an earlier version of this work, made very useful suggestions along the way.

Julia Steward and Frances Arnold, my editors, have offered both encouragement and practical suggestions.

Last in my list, but first in importance, come my parents and those to whom this book is dedicated. My father and mother offered support and tolerance over the years and to offer them my heartfelt thanks is to understate my gratitude. My debt to Juliet McLauchlan and Peggy Cattell is enormous. Their commitment to the subject of English literature, their enthusiasm and humour, along with their continued concern for their former pupils, may find some small memorial in this work. It was promised to them long ago and I hope they will be pleased with some of it.

Valerie Dodd
Brill

Introduction

> every artist, poet or novelist is also a thinker whether he
> chooses or not . . . . The imagination is not a faculty
> working apart; it is the whole mind thrown into the act of
> imagining; and the value of any act of imagination . . .
> will depend on the total strength and total furnishing of
> the mind.[1]

The awareness that George Eliot was an intellectual turned novelist informs most discussions of her life and work. She was exceptionally well-read in philosophy, theology and science; she and her
associates discussed such subjects in conversations, letters, journalism, and their substantial books. She has thus been lauded as a sage
articulating universal truths; her imagination has been seen to
operate in terms of a conflict between intellect and emotions; her
novels have been analysed as vehicles for the discussion of philosophical ideas.

To all three views, objections present themselves. The enigmatic
quality associated with oracular utterance endows the speaker
with a mysterious quality: George Eliot, because of her retiring
personality, and Lewes, because of his protective attitude towards
her, contrived, wittingly or otherwise, to promote the image of
remote prophetess. F. W. H. Myers described the voice which
'seemed to environ her uttered words with the mystery of a world
of feeling that must remain untold'; Oscar Browning hung her
portrait over his desk in Cambridge, and confessed, 'scarcely a day
passes that I do not seek to draw from it some portion of that
spiritual strength for which I am so deeply indebted to her during
my life.'[2] Mrs Linton, contrastingly, commented acidly that for
many literary women, 'the echo of their fame filled their own ears
with overpowering music, and translated their humanity into
something half divine': George Eliot, she thought, posed as a sybil,
never forgetting a 'self-created Self'.[3] Many thinkers in the latter
half of the nineteenth century possessed a melancholy consciousness of inner confusion. Europe was enduring the 'night of the
Brocksberg'[4] and 'nearly all our powerful men in this age of the
world are unbelievers; the best of them in doubt and misery; the

1

worst in reckless defiance; the plurality, in plodding hesitation.'[5]
Anguished unbelief prompted the search for prophets and ironically, it was often writers racked with scepticism who were reverenced as seers. Novelists saw themselves as prophets;[6] in 1878,
George Eliot conceded 'every writer was *ipso facto* a teacher'.[7]
George Eliot became the luminary of the Priory, Carlyle assumed
the role of the sage of Chelsea, and J. S. Mill mourned his wife
Harriet's death in his guise of the saint of Avignon. Something may
be gleaned of George Eliot's personality, and of the intellectual
atmosphere from this. As translator and journalist, as well as
novelist, she manifested an articulate seriousness of intent. Walter
Bagehot, confined to bed in 1870, asked for 'something to read
from Smith's Library; but not George Eliot – that, he said, was
work'. Trollope found her novels difficult reading, and her ever-
tactful publisher, John Blackwood, said to her of *Adam Bede*, 'I am
required to give my mind to it, and I trembled for that large section
of hard readers who have no mind to give.'[8] Her novels were not
seen primarily as entertainment. But the view of the writer as
mentor to a troubled age was a widespread phenomenon, and the
assigning of such a role to George Eliot fails to illuminate the
idiosyncratic nature of her development into a novelist.

The analysis of her imagination in terms of conflicting emotional
and cerebral tendencies is also unsatisfactory. It stems partly from
the pinpointing of an important difference between George Eliot
and contemporary novelists such as Thackeray, Dickens, Mrs
Gaskell and the Brontës. One important function of the Victorian
novel was to provide a 'critique of the philosophers'[9] via its sustained scrutiny of the social implications of Benthamism and capitalism, and its onslaught on dogmatism. George Eliot's
contemporaries, however, patently hewed their novels from the
raw materials of experience and observation. Whilst George Eliot
drew upon similar sources of inspiration, she also brought to
fiction an absorbing, lifelong interest in theology, philosophy and
science. Notebooks record her philosophical studies and omnivorous reading.[10] In the eyes of her friends, Oscar Browning and
Frederic Harrison, this set her apart.[11] After her death, her name
was bracketed with those of Newman, Carlyle and Ruskin; her
superior mental culture was remarked upon then, and has mer-
ited comment ever since.[12] Her intellectuality has suggested that,
given the vital connection seen to exist between experience and
creation, particularly in the work of female writers, George Eliot's

work must manifest a tension between a positive source of inspiration in emotion and observation, and a negative creative impetus, stemming from her fascination with ideas.[13]

George Eliot's failure to conform to nineteenth-century ideals of womanhood is seen to intensify this conflict between the emotional and cerebral tendencies of her imagination. It is implied that, in an age when women were seen as emotional and weaker beings, she must have had ambivalent feelings about her character and life. George Eliot had a will of her own, and mocked female passivity. But middle-class women were brought up 'on the old lines of childish effacement and womanly self-suppression'; they were told that their nature was 'to live for others', to make 'complete abnegation of themselves'.[14] Women, wrote Ruskin, should be educated to become the passive moral and emotional centre of the home.[15] George Eliot was a spinster, a situation which she did not see as unbearable, and then a mistress. Yet spinsters were a 'kind of execrescence on the surface of society'; marriage was woman's destiny.[16] In *Mary* and *The Wrongs of Woman*, Mary Wollstonecraft demonstrated how women's freedom was curtailed by their economic dependence upon men; the law assigned women no property rights and society offered them little chance of making a living. A timid conformity was the norm. 'Respect for the opinion of the world, has . . . been termed the principal duty of woman'; the inculcation of 'social conformity' was one of the aims even of a bold educational experiment such as Queen's College, founded in 1848.[17] George Eliot lived alone in London and Geneva; she earned her own living; her liaison with Lewes shocked many.

The education most women received reinforced these norms. Intellect was regarded as unfeminine. Middle-class women, like Rosamond Vincy, were taught those useless 'accomplishments' which Maria Edgeworth attacked in *Practical Education* (1798). Rousseau urged, in the influential *Emile*, 'do not turn your young women into theologians or logicians'; the implementation of Hannah More's ideas on women's education would produce, 'The hoyden, the huntress, the bold heroine', and 'masculine manners' would become 'all the rage'.[18] The literary heroine with 'thinking powers' was unusual, and intelligent women were difficult.[19] Such views were held even by the young Lewes, who was later to abandon the myopia which led him to write lengthily and sentimentally about women's emotionality in *Ranthorpe* (1847).[20] Herbert Spencer, at times, saw George Eliot's intellect as a masculine quality, as abnormal and damaging, as did Mathilde Blind, one of her early biographers.[21] The Tennysonian view, 'Man with the head and woman with the heart', even found medical sanction, for in 1868, *The Lancet* pontificated, 'any woman who is logical, philosophical, scientific departs from the normal woman in her physical as well as her mental characteristics'.[22]

To note George Eliot's deviation from social norms is one thing: to see such deviation as producing in her a sense of conflict is another.[23] For much of her life, she was blessed with friends, and in Lewes with a lover, who fostered and ratified by their own actions her unorthodoxy. If she did sense, at times, conflict between her equally demanding emotional and intellectual appetites, this does not automatically presuppose that this personal conflict would influence the themes of her novels, nor the mode of perception they articulate. Whilst art may mirror personal conflict, it may also transcend it, even operate in relation to a serenity of apprehension which the turmoil of our feelings and actions can rarely and inadequately reflect. Terminology appropriate to the description of psychology cannot always be translated into the realm of aesthetics. That George Eliot's creations have 'something of the life-like complexity of Shakespeare's', argues her capacity to rise above personal concerns.[24] Literary notions suggesting that writers must find inspiration in the known and the felt, social norms proposing female emotionalism and conservatism, these have helped to relegate George Eliot's intellectuality to the category of etiolating influence. J. W. Cross's biography, with his idealised picture of a sensitive soul who also read endless heavy tomes, and with his editing out of her sexual indiscretions and her sense of humour, both equally heinous to her mourning widower, was rightly seen by Gladstone as 'a Reticence – in three volumes'.[25] Yet Cross's portraiture set an influential precedent. George Eliot as oracle, or as writer and woman torn between the claims of head and heart have become time-hallowed icons.[26] The concepts of 'head' and 'heart' have been applied differently from one critic to another, providing key terms in critical analysis, and yardsticks of evaluation.[27]

The approach which relates George Eliot's life and work to the philosophical movements of her age is comparatively recent, although her contact with the English admirers of Comte was the subject of much speculation during her lifetime.[28] Yet if seeing her novels as valuable in their spontaneous reworking of personal

recollections was a partial view, so is the fashion for seeing Deronda or Ladislaw as concepts made flesh.[29] Her vision was more
muddled, and also more complete. To prove points about intellectual and emotional tendencies, which are assumed to be dichot-
omous, leads to the ignoring of the artistic logic of an autonomous
creation. Acclamation of the rich vision of life at Dorlcote Mill, or in
Middlemarch, must have regard to George Eliot's growing up in
the Midlands, but also to the careful research which underpinned
her descriptions. The George Eliot who was startled by the gipsy as
a child, also went to inspect mills before she wrote *The Mill on the
Floss*,[30] the novelist who could draw upon her childhood memories
of election riots also diligently took notes on the history in England
in the 1820s when preparing to write *Middlemarch*.[31] Like Scott, her
lifelong idol, she saw accurate facts as an aid to the unavoidable
limits of the imagination.[32] When reading George Eliot at her best,
the so-called intellectual and emotional tendencies are separable,
but not, ultimately, separate. On a structural level, seeming spon-
taneity and intellectual control also coexist. She patterned narrative, via imagery, via paralleled and contrasted episodes, but she
also, at will, relaxed control over her material. In *Adam Bede*, she
drew attention to the change in Adam's and Dinah's relationship
by reiterated title to Chapter 11 and 50, but in Book 4, she worked
on a simpler, suspenseful narrative principle, as she took the
reader from the meeting of Arthur and Hetty in the wood, to Hetty's
fear that she was pregnant. To focus solely upon the presence of
intellect in the novels, whether it be seen as the source of characters who are embodied concepts, as prompting an erudite, quasi-
archaeological tendency, or as the force which leads to authorial
patterning of material, oversimplifies the experience of reading the
novels, and the way in which they were written.

If her novels are intellectual they are so in a complicated fashion.
In the 1840s, when she was seriously thinking of writing a novel,
she witnessed the evolution of George Sand's views on the novel's
relationship to philosophy, and she accounted George Sand an
important influence on her thought.[33] More centrally, Marian
Evans formulated, before she turned to fiction, a definition of art
rooted in a larger attempt to define knowledge itself, both its
processes and the objects of its concern. In this respect, the very
genesis of her decision to write fiction was philosophical. In defining knowledge, she drew upon the works of philosophers, and she
shared the strenuousness of their endeavour. Perhaps even more

to the point, as regards her turning to the novel, she found in the philosophers she read an increasing scepticism about the value of philosophy.

Henry James's reflection upon the mystery of the process whereby George Eliot produced 'rich, deep, masterly pictures of the multifold life of man' thus poses a question worth asking.[34] The reverential scepticism which James's remark suggests is the striking quality of her vision, is a mode of perception to which her reading of philosophers habituated her. It developed out of the debate between the empirical and intuitionist logics, which Marian Evans first encountered in her days of solitary reading at Griff. On 27 October 1840, she first referred directly to her interest in Carlyle, although she may have read his work as early as the mid-1830s. She was reading Coleridge in 1841 at Foleshill. The Rosehill circle, which she entered in November 1841, introduced her to a reassessment of empiricism; she read Charles Bray's *The Philosophy of Necessity* (1841) and discussed Mill's *A System of Logic* (1843) with John Sibree.[35] 1840 was a key date in Marian Evans's development, but it marked not only a turning-point for her, but also for Mill and Carlyle, for in 1840 they both reached significant stages in their developments of the philosophical tradition they exemplified. This was to be crucially important.

Part One
The Philosophical Debate in England

1

Intuition and Experience

> logic . . . instructs us in fallacies as often as the imagina-
> tion teaches us errors. It is because of this that observation
> is such a lengthy process and the imitation of life such a
> difficult task.[1]

The philosophical debate George Eliot encountered originated in
the eighteenth century, for, after David Hume's death in 1776,
there seemed to be a choice between 'profundity with a certain
amount of madness, or sanity coupled with or based on
superficiality'.[2] The mutual hostility of the schools of Intuition and
Experience was 'full of practical consequences' which lay 'at the
foundation of all the greatest differences of practical opinion'.[3] The
Scottish school of Intuition centred upon Sir William Hamilton,
whose views J. S. Mill attacked in 1865. Following Thomas Reid,
Dugald Stewart, and Thomas Brown, Hamilton offered a critique
of Hume.[4] The Scottish philosophers saw mind as an active force,
able to apprehend directly an external reality which had an independent existence. Despite an affinity to Idealism, these thinkers
attacked the German metaphysics from the standpoint of near-
ignorance. Stewart and Brown condemned Kant, although Hamilton's references to the Germans stimulated a wider interest in
them.[5]

The German philosophy was slow to make headway in England.[6] Commentaries on, and translation of, Kant appeared in the
1790s, but the first major translation of Hegel did not come until
1855 with H. Sloman and J. Wallon's *The Subjective Logic of Hegel*.
There were isolated attempts to popularise German aesthetics,
which was linked to Idealism: translations of F. W. von Schlegel's
works were published in 1815, and Sarah Austin, J. S. Mill's friend,
translated similar works which started to find a market in the
1830s.[7] Mme. de Staël's *De L'Allemagne* was rendered into English
in 1813, and Volume III dicussed Kant, Fichte, Schelling and F. W.
von Schlegel, and considered the influence of Idealism on science,
the arts and moral questions. Prejudice against foreign ideas long

persisted, manifesting itself in Thackeray's *The Paris Sketch Book*
(1840) and shocking Hippolyte Taine in the 1860s.[8] To the innate
insularity and conservatism of the English mind,[9] political factors
gave sanction. Germany had little international prestige: England
was at war with France from 1735 to 1815, and then followed the
domestic unrest of the agricultural riots of 1825, the ostensibly
pre-revolutionary agitation for the 1832 Reform Bill, and the rise of
Chartism. French ideas were seen as a political threat.[10] The brutali-
ties of the 1789 Revolution were attributed to the influence of the
Encyclopaedists; the Terror haunted the imagination of many
writers who had entertained progressive ideas, surfacing in works
as diverse as Carlyle's *French Revolution* (1837), Wordsworth's
Prelude (1850) and Dickens's *Tale of Two Cities* (1859). Modern languages were rarely taught in English schools, although Dissenting
Academics and Scottish universities employed a less hidebound
curriculum. In 1855, Mark Pattison found in Oxford a faction,
'whose term of abuse is "German" and yet have less than a child's
knowledge of the nature of German institutions.'[11]

It fell to Coleridge, whose works Marian Evans first read in 1841,
to be the most prominent and idiosyncratic pioneer of Idealism.
Coleridge proposed his childhood love for fairy-tales as the reason
why his mind was 'habituated *to the Vast,* – & I never regarded *my
senses* in any way as the criteria of my belief. I regulated all my
creeds by my conceptions, not by my *sight'.*[12] Fascination with
ideas and mysticism characterised him as a schoolboy; at Cambridge, Unitarianism showed him the possibility of reconciling
Christianity and scientism.[13] By 1801, he was reading Kant. At the
heart of Coleridge's work existed a distinction between two modes
of perception which was to dominate much of the nineteenth-
century philosophical debate. In a note Coleridge added to *The
Statesman's Manual* in 1827, he reflected, 'It is! – is a sense of reason:
the senses can only say – It seems!';[14] to him, this evaluative and
descriptive contrast imaged the history of western thought. It was
'the highest *problem* of philosophy'[15] and pervaded his discussion
of associationism and dualism in Chapters 5–9 of *Biographia Literaria.* Yet Coleridge yearned to reconcile the warring philosophies,
noting that sensation was 'but vision nascent',[16] seeing Locke as
half-true.[17] He found a synthesis of the opposites represented by
empiricism and intuitionism as sensation and vision, objective and
subjective, head and heart, in his ideals, in Christianity, in art, in
Kant's *Reason and Understanding.*[18] He also found it in the optimum philosophical process, which would 'intellectually separ-

ate . . . distinguishable parts' and 'restore them in our conceptions to the unity, in which they actually co-exist'.[19] Coleridge was
not merely a propagandist for Idealism or a critic of empiricism; he
advocated a widened, definitive philosophy.[20] He asserted the
importance of philosophical thinkers and wished to merge all
systems into an irrefutably true synthesis.[21] He was arguably the
first nineteenth-century eclectic *par excellence*.

Coleridge also asserted the relevance of philosophy to life, insisting
that it must have 'in its first principles . . . a practical and moral, as
well as a theoretical or speculative side'.[22] In *Biographia Literaria*, he
defended Christianity; in *Confessions of an Inquiring Spirit*, he re-
explained Biblical infallibility; in the *Lay Sermons*, he suggested a
new way of assessing the merit of political institutions.[23] Coleridge's
writings also attested how he sought in synthesis consolation for
his own psychological turmoil. His poetry, with its anguished
description of self-division, exposure and isolation, shows a pierc-
ingly alert contemplation of his inadequacy. Intellect threatened
happiness and vitiated vision; the outpourings of his verse were
echoed, sometimes almost verbatim, in his prose musings.[24] Non-
empirical philosophy kept the heart alive: Idealism gave play to
both thought and feeling, and satisfied that tendency Coleridge
spoke of in 1796; 'I feel strongly, and I think strongly; but I seldom
feel without thinking, or think without feeling'.[25]

Obscurity was a charge levelled against Coleridge by Leigh
Hunt, Byron and De Quincey,[26] and Coleridge did fail to produce
the systematic exposition of Idealism he aspired to provide.[27] But it
was his proclamation of the relevance of Idealism to public issues
and to his own inner tumult which drew attention to the fact that
empiricism was neither asking, nor answering, the right questions.
For Coleridge, philosophy was bound up with the problems of
society and the individual. Moreover, in his attempt to synthesise
logical methods, he manifested that concern for the process of
knowledge which was to characterise speculation in the nineteenth
century.[28] In both of these respects, his work had profound implications for later writers, including Marian Evans.

The empirical school helped inspire the work of Marian Evans's
friend, Charles Bray. It was made up of Jeremy Bentham and his
followers, and exerted an influence out of proportion to its
numbers.[29] Bentham, who was a semi-recluse, did little to dissemi-
nate his views; his works only became readily available with the
publication of the incomplete Bowring edition between 1838 and
1843. However, he attracted disciples; Lord Shelburne sought him

out in 1781, and, in 1788, began his friendship with Samuel Romilly, who expounded Benthamite theories in Parliament. In 1804, the *Edinburgh Review* paid attention to Pierre Dumont's *Traité de Législation* (1802) which mingled translation and exposition of Bentham's writings on jurisprudence, and in 1807, the same periodical praised his theory of law. In 1808, Bentham met James Mill who was to devote much of his life to spreading Bentham's views, writing on them in the *Encyclopaedia Britannica* between 1816 and 1823, and founding the Political Economy Club. In 1824, James Mill purchased the *Westminster Review* which became the voice of the Radical Party, which sent nearly sixty members to the first Reformed Parliament. John Stuart Mill and Carlyle were to ponder the value of Radicalism; Marian Evans, in the 1850s, was to edit the *Westminster Review*.

Benthamism had a slender claim to originality, owing much to Locke, Newton and Hume, to Gay's *Dissertation concerning the Principle and Criterion of Virtue and the Origin of the Passions* (1730) and to Hartley's *Observations on Man, his Fame, his Duty and his Expectations* (1749) as regards the theory of association. Paley's *Principles of Moral and Political Economy* (1785) had applied the test of utility to morals and theology. Bentham also introduced into England the ideas of Helvétius, who had expounded legislative theory in relation to the notion of utility in *De L'Esprit* (1758); he corresponded with D'Alembert and Abbé Morellet. Bentham, like Coleridge, placed a description of mind at the centre of his philosophy, but, unlike Coleridge, he emphasised the mind's passivity as a recipient of sensations. Abstract ideas were built up from the convergence of sensations; moral principles were formed by the association of certain acts with plain or pleasure. The mind's powers were limited: 'All events seem entirely loose and separate. One event follows another, but we can never observe any tie between them. They seem *conjoined*, but never *connected*'.[30] Knowledge was slowly accumulated. Like Coleridge, the Benthamites applied their philosophical principles in the fields of private and public activity. Spurred on by his painful childhood experience of the courts,[31] Bentham concerned himself with law, and designed, in 1793, his model prison, the Panopticon. If the mind was passive, the influences of environment and education upon the individual were crucial. Benthamites campaigned for non-sectarian education and applied the test of utility to Christianity. Bentham wrote *Cresthomathia* (1816), a treatise on education, and contributed ma-

terial to Grote's pseudonymous *Analysis of Natural Religion* (1822).
James Mill suggested churches should become educational and
political centres.

The limitations of the Benthamites were obvious. Despite their
noisy claims to scientific method, important notions were merely
asserted, but not established by deductive analysis. They posited
an average sensibility in the pain/pleasure psychology; they
echoed eighteenth-century notions of egoism and benevolence,
and assumed the truth of the notions of utility and inevitable
progress. The psychological theory overlooked the fact that pleasures vary in quality, that the same experience was not equally
pleasurable to all. James Mill scorned 'the great stress laid on
feeling' as 'an aberration of the moral standard of modern times'.[32]
The early Benthamites resisted the psychological and philosophical
insights afforded by both European Romanticism and the English
Protestant renaissance, which showed themselves in Tractarian-
ism, Evangelicalism and Methodism. Literature was considered
unimportant.[33] An ideal of clarity in expression provided 'the best
notation for describing a fragment of the Universe that is within
the Human Intellect's grasp. But the poetic usage is the best for
reconnoitring this foreground's mysterious hinterland.'[34]

J. S. Mill, Carlyle and Marian Evans were not alone in detecting
weaknesses in Benthamism. Dickens, Matthew Arnold and others
caricatured the Benthamites for forensic effect, and ignored their
successes. Legal reforms came in the 1820s and 1830 from Brougham's efforts; Francis Place helped revise the Conspiracy Laws in
1824. The movement gave intellectual substance, and a degree of
middle-class respectability to the clamour for social change which
marked the first half of the century. A philosophy of reform, not
revolution, was a stabilising force when cataclysm seemed immi-
nent, even if the Benthamites were able to be moderate because
they, unlike working-class agitators, had little direct experience of
the seemingly insoluble problem of poverty.[35] The early Benthamites part-created, part-embodied, that very English mentality
which 'feels no need to start building itself a moral and intellectual
dwelling from the ground up'.[36] By steering a middle course, both
politically and philosophically, they attracted hostility from all
sides, from Tories, Whigs, and Socialists such as Thomas Spence,
Charles Hall and Robert Owen.

Although J. S. Mill saw a stark opposition between the schools of
Intuitionism and Associationism, his distinction overlooked their

similarities. Neither school advocated social revolution. Coleridge sought to reconcile scientific and intuitive modes of perception: the Benthamites claimed to operate a deductive method, but assumed the existence of certain truths. Both schools were fighting the conflict Coleridge described as being between Aristotelianism and Platonism,[37] and the definition of the process of knowing was central to the efforts of both. The school of Experience was also convinced, as Coleridge was, of the important implications speculation had for human experience. Coleridge would have assented to Bentham's observation that there is 'a very dry . . . branch of art and science, denominated *Logic*: – upon it . . . hangs life and everything else that man holds dear to him'.[38] This axiom was not to be disputed by the inheritors of the incipiently eclectic traditions established by Coleridge and the early Benthamites. John Stuart Mill, Thomas Carlyle, and Marian Evans were to look at the question of the process, scope and purpose of knowledge in ways which owed much to, but differed radically from, their predecessors.

2
Mill and Carlyle to 1828

Whereas ancient philosophy chiefly investigated the nature of Being, modern philosophy has more and more concentrated . . . upon the nature of Knowing.[1]

I

By the early nineteenth century, applied eclecticism had taken root in philosophy: the question of perception, which determined how men viewed, and acted in, the world, had shifted to the centre of the speculative discussion. As Hippolyte Taine later remarked despairingly, 'You have learned men, but there are no thinkers amongst them'.[2] In 1837, Carlyle's *History of the French Revolution* propounded a theory of perception which took as its starting-point Carlyle's antagonistic reaction to enlightenment philosophy, and its historical manifestation rational revolutionism, and this theory had important implications regarding the function of literature. For Mill, 1840 marked the end of his 'mental changes'.[3] And in the early 1840s, Marian Evans encountered the works of Mill and Carlyle.

Early in their careers, Mill and Carlyle became dissatisfied with Benthamism, and, ultimately, with all doctrinaire systems. Although ostensibly attacking empiricism from opposite standpoints, both wished, firstly, to break through the sterility of the debate between Associationism and Intuitionism, and to forge a new theory of perception, in which reason and intuition, intellect and emotions, merged. Secondly, both wished to anchor philosophical speculation even more firmly in the issues of life, for they recoiled, as their parents had done, from the inert abstractions of conceptual thought.[4] They sought out, and championed, writers who avoided the bloodlessness of earlier speculation; they supported political causes. They responded with acute sensitivity to the social atmosphere in terms of their philosophical preoccupations. Not only did their thinking attempt to illuminate contemporary reality; historical events, and their own contexts, endowed

15

their thought with urgency. Marian Evans' intellectual odyssey often echoed this pattern.

Emerson and Taine were struck by this English tendency to scepticism and pragmatism in the face of theory.[5] Yet although Mill, Carlyle and Marian Evans were sceptical of theory, they were also sometimes seduced by it. Nor did they dismiss intellect: rather, they attempted to effect vital unions whereby knowledge illuminated life, reality ratified concepts. Dissatisfaction with rationalism led them to stake out larger claims for the mind; their stand against reason posited the absorption of empiricism into a greater whole. They wished to claim more, not less, for the powers of perception.

In her contact with Idealism and the attack upon Benthamism by a second generation of empiricists, Marian Evans can be seen working within a philosophical tradition in which perception availed itself of both rational and emotional capacities; this tradition also prompted questions about human existence and learnt from non-philosophical sources. In this sense, the influence of Mill and Carlyle upon her evaluation of philosophy was pervasive. Contact with this tradition also directed her to specific writers Mill and Carlyle found illuminating, and who operated within the same field of eclectic and pragmatic endeavour, such as Saint-Simon and Comte. She was also drawn to literary works by writers like George Sand and J. A. Froude, which existed in a vital, but often adversarial, relationship to philosophy.

Every intellectual progress is individual and complex. Mill and Carlyle were not the sole influences upon Marian Evan's development in the years before she wrote her novels; her reception of their work was conditioned by her other reading of other writers, and Mill's and Carlyle's stand against dogmatism and abstraction directed her towards works which modified their positions. Suggestions of mental affinities should not obscure differences: if all three writers may be designated *philosophes*, Mill is also rightly termed a philosopher, George Eliot a novelist, and Carlyle a social and literary critic, historian and biographer. The reading of philosophy alone did not lead Marian Evans to the novel: that she was a thinker is without dispute, but the story of how she came to write novels cannot be simply the story of her thought. Yet her nervous desire to write fiction was strengthened by, for instance, the quasi-philosophical theory of the novel expounded by Lewes in the late 1840s and 1850s, and by Comtist-inspired articles in the

Westminster Review on the important function fiction might perform. In their criticism of speculation divorced from life, in their distrust of dogmatic modes of perception, a position both were articulating by 1840, Mill and Carlyle announced the incompleteness, and heralded the obsolescence of, the form of thought known as philosophy. They often proposed the superior value of literature, and this view was echoed by the writers Marian Evans read. The novel was, for George Eliot, the most fluid genre available in which to embody a new, enlarged mode of perception, in which to contemplate the relevance of concepts to life.[6] In 1856, when Marian Evans settled down to write *Scenes of Clerical Life*, her action tacitly acknowledged the rightness of the conclusions reached by Mill and Carlyle, who questioned the value of speculation as activity, and of any single logical system as an entrance into the realms of truth.

II

The intellectual journeys by which Mill and Carlyle reached their 1840 position were complex and painful. By 1828, both writers had reached turning-points, and became temporarily enthusiastic about Saint-Simonianism, which also attracted Marian Evans's attention when she found references to it in *Chartism* (1840) and *The Philosophy of Necessity* (1841). In this early period, the psychological crises of Mill and Carlyle were enacted and defined, as Coleridge's had been, in relation to the debate between Associationism and Intuitionism, but these crises were also conditioned by their respective personal and cultural circumstances. The problems of logic were entrenched in the problems of life.

For Carlyle, the years before he settled in London were restless and solitary. After being educated at Annan Academy and entering the University of Edinburgh in 1810, he soon abandoned divinity for law; in 1822, he became tutor to the Buller children. In 1824, he met Coleridge in London, and scientists and mathematicians like Legendre and Laplace in France. In 1825 he returned to Scotland, married Jane Welsh in 1826, and, in 1827, settled at the bleak remote farmhouse of Craigenputtock, Galloway, where he remained until 1834. Carlyle had been reared within a sect known as the Burghers, and noted in 1866 that Dissent attracted the man who 'awoke to the belief that he actually had a soul to be saved'.[7]

This intense awareness of a spiritual dimension and ethical obligation remained with him all his life. He was conversant, from an
early stage, with the rival philosophies of empiricism and intuitionism. In Edinburgh, he was drawn to Thomas Brown's ideas as
an alternative to empiricism, and as vindication of the ethical
emphasis of his childhood religion.[8] Edinburgh was alive with talk
of the German philosophy, and German was taught in the Scottish
educational system. The Scottish capital was enjoying an intellectual revival; from that city, B. G. Niebuhr wrote that Kant was
discussed at a lunch he attended.[9] In 1816, Carlyle read Coleridge's
works and Dugald Stewart's attack on Kant in the *Encyclopaedia
Britannica*. By 1819 he was speaking of his German studies as being
of long-standing. In the same year, he also read D'Alembert,
Diderot and Voltaire. At Annan Academy, where he was now
teaching, mathematics was a speciality, and Carlyle worked hard
at natural sciences.[10]

By 1818, Carlyle was doubting the Bible's historical accuracy, its
interpretation of life, and capacity to guide conduct.[11] His descriptions of a sudden 'conversion', in June 1821, dramatised a gradual
process, for his reading of determinist works overlapped with his
perusal of the German writers who helped him re-establish his
faith on a new basis. For Carlyle, as for Coleridge, empirical
doctrines had agonising personal implications. Carlyle's despairing vision of the world as 'one huge, dead, immeasurable Steam-
Engine, rolling on, in its dead indifference, to grind me limb from
limb',[12] seized upon the sombre applications of a logical method
which pictured a world governed by an endless sequence of cause
and effect, which the mind could observe, but whose nature it
could never comprehend. This mechanistic universe possessed no
spiritual dimension; a merely observable chain of cause and effect
argued a limitation in the powers of human perception. The
exertion, even the existence, of human will seemed impossible in a
determined universe; without God, there was no sanction for
morality. The mind, forming ideas from the passive reception of
sensations, was but a microcosm of a universe governed by
necessity. Yet, asserted Carlyle, although his 'eyes' (that mode of
perception which operated in terms of Benthamite logic) could not
see God, 'in my heart, He was present, and His heaven-written
laws stood legible and sacred there': thus, 'living without God in
the world, of God's light I was not utterly bereft'.[13] He reaffirmed
man's spirituality on a new basis, and respect for his parents'

Christianity remained for the rest of his life, even if they would not have understood the terminology in which he expressed his religiosity.[14]

After 1821, his contact with determinism continued, with the translation of Legendre in 1821, but from 1824 to 1825 after meetings with Coleridge and Hamilton, he turned his attention to Kant.[15] For the 1825 edition of *The Life of Friedrich Schiller*, he wrote sections on Kant, and tried, unsuccessfully, to calm his nerves before his wedding by reading *Critique of Pure Reason*.[16] He approached Idealism via German literature, which was to be his main interest after 1821. He responded enthusiastically to the view that 'the truths of philosophy have some application to Munich and Berlin', and to German literature's concern with philosophical problems which were 'not those of the most purely theoretical interest', but, 'the great practical problems of life'.[17] By 1824, he had the monopoly of the field, and was working in an atmosphere of spiritual calm. Sectarian philosophies, mathematics and intellectual activity had failed to provide Carlyle with an adequate 'theory of man; a system of metaphysics, not for talk, but for adoption and belief', but Kant's vindication, as Carlyle saw it, of a vision of a material universe interpenetrated with spirit, fraught with ethical obligations, ratified his early Christian beliefs.[18]

Carlyle's propaganda for German literature during this period focused upon the issue of perception, although, a critical, anti-dogmatic note sometimes surfaced. He pleaded the importance of German literature which incorporated reference to Idealism, yet also assessed its weaknesses, most notably in 'State of German Literature' (1827). He saw the critic as explicator of the prophetic tendency in literature, as one who applied principles 'deduced patiently . . . from the highest and calmest regions of Philosophy';[19] he identified with, and shared, the artist's heightened perception. Carlyle showed little concern for, or understanding of, the technicalities of Idealist logic, but praised its suggestion of a new way of seeing the world, its capacity to 'open the inward eye to the sight of this Primitively True . . . to clear off the Obscurations of Sense', its seeking of truth, 'by intuition, in the deepest and purest nature of man'.[20] Dissent gave Carlyle intense awareness of a complex reality and ethical certainty; he saw the intuition of Idealism as likewise implying a unity of consciousness, which endowed the world with the wholeness of its vision, which was a counterpart of an integrated reality.[21]

In this psychological idealism, there was implicit criticism of the Benthamite view of world and mind, whose reverberations had caused Carlyle such inner turmoil. German literature allowed Carlyle to claim much for the powers of human vision, whereas in both Associationism and the Scottish school, there was 'a fundamental distrust in the power of human thought'.[22] The imaginative acts of the Germans reconciled observed and felt truth, and revealed the 'contradiction and perplexity', but also the 'secret significance' and beauty of the age.[23] Their works, like Christianity, wove together intellect and moral feelings, combined descriptive and didactic functions. Carlyle was 'endlessly indebted' to Goethe for the resolution of his spiritual crisis in the 1820s, but also found comfort in the ethical idealism of Ludwig Tieck and Richter, who reverenced the beauty of the actual.[24] In literary articles, Benthamite notions were criticised, and German philosophy praised, save when it descended to obscurity, abstraction and theorising, when, it might be argued, it was most obviously like philosophy.[25] Literature, it was implied, was saved from such defects, because it dealt with character and event, and thus might express a mode of perception more effectively than the philosophy which supplied that perception's theoretical basis. Carlyle's exaltation of literary perception was to have a profound influence upon his admirers, Marian Evans and George Lewes. Carlyle emulated the mode of perception he found in the German writers. In 'Burns' (1828) he saw character as a 'living unity', commented that the artist must discern the ideal in the actual, and insisted, 'It is not the dark *place* that hinders, but the dim *eye*'. Poets might be seers.[26]

To Carlyle, the applications of Idealism were more important than the actual philosophy. The German resolution of the problem of perception had important personal implications. He reflected that psychological emancipation came with a realisation that man might triumph over necessity.[27] At Hoddam Hill, the remote Solway farmhouse where he settled in 1825, Carlyle thought that he won, with Goethe's help, 'an immense victory', in going beyond an obsessive concern with sectarian philosophical debate. Art became a means to psychological health.[28] The German Enlightenment, unlike the French, had not vehemently opposed Christianity; art was assigned 'a central part to play in the realization of human nature, in the fulfilment of man' and, by the 1770s, had taken on, 'a function analogous to religion . . . to some extent replacing it'.[29] Carlyle came to believe that literature, when informed by Idealism, could, like Christianity but unlike empiricism, interpret, console and teach. Yet the seeming change masks thinly a continuity in his mental cast. His emphasis upon the spiritual dimension in reality, and his stern moralism, show not only that he read Kant, but that he remained true to his origins in Scottish working-class Dissent.[30] Idealism and Dissent vindicate each other in an unlikely, but fruitful, reciprocity: the German critique of rationalism is ratified by the inner experience of the son of a Burgher and a peasant.

III

Ideologically, John Stuart Mill was, like Carlyle, his father's son. But whereas early Benthamism contained its paradoxes, Mill confronted them, and attempted a reconciliation of logical methods, so that, 'in an age of eclectics he has considerable claim to be regarded as the arch-eclectic'.[31] He was soon familiar with the Benthamite argument that 'speculative philosophy' is 'in reality the thing which most influences' men, and which 'in the long run overbears every other influence save those which it must itself obey'.[32] In Mill's early years, the philosophical debate was bound up, as it had been for Coleridge and Carlyle, as much with his own psychological survival as with the fate of humanity. The speculative tendency of Benthamism, and his 1826 crisis, raised for him questions about feeling and individuality which were often not congruent with his efforts for the cause of reform. The crisis led him to re-evaluate the associationist doctrines which caused it: he deemed Benthamite psychology inadequate, for it made 'the complex motives of humanity appear simple'.[33]

Mill's formal education ended at the age of fourteen, and possessed elements which encouraged anti-Benthamite tendencies. It was based on the theory that 'Anything which could be found out by thinking, I was never told.' Yet the training was sectarian, for James Mill explained the significance of the material his son memorised, often in the light of utilitarian principles. John Mill studied Benthamite topics, such as mathematics, political economy and logic, and considered logic an invaluable discipline. The scheme was not, however, illiberal: he wrote history for his own amusement, and chose his own topics for verse composition. Although he contended that Benthamism undervalued poetry, feeling and imagination as elements of human nature, Mill read Aesop, Homer, Scott, Spenser, Dryden and Cowper, and his father borrowed novels for him. Although Mill insisted he never had any religious belief, his father's agnoticism did not emerge until 1816: he discussed religion with his child, and had him read religious histories. Mill also admitted to the disturbing influence of his father's personality, which was, paradoxically, energetic yet stoical, unemotional yet pessimistic; James Mill was a guardedly passionate man, who 'threw his feelings into his opinions'.[34]

The period he spent in France from 1820–21 released Mill into the 'free and genial atmosphere of continental life'. He was exposed to new teachers at the University of Montpellier, and to unBenthamite subjects, such as French literature, fencing, singing and piano-playing.[35] A visit to the liberal economist, J-B Say, encouraged 'a strong and permanent interest in continental liberalism'. France offered Mill a fresh perspective on his father's views. Back in England, he dutifully helped him with *Elements of Political Economy* (1821) and studied law with John Austin. But he developed reservations about Condillac's associationist psychology. It was a time of political unease caused partly by the Cato Street Conspiracy of 1820. 'Radical' became a term of abuse, and John Mill turned to a study of the French Revolution, and to Dumont's *Traité de Législation*, which provided him with a 'religion'. Bentham's works were no longer a matter of duty, but 'private reading'. Mature assessment was possible: the 'greatest happiness of the greatest number' principle 'burst upon me with all the force of novelty'.[36] From 1821 to 1826, Mill engaged in Benthamite propaganda, when 'to advocate peaceful reform was . . . almost as great an offence as to plot rebellion'.[37] He wrote for the press, and founded, in 1822, an unashamedly 'sectarian' utilitarian Debating Society. But he also encountered that intellectual individualism in his friends which was to motivate the deliberate eclecticism of the Philosophical Radicals, and which the speculative, eclectic tendencies of early Benthamism unconsciously encouraged. He debated with the Coleridgians, F. D. Maurice and John Sterling; the social sciences discussion group he inaugurated in 1825 launched his career as 'an original and independent thinker'.[38]

Like Carlyle in Edinburgh, Mill inhabited two mental worlds. In 1826, he was still campaigning for Benthamism, but his inner sectarianism was being eroded. Publicly, he was committed to utilitarianism: privately, he was full of troubling speculations. 1826

found him in 'a dull state of nerves' and his exhausting schedule of
the India Office, discussion groups, and writing was a contributory
factor. James Mill worked earnestly for the future, yet contemplated the attainment of utopian ideals with little enthusiasm. His
son now experienced familiar joyful emotions, but their 'charm'
(the word was repeated and connoted both magic and desirability)
had vanished.[39] A sense of distance from his emotions made him
question the Benthamite concept of mind as a malleable entity, in
which the correct environment produced, by a process of association, valid ideas of good and evil. Once, however, (and here
Benthamite logic was turned upon Benthamite psychology) Mill
scrutinised his feelings, it became apparent that the links of association were artificially imposed. Analysis might remove illogical
associations which created prejudice,[40] but it also erased valuable
associations which were 'a *mere* matter of feeling'.[41] Uncritical
acceptance of the associationist psychology, Mill concluded,
ruined the capacity to feel, and it was only his private, spontaneous act, in responding to Marmontel's description of his father's
death, which revealed to him his capacity imaginatively to grasp
another's situation. This convinced him not only of his capacity to
feel; it confirmed the independent existence of the emotional self.

The crisis may have been 'not so much a revolution as an
enlargement', but it made Mill more receptive to ideas he might
otherwise have rejected.[42] It encouraged his first conscious step
towards a modification of Benthamism. The self-interested pursuit
of happiness was not a valid end: rather, happiness was to be
found in forgetting self. Active intellectual analysis must be balanced by cultivation of the 'passive susceptibilities'; reform must
deal not solely with man's environment, but with the 'internal
culture of the individual'. Mill's interest in poetry and music
intensified.[43] He saw as did Carlyle, and later Marian Evans, that
non-empirical modes of inquiry and expression attain and tell
truths unavailable to sectarian Benthamism.

Mill's crisis helped initiate that philosophical trend which attempted to learn from both Benthamism and Idealism. In granting
an independent existence to feeling, in stressing the inner life, Mill
questioned fundamental tenets of Benthamite psychology. His
experiences gave partial ratification to Intuitionist arguments about
the nature of mind and, hence, of human perception, and showed
him limitations in the applied rationalist tradition, which could not
interpret, or solve, his traumatic dilemma. From this stemmed the

aspiration he described to Bulwer Lytton in November 1836, 'to soften the harder and sterner features of . . . Radicalism and Utilitarianism, both of which in the form in which they originally appeared in the *Westminster* were part of the inheritances of the eighteenth century'.[44] Empiricism, as in Carlyle's case, propelled Mill into a personal agony, which called into question that same philosophy. The quest commenced for a philosophy which embodied a form of perception corresponding more closely to human experience, better able to describe man's perception of existence and, ultimately, to resolve some of man's problems in the world of human action.

3
Saint-Simonianism

To have been hurried by a generous enthusiasm into any
vagaries, however strange or absurd, does no permanent
injury to any man's reputation or prospects in life, when
once the delusion is over.[1]

The notion of a 'quest for truth' prompted contradictory responses.
Inherent in the concept was the notion which emerged in the
nineteenth century that truth resided in the process of open-ended
inquiry, for that process reflected the reality of mind and world.
Solutions were not to be found.[2] Yet 'quest' alternatively implied
an attainable goal, and thence derived systems which initially
defined the knowing process, and explored the implications that
definition had for private and public issues. The rejection of doctrinaire eighteenth-century philosophy spawned both scepticism and
new, dogmatic systems, and the attraction of Mill and Carlyle to
Saint-Simonianism shows this movement in action. Likewise,
Marian Evans was to oscillate between the views that truth resided
within process or within system: the examples of Mill and Carlyle
prompted her consideration of the problem, and her final assent to
the view of truth as process led her to literature as the genre which
could best express this hard-won philosophical position, and encourage others to adopt it.

Mill and Carlyle first became interested in Saint-Simonianism
because it seemed to correspond, with its eclectical logical method, to
their anti-doctrinaire stances. According to Caroline Fox, Mill thought
there was a 'tremendous duty to . . . admit always a devil's advocate
into the presence of your dearest, most sacred truths.'[3] The Saint-
Simonian use of a new logic as the basis for an interpretation of life,
and a solution to its problems, also spoke to the need of Mill and
Carlyle to wed ideas to existence. The associationist psychology's
emphasis upon self-interest was the starting-point for political *laissez-
faire*: Mill and Carlyle questioned Benthamite psychology, and attacked
its accompanying political stance. Saint-Simonianism confirmed

some of their own preoccupations and conclusions. Yet the individualistic critical spirit fostered by their crises prevailed; they rejected adherence to Saint-Simonianism, and also, after a curiously incongruous friendship, each other. They focused upon different aspects of Saint-Simonianism; it inspired them to different kinds of writing. They temporarily influenced each other's work, but the *rapprochement* was made by each in terms of personal experience.

Saint-Simon, who was born in 1760 and died in 1825, was tutored by d'Alembert, and proposed marriage to Mme de Staël; his work blended the Encyclopaedist tradition with insights afforded by the reaction against that tradition. He praised Newton's method, but realised that, 'between the formal generalities of metaphysical philosophy and the narrow specialization of the particular sciences, there was a place for a new enterprise'.[4] Central to his 'untidy, unsystematic, capricious' and influential philosophy was the plea for a logic which would examine questions 'first *a priori* and then *a posteriori*'.[5] The Saint-Simonians were heirs to an eighteenth-century tradition, for they 'believed that ideas and doctrines would be the agents of social transformation'.[6] Saint-Simon aimed to link all branches of knowledge, for he admired the unity of the *Encyclopédie*, but his own synthesis would be brought about partly by an *a priori* method. He theorised on ethics, relating the 1789 anarchy to the prevalence of selfishness; he put forward proposals for the reorganisation of the Institut de France and of Europe. The eighteenth-century notion of history as unending progress, which was echoed by the Benthamites, was also modified. Saint-Simon praised medieval Catholicism for its concern with learning and the poor, for its balancing of national and international interests.[7]

Saint-Simon also dealt with two urgent new problems, the industrial revolution and religion. His views on the urban proletariat were implicitly anti-Benthamite, for he suggested that, 'the discussion of the relations between producer and consumer, or between capital and labour, was more important than argument about constitutional forms and political institutions'.[8] Gustave D'Eichtal, who was, like Marx, a disciple of Saint-Simon, similarly saw the dangers of utilitarianism. He thought that England would be the first nation to confront the dire consequences of Benthamite *laissez-faire*, and chose to proselytise there. The errors of Benthamism which provoked the personal agony of Mill and Carlyle were seen to promote 'the injustice in life', and thus inspired alternative political theories.[9] In the hungry forties, Marian Evans, too, like Mill and Carlyle in earlier years, turned to the French political theorists. Saint-Simon, whose work dated from the period immediately after the 1789 French Revolution, had come to think that speculation should culminate in new beliefs, and he conformed to that post-revolutionary trend in French philosophy which linked religion and politics to promote 'an apocalyptic belief that the Kingdom of God could be brought to this earth'.[10] The 1789 experiments, Robespierre's cult of the Supreme Being, and La Revellière's Theophilanthropy had failed, and Saint-Simon considered Deism outmoded.[11] *Nouveau Christianisme* (1825) recalled the enthusiastic impulse of the turn of the century. Saint-Simon isolated the notion of brotherly love, and was antipathetic to the historical development of dogma, as a perversion of the simple precepts of the early Church. An élite would spread the new gospel, promoting learning and improving man's lot. The distinction between religion and theology was to become common in the nineteenth century: Feuerbach, whose work Marian Evans translated, learnt from this aspect of Saint-Simonianism.[12]

Despite an incoherent prose style, and the looseness of his synthesis, Saint-Simon's work aroused much enthusiasm. He was not an active propagandist, but a sceptical Thackeray noticed that the sect which was formed after his death was 'followed by a respectable body of admirers'.[13] *Le Producteur* was founded in 1825 to expound the Saint-Simonian philosophy; in 1828, the College of Apostles was established, and Bazard gave public lectures. The *Globe* replaced *Le Producteur* in 1830, and Bazard and Enfantin set up a community which drew Liszt to its gatherings. When George Sand arrived in Paris in 1830, the sect was much talked of, and *An Address to the British Public, by the Saint-Simonian Missionaries* (1832) emphasised that, in two years, the group had grown from obscurity to strength. But in 1832 came a schism, when Enfantin founded a separate community, Ménilmontant. Only two years after a revolution, it immediately attracted suspicion as a dangerous social and political experiment. After a spectacular, farcical trial at the end of 1832, Enfantin was imprisoned, having been convicted of immorality.[14] In England, the movement had a mixed reception: it was widely discussed, yet 'too soon forgotten'. The 1831 mission to London, aided by John Stuart Mill, was suspected of being a recruiting centre for prostitutes. Saint-Simon's personality was attacked. The movement's élitism was denounced, its mysticism

dismissed as 'spurious'. By 1843, it could only be recalled by 'One
who has a Good Memory'.[15] The panic-stricken tone in the English
press stemmed from the political atmosphere. In 1829, the passing
of the Roman Catholic Relief Bill narrowly averted civil war in
Ireland; agrarian and industrial unrest were quelled by savage
methods. In 1830, Wellington declared that the reform of the
Commons was unnecessary; the same year, Charles X of France
was deposed for attempting to restrict the franchise. The discontent in the rapidly growing industrial centres showed the limitations of *laissez-faire*, yet such places were unrepresented in
Parliament. Attwood's Birmingham Political Union united the
working-class and the middle-class in their demands for political
reform, and, in 1830, when the Reform Bill failed to pass, Birmingham seemed on the verge of rebellion. The 1830s were fraught with
dangerous discontent, and the early part of the decade saw the
working-class arming themselves against oppressors. With the
notable exception of *The Monthly Repository*, Saint-Simonianism
was seen as an attempt to import yet more anarchy.[16] The movement made its impact upon isolated members of the *avant-garde*,
such as Robert Owen and Harriet Martineau. The latter, like Mill,
Marian Evans and Lewes, was to progress from interest in Saint-
Simon's work, to concern with that of his heir, Comte, although
Comte never won Carlyle's approval.[17]

In 1828, Carlyle was writing enthusiastically about those German writers who had provided a new basis for his faith. Articles on
Heyne, Werner and Goethe in 1828, and on the German drama in
1829, reiterated the methods and preoccupations of earlier works.
In 1829, however, spurred on by the troubled political climate, he
explored, in 'Signs of the Times', the social implications of sectarian perception. The article was characterised by an eclectic striving
to promote an ideal of balance. Externality, superficiality, lack of
directness prevailed in the English metaphysical tradition, in religion, political philosophy and government, literature and morality.
The Mechanic Principle of the Benthamites must be modified by
the Dynamic Principle, for 'only in the right coördination of the
two, and the vigourous forwarding of *both*, does our true line of
action lie'.[18] It was this merging of logics, and its panoramic
application, which caught the eye of the Saint-Simonians, to
whose hierarchical synthesis it bore some resemblance. Carlyle
had taken notes on the sect from the *Revue Encyclopédique* in 1827;
Charles Buller, his former pupil, knew Gustave d'Eichtal, and his

brother, John Carlyle, had stayed with d'Eichtal's uncle in Munich. *L'Organisateur* printed a long commentary on 'Signs of the Times' in March and April 1830, and the sect started to send Carlyle their works.[19]

Goethe warned Carlyle against the Saint-Simonians, and Carlyle was initially wary, but, throughout 1830, his enthusiasm increased and, by the end of the year, he had read their works, and had translated *Nouveau Christianisme*.[20] Saint-Simonianism united and clarified ideas which were familiar to Carlyle. Its reaction against rationalism was in line with his own impulses. He had considered Werner's plans for a new religion, and Goethe's religious specula-tions. Novalis, whose works Carlyle had also read, saw religion as countering egotism, and the consequential social fragmentation. Carlyle had defined ideal perception as akin to 'religious wisdom', speaking to the entire soul, glimpsing the union of Ideal and Actual, wedding knowledge to faith. His arguments against intel-lectual sectarianism distinguished between essential truth and historical form; he wished to expand the concept of religion.[21] Lessing, Novalis and Goethe had spoken of historical periodicity: Carlyle echoed their notions in his Diary in 1829.[22] Politically, Benthamism was becoming still more unconvincing, and Carlyle was reflecting upon human interdependence. His reading of Saint-Simonian works in the turbulent 1830s politicised Carlyle's thought. He saw democracy as 'a thing inevitable, and obliged to lead whithersoever it could', but described himself as 'utterly mystical and Radical'. He seized upon the spiritual and intellectual implications of Saint-Simon's theory, puzzling the Whig, Francis Jeffrey, with his views.[23] In 'On History' (1830) Carlyle explored Saint-Simonian ideas about the historical process, and tried to reconcile their emphasis on collective experience with his own individualism, showing the influence of the historical context upon man's spiritual experience. Yet he saw not the alternation of critical and organic periods, but 'the coming Time . . . unseen . . . in the Time come', and argued against historiography's simplification of human motive.[24]

Sartor Resartus (1833–4) was, in one respect, an eclectic land-mark, in its attempt to reconcile French and German thought: it also applied that reconciliation to comment upon the 1830s. It was, moreover, telling that it was a disguised autobiography, in which philosophical and social problems were mirrored in the agonised individual consciousness. Carlyle was, as in the incomplete *Wotton*

Reinfred (c. 1826), taking stock of his position, and neo-collectivist
Saint-Simonianism made scant impact upon his individualism. The
complicated way in which the work was autobiographical, its
confusion of argument, tumultuous prose style, the intermittent
presence of the central figure, its deliberately unsystematic mode
of exposition, puzzled editors, admirers, like Joseph Mazzini, and
perhaps even Carlyle himself.[25] Yet its chaotic quality served
directly to render the turbulence of the age; indirectly, it suggested
Carlyle's lapse from the dearly-bought equilibrium of 1827.

Ideas from German literature and Saint-Simonianism jostled
each other: they were contrasted, compared, sometimes reconciled. Familiar themes recurred. There were pleas for the valuable
serenity of German thought, criticisms of the sceptical and doctrinaire tendencies of Utilitarianism. Carlyle argued against Necessity, for the existence of unseen laws, and for the unity of true
perception. Yet a strongly critical note entered when he considered
Idealist terminology.[26] The German ideal of balanced perception
was echoed by the Saint-Simonian synthesis which started with
science, and ended with religion. Carlyle argued for detached
inquiry into, and reverence before, Creation, and in his view of
reality matter and spirit were reconciled.[27] Finite and Infinite met
in his theory of symbols (III,3). The symbolism of clothes fused the
notions of the changing historical form, and the unchanging nature
of mankind, and, with an eye to his reaffirmations of childhood
beliefs in a new terminology, Carlyle saw this contrast as crucial in
any discussion of ecclesiastical history.[28] Specific notions associated with the German and French philosophies were also fused.
That unbelief led to belief echoed Goethe, Fichte, and Saint-
Simonian notions of critical and organic. Saint-Simonian vindication of the flesh reiterated Novalis; the German notion of the
divine essence of mankind supported neo-Socialist arguments for
equality. Saint-Simon's idea of a reborn society merged with Werner's image of the Phoenix.[29]

Like Mill's, Carlyle's response to Saint-Simonianism was one of
assent where it confirmed ideas with which he was familiar, or
where the French philosophy spoke to deep-rooted intellectual
tendencies. But his past experience made him suspect specific
nostra. Gustave d'Eichtal told Enfantin that Scotland offered a
more fertile ground than England for Saint-Simonianism, because
'Christian traditions fused with thoughts of social regeneration
were sure to find an echo there', and *Sartor Resartus* gave truth to

this. The Saint-Simonian concern for the masses inspired harrowing descriptions of the Irish plight. Yet the sect made a 'false application' of the notion of human dignity, and Carlyle queried their religious doctrine and its hold over the head and the imagination.[30] In *Sartor Resartus*, fusion of French and German ideas was effected in the hero's mediating, tormented consciousness, as he searched for solutions. Each system was eclectic in its own fashion, and confirmed that tendency in the other. They ratified not only each other's method, but also Carlyle's. Both systems sought a wholeness of vision beyond sectarian logic; they applied this vision to defined areas of concern, and Carlyle saw that some of their doctrines might be reconciled. The eclecticism and pragmatism of the Saint-Simonian endeavour reinforced and informed Carlyle's method of seeing the logical problem as at the heart of all other problems. Yet if Carlyle approved of the ideas about the process and application of knowledge he found in Saint-Simonianism, his abhorrence of dogmatism led him to reject its specific solutions. The German concept of the fluid, comprehensive consciousness sharpened his awareness of the inadequacy of Benthamite psychology. The 1830s also made him realise that political solutions failed to meet the demands of complex, individualistic human nature. Individualism played little part in Saint-Simonianism, and Carlyle never responded to, or comprehended, the notion of collective life.[31]

In *Sartor Resartus*, Carlyle's distrust of dogmatism began to enlarge into an anti-intellectualism which anticipated his mature philosophy of Silence and Action. He began to see man's function as action, not thought, and to insist that literature must be a social and moral act. He also started to ponder the split between thought and action, prompted, perhaps, by the looseness of their connection within Saint-Simonianism. He had rejected the narrow abstractions of philosophy; he had hoped to evolve the perfect logic which would illuminate life. He now wondered whether, 'all Speculation is by nature endless, formless, a vortex amidst vortices: only by a felt indubitable certainty of Experience does it find any centre to revolve round, and so fashion itself into a system'.[32] This hypothesis as to whether life eluded thought raised further questions about the relative importance of the life of action and thought, and the way in which the two were, or might be, connected, so as to save philosophy from the aridity of speculation. Marian Evans, reading *Sartor Resartus* in solitude at Griff, encountered a work which questioned the value of speculation at the same time that it introduced her to the philosophical debate of the age, and suggested to her its importance.

In the 1830s, to John Stuart Mill, whose father believed philosophy could be converted into action, Carlyle's question was also a burning one. Mill, like Carlyle, considered that his psychological crisis, which involved a personal response to issues raised by the philosophical debate, had a general truth to tell: he 'felt that the flaw in my life, must be a flaw in life itself'. Mill sought in non-philosophical sources illumination of the problems philosophy raised. Carlyle found in German literature a theory and embodiment of unified perception; Mill discovered, in his 1829 reading of Wordsworth, 'thought coloured by feeling, under the excitement of beauty'. Coleridge also had commended in Wordsworth 'the union of deep feeling and profound thought', but his phrasing suggested the method of the synthetic Idealist logic which was alien to Mill.[33] Wordsworth's poems appealed to Mill's love of the countryside, fostered by childhood tours of England, and visits to Bentham at Ford Abbey: experience of nature's beauty had alleviated his depression, although he deleted from the draft of his autobiography an account of the healing effect of the Thames landscape in 1828. Arguing with Roebuck, Mill was to contend that an emotional response to nature could exist independently of, be unmarred by, a capacity for scientific analysis of phenomena. Wordsworth also showed how response to landscape encouraged thoughts of mankind; he seemed to vindicate Benthamite concern for humanity by founding it on feeling. The 'Ode: Intimations of Immortality' described emergence from a depression caused by the loss of hopeful visions. After reading it, Mill's melancholy diminished: he seemed determined, like Wordsworth, to abandon sorrow, and to build a revised philosophy upon the foundations of the new vision of life he had discovered during his crisis. Mill also turned to the English heirs of Idealism. He disagreed with convinced Utilitarians like Roebuck, and sought out F. D. Maurice and Sterling. He read Goethe, other German writers and Coleridge. Yet he evolved his concept of the value of feeling independently, from experience, although admitting that it gave him 'points of contact' with the Coleridgians. It was the radical Idealism of Sterling which he admired.[34]

Mill saw this period as one in which adherence to doctrinaire views gave way to conscious eclecticism; he was 'incessantly

occupied in weaving . . . anew' the fabric of his opinions, relating new ideas to old ones, using them to modify or replace
earlier beliefs.[35] The 1828 speech, 'On Perfectibility', emphasised
that progress came from constitutional and educational reform,
but also stressed the value of feeling as a potential auxiliary of
the moral principle.[36] At this point, Mill encountered Saint-
Simonianism, having already, in 1820, glimpsed its founder in
Paris, 'slaving away at his evangelical socialism in suicidal poverty.' Continually under pressure from the spring of 1828 to give
allegiance to the movement, his scepticism made him hesitate over
the extent of the practical support and intellectual assent he was
prepared to give.[37] Mill's attitude was influenced by his preoccupation with revising the implications and method of Benthamite
logic. He was attracted to the Saint-Simonian theory of history,
with its tolerant attitude towards the past, as an alternative to the
cruder progressivism of his father and Macaulay; he especially
admired a paper by Comte on the subject. The Saint-Simonian
analysis of periods of doubt and belief provided a macrocosmic
image of Mill's own experience, and he looked forward to a future
which would combine free discussion and firm convictions, an
ideal early Benthamism had supposedly proposed. The Saint-
Simonian notion of the ideal society also found favour with Mill
and his meeting with Mrs Taylor in 1830 probably made him more
receptive to arguments for sexual equality.[38] The Saint-Simonian
political doctrines combined attention to a complex economic mechanism, demanding specific recommendations, and the expression of an imaginative impulse towards a utopian vision, 'prompted
by moral and timeless reasons'.[39] Their attention to new sociological factors made Benthamism seem outmoded; the visionary quality touched Mill's newly-aroused imagination. An imaginative
ideal, he felt, could stir men to action. He helped the Saint-
Simonian mission, though he did wonder, significantly, whether
its methods might be 'inefficacious'.[40]

It was, however, the fluidity of the movement's views which
most attracted Mill. He disputed their theory of property, and
urged the value of philosophical eclecticism to a group who had
initially embraced it. He suggested they learn from the English
political economists, and from German writers, about 'the philosophy of history, literature and the arts'.[41] Mill merged the Saint-
Simonian notion of an élite with Coleridge's concept of a clerisy in
a paper in *The Jurist* in February 1833 and saw the Saint-Simonians

as coming to his notice at a time of profound personal change, and as giving 'order and system to the ideas which I had already imbibed from intercourse with others, and derived from my own reflections'.[42]

'The Spirit of the Age', which appeared in the *Examiner* between 6 January and 29 May 1831, showed both Mill's emergent independent stance, and his selective indebtedness to the application of the Benthamite and Saint-Simonian logics to specific problems. His eclectic's unwillingness to come to firm conclusions was evidenced by the fact that he never carried out his plan to complete the series when the Reform Bill was passed. Mill's view of the age as 'critical' derived from Saint-Simonianism, and he echoed Comte's notion of the predictive function of sociology.[43] He proposed the value of an intellectual élite, and spoke of the historical conditioning of character. His views of the Middle Ages and the Roman Catholic Church were also influenced by Saint-Simon.[44] Yet individualistic preoccupations remained. His concern for the Church/State relationship, his view of the ruling class, and the comparisons between English and ancient civilisations revealed an English, and Benthamite, slant. The lack of convictions was an 'enormous' evil, and he suggested that the work of others could not provide them, for 'in an age of transition the source of all improvement is the exercise of private judgment'[45] Truth could not be found within any one system, and he seemed to evoke *Aids to Reflection*[46] when he commented sadly on mankind's 'invincible propensity to split the truth and take half, or less than half of it; and . . . habit of erecting their quills and bristling up like a porcupine against any one who brings them the other half, as if he were attempting to deprive them of the portion which they have'.[47] This comment serves as his epitaph on the Saint-Simonian movement and a firm statement of his own eclecticism: it also provides a summary of what was to be his reaction to Carlyle as their friendship drew to a close.

4
The Personal Debate

The rift between Mill and Carlyle came in 1840, when Carlyle delivered an onslaught on Bentham in 'The Hero as Prophet'.[1] Their parting demonstrated how, although they were both striving to escape the sterility of sectarian philosophical debate, they did so in terms of dissimilar personal experiences, which gave them irreconcilable perspectives on both logic and life. In 1831, Empson mentioned Mill to Carlyle as 'a converted Utilitarian who is studying German', and this elicited an enthusiastic response from Carlyle: in 1832, Carlyle claimed Mill was his 'partial disciple'.[2] The friendship flourished at a time when both were cultivating open-mindedness; they shared, said Carlyle, 'a common recognition of the infinite nature of Truth'.[3]

Specific interests related to the debate on logic drew them together. Carlyle was writing on Voltaire, and Mill spurred on his interest in the Encyclopaedist tradition, and sent him material from his own collection on the French Revolution. Yet the nature of their interests in eighteenth-century France varied. The articles on French themes which Mill contributed to the *Examiner* from 1830 onwards, drew didactic parallels with events in England: Carlyle uttered aphorisms, saying that the 'right *History*' of the French Revolution 'were the grand Poem of our Time', and commented that the Revolution had revealed the essential human character. Initially, Carlyle conceded limited approval to Utilitarianism, as affording some kind of belief, but he overestimated Mill's hostility to Benthamism.[4] On the value of speculation, they also differed. Carlyle wrote that in an age of transition, 'speculation is not wanted, but prompt practical insight, and courageous action'; he complained that Mill's letters were 'too speculative', and then modified his opinion, deeming speculation tolerable, if 'it is of the very highest sort; or when, as itself a historical document, I find it interesting for the sake of its interesting author'.[5]

Concern for the Saint-Simonian troubles of 1830 also drew the two together; Mill supplied news of the sect, and material for Carlyle's projected articles on the subject. They agreed about the movement's imaginative appeal, and suspected Enfantin's methods. Both countered Socialist theories with pleas for the importance of the individual.[6] Yet the looseness and breadth of the Saint-Simonian synthesis allowed them to stress varying aspects of it. Mill focused upon its political and historical ideas, Carlyle upon its religious notions and implications for perception. Saint-Simonian historicism influenced Mill's views on representative government, Carlyle translated *Nouveau Christianisme*. Both transformed Saint-Simonian ideas: Mill's ideal society merged critical and organic trends, and Carlyle assimilated the critical/organic thesis to Goethe's notions on belief and unbelief.[7]

Over specific issues raised by Saint-Simonianism, they disagreed. Carlyle saw little value in political machinery: if truth was ever-evolving, the perfect society could never be realised. Mill was committed to the political process. He did not share his father's enthusiasm for the Reform Bill, but he had friends in the Commons, and, from 1833 onwards, was a political journalist.[8] On religious issues, the two also revealed significant differences. Carlyle pleaded, like an Old Testament prophet, for sternly moral beliefs; Mill came close to the Unitarians, whom Carlyle disliked. Mill fell in love with Harriet Taylor, and wrote for the *Monthly Repository*. He was also sympathetic to the Coleridgian latitudinarianism of F. D. Maurice and Sterling, whilst Carlyle always abhorred the Broad Church and admired the Scottish Church. Mill was severely critical of established churches. Their vision of the surrounding world also differed. Mill considered that mind endowed nature with beauty: *Sartor Resartus* incorporated a powerfully-expressed pantheism, which Carlyle continued to propound.[9]

The writings of the two men between 1831 and 1834 show common areas of interest. On the eve of the Reform Bill, both surveyed contemporary society – Mill in 'The Spirit of the Age', and Carlyle in 'Characteristics'. Their analyses, terminology and conclusions were, however, strikingly different. Mill wrote on the French Revolution in August 1833 in the *Monthly Repository*, whilst Carlyle was reading French history, but Mill's reflections on the Encyclopaedist tradition were channelled into articles which dealt with issues current in English political life.[10] There was also obvious divergence of interests. Carlyle wrote six articles on Goethe in 1832, and still considered that the Germans had made belief possible. Mill's interest in German, which he had learnt in the 1820s and to which he had returned just before he met Carlyle, revived under the latter's influence, but his bias remained towards the French tradition. His work on a new Logic, a project evolved in the 1830s, would not have commended itself to Carlyle, and Mill only read Hegel and other German logicians grudgingly in 1841.[11] Their reactions to 'The Spirit of the Age' showed their contrary perspectives. Mill retrospectively dismissed his own articles as badly-written and 'ill-timed': Carlyle proclaimed the appearance of 'a new Mystic', and refused to listen when Mill denied the accolade. Mill's training in deductive logic is at odds with Carlyle's intuitive perception of a kindred spirit of endeavour. Mill was slow to appreciate Carlyle's work, and felt that he had little to contribute to any technical endeavour: he valued his writings as 'poetry to animate' but 'not as philosophy to instruct'.[12] In 1833, both composed articles on historiography, which incorporated Saint-Simonian notions. Mill quoted Carlyle at approving length. But whereas Mill saw history as embodiment of the empirical, logical process, Carlyle saw it as a chaotic river. Carlyle spoke of the inevitable subjectivity of the historian, searching for irrecoverable facts, and made large claims for the poetic and religious functions of historiography, the magnitude and terminology of which claims Mill would surely have disputed, given his views on the historical process as conforming to the patterns of empirical logic.[13]

Mill's articles on poetry also showed how his thought remained untouched by German aesthetics. He repeated commonplace English notions of the poet as solitary, echoed Shelley's *A Defence of Poetry*, *Biographia Literaria* and Wordsworth's 1800 Preface.[14] He valued poetry in the light of his 1826 crisis, speaking of the importance it assigned to the inner life, and its union of intellect and feeling which could encourage the pursuit of philosophical truth. Mill praised the eclectic quality of the poetic temperament: truth 'is more certainly arrived at by two processes, verifying and correcting each other, than by one alone'.[15] The terminology, the level tone, the personal preoccupations which underpinned the comment were distinctively Mill's: only in broad terms did he approach Carlyle's attempt to reconcile deduction and intuition. Carlyle could not have written so unemotionally about literature, for his psychological debt to it was much greater than Mill's.

After 1834, Mill, urged on by the political situation, and his nurturing in a context of social awareness, was once more to attempt to wed logic to life in his writings on current affairs.

Carlyle was to show, conversely, that there was no logical pattern to be imposed on the political process, that reality eluded the descriptive powers of any philosophical system. From 1834 to 1840, Mill spent much of his time working for the kind of ideological revolution which Carlyle castigated in *The French Revolution*. Carlyle's political action took the form of showing that such a revolution was doomed to failure because of the short-sighted vision of the protagonists, who ignored the presence of intractable, complex reality at their own, and the nation's, peril. Mill, in temporarily embracing specific issues, lost sight of the notion of truth as process: Carlyle saw reality as resistant to any conceptualisation, however eclectic and sceptical in intent.

5

J. S. Mill (1834–1837): Logic and Politics

No sagacious man will long retain his sagacity, if he live exclusively among reformers and progressive people[1]

Writing to d'Eichtal in 1829, Mill remarked of his fellow Englishmen,

> To produce any effect on their minds, you must carefully conceal the fact of your having any system or body of opinions, and must instruct them on insulated points, and endeavour to form their habits of thought by your mode of treating single and practical questions.[2]

During the early 1830s, he concentrated on 'practical questions', yet also seemed progressively to ignore the untheoretical bias of the English mind. The reassertion of Benthamite truths intensified. After the passing of the Reform Bill, he expounded in the press a theory of Radicalism based upon a Benthamite philosophy of mind. However, as the fortunes of the Radical Party, and political conditions changed, Mill's eclecticism reappeared. His political writings became more impassioned as he dealt with current events, yet they were also deliberately individualistic as he set about the urgent task of redefining the philosophy of reform. Finally, he turned to a reconsideration of the nature of perception, and the philosopher's role, as he discerned, in the growing conservatism of the newly-enfranchised, and the burgeoning of populist movements, an implicit rejection of radicalism. The failure of Benthamite logic to carry conviction in the nation led Mill to flirt with the notion of rejecting logic itself. Likewise, the events of the hungry forties were to propel Marian Evans's thinking about the logical problem in new directions.

The years from 1833 to 1835 found Mill in optimistic mood. In 1833, when Parliament reassembled, the Whigs, under Lord Grey, a celebrated reformer in his youth, were in the majority. Opposed to the Whigs and Peel's Tories, were nearly sixty Radicals, many of whom were Mill's associates, and the Irish MPs, led by Daniel O'Connell. The government, formed of a 'scratch team of aristocrats', was forced to find its allies amongst the Tories, with whom they shared an aristocratic tradition James Mill considered 'frivolous and effete.'[3] The Whigs' progressive instincts were intellectual in origin; they stood firm for law and order, and had little sympathy for, or understanding of, working-class poverty, or egalitarian aspirations. Their enclosed society was confident in its old-fashioned values: Elizabeth, Lady Holland, castigated Rousseau's self-indulgent emotionalism, and admired Voltaire and D'Alembert. Her husband represented to her the Whig ideal, for 'Toleration was his darling object. Peace, amity & indulgence to all mankind were the predominant feelings of his heart.'[4]

Grey's administration was constantly in a difficult position, being too progressive to please the Tories and too reactionary for the Radicals. The Tories opposed Palmerston's co-operation with the liberal French government, and forced the government to modify its proposals for emancipating slaves. The Radicals were angered by the government's failure to reintroduce income tax, and to implement Roebuck's plans for state education. They also wielded some power over the Whigs. They influenced the framing of the 1833 Factory Act: Brougham introduced legal reforms, and the appointment of three Commissioners to administer the 1834 New Poor Law Act was inspired by utilitarian views. The question of the Irish Church widened the rifts between the parties. Radicals saw the established church as 'an organ of class government'[5] and, in alliance with dissenters, called for a separation of Church and State and measures to diminish the income of the Irish Church. The Bill of February 1833 did little to meet their demands. Yet the reduction of the Irish bishoprics from twenty-two to ten prompted Keble's Assize Sermon at Oxford on 14 July 1833, which initiated the ultra-Tory Oxford Movement. The government had, once more, offended both sides, and, in the intensely sectarian debate which followed, the Anglican Church was split, and, with Radical support, dissenters campaigned even more vigorously for civil rights. Irish affairs finally led to Grey's resignation in 1834. Daniel O'Connell revealed that the Irish Secretary , E. J. Littleton, had promised him, in return for a cessation of agitation, that the Coercion Act would not be continued beyond 1 April 1834. Grey was about to renew the Act. He was succeeded briefly by Melbourne and Peel. A reluctant Melbourne then came to power again in 1835 to lead a Whig administration which was to last until 1841.

In July 1833, Mill wrote to Sterling, 'I am becoming *more* a Movement-man than I was, instead of less.' For a time, he abandoned the incipient scepticism which would have horrified his father: like Joseph Mazzini, he seemed to see no complications inherent in the rhetorical question, 'What good are ideas . . . unless you incarnate them in deeds?'[6] Delighted by the position of his Radical friends in Parliament, he urged them on, trying to 'put ideas into their heads and purpose into their hearts'.[7] Mill's propaganda appeared in two periodicals. His articles in the *Monthly Repository* illustrated the alliance of religious and political dissent so prominent during this time, which nurtured the radicalism of Marian Evans and her friends in the 1840s. The views of Coleridge, Carlyle, Saint-Simon and Mrs Taylor had increased Mill's toleration for liberal Christianity. W. J. Fox, the editor of the *Monthly Repository*, freed the periodical of unitarian sectarianism and transformed it into a broadly liberal journal, which had long-standing links with the Benthamites, from whom it derived its social philosophy. Fox promoted the Saint-Simonians in 1831, and printed articles on divorce reform and female emancipation in 1833. He was one of the first to commend Browning's poetry.[8] As well as writing for Fox's journal, Mill also edited the *London Review*, founded in 1834, as the 'organ of philosophic radicalism': its tone was heavily influenced by James Mill.

John Stuart Mill transformed the most unlikely material into propaganda. His articles on Plato, published between February 1834 and March 1835, aired views formulated in an uncritically Benthamite phase.[9] He agreed with his father in recommending the *Dialogues* as exhibiting the value of 'a particular mode of enquiry', defining terms, and using examples in the conduct of an argument.[10] Mill also propounded Benthamite opinions: he attacked the ancient universities, discussed justice and punishment, highlighted Plato's views on utility, and pleasure and pain, and showed the limitations of speculation, the need for political involvement. Yet he also argued against Plato: in inculcating love of virtue, 'the imagination and the affections' must play a part.[11] Forensic propaganda for Radical views appeared overtly in 'Notes on the Newspapers' which provide a commentary on the tumultuous year of 1834. Mill recommended payment of MPs, pleaded for a free press, and a centralised administration of the New Poor Law. He censured repressive policies towards the trade unions and the Irish.[12] To four areas of Benthamite concern, the people, church establishment, legal reform and education, he constantly returned. He saw the dangers of a government out of touch with a poor, uneducated proletariat. He supported the reduction of the income of the Irish Church, and criticised discrimination against dissenters and unbelievers. He approved law reform in relation to land ownership, prisons and the penal code, and flogging in the army. He supported Roebuck's scheme for national education, and the reform of higher education.[13] Political preoccupations such as his sense of living in a time of accelerated change, and the status of intellectuals, surfaced in articles ostensibly unconcerned with current affairs.[14] 'Close of the Session' summed up his optimism. He hoped for more action from the government, but praised its recognition of a widespread desire for reform. 1834 had shown that the wishes of the people may be represented by the legislature; James Mill's particular bugbears, the aristocracy and the Established Church, faced annihilation. The Benthamite golden age was about to dawn: 'What the ten days of May 1832 rendered probable, the session of 1834 has made certain; that the English revolution will be a revolution of law, and not of violence.'[15]

Events were soon to prove Mill wrong although, when Melbourne took office in 1835, the composition of the Commons bore out his optimism. Whigs and Tories had an almost equal number of MPs, but the Radicals had doubled their representation, taking nearly all the metropolitan seats. Melbourne's mellow cynicism and melancholy temperament made him unconvinced of the value of reform; he once remarked casually 'Benthamites are all fools'. His efforts were, anyway, checked by Peel on one side and O'Connell on the other. Progressive legislation, such as the 1835 Municipal Reform Acts, and the 1836 Marriage Act, arrived on the statute book, 'often in so modified a form as to defeat the intention of their original promoters'.[16] By July 1837, desire for change had waned, and, in the election, the Whigs suffered heavy losses and the Radicals retained only nine seats. Ominously, in the same year, the Birmingham Political Union, which had agitated violently for reform before 1832, was revived, suggesting that Mill's vision of peaceful change and the representative nature of the new franchise was illusory.

During 1835, Mill clung to his role as propagandist, a Socratic stinging insect, sent to goad and reproach the Radicals.[17] He urged them to commit themselves wholeheartedly to reform and an independent stance, and criticised the Whigs for a lack of coherence in their plans for reform. He wrote about trade unionism and legal reform, bestowing lavish praise on Bentham.[18] Yet new political trends disturbed him. By 1835, the newly-enfranchised, who were dependent on Tory landlords, were giving support to Peel, which marked a shift from their 1833 position. Public opinion seemed on the side of progress, but leaders were lacking. Still more worrying was the absence of intellectual deliberativeness: events were, 'daily shaping themselves forth under the plastic power of that irresistible Necessity, wrought by the natural laws of human civilisation'.[19] In the light of these depressing trends, Mill sought out new subjects for his journalism. The champion of radicalism turned, as he had done in 1826, to poetry, contributing a pioneering article on Tennyson to the *London Review*: Tennyson was praised for his merging of 'reason' and 'imagination'.[20]

Mill also wrote three articles which attempted a theoretical explanation of the Radical position. The Whigs were content to operate 'by . . . the rule of all unscientific craftsmen, the rule of the thumb', but Mill was determined that Radicalism should be founded on a system of ideas, forgetting his comment to d'Eichtal that it was precisely ideology to which the English were antipathetic. Reviewing *The Rationale of Political Representation*, Mill argued that the aim of government was to enable 'mankind to live in society without oppressing and injuring one another', and contemplated the difficult relationship between a governing, educated élite, and the people.[21] He returned to this theme in an article on de Tocqueville, and to the linked question of the need to educate for democracy, in the face of the rise of popular power. The choice was no longer between despotism and democracy, but 'between a well and an ill-regulated democracy'.[22] Mill's article on Sedgwick was even less concerned with specific issues, and the breadth of view recalls 'The Spirit of the Age'. Mill described the article as a defence of his modified Utilitarianism. He praised in Utilitarianism the speculative 'investigation of truth *as* truth . . . the prosecution of thought for the sake of thought', and emphasised that education must develop both imagination and reason. The nature of thought

and truth resumed a central position in Mill's writing. He discussed the ethical systems of Intuitionism and Associationism, and
offered modifications to utilitarian precepts. He praised autobiog-
raphers, novelists and poets for providing raw material for moral
philosophy, and saw an 'act of imagination, implying voluntary
attention' to others' pain as an essential constituent of the moral
sense, recalling, perhaps, his response to Marmontel's *Mémoires* in
1826. The moral sense was seen to change with historical circumstances. Mill thus defended an intellectual position, and then
moved outwards to specific issues. The focus shifted from practice
to theory within the structure of his argument; crucially, he also
suggested that works which recorded human experience and acts
of the imagination had truths to tell philosophers. Paley, Mill
noted, failed because he lacked, 'the single-minded earnestness for
truth, whatever it may be – the intrepid defence of prejudice, the
firm resolve to look all consequences in the face, which the word
philosopher supposes, and without which nothing worthy of note
was ever accomplished in moral and political philosophy'. The
eloquence of those idealistic words in defence of eclecticism provides a poignant contrast to the note of growing scepticism and
anxiety in Mill's political writings.[23]

Upon the death of his father in June 1836, Mill decided to use the
London and Westminster Review, 'to give full scope to my own
opinions and modes of thought, and to open the Review widely to
all writers who were in sympathy with Progress as I understood it',
for he sought to rid Philosophical Radicalism of elements of 'sectarian Benthamism'. As he had foreseen, Radicals were shocked
when he asked Carlyle and Sterling to write for the periodical.[24]
1836 showed a continuation of the trend of the previous year: Mill
was less preoccupied with current affairs, increasingly interested
in the theory of Radicalism. His growing disappointment with
English politics was obvious. Whilst still praising the capacity for
peaceful change, he urged Radical MPs to form a stronger pressure
group.[25] He criticised the vague terminology of the Tory, Sir John
Walsh, and the failure of the Whigs as a party of reform, but he
also castigated Radical inactivity, and repeated the insight he had
offered d'Eichtal in 1829, when he remarked, 'There is no passion
in England for forms of government, considered in themselves.
Nothing could be more inconsistent with the exclusively practical
spirit of the English people'.[26]

Mill nevertheless turned to a critical and theoretical analysis of modern society, as he considered the structure and values of American society.[27] 'Civilization' embodied a patently theoretical viewpoint. The careful definition of the term, the use of examples, followed the Platonic method both Mills praised. Mill saw the hallmark of a civilised society as the existence of unselfish corporate action; he argued for reform of institutions, the education of the masses. Yet he argued against progressivist assumptions, seeing the wane of the heroic spirit, the decay of regional culture, and the swamping of individual literary talent as evils an advanced civilisation would bring. Mill's answers to these difficulties drew upon his experience, his reading of Saint-Simon and his sad contemplation of current affairs. Individuality must be fostered, more effective forms of co-operation evolved. Even more important as regards the re-emergence of Mill's central concern with truth as process was his suggestion that teaching should be 'in the spirit of free inquiry, not of dogmatic imposition'. Logic and the philosophy of mind must occupy a central position in education, 'the one, the instrument for the cultivation of all sciences; the other, the root from which they all grow'. Logic must not, however, be taught as a set of technical rules, nor the philosophy of mind as a series of abstract propositions. Drawing upon a tradition of introspection sanctioned by Idealism, Christian dissent, and literary romanticism, Mill suggested, 'The pupil must be led to interrogate his own consciousness, to observe and experiment upon himself; of the mind, by any other process, little will he ever know!'[28] Between 1834 and 1840, the truth of the Benthamite system which Mill expounded was tested pragmatically in the context of an unpredictable and complex historical reality, and was found wanting. His sense of the need to redefine the nature of perception, and the ways in which it might operate to attain truth, reasserted itself. In 1837, he resumed worked on *A System of Logic*.

6

Mill (1837–1840): The Limitations of Logic

Looking back on his life, Mill decided that, after 1840, there were 'no further mental changes to tell of'.[1] Mill's personal experiences, as well as his intellectual interests, are at issue here, and they are closely linked. By 1840, the 1826 crisis was far away; his father was dead, and his relationship with Harriet Taylor was more settled. He had critically scrutinised Benthamism, English Idealism, and the post-Encyclopaedist developments in French thought. Despite the anguished tone of some of the articles written in the late 1830s, Mill became more confident in his search for the optimum definition and mode of perception, and his consideration of the implications perception had for action. By 1840, the *Logic* was finished: in the early 1840s, via that work, and those of Charles Bray, who was inspired by Mill's endeavour, Marian Evans encountered a crucially modified empiricism, and view of the function of speculation.

Mill's naming of 1840 as a terminal point coincided, not accidentally, with the end of a phase in English political life. By 1840, the Philosophical Radicals were a spent force. The late 1830s were dominated by the 'condition of England' question; England's notorious class divisions prevented the emergence of a broadly-based party of reform. The Philosophical Radicals were upper-middle-class intellectual Londoners, with little knowledge of the problems of the industrial working-class in the north and the midlands. In the election of July 1837, only nine retained their seats, and Durham's death weakened the party. Working-class disillusion with the Reform Bill was discussed by Charles Bray in 1841; Crossthwaite, in Kingsley's *Alton Locke*, described the lack of understanding shown by a Liberal MP to a deputation of poor tailors.[2] The working class turned to the Chartists whose leaders, ironically, derived their six points from the Radicals. In 1838, the People's Charter was published, and the Anti-Corn Law League

46

established. 1839 saw the Chartist Convention, viewed by sup-
porters and opponents alike as an alternative Parliament, meeting in
London and Birmingham, and the presentation of the first Chartist
petition. The incendiary riots in Birmingham in July of the same
year were a reminder that Chartism was 'a protest as incoherent as
the life that had provoked it'.[3] By 1841, England had a Conservative government led by Peel. Radicals, Whigs, Tories, and the
working class, all gave Mill grounds for despair: none were capable
of introducing reforms by peaceful methods, or of basing those
reforms upon a coherent philosophy. Mill's disengagement from
his journalistic mission stemmed not solely from a conscious
choice to return to the problem of logical method; such decisions
were imposed upon him by a political situation which rendered his
propagandist efforts null and void. The unexpected turns of events
forced him to doubt whether truth could be contained within a
system of ideas such as that which he had canvassed: he attempted
to revise the theory of perception, and the logical method upon
which that system was based. In his contemplation of both action
and thought, Mill's pragmatism and eclecticism both became more
deeply sceptical. In 1840, he handed the *Westminster Review* over to
W. E. Hickson. Since 1837, he had devoted much of his time to *A
System of Logic*, which he had started in 1830 and put aside in 1832.
By 1840, the *Logic*, which showed an apparent attempt to reconcile
Intuitionism and Associationism, was finished.[4]

Mill's rejection of a dogmatic theory of perception and logical
method, and his disillusion with Radical practice, encouraged his
interest in writers who were attempting to link a new logical
method to novel political models. In 1837, Wheatstone brought to
England the first two volumes of Comte's *Cours de philosophie
positive* (6 vols, 1830–42). Mill had admired Comte's method when
he read one of his papers in 1829 or 1830, and when, like Comte,
Mill was involved with the Saint-Simonians. He had modified the
Saint-Simonian concept of historical periodicity by reference to
Comte's outline of theological, metaphysical and positive stages.[5]
Mill found Comte's discussion of logical method invaluable, and *A
System of Logic* (1843) established Mill's role as a pioneer propagan-
dist for the *Cours* in England.[6] George Henry Lewes and Frederic
Harrison both came to Comte via the *Logic*, and it extended Marian
Evans's knowledge of Positivism.[7] Reading the *Cours* also directed
Mill back to the Saint-Simonians, and their ideas re-entered his

writing, especially when he discussed Chartism. Such ideas were
to be similarly present in Carlyle's *Chartism* (1839), the book in
which Marian Evans first encountered the French philosophy.
From 1838 to 1845, a contemporary witness noted, 'Great Britain is
in a permanent state of revolution';[8] five out of six adult males had
no vote. The Chartists talked openly of violent revolution, and, in
1838 and 1839, there were rumours of the working class taking up
arms. The Saint-Simonian focus upon the problem of the masses
may have made Mill perceive a crucial hiatus in Radical theory: in
1841, he still spoke of the Saint-Simonians as his friends.[9]

The rise of populist movements, and the reconsideration of
Saint-Simonian views, led Mill to pursue certain lines of inquiry
with harsh urgency, and Radicalism lacked adequate answers to
the problems he contemplated. Mill's harrowing picture of the
working class resembled that in *Sartor Resartus*, also inspired by the
French sect. In 1837, Mill realised the failures of the 1832 Reform
Bill:

> The great mass of our labouring population have no representa-
> tives in Parliament, and cannot be said to have any political
> station whatever; while the distribution of what may be called
> social dignity is more unequal in England than in any other
> civilized country of Europe, and the feeling of communion and
> brotherhood between man and man more artificially graduated
> according to the niceties of the scale of wealth.[10]

This is in striking contrast to his comments at the end of the 1834
Parliamentary session. In 1838, he saw a working class attracted by
Owenism, preoccupied with worker/employer relations, estranged
from middle-class Radicals. Mill could only echo Durham's wan
prescription that the working class should seek power by showing
themselves worthy of it.[11]

He thus tried to redefine the role of the Radical party. The
aristocratic principle must be opposed, for a 'Radical Party which
does not rest upon the masses, is no better than a nonentity'.[12]
Later, he suggested that a Radical's motto should be 'Government
by means of the middle for the working classes'. Yet a mode of
philosophical perception now, even more obviously, informed his
definition of Radicals as 'those who in politics observe the common
practice of philosophers – that is, who, when they are discussing
means, begin by considering the end, and when they desire to
produce effects, think of causes'.[13] His pleas for Radical action

became, however, more urgently pragmatic, and operated independently of a theoretical basis. In 1837, he recommended action:
in 1839, he echoed Carlyle, commenting impatiently, 'Radicalism
has done enough in speculation; its business now is to make itself
practical'. He begged for constructive, independent moves, pleaded
Durham's case, and said that the leader of a popular party needs
'not solely . . . the ability to talk, nor even merely to think, but . . .
the ability to *do*'. The Radicals lacked men able to avail themselves
of opportunities.[14] The split between thought and action was
reopened. Mill castigated mere speculation in the political arena,
yet felt that theory must underpin political practice, and that the
formulation of a new logic was imperative.

In relation to the latter task, Mill focused upon the claims of the
rival logics, and attempted a redefinition of the philosopher's role.
The obviously philosophical articles on Bentham and Coleridge,
seen by Mill's associates as a surrender to German mysticism, were
examples of this venture, but Mill saw this theme as permeating all
his work during this period.[15] His assessment of Intuitionism and
Associationism was eclectic, both as regards their theories of perception, and application of them. He censured Carlyle's antipathy
to Benthamite method and reform, and criticised Idealist terminology, which concealed 'much genuine philosophy'.[16] He attacked
Coleridge's 'attempt to arrive at theology by way of philosophy'.
Yet Mill admired Carlyle's merging of opposites in both method
and vision. He commended his painstaking investigation of facts,
coupled with imaginative power, his depiction of 'the confused
entanglement of the great and the contemptible' which is 'precisely
what we meet with in nature'. He saw that Coleridge shared with
Bentham a quality of earnestness, and Mill's eclecticism extended
to Coleridge's systematisation of Conservative thought, which
revealed 'much in it, both of moral goodness and true insight'.[17]

Bentham was assessed in even more detail, because his work
provided the starting-point for Mill's *Logic*, and for the political
stance of the Radicals. He praised the analytical method, yet noted
how Bentham lacked imaginative sympathy, seeing 'the incompleteness of his own mind as a representative of universal human
nature'. He was most impressed by Bentham's revelation that
philosophy was not 'remote from life', but crucially influential.
Although he often defended Benthamism in his political writings,
Mill spoke of its failure to deal with the education of the feelings,
the fostering of individuality. He praised Coleridge for his attack
upon Condillac's psychological theory.[18]

Mill's championing of eclectic modes of perception was shown as he praised or criticised writers in the light of ideas associated with the similarly eclectic Carlyle and Saint-Simon. He often fused ideas from the two sources. He saw the journalist Carrel in the way Carlyle saw some writers, as 'a man of action, using the press as his instrument', but also echoed the Saint-Simonian idea that Carrel appeared at a critical period which facilitated such a role. Sympathy for Saint-Simonian ideas was often obvious, but he differentiated between the value of their theory and the unfeasibility of their practice, and his contemplation of the failure of the Radicals gave weight to such a distinction. He praised Scott's historical sense, and lamented Bentham's lack of it. He commended the historiography of Michelet as providing a firm basis for predicting social change, a point also made by Comte and the Saint-Simonians.[19] Carlyle's influence pervaded Mill's discussion of writers and philosophers. Carrel was a reminder that heroism could exist amidst 'the pettiness of modern civilization'. His view of figures as disparate as Carrel, de Vigny, Carlyle, Coleridge and Bentham, incorporated the Carlylean notion that all writers performed a seer-like function: all searched for, and tried to articulate a valid mode of perception, a premise upon which Carlyle based *On Heroes and Hero-Worship* (1840). Mill also crucially modified utilitarian pragmatism to suggest, as Carlyle had done, as George Eliot was to do in the Epilogue to *Middlemarch*, the limited effectiveness of human actions, the elements of feeling and beauty in ethics. Action has also its '*aesthetic* aspect, or that of its beauty; its *sympathetic* aspect, or that of its *loveableness*'.[20] Awareness of such intangible qualities was an important component of the scepticism of the generation which reacted against rationalism. Eighteenth-century English philosophers were unable to imagine any of the more complex and mysterious manifestations of human nature.[21]

Mill's definition of the philosopher's role was finally formulated by reference to literary, as well as philosophical, sources. Anti-dogmatism characterised his ideal of perception. He criticised Bentham's ignoring of minds unlike his own. The philosopher should strive, 'To start from a theory, but not to see the object through the theory; to bring light with us, but also to receive other light from whencesoever it comes'. He praised Carrel as 'an intellect capacious enough to appreciate and sympathise with whatever of truth or ultimate value to mankind there might be in all theories'. Systematic 'half-minds' opened up new veins of speculation, but 'no whole truth is possible but by combining the points of view of all fractional truths'. Behind such statements lies a zeal for thought as process and flux, rather than rigid method, a conviction that truth is complex, and not to be confined into a dogmatic system. The philosopher's task was 'to expose error, though it may happen to be accredited – to elicit and sustain truth, known or unknown, neglected or obnoxious'.[22] In *Fragment of a System* (1800), Hegel reflected,

> Reflection is thus driven on and on without rest; but this process must be checked once and for all by keeping in mind that . . . what has been called a union of synthesis and antithesis is not something propounded by the understanding or by reflection but has a character of its own, namely, that of being a reality beyond all reflection.

The Hegelian notion of the world and truth as process, of all knowledge as limited, because historically conditioned, forestalled 'the demand for final solutions and eternal truths'.[23] The notion of thought as endless quest, the rejection of final solutions, whether in the system of Bentham, Saint-Simon or the neo-Idealists, aligned Mill with Hegelian views.

Hegel's notion of 'a reality beyond all reflection' provides an appropriate key to Mill's position, and sheds light upon his scepticism about speculation's inability to decipher the world and solve its problems. He envisaged valid perception as humble in the face of reality. He praised de Vigny because he 'looks life steadily in the face', and had 'no point to carry, no quarrel to maintain over and above the general one of every son of Adam with his lot here below', and, bracketing him with de Tocqueville, commended their reverential scepticism, which saw reality as supplying its own truth. In describing them as unable to 'satisfy themselves with either of the conflicting formulas which were given them for the interpretation of what lay in the world before them, they learnt to take formulas for what they were worth, and look into the world itself for the philosophy of it', he might have been describing himself.[24]

The political events of the late 1830s were the reality which called into question the Benthamite logic; they intensified Mill's non-doctrinaire stance. The 1826 crisis bore its final fruit: Mill's sceptical eclecticism and uneasy pragmatism issued in a drastically reformulated definition of the nature and function of philosophical thought. The speculative method was to be freed from the constraints of sectarian logic, and was to learn from other disciplines, avail itself of faculties other than reason. It was also to retain a sense of the supremacy of external reality, and to reject final solutions. Mill's application of a theory of perception to action waned. The process of thinking was more complicated than Bentham had thought; its discoveries, less certain, if attainable at all. Marian Evans's approving quotation of Gruppe's dictum, 'The age of systems is passed . . . System is the childhood of philosophy; the manhood of philosophy is investigation' summed up the radical shift in emphasis. In the same article, she also paid tribute to Mill.[25]

7

Carlyle (1834–1840); Alternative Revolutions

> As human nature is eternally active, the innovator is but
> the conservative with more perplexing facts before him,
> and the conservative only the upholder of revolution who
> has now, at length, no more worlds to conquer.[1]

The melancholy experience of isolation united Mill and Carlyle in
the years after the 1832 Reform Bill. The originality of Mill's
intellectual quest was fed by, and contributed to, his solitude. As
the prospects for peaceful reform became less hopeful, and the
Radicals a less effective force, so did Mill's role as sympathetic
critic of the group become less viable. He redefined the nature and
function of speculation and found for himself a new role. Productive though his associations with the neo-Idealists and the Saint-
Simonians temporarily were, they ultimately re-accentuated his
solitary position. He could not exchange allegiance to Benthamism
for adherence to another system. The middle of the road was a
lonely, albeit fruitful, position. Mill's isolation was, however, to
some exent, a shared one, for the Radicals as a group came to
experience an isolation akin to Mill's after the 1837 election. In the
1830s, Carlyle, like Mill, was concerned with a critique of logical
method closely allied to a contemplation of Radicalism. Carlyle's
isolation was, however, more profound than Mill's. His nurturing
within Scottish Dissent had encouraged his role as a propagandist
for Idealism. His move to London reawakened awareness of his
national identity, so that not only did Idealism confront empiricism, but working-class Scottish Radicalism and Dissent questioned
the secular reformism of the English upper and middle classes. In
the English capital, Carlyle was culturally uprooted, solitary in his
religious viewpoint, politically segregated.
  Despite the 1770 Act of Union, Scotland possessed a social
structure very different from that of the adjoining country. Its
cultural tradition was largely independent of English influence;

Edinburgh was the centre of a thriving national literature, and
Scottish thinkers considered German Idealism before English
thinkers paid it any attention. Scottish schools and universities
included natural sciences and modern languages in their curricula,
and were open to all social classes. In England, it was not until
1833 that the first grant was made by Parliament for elementary
education; the English public and grammar schools were decaying
institutions, devoted to the teaching of the classics. Oxford and
Cambridge were training schools for the aristocracy and Anglican
clergymen. Carlyle's move to London embodied a decision made
by many Victorian authors. The vitality of an autonomous provincial culture provided stimulus for many of these writers, but
London, with its opportunities for work and fame, had a magnetic
power. Prior to the move, Francis Jeffrey, editor of the *Edinburgh
Review*, had refused to procure for Carlyle the Chair of Astronomy
at Edinburgh University, and Carlyle relinquished his efforts to
acquire an income by conventional means. Carlyle spoke of his
memories of the difference between the two periods: 'The London
years are not definite, or fertile in disengaged remembrances, like
the Scotch ones: dusty, dim, unbeautiful they still seem to me in
comparison'.[2] The terminology associated his life in Scotland with
qualities of optimism and proximity to a fruitful cultural inheritance: the London years were described with adjectives suggesting
an Arnoldian weariness of perception inherent in urban life.

The death of Irving, in what Carlyle termed, 'the first months of
our adventurous settlement', intensified the sense of severance
from Scottish roots. Just as Scotland failed to provide a role for
Carlyle, so Irving, in 1833, had been rejected by the Kirk. Yet
Carlyle also saw Irving and himself as unique in being the last
products of a Scottish tradition of Dissent.[3] That inheritance
enabled Irving to be 'a genuine man sent into this our *un* genuine
phantasmagory of a world', but it also alienated him from English
metropolitan values. He was aloof from 'our mad Babylon . . .
with all her engines', and 'the Spirit of the Time, which could not
enlist him as its soldier, must needs, in all ways, fight against him
as its enemy'.[4] In the death of Irving, a distinctly Scottish genius,
alienated from both his homeland and England, Carlyle glimpsed a
gloomy premonition of what might be his own fate.

In his cultural uprootedness, Carlyle pinpointed his idiosyncratic mental cast in terms of nationality. Scottish Dissent was at the
forefront of his mind; in 1833, he contemplated writing a book on
John Knox. Politically, Carlyle defied categorisation. He was aware

that the Scottish flavour of his Radicalism gave him little mental affinity with the Benthamites with whom he socialised. Carlyle's Radicalism was 'a bitter inheritance from the Covenanters'; whereas Mill and the English populist movements flirted with the notion of revolution, the sects of the late eighteenth-century religious revival in Scotland rejected 'the radicalism of those who uproot old institutions'.[5] The Benthamites shared with Carlyle a *déclassé* status because of their education, but although Carlyle attracted their attention, he sensed a gap between their views and his preoccupations and spoke, in later years, of their one-sided outlook.[6] Carlyle's radicalism did not extend to personal morality; he saw the London radicals as antipathetic to the notion of duty, lax in sexual behaviour. At a radical meeting in 1834, he was bored and angered by the speeches; in 1837, he felt weary contempt for 'electioneerings and screechings'.[7] Carlyle became slowly disillusioned with Mill, and his break with him demonstrated, and increased, his political isolation. In 1835, he spoke of Mill as 'the nearest approach to a real man that I find here'. By the middle of 1836, he had determined to see less of him, for Mill had 'withered into the miserablest metaphysical *scrae*, body and mind'. In 1835, Carlyle confessed to his mother his disgust at London politics and the government's failure to improve the lot of the poor, yet he insisted that he was 'one of the deepest, though perhaps the quietest, of all the Radicals now extant in the world'.[8] As Mill redefined the public role of radicalism in the press, Carlyle defined radicalism privately and idiosyncratically, as a personal creed.

Carlyle's dislocation, spiritual isolation and political heterodoxy conditioned the viewpoint which governed the composition of *The French Revolution*: the writing of the book started only after he settled in Cheyne Row. At a psychological level, solitude accentuated Carlyle's nervous sensitivity, prompting a vision in which extremes were surrealistically juxtaposed. In 1835, London as microcosm bodied forth this juxtaposition, and Carlyle's reflections suggested his preoccupation with his provinciality:

> The world often looks quite spectral to me; sometimes as in Regent Street the other night (my nerves being all shattered), quite hideous, discordant, almost infernal . . . Coming homewards . . . through street walkers, through – *Ach Gott!* – unspeakable pity swallowed up unspeakable abhorrence of it and of myself. The moon and serene nightly sky in Sloane Street consoled me a little.[9]

Carlyle's eclecticism also emerged as a deliberately formulated viewpoint, a counterpart of, and element within his isolation. Refusing to be of one party, he derived enlightenment from all. In 1835, he pronounced his 'most decided contempt for all such manner of system-builders or sect-founders' and determined to strip himself of all formulas.[10] His mode of vision was distinct from the Intuition he had praised in the 1820s, a faculty validated by German thought. The vision of the 1830s lacked even a misread or transformed logical basis. Carlyle rejected the schematic intellectuality of philosophy and theology, because they revealed only 'the shadow projected from an everlasting reality that is within ourselves. Quit the shadow, seek the reality!' He saw truth as residing not in theory or conceptualisation, but in the fully-apprehended texture of a complex event. Hence sprang his 'passion for the concrete', his comment that 'the highest kind of writing, poetry or what else we may call it, that of the Bible for instance, has nothing to do with fiction at all, but with belief, with facts'.[11] The juxtaposition of beliefs and facts pinpoints the originality of Carlyle's vision which Mazzini termed 'imperfect and fugitive *realism*'.[12] Carlyle envisaged a perception and treatment of events which gave equal emphasis to concrete and spiritual realities. It was this blending of poetry and fact which Mill praised when reviewing *The French Revolution*.

For Carlyle, the quest for truth was not merely intellectual but moral and possessing strong religious overtones. He associated his mode of perception, in which vision, knowledge and belief were linked, with his Christian heritage: 'By God's blessing one has got two eyes to look with, also a mind capable of knowing, of believing. That is all the creed I will at this time insist on'. Carlyle's notion of reality had its roots in the Dissent of his parents, a religious tradition alien to metropolitan culture. Carlyle modified the position of the mother in *Wotton Reinfred* who 'felt as if the whole material world were but a vision and a show, a shadowy bark bound together only by the Almighty's word', and adhered closely to the view of his father who 'could not tolerate anything fictitious in books, and walked as a man in the full presence of heaven and hell and the judgment'.[13] Carlyle, similarly, acknowledged two types of 'fact', the historical and the spiritual, but did not link them by logical argument or philosophical theory: he posited them within a Christian tradition.

The transformation of such a vision into words presented Carlyle with the massive problems of language and form which had been unconsciously broached in *Sartor Resartus*, a work which, like *The French Revolution*, articulated a forensic eclecticism, and bore witness to Carlyle's confrontation with social chaos. The difficulty was obvious to J. A. Froude and Taine, and it haunted Carlyle, who spoke of his aims in terms which recalled the Herderian notion that thought was inseparable from the language in which it is expressed.[14] In 1836, he told Mill the stylistic problem was the largest one he faced; in 1837, he said style must be 'the product and close kinsfellow of all that lies under it'.[15] In *The French Revolution*, he lamented the fact that words were a 'poor exponent' of thought, and that thought itself was 'a poor exponent of the inward unnamed Mystery'. In 1839, he framed the antithesis sadly: 'Nature is solid, with six sides; language is superficial, nay linear.'[16]

Carlyle believed himself to possess a lonely vision of the truth, and he solved his problem by recourse to Scottish precedents. *The French Revolution* contained a forensic note, whereby Carlyle relied upon a pedagogic author/reader relationship, a technique learnt partly from Richter. The distinctiveness of the 'voice' of the work also, however, went back to a Scottish oral tradition.[17] The authorial voice was sometimes self-effacing, half-content simply to express its vision via idiosyncratic syntax and vocabulary. This method resembled that employed by Professor John Wilson, who lectured at Edinburgh in Carlyle's student days. Carlyle praised the 'solidity' of Wilson's vision, contrasting it to the 'purely metaphysical' exegeses of Dr Brown. Wilson would illustrate his lectures with 'Glowing pictures, dashed off in rapid powerful strokes, often of a fine poetic and emphatic quality . . . snatches of human portraiture', and would

> launch into blazy high-coloured delineations of distinguished men; *dramatising* his ideas, often enough . . . giving you a singularly vivid likeness in caricature. Caricature essentially good natured almost always, with brushfuls of flattering varnish exuberantly laid on, – tho' you felt, nearly always too, that there lurked something of the satirical *per-contra* at the bottom, and a clear view of the seamy side withal.[18]

In writing his masterpiece, Carlyle was indebted to Scottish precedents for both vision and method.

During the four years he spent writing *The French Revolution*, Carlyle was sustained by his enthusiasm for what he called, in 1833, 'the subject of subjects'. His reading in transcendentalism diminished after 1834.[19] Despite the success of his 1837 lectures on German literature, he did not bother to publish them, although his financial position was precarious. He published, instead, three articles which foreshadowed the themes and methods of *The French Revolution*. They spoke of the divine mystery of the world, the strangeness of human psychology, the romance of the actual. The revolution was 'a thing waste, incoherent, wild to look upon; but great with the greatness of reality; for the thing exhibited is no vision, but a fact'. Carlyle defined the aim of intellectual effort as to make 'one *see* something: for which latter result the whole man must coöperate', yet the sectarian writing of history left reality unapprehended, for, 'the Phenomenon, for its part, subsists there, all the while, unaltered; waiting to be pictured as often as you like, its entire meaning not to be compressed into any picture drawn by man'.[20]

Carlyle perceived both the event he described, and his book as an unstructured unity: the historical reality did not conform to the laws of logic, and likewise the imagination, in recreating history, could not be explained by, or function in relation to, logic's laws. His unified vision of both the event and book is indicated by his ability to rewrite part of the work after the burning of the first volume of draft by Mill's housemaid in 1835. He strove for overall effect, determining 'to splash down what I know in large masses of colours, that it may look like a smoke-and-fire conflagration in the distance, which it is'. He rarely spoke of details, but described his conception as 'quite an epic poem of the Revolution: an apotheosis of Sansculottism!'.[21]

Carlyle considered he 'put more of my life into that than into any of my books' and he was emotionally exhausted when he finished its composition.[22] In his strenuous scrutiny of the event, he confronted directly many personal preoccupations which had crystallised and intensified in his isolation. He saw the book as a tract for his times: from the Revolution's 'endless significance' we should 'endeavour to extract what may, in present circumstances, be adapted for us'. The Girondins resembled 'our present set of respectable Radical Members', and his demonstration of the irrelevance of the Girondist solution to the problems of France was correlative to the reasons for his disillusion with metropolitan radicalism. He compared the hunger of the French to the Irish plight in the 1830s.[23] Published as the book was when both Whigs and Radicals had failed to cope with the practical problems, and intellectual implications of populist movements, its depiction of the anarchical French mob afforded sobering parallels. The tone of mingled sorrow and urgency with which Carlyle spoke of the working class showed him dealing obliquely with a problem Mill considered directly and theoretically during the same period. The work also incorporated an analysis of the rational philosophical basis of Girondism; the tone and nature of the criticism had much in common with Carlyle's indictment of Utilitarianism. Carlyle's heroes, Danton and Mirabeau, perceived spiritual and material realities; the latter had 'not . . . *logic-spectacles*; but . . . an *eye!*', which Carlyle contrasted to the Girondists' 'fatal shortness of vision'.[24] True vision was contrasted to a perception limited within the confines of a logic which led to damaging actions. Mill and Carlyle insisted that perception was linked to action; both critically scrutinised the nature of perception in the face of the failure of a radicalism underpinned by rationalist logic.

The wave-like pattern Carlyle sometimes discerned in the events of the revolution afforded a macrocosm of his spiritual odyssey, as hope and stability gave way to despair and chaos, after the Saint-Simonian and Goethean models. The French Revolution was an event not merely in history, but in each man's mind; describing the Battle of Argonne, Carlyle quoted Goethe's *Campagne in Frankreich*, and saw in Goethe's mind, 'this same huge Death-Birth of the World; which now effectuates itself, outwardly in the Argonne, in such cannon-thunder; inwardly, in the irrecognisable head, quite otherwise than by thunder'. Yet, this oscillation was governed by a mysterious providence. 'Despair, pushed far enough . . . becomes a kind of genuine productive hope again.'[25]

These political, philosophical and spiritual preoccupations merged, however, into Carlyle's overriding aim, which was to body forth the complex reality of the event. An anti-doctrinaire stance was consistently apparent. Carlyle was explicitly didactic, in urging upon the reader a certain view of the revolution, but also implicitly didactic, for, by viewing the event correctly, the reader learnt the value and practice of a particular mode of perception. Life was shown not to conform to logic; perception, based on logic, failed to apprehend life. Explicit didacticism operated as Carlyle interpreted events in an eclectic fashion. The isolable themes in *The*

French Revolution did not show Carlyle indicating a single meaning in, or imposing a single interpretative theory upon, events. Rather, he used varying interpretations to spotlight events from different angles, and in different colours. Such a method pointed to that tendency in Carlyle's work which Mazzini saw as encouraging scepticism, yet *The French Revolution*, because of its non-doctrinal stance, attracted fulsome praise from ideologically opposed groups.[26] The revolution was an enigma, so all types of knowledge must be brought to bear upon it: 'in every object there is inexhaustible meaning; the eye sees in it what the eye brings means of seeing'. It was a problem which 'the best insight, seeking light from all possible sources, shifting its point of view whithersoever vision or glimpse of vision can be had, may employ itself in solving; and be well content to solve in some tolerably approximate way'.[27]

Carlyle utilised many theories, and merged disparate doctrines. His generalisations about the historical process were not logically reconcilable, and his stand against formulas would have been vitiated if they had been. He spoke of history as man's emergence from time, and descent into death, and, a few pages afterwards, combined, in an alternative definition, rewritten Idealist notions with Saint-Simonian and Goethean ideas about periodicity. When he utilised the image of man existing 'as we all do, in the confluence of Two Eternities',[28] he indicated the transient nature of human experience, and he was fond of invoking Prospero's speech in Act IV, Scene 1 of *The Tempest*. He located man at a point in time, emphasised the inexorability of cause and effect, and gave to the historical process connotations of a Nemesis-governed Greek tragedy. The view of humanity in relation to the sweep of time was utilised variously and movingly. He singled out the clergy in describing the procession to Notre-Dame, and remarked how they had 'drifted in the Time-Stream, far from its native latitude', and similarly considered the bizarre fate of Bishop Talleyrand-Périgord. Marie-Antoinette was both faded beauty and emblem of hope. Such a perspective was resonant with multiple meanings. It pointed to human transience; it invoked a medieval concept of fortune; it preluded the onset of despair. Describing Robespierre's solitude during the Terror, Carlyle recalled the 'young Advocate of promise . . . [who] gave up the Arras Judgeship rather than sentence one man to die'.[29] This suggested the melancholy failure to fulfil youthful promise, the strange psychological development of men in times of crisis. The notion of man as a speck in eternity was deployed to sound notes of both irony and sadness.

Carlyle also offered a panoramic vision which was implicitly didactic. Its meaning resided in tone, being conveyed by the sound of terminology and syntax, as much as by the cognitive power of the words. In this respect, his presentational method drew upon the view of Ranke and his associates, who had insisted that there was no pattern in history, and saw the historian's task as that of objective fact-collector, concerned to show 'how things in actuality were'. In 1824, Barante's history of the Dukes of Burgundy bore, on its title page, Quintillian's axiom, 'History should be written to tell stories, not to prove points'.[30] Carlyle taught the reader implicitly by the presentation of a series of events upon which he imposed no pattern, only suggesting tentatively that 'laws of action . . . work unseen in the depths of that huge blind Incoherence', or seeing the revolution, like the National Convention, as 'a black Dream, *become real*'. Amidst the chaos, 'In startling transitions, in colours all intensated, the sublime, the ludicrous, the horrible succeed one another; or rather, in crowding tumult, accompany one another'.[31]

The revelation of chaos found a counterpart in Carlyle's presentation of people and events as embodying and fusing mysterious contradictions, a vision unlike the early utilitarians' 'picture with hard, positive outlines . . . unsoftened by the changing effects of mist and cloud'.[32] Carlyle's focus turned from political tumult to an ordered world of toil, and the silent progress of the seasons. A royal procession was 'comico-tragic', 'most fantastic, yet most miserably real'. On one event, he commented, 'So strangely is Freedom . . . environed in Necessity; such a singular Somnambulism of Conscious and Unconscious, of Voluntary and Involuntary, is this Life of Man'. 'Nature fathered both Marat and Charlotte Corday; within one man 'there are depths . . . that go the length of lowest Hell, as there are heights that reach highest Heaven; – for are not both Heaven and Hell made out of him, made by him, everlasting Miracle and Mystery as he is'. A note of lamentation, Hamlet-like in its synchronism of questioning and acceptance, accompanied such a vision of paradox: a statement of fact shifted into a minor key of reflection, as Carlyle asked, 'O why was the earth so beautiful, becrimsoned with dawn and twilight, if man's dealings with man were to make it a vale of scarcity, of tears, not even soft tears?'[33] The rhythm, repetition of key words, alliteration, deployment of long vowels, and liquid and sibilant consonants imported the implicit lesson. The meaning of the vision was, in Herderian terms, the words Carlyle chose.

Didacticism and revelation worked together to convey to, and absorb the reader in, Carlyle's vision. Carlyle imagined his reader as a distant 'beloved shade', himself as 'but a voice'. Yet the reader was also the 'not yet embodied spirit of a Brother': Carlyle spoke of 'our journeying together'. As the exponent of eclecticism, Carlyle explained events to the audience, but, in reading Carlyle's words, the audience also came to see with Carlyle's eyes. Knowledge and vision were identified. That Carlyle found inspiration for this method in a peculiarly Scottish tradition is shown when he remarked in punning, archaic dialect 'What a man *kens*, he *cans*'.[34] Such words find an echo in the Hegelian notion that 'Truth lay now in the process of cognition itself'.[35] Carlyle created a complex world with which Benthamite logic and its schematised view of reality, failed to reckon. Of the Benthamites, as of the Girondists, Carlyle noted, 'they and their Formula are incompatible with the Reality'.[36] In the light of the failure of the reformist philosophies of late eighteenth-century France, and of the Whigs and Radicals of the 1830s, Carlyle's book was political in its implications. The French Revolution, as Carlyle viewed it, proved that those who live by formulas will perish by reality; the rise of populist movements, and the defeat of the Radicals in 1837, led Mill to a similar conclusion. The reading of *The French Revolution* taught this historical fact, and suggested this contemporary parallel.

The rationalist tradition had also suggested the limitations of the mind. Carlyle demonstrated a new way of looking, whereby mind might view reality more comprehensively, so that the rationalist error might be avoided. In 'journeying together' with Carlyle, the reader became involved in a protracted attempt to avoid the Girondists' and the Benthamites' mistake, for he was made to see the world with Carlyle's eyes, and their vision was unobscured with formulas. Defining the 'objectivity' of *The French Revolution*, Mazzini noted how Carlyle identified himself with 'the things, events, or men which he exhibits', to produce 'not imitations, but reproductions'. As Carlyle forged his method to articulate his vision of a complex reality, so Mill praised de Vigny's attempt to look 'life steadily in the face', to gaze 'into the world for the philosophy of it'.[37] *The French Revolution* enacted a direct confrontation with reality such as Mill envisaged. Carlyle described the work as 'a wild savage book, itself a kind of French Revolution',[38] for it was intended to transform men's way of viewing the world. *The French Revolution* embodied the protest of an idiosyncratic perception which owed much to Scottish Dissent. The working-class Burgher's son from the remote provinces challenged the mental preconceptions, and resultant political actions, of aristocratic Whigs, intellectual metropolitan radicals, and anarchistic populists. Carlyle concluded that their incorrect understanding of reality caused the chaos he witnessed in England in the 1830s, yet 'If all wars, civil and other, are misunderstandings, what a thing right-understanding must be!'[39] Acceptance of Carlyle's rebellion against the vision of reformist orthodoxy would, paradoxically, bring the peace which the groups he castigated had failed to effect.

The attempts of the rational reformists to translate logic into political action had led to disorder and suffering, because reality did not function in accordance with logical laws, and could not be logically explained. Mill and Carlyle, by the late 1830s, were beginning to see sectarian philosophies as barriers the mind must pass beyond to attain true understanding. Yet Carlyle persisted, as had the earlier Utilitarians, Coleridge and Mill, in seeing the problem of perception as the root of all other problems. He insisted that only a correct view of reality could avert social chaos. Art, rather than inadequate and narrow philosophical systems, may express a valid mode of perception, and this endowed the imaginative vision with a status elevated above that of the philosophical. Carlyle thus claimed a serious social role for the artist. The rejection of philosophy was the prelude to more important tasks. It was in relation to this critique of philosophical speculation in the work of Mill and Carlyle that Marian Evans was to formulate her decision to write novels.

Part Two
Marian Evans

8

Marian Evans (1819–1840)

Men do not fathom intellectual history if they ask about nothing but the intellect.

originality, in any high sense of the word, is now scarcely ever attained but by minds which have undergone elaborate discipline, and are deeply versed in the results of previous thinking.[1]

In their consideration of Intuitionism and Associationism, Mill and Carlyle moved beyond the confines of a philosophical debate about logical methods. Firstly, the logical problem raised questions about such issues as the historical process, the individual's political, moral, and religious positions, and, centrally, the nature of perception. Secondly, both writers brought to bear upon philosophical problems insights afforded by literature and, in Carlyle's case, by religion. Thirdly, their attempt to extricate themselves, for psychological reasons, from the destructive sectarianism of the debate, led them to attempt a merging of logical methods, and also to have recourse to other writers who were working towards similar ends. By 1840, Mill and Carlyle were speaking of reality as resisting doctrinaire interpretations of the world, and of the mind confronting reality in a way which refuted the formulas of philosophers who attempted to define how the mind apprehended the world. From 1840 onwards, Mill's and Carlyle's intellectual efforts were also diffused. Carlyle produced works which cannot be categorised as to genre, such as *Chartism* and *Past and Present*. *Heroes, Hero-Worship and the Heroic in History* repeated, more dogmatically, insights contained in his earlier works. The historian's skills of sifting and synthesising facts were turned to account in biographies of Cromwell and Frederick the Great. Mill became an MP; he wrote on logic; he defined liberty. He campaigned for female emancipation; he wrote his autobiography and essays on religion. They both produced their mature works when a preoccupation with the problem of logical method ceased. By contemplation of the problem they were led away from it: ultimately, they entertained

doubts about the validity of philosophical methods and conclusions. In the wide tradition of eclecticism and pragmatism
which they and other writers echoed and strengthened, Marian
Evans witnessed a disentanglement from the preoccupations of
philosophy which, in broad outline, her own development was to
repeat, but which produced very different results. She was of a
later generation, and from a different cultural tradition, and this
proved crucial. The similarities between George Eliot, Mill and
Carlyle struck George Eliot's contemporaries. George Sarson noted
that the three writers shared 'a similarity in their aim and drift', and
Frederic Harrison commented that George Eliot, 'in mental equip-
ment stood side by side with Mill, Spencer, Lewes, and Carlyle. If
she produced nothing in philosophy . . . quite equal to theirs, she
was of their kith and kin, of the same intellectual quality'.[2] Marian
Evans read voraciously, pursuing, a 'systematic study of subjects . . . an admirable balance of art, science, and philosophy'; in
March 1839, she commented, 'We cannot, at least those who ever
read to any purpose at all . . . help being modified by the ideas
that pass through our minds.' She yearned for synthesis, and
spoke of her youthful sense of 'only needing to apply myself in
order to master any task – to conciliate philosophers whose systems were at present but dimly known to me.' Yet, although her
life was lived in close relation to ideas, her scepticism was profound; she felt 'a constitutional repugnance for systems and codes
of life'.[3]

She was born in 1819, into a turbulent England. The Napoleonic
Wars had ended four years previously with the battle of Waterloo;
the Peterloo massacre occurred in the year of her birth. Her
adolescence, and early adulthood, coincided with one of the most
harrowing decades of the century, a time of bad harvests, economic depression, and the rise of Chartism in the wake of disillusion with the 1832 Reform Bill. The nearby city of Birmingham
became, in 1832, the self-elected centre of revolution. The area
around Coventry juxtaposed trim, neat villages, dependent
upon agriculture, and mining and weaving settlements, whose
prosperity was linked to that of the industries of the Midlands, and
especially the ribbon-weaving trade in Coventry. The cottage-
based weavers were the first to be laid off in a recession; they were
poorly housed, and were, reputedly, heavy drinkers with lax
morals. An 1840 Government Commission noted that their low
wages had as demoralising an influence on the working class as

poor relief.[4] It was also a time of a drift from the land; by 1840, urban workers outnumbered rural workers by two to one. The rural areas, such as that in which Marian Evans lived, were little affected by the reforms initiated by the Benthamites, but her Griff environment nevertheless embodied the contradictions of an age of transition. Through her father and the aristocratic Newdigates, she glimpsed a world of uncontroversial Anglicanism, and the time-hallowed privileges of the landed classes. Yet Robert Evans and his employers embraced change. Marian Evans's father supervised the mining of the Arbury coal seam: to this day, the Gothic plaster ornamentation of Arbury Hall, and the cracks in it caused by mine-workings, physically image the Newdigate responsiveness to new trends. Marian Evans's surroundings were such as might well prompt thoughts about the social mechanism. The pastoral peace Henry James found in Warwickshire in 1877 fulfilled the American dream, but Warwickshire in the early decades of the nineteenth century was also accurately described by James as somehow representative: it was 'the core and centre of the English world; midmost England, unmitigated England'.[5] It contained stark contrasts between the old and new worlds of conservatism and radicalism, aristocracy and proletariat, a rural and an industrial civilisation.

Mary Ann Evans was the last of six children born to Robert Evans by two wives between 1802 and 1809. As the youngest child in the family, she acquired a somewhat forbidding, precociously grown-up manner, setting her apart from the other pupils at the Miss Franklins' school. She had more in common with her teachers than her schoolfellows; she was highly emotional, yet also timid.[6] For Chrissey, her sister, five years her senior, she felt a strong affection. In 1852 she abandoned the unfinished proofs of the January number of the *Westminster Review* to visit Chrissey when Chrissey's husband, Edward Clarke, died on 20 December. Isaac, her brother, the adored childhood playmate, was to prove the aloof and censorious critic of her maturity. She had fond memories, in later years, of the kindness of her half-sister, Fanny. The outlook of Robert Evans, her much-loved father, was highly conventional. As land agent for the Newdigates, he shared their views; he was a High Anglican and a Conservative, who looked back with horror to the French Revolution, and, in 1832, arranged for the Newdigate tenants to vote against populist candidates. He was not a man of great education, and his Journal reveals no

literary talents. Yet Robert Evans's career confirmed the emergence
of a meritocracy in the nineteenth century. Having started out as a
carpenter, he progressed to the study of scientific agriculture, well
before that subject gained recognition in the late 1830s.[7] He was a
man with considerable technical expertise, knowing about mining,
surveying, and building. His success gave his daughter an indeterminate social status, which freed her thought from the preoccupations of any particular class.[8] It was also his hard-earned
respectability which indirectly led his youngest daughter to that
unorthodoxy which her highly respectable family so abhorred. The
family background was not intellectually stimulating: Marian
Evans was not eager to learn to read, and the household contained
few books. Robert Evans decided, however, for motives of prestige
and convenience, to send his daughter to boarding-school, and her
mother was anxious that she should have a good education.[9] Mrs
Evans's health was also poor after giving birth to twin sons who
only lived for ten days in 1821. It doubtless suited the parents to be
relieved of the care of their other two children: in 1824 both Isaac
and Marian Evans were sent away to school.

Education for girls in the early nineteenth century was usually of
a poor standard. Dame schools, such as the one Marian Evans
attended in 1824, were usually inefficient nurseries. Rote learning
was the method usually employed by inadequate teachers of older
children. The course of studies for young women was unintellec-
tual, for demanding subjects were seen to be incompatible with
feminine frailty. Such a system George Eliot was to satirise in the
description of Rosamond Vincy's education in *Middlemarch* and,
sceptic though George Eliot was, she never doubted the importance of higher education for women.[10] Marian Evans was fortu-
nate, however, for the schools she attended were of the rare kind
which produced the sensible, serious women who favourably
impressed Taine on his tours of the English provinces. Lewes, in
1860, strongly denied that George Eliot thought of herself as
'self-educated', and she spoke to Cross of the excellence of the
Miss Franklins' instruction.[11] She received encouragement from
the Newdigates, who allowed her access to their library; her father
gave Miss Lewis, her teacher at Mrs Wallington's boarding school
in Nuneaton, twenty pounds to spend on books for his daughter.
Her friend, Bessie Belloc, saw the mature George Eliot as 'the
living incarnation of English Dissent', noting especially her in-
dustriously diligent use of her talents, a virtue imbibed from the
liberal dissenting tradition of the Baptist Miss Franklins, whom

Marian Evans's father erroneously saw as no threat to the influence upon his daughter of his own conservative views. From this education, Marian Evans acquired a taste for omnivorous reading which sowed the seeds of both her intellectuality and her scepticism. It also taught her a speculative ambitiousness, which her adult sense of the difficulties of the quest for truth mocked ironically.[12]

At Mrs Wallington's school in Nuneaton, which she attended from 1828 to 1832, Marian Evans met Maria Lewis who, although still only in her early twenties, was principal governess of the establishment. Miss Lewis was an evangelical Anglican, a member of a group who, like enthusiasts of other sectarian persuasions, offered 'a concerted system of ideas, aspirations, and practices to be imposed upon society'.[13] The evangelicals' pragmatic reformism was encouraged by the horror aroused by the atheistic French Revolution, and they reached the peak of their influence during the profound social unrest of the 1830s. They set up missions, initiated a campaign of church-building, championed the abolition of slavery and prison reform. The group was not merely pragmatic: it was even, in a sense, anti-intellectual. It had originated from the reintensification of the Protestant tendency which emphasised the individual's duty to scrutinise his conscience. With its focus upon vital spiritual experience, it spoke to what Newman called 'the spiritual awakening of spiritual wants', and it dwelt upon the mystic union of the soul with God. Its unlearned pastors were not 'the fittest teachers for inquiring minds', and they appealed to the emotions and the consciences rather than the intellects of their lower and middle-class congregations. An emphasis on scriptural authority led to a neglect of critical Biblical scholarship.[14] Evangelicalism introduced Marian Evans to the notion that ideas could govern an individual's interpretation of the world and conduct within it. George Eliot was retrospectively to describe herself at the age of seventeen as 'earnestly endeavouring to shape this anomalous English Christian life of ours into some consistency with the Spirit, and simple verbal tenor of the New Testament'. She showed herself, for the first time, unable to 'rest content with ideas that remained quietly in the realm of thought'.[15] She responded to both the pragmatic and non-intellectual aspects of the movement. She took up good works. She cultivated her soul by copying pious verses into a notebook and by organising prayer meetings. The systematic control over belief and action which the movement offered counterbalanced the liberating effect of her education.

Around 1827, she read *Waverley*. Scott's novels were to be a life-long passion. On 1 January 1860, Lewes presented her with forty-eight volumes of The Waverley Novels, describing Scott, in his affectionate inscription, as 'Her longest-venerated and best-loved Romancist'. Her late essay, 'Authorship', defended Scott against charges of commercialism.[16] Her reading of Scott increased the tendency towards sceptical inquiry which had been encouraged by her education, and by that other aspect of evangelicalism which spoke of the importance of private judgment. Balance and tolerance were the keynotes of Scott's vision. His narratives introduced Marian Evans to the opposing concepts engendered by the rival logics, but also suggested how they might be reconciled. His was an imagination which effortlessly blended heart and head, compassionate sympathy and dispassionate analysis, and he utilised both qualities in an attempt to understand, rather than to judge. Scott offered a revolutionary view of character in relation to its historical context. He thus afforded a contrast to evangelicalism, which had seen character in relation to spiritual realities, and foreshadowed the contemplation of determinism Marian Evans was to encounter in Charles Bray's *The Philosophy of Necessity*. He often probed the problem of historical determinism in relation to the same historical period, dealing with medieval civilisation in *Ivanhoe, The Talisman* and *Quentin Durward*. He was fascinated by what Saint-Simon called critical periods: he charted the minute changes wrought upon manners by social change within a short period, and even in a novel with a contemporary setting focused on '*shifting* manners'.[17] Yet he also sceptically asserted the existence of an unchanging human nature, and showed how character was influenced by 'family connexions, and early predilections'.[18] Scott's unprejudiced treatment of political viewpoints also helped to mould Marian Evans's scepticism. He eschewed party bias, because it led to intolerance and narrowness of vision, and his political views were governed by a pragmatic, historical sense.[19] At a time when political groups were polarised into the extremes of radicalism and conservatism, Scott arbitrated judiciously between concepts of progress and decay. He conceded the possibility of human improvement through increased knowledge, yet he also possessed a sense of the frailty of human wisdom and virtue. He responded to melancholy images of decayed grandeur, but also deromanticised the past.[20] His contemplation of the nature of change may well have sharpened Marian Evans's sense that her own environment was in a state of flux. She saw the coming of the railways in 1838 and the changes wrought by the 1835 Municipal Corporations Act. At the Miss Franklins' school, she lived in a row of gracious houses which was close to appalling slums; when engaged in charitable acts, she met unemployed weavers, driven from work by technological progress.[21] Scott's non-doctrinaire view of change also seems to echo on in the Epilogue to *The Mill on the Floss* and the opening chapter of *Scenes of Clerical Life*.

In his treatment of events, Scott blended reality and romance. He retained a sense of wonder, for he asserted that the future could not be 'subject to the rules of arithmetic', and that there were 'mysteries . . . beyond the knowledge of philosophy'. Julia Mannering found that reality could conform to the imagined events of fiction; sensational events were justified by reference to historical fact.[22] But Scott also showed that belief in the supernatural might be historically conditioned, or the product of an anxious mind, or a misguided interpretation of natural circumstances.[23] His sympathetic treatment of sensibility was also tempered by a respect for reason. The heroes of *Waverley* and *The Antiquary* reached maturity when they relinquished passionate enthusiasms and belief in romance. The egotism of sensibility was criticised, and real grief distinguished from assumed melancholy. Scott was more moved 'by the distress under which a strong, proud, and powerful mind is compelled to give way, than by the more easily excited sorrows of softer dispositions'.[24] His ability to learn from rationalist and romantic traditions was also obvious in his treatment of religion: he saw the dangers of both cold liberalism and passionate enthusiasm. He was fascinated by enthusiasm, by Catholicism in *The Black Dwarf* and *Rob Roy*, by conflicts between Christians and Muslims in *The Talisman*, and between Puritans and Anglicans in *Woodstock*. Belief was, however, explained by reference to environment and individual psychology.[25] He lamented sectarian divisions which ignored men's common humanity, and he proposed the reading of the Bible for its 'general tenor'. Beliefs must not dictate 'a line of conduct contrary to those feelings of natural humanity, which Heaven has assigned to us as the general law of our conduct'. He suggested that 'goodness and worth were not limited to those of any single form of religious observance'.[26]

Towards the end of his life, Scott comforted himself that 'I have tried to unsettle no man's faith, to corrupt no man's principle'.[27] Yet Marian Evans's defiant tolerance found some of its origins in

Scott's historical perspective. Scott possessed the historian's desire to see things as they were, and he aimed to 'do justice to all men'.[28] George Eliot was to tell Mrs Congreve that Scott prompted her emancipation into creative scepticism because 'he was healthy and historical and it would not fit onto her creed'. He diminished her willingness to embrace any single interpretative doctrine by presenting an historian's view of belief which took into account its complex causes. He directed her towards the marshalling of evidence and an examination of problems, and she echoed such notions in a letter written in 1840.[29] In her last work, she paid tribute to Scott's enquiring method, and its social effect, when she noted 'Utopian pictures help the reception of ideas as to constructive results, but hardly so much as a vivid presentation of how results have been actually brought about, especially in religious and social change'.[30]

Her contact with the Evangelical movement, and her reading of Scott, belong to the schoolgirl years. Upon the death of her mother, the sixteen-year-old girl was summoned back to Griff House, a tall, mostly eighteenth-century building near the local church. Nostalgia for her childhood days pervades the *Brother and Sister* poems, written in 1869, but her memories of her adolescence were mainly melancholy. Her girlhood, she said, was much unhappier than Maggie Tulliver's. There were some pleasures. She loved the unsensational Midlands landscape; she continued her good works, and there were visits from friends and family. She was, however, torn between her longing to study and her obligations to her father. In 1869, she told Mrs Pierce, 'I enter into those young struggles of yours to get knowledge, into the longing you feel to do something more than domestic duties while yet you are held fast by womanly necessities for neatness and household perfection . . . . I have known what it was to have close ties making me feel the wants of others as my own'.[31] Hers was also an isolated existence from an intellectual point of view. She devoted three days a week to energetic self-education and her father provided money for books. Yet letters to old friends were the sole outlet for discussion of her ideas, and, as these ideas changed, Patty Jackson and Miss Lewis were an unreceptive audience. Her reading of Scott unsettled her beliefs, and the years at Griff saw the process accelerate. She eagerly explored a wide variety of subjects, proof of the intellectual curiosity stimulated by the Miss Franklins. Even on her first visit to London, at the age of nineteen, she spent the evenings reading.[32] She turned to the English classics: Young's *Night Thoughts*, Cowper, Shakespeare, Defoe, Pope and Bacon, and romantic writers such as Southey, Byron and Wordsworth.[33] Theology, as Ruskin noted, was a dangerous subject for women, and Marian Evans read religious works written from a variety of viewpoints.[34] She perused memoirs, scriptural commentaries, works on the relationship between geology and the Bible. She subscribed to Isaac Taylor's *Ancient Christianity*, which expounded a critical view of the early Fathers. In 1840, animated perhaps by Scott's historical perspective, she tried to compile a chart which would provide a 'chronological view of Ecclesiastical History'. In the same year, she was deep in the literature of the Oxford Movement, reading books by William Gresley, the Tracts, *Lyra Apostolica* and Keble's *The Christian Year*.[35] These works were in tune with her reading of Romantic writers, for the Oxford Movement had much in common with romanticism, but they were remote from the evangelical commitment to practical Christianity in a troubled decade.

Such reading might have seemed suitable for a pious, serious and respectable girl but, coupled with a fascination for Scott, an excursion into differing sectarian viewpoints led to a questioning of the rightness of any one of them. Whereas the scepticism of Mill and Carlyle emerged from their disenchantment with one-sided philosophical creeds, Marian Evans defined her scepticism in relation to the noisy religious disputes which multiplied after the attempts of Grey's government to reform the Irish Church in 1833. In 1839, she remarked to Miss Lewis, 'however congruous a theory may be with my notions, I cannot find that comfortable repose that others appear to possess after having made their election of a class of sentiments'. She spoke of the difficulty 'really honest minds' found in attaining 'a resting place amid the foot-balling of religious parties', and suffered a fit of hysteria at a party because of her 'conviction that I was not in a situation to maintain the *Protestant* character of the true Christian'.[36] Her letters, nevertheless, abounded in pieties. She announced the birth of Chrissey's third child with a reference to the Collect for the fourth Sunday after Easter, and her letters to her Methodist aunt and uncle, Mr and Mrs Samuel Evans, strung together, or paraphrased, Biblical quotations. She criticised oratorio for turning the Scriptures into entertainment.[37] But the letters also hinted at a mental and emotional unrest which her correspondents ignored or misinterpreted. Her remarks about her spiritual difficulties and imperfections were probably taken as an indication of the enthusiast's self-castigating conscience. In February 1839, she wrote to Miss Lewis, 'I think there are few who know much of mental conflict that would not choose external trial in preference to it.' She told her Methodist aunt, Mrs Samuel Evans, that she had 'too high an opinion . . . of my spiritual condition', and spoke of her own mind as 'a stranger to the continuous enjoyment of that peace that no man can take from its possessors'. In discussing her hysteria in 1840, she admitted, 'I have not referred to realities that I desire to have nearest my heart, for several reasons'. Her sense of inner unease was often expressed in misleadingly religious terminology: she used Biblical texts and imagery which hinted that she felt isolated, desperate, uprooted and confused.[38]

This turmoil was brought about, however, not merely by contact with the 'healthy and historical' mind of Scott, and her weariness with sectarian disputes. Marian Evans had started to read Carlyle, and those who grew up in the 1840s described the first reading of his works 'in terms that seem drawn from the revival experiences of Methodism'. He was 'the yeast-plant, fermenting the whole literary brew as it had not been fermented for centuries'.[39] Marian Evans's first direct reference to his work came in a letter written to Miss Lewis on 27 October 1840, when she quoted from *Chartism*. Yet it seems possible that she read his works earlier than this. In November 1838, she referred to Edward Irving, which may indicate that she had read Carlyle's article.[40] Stronger evidence of an early contact with Carlyle's work is, however, provided by the comments she made in March 1839 on Lockhart's biography of Scott. Like Carlyle, in his review of Lockhart, she expatiated on the value of biography. Carlyle had remarked of Scott, 'His life was worldly; his ambitions were worldly. There is nothing spiritual in him; all is economical, material, of the earth earthy', and Marian Evans noted, 'The spiritual sleep of that man was awful; he does not at least betray if he felt anything like a pang of conscience'. Carlyle's comment that Scott 'must kill himself that he may be a country gentleman, the founder of a race of Scottish lairds' also seems to be echoed by Marian Evans's view that Scott 'sacrificed almost his integrity for the sake of acting out the character of the Scotch laird'.[41] At the time she wrote these comments, she had read only the first volume of the biography. Devoted to Scott though she was, she echoed Carlyle's evaluation of the later years of Scott's life. Miss Lewis, the recipient of the letter, presumably read these criticisms of worldiness as entirely appropriate to her pupil's evangelical principles. Marian Evans, at this juncture, also conceived the desire to learn German. She had received her second lesson from Mr Brezzi by 23 March 1840, and seven months later confessed that of all the languages she had learned, it was with German that she felt the greatest affinity.[42]

She was soon openly expressing her enthusiasm for Carlyle. She wrote to Patty Jackson, urging her to read *Sartor Resartus*, for Carlye's 'soul is a shrine of the brightest and purest philanthropy, kindled by the live coal of gratitude and devotion to the Author of all things'. She added, significantly, 'I should observe that he is not "orthodox"'. Carlyle's philosophical anti-sectarianism confirmed the tolerant scepticism she found in Scott. Marian Evans became openly impatient with doctrinaire stances. She told Miss Lewis that John Williams was 'a dissenter, but the B[ishop] of Chester highly commended his work. . . . If you have any bigots near you there could not be a better book for them'. It was probably Carlyle's idiosyncratic Christianity which also encouraged her interest in the work of Mrs Jameson who had a 'liberalising, philosophising manner of speaking about religion and morals', and the writings of Louis Aimé-Martin, 'a soi-disant "rational" Christian'.[43] Marian Evans described spiritual experiences in terms which recalled Carlyle's in *Sartor Resartus*, and the passages on natural supernaturalism in that same work informed the language in which she spoke to Miss Lewis in 1840 of her delight in nature. She also echoed the clothes imagery from that work, and merged Carlyle's ideas with Wordsworthian notions.[44]

Marian Evans's reading of *Chartism* was especially important. The work was written on the eve of the hungry forties and was considered too polemical for any respectable periodical. It dealt with a contemporary reality of which Marian Evans could not have been unaware, for Birmingham was an important centre of Chartist activity. Faucher cited the book to support his own portrayal of ferment beneath the surface of society, and anxiety in the circles of power; it was quoted approvingly by Engels.[45] The work would have sharpened Marian Evans's sense of social change and, as the last of Carlyle's works to show any sympathy with radicalism, it introduced her to certain advanced social theories before she met the Brays, who were to extend her interest in such matters. Marian Evans, moreover, when she quoted from *Chartism*, spoke also of the individual's duty to mankind: 'We should aim to be like plants in the chamber of sickness, dispensing purifying air even in a region that turns all pale its verdure and cramps its instinctive propensity to expand'. This might have seemed an innocuous plea for evangelical good works, but she continued 'Society is a wide nursery of plants where the hundred decompose to nourish the future ten, after giving collateral benefits to their contemporaries destined for a fairer garden. . . . Events are now so momentous, and the elements of society in so chemically critical a state that a drop seems enough to change its whole force'.[46] The first sentence suggested the continuity of the historical process; the second, with its reference to a 'critical' period, implied a cyclical view of time. She eclectically blended two logically irreconcilable notions in an urgent attempt to interpret the problems of her environment. This was the method of Carlyle. She also echoed the terminology of heart and head employed by Carlyle: his works introduced her to the attempt to resolve the debate between Associationism and Intuitionism, and demonstrated the ramifications of this debate in experience itself.[47]

Matters came to a head in 1842 when she refused to accompany her father to church, the first public sign of a process which started in her late teens. Close friends, such as John Chapman and Frederic Harrison, spoke of a slow erosion of her beliefs. Belief is destroyed, Chapman noted, 'in the silent hidden way which characterises the excavations of termites; it is not until the once solid beams have been reduced to the thickness of an eggshell that the edifice is perceived to be in danger'.[48] Marian Evans spoke of the move from Griff to Foleshill as 'a deeply painful incident – it is like dying to one stage of existence'.[49] At Rosehill, she was to find the intellectual companionship she lacked in her rural seclusion. Only in providing this companionship did the Brays and the Hennells change her life: her scepticism had already taken root.

9

Marian Evans (1841–1843): Coventry

Strengthen the female mind by enlarging it, and there will
be an end to blind obedience.[1]

I

Marian Evans moved to the outskirts of Coventry at the start of the
hungry forties. There were some hopeful political signs. In 1843,
after O'Connell was imprisoned, and then released by the Lords,
agitation for the repeal of the union of Ireland subsided. Peel's free
trade budget of 1842 laid the basis for future prosperity. Some
developments bore directly upon Warwickshire. In 1841, a Committee was set up to investigate the plight of the handloom weavers. In 1842, Ashley's Women and Children in the Mines Bill was
passed, and Chadwick inquired into the sanitary condition of the
labouring population. Yet moves to improve the lot of the poor
were accompanied by the rebellion of the poor against their fate.
The first half of 1842 also saw the second climax of Chartist unrest
at a time of grave economic depression. The movement was
changing its base, however, away from the Midlands. By the time
the second National Chartist Convention met in London on 12
April 1842, the movement had become centred on Manchester.
The Chartist petition was rejected on 2 May 1842 and the following
August saw the outbreak of the Plug Strikes.

The move from Griff signalled a radical change in Marian Evan's
environment, which, together with her contact with the Rosehill
circle, sharpened her concern for social issues. Foleshill itself
expanded rapidly between 1820 and 1830 and was turning into a
suburb of Coventry. Its inhabitants were engaged in mining,
weaving and agriculture, and a government report of 1840 spoke of
Foleshill as a lawless, depressed area, especially notorious for ignorance, immorality and drunkenness. The Church of England exerted
little influence over the unruly population, and that population

79

had little faith in the efficacy of government legislation. Progressive political sentiments and a working-class tradition of self-help
were, however, in evidence amongst the Foleshill weavers. By
1840, seven co-operative shops had been established: one boasted
a small library of works on socialism, political economy and political science. The dissenting chapels set up schools, and pressed
politicians for a scheme of national education.[2] The centre of
Coventry was less than a mile away from Marian Evans's new
home. Coventry had ceased to be of regional importance before the
start of the nineteenth century, and, in 1842, the County of Coventry was returned to Warwickshire, and the city's prestige was
further diminished. It still possessed, however, the vitality of
many provincial cities. The top ranks of its society were occupied
by the professional classes, and, just below them, came the large
ribbon manufacturers, such as Charles Bray. For these groups,
there were learned societies, race meetings, concerts and plays.
Coventry also had a vigorous liberal tradition from which both
Marian Evans and the Rosehill circle profited. Even before the 1832
extension of the franchise, all those who had served an apprenticeship were entitled to become freemen of the city, and all freemen
had the vote. Between 1832 and 1867, these artisans regularly
returned Liberal and Radical MPs. After the 1835 Municipal Corporations Act, local elections were bitterly contested, and the city
acquired a reforming corporation. Holyoake noted in 1843 'Infidelity in Coventry . . . is not a ricketty, but a fine-grown boy. More
is done than is recorded, and liberal views extend farther than is
supposed'. In 1848, an active Socialist group still existed in the city,
and freethought organisations flourished between 1838 and 1862,
although by the late 1840s such associations had waned in most
provincial areas. The forties in Coventry were not exceptionally
hungry, but the slump in the ribbon trade from 1840 to 1843
brought awful living conditions for the weavers. The ribbon manufacturers had to cope with a worsening of industrial relations,
which led to disputes about wages, strikes and picketing. The wide
working-class franchise, and the absence of an aristocratic ruling-
class, did, however, save the city from the worst excesses of
Chartism, and the political agitation associated with dissent.[3]

Marian Evans moved to Foleshill on 17 March 1841; Isaac married Sarah Rawlins on 8 June in the same year. Robert Evans and
his remaining unmarried child settled down to a quiet existence,
punctuated by visits to, and from, his other children. She had few

outside distractions in these first eight months, save for trips to church, the occasional lecture series, her language lessons, and running a clothing club for miners' families. Bray told Combe in 1854 that she was, of all daughters, 'the most devoted I ever knew'; she also doted on Clara Clarke, her small niece.[4] Her intellectual life continued to be energetic, but she wrote to Miss Lewis of her feeling of isolation, and yearned for intellectual companionship.

She ventured in new directions. At Griff, she had been interested in the physical sciences, in geology, in phrenology. At Foleshill she read John Pringle Nichol's *View of the Architecture of the Heavens* (1838) and *The Phenomena and Order of the Solar System* (1838) which gave her insight into Newtonian scientific determinism, and works which considered the relationship between science and religion also attracted her attention. She became, however, more closely acquainted with critiques of determinism. Her reading of Carlyle persisted.[5] She turned also to the works of Coleridge, and encountered an eclectic philosophical stance, and a mind which seized upon the relationship of this stance to specific issues. His reconciliation of religion and science was largely ignored at this time, and Marian Evans's early encounter with his ideas helps to explain why she was little disturbed by the Darwinian controversy in the middle of the century. Coleridge also rooted Christian belief in philosophical proof. Following his example, Marian Evans contrasted intuition and induction, and facetiously employed the language of metaphysics in a letter to Patty Jackson. Whilst she continued to express impeccable feelings of self-recrimination, and plans for prayers, the broadly-based Christianity of Coleridge impressed her. She offered to make Miss Lewis extracts from his writings; she attacked sectarian controversy. Coleridge suggested that the Bible was not important because it contained historical truth, and Marian Evans echoed the method of reading the scripture proposed in *Confessions of an Inquiring Spirit* (1840). She suggested that Miss Lewis's pupils should start 'taking the parables or other portions of the New Testament for analyzation – writing in words other than those of Scripture the general truths contained or implied in the passage'. Her religious reflections were couched in the terminology of non-sectarian moral idealism.[6]

The solitude in which she contemplated such ideas ended towards the close of her first year in Foleshill. On 2 November 1841, she went to Rosehill for the first time with her neighbour, Mrs Pears, who was Charles Bray's sister. The Rosehill circle was sociable, philanthropical, much interested in speculation, composed of 'superior and interesting persons'. Miss Lewis soon became jealous of the fascination these new acquaintances held for her former pupil.[7] At the centre of the group was Charles Bray. He had met Marian Evans when she was a child at Griff, and was eight years her senior. At the age of twenty-four, he had inherited the family ribbon firm. His interests ranged over a daunting variety of subjects. In the 1830s, after his conversion to phrenology by George Combe, a leading exponent, he had travelled England, lecturing on the science. Despite the poor reception his pessimistic views were accorded, he was willing to expound them to small groups, and to pay his own expenses. He eventually became one of the most influential phrenologists in the Midlands. In the early 1840s, as the fashion for phrenology waned, he gave cautious approval to the new craze for mesmerism. In the late 1830s and 1840s, at a time when religious objections to Socialism were vehement, Bray was interested in Owenite theories during the heyday of that movement, and he attended the 'Opening of the Millenium' at Queenswood in Hampshire.[8] He was always eager to make his views known, and to convert them into action. In 1846, he bought the Coventry *Herald*, the newspaper which published Marian Evans's earliest journalism. Bray transformed it into a force in the formation of local opinion; it was used as 'the organ of the new philosophy and its applications, as far as public opinion will allow'. It was liberal in politics, nonsectarian in religion. Bray's fortunes were subject to the fluctuations of trade caused by changing fashions and seasons, but his reputation was that of an honourable employer, who was concerned for the welfare of the working class. He involved himself in local issues such as the 1843 controversy over the enclosure of the Lammas and Michaelmas Lands and helped to form a society to provide gardens for the workers in the same year. In 1853, with hindsight, Marian Evans, from the standpoint of one surrounded by like-minded metropolitan liberals, commended Bray's 'solitary labours at Backward Coventry', noting 'He really has managed to sow some good seed there, and some of it has already sprung up'.[9] Those around Charles Bray also attracted Marian Evans's attention. Sara Hennell, Bray's sister-in-law, was to write such books as *Thoughts in Aid of Faith* (1860), which attempted to reconcile scientific and mystical thought. George Eliot preserved such works in her library, more out of affection for the author, than enthusiam for their reasoning.

Cara Bray, Charles's wife, became a treasured friend. When she was in her early forties, George Eliot recalled fondly in a letter to her 'all the tenderness, forbearance, and generous belief that made the unvarying character of your friendship towards me when we used to be a great deal together'. With faultless tolerance, Cara Bray agreed to her husband's liaison with Hannah Steane, which produced six children, three of whom were born when Marian Evans was a frequent visitor to Rosehill, and one of whom was brought up by Cara as her own child.[10]

Marian Evans's contact with the Rosehill circle seems to have been a factor in prompting her, perhaps in emulation of Charles Bray's vaunted progressivism, into converting her inner scepticism into action. In January 1842 she refused to attend church, and was 'on the brink of being turned out of [her father's] house'.[11] Her father planned to move from Coventry. She planned to leave home, and look for a job as a governess. She was sent to stay with Isaac at Griff. On 15 May she resumed church-going. For the first time, Marian Evans was made to realise that religious unorthodoxy was socially unacceptable, and politically suspect in the eyes of respectable people. Finding a suitable husband was partly the issue. Familial despotism shocked champions of women's rights like John Stuart Mill and Mary Wollstonecraft, but a conventional family of modest means, like the Evanses, justifiably feared for their daughter's future if she persisted in such behaviour. Marriage was thought of as women's destiny; spinsters were seen to have no useful role to play in society, and could rarely support themselves financially. Isaac priggishly remarked, 'Mr. Bray, being only a leader of mobs, can only introduce her to Chartists and Radicals, and . . . such only will ever fall in love with her if she does not belong to the Church'.[12] Isaac was not unusual in seeing a connection between religious apostasy and political radicalism, and in abhorring both as marks of a dangerous lack of respectability. The laws, public opinion and institutions upheld the notion of England as a Christian country. Freedom of discussion was associated with a subversive continental tradition, and English liberals were dubbed *les libéraux* or *los liberalos* to indicate their lack of patriotism. An eminent mind such as Newman, well-read in Gibbon, Hume and Paine, revealed how conservatism had become the hallmark of much educated opinion in the 1840s: Newman described the spirit of liberalism as 'the characteristic of the destined Antichrist'. Mark Rutherford's republican grandfather, living in the English provinces, encountered a mob bent on showing him 'the folly of his belief in democracy by smashing every pane of glass in front of his house with stones'. To Robert Evans, as to many of his generation, the unorthodoxy of youth seemed criminal, and was 'unintelligible . . . except as a result of a wicked heart, a weak head, or that universal solution to the problem of theological aberration – Satanic possession.'[13]

Yet although within her own family she confronted the strictures on unorthodox belief and behaviour, Marian Evans found at Rosehill an openness of debate which kept her in touch with the latest intellectual developments. Before the railways opened up cities such as Coventry to metropolitan influences, provincial centres often contained small groups of people providing for themselves, for newcomers and visitors, an intellectual environment whose stimulating earnestness was partly the result of the disapproval which progressive views aroused in conservative circles. Those writers Marian Evans was to admire, and the friends she was to make in London, were often products of such a setting. Carlyle had been nurtured by such a regional culture, and swiftly recognised the phenomenon on a visit to the Midlands in the 1820s. Harriet Martineau grew up in a similar circle in Norwich, and the Baptist John Foster, whose biography was soon to attract Marian Evans's attention, had known such a group in Bristol in the 1790s. Herbert Spencer, as a young man in Derby, benefitted from the 'rich variety, creativity and seriousness' of the English provinces.[14] At Rosehill, there was discussion of vexed questions of philosophy, politics and literature. It was a centre for visiting progressive intellectuals and there Marian Evans met Richard Cobden, George Combe, Emerson and J. A. Froude. She encountered liberal Christians, such as W. J. Fox and George Dawson, the friend of Carlyle, who advocated a creedless Christianity, which insisted upon a Christian duty to convert beliefs into conduct, and to perform charitable acts towards the poor.[15]

Marian Evans came into the Rosehill circle during 'the period of its highest mental activity'. Charles Bray had just written *The Philosophy of Necessity* (2 vols, 1841) which she seems to have read soon after meeting its author. Bray claimed in later years to have formed her mind but this is not borne out by his own account, for he was impressed by her impartiality, erudition, and movement towards freedom of thought when they first met.[16] *The Philosophy of Necessity* attracted her approval because it drew together ideas with which she was slightly familiar, and revealed a mind which looked at life in a way which corresponded with many of her own intellectual tendencies. Bray was preoccupied, as were Coleridge and Carlyle, with the implications of philosophical determinism, but his bias, as his political views revealed, was Benthamite. He was interested in science from an early age, and found Neil Arnott's *Elements of Physics*, with its discussion of 'the connection and relation of the sciences', of 'more use to me in directing and classifying my studies, when I was young, than any other single production'.[17] Bray attempted to revise, however, the Benthamite psychology of action. Implicit in the phrenological theories to which Bray subscribed was the notion that 'Man could improve only within the bounds of the character which Nature gave him at birth. Hope and determinism, in unequal measures, were the dual components of phrenology'. Bray was to stress the importance of the quality phrenologists termed Benevolence. He also modified the implications of determinism by giving due weight to individualism: in *The Education of the Feelings* (1838) he tried to reconcile 'Philosophical Necessity with Morality and True Responsibility'.[18] In *The Philosophy of Necessity*, Bray argued that freedom consisted, not in the possession of free will, but in the range of actions open to men, that action was not wholly conditioned, for reason might be brought to bear upon instinct. Instinct was also not equated with self-interest, for the animal feelings included 'those that are so intimately connected with him that they may be said to form a part of himself; viz., his wife, children and friends'.[19] Bray also considered how determinism had implications for the psychology of perception, which had ethical repercussions. He linked acceptance of deterministic theory to an impartial scrutiny of phenomena; this was seen to foster moral tolerance and stoicism.[20] Bray's ethical idealism stemmed from an encounter, at the age of seventeen, with a highly intelligent Evangelical dissenter. Following Spinoza, Bray saw evil as a corrective reminder of man's ignorance, and suggested resignation to the inevitable. He repeated age-old ideals, such as 'Know Thyself' whilst claiming that his scientific method of exploring behaviour made the fulfilment of this injunction possible.[21]

Bray's religious views were indebted to an eighteenth-century tradition of modified rationalism. Those movements to which he gave support, phrenology and Owenism, propounded a conservative deism and a non-sectarian Christianity. Adherents to phrenology often embraced Unitarianism, and Bray's friendship with a Unitarian minister was an important influence on his youthful development. In 1838, a meeting of Unitarian congregations had passed resolutions urging the 'essential worth of that principle of free inquiry to which we are indebted for our own form of Christianity and of that spirit of deep and vital Religion which may exist under various forms of theological argument'.[22] Bray rested his argument for the existence of God on the notion of Design; he argued that enquiry provided a firm basis for belief, for the 'existence of God, of the pervading spirit of Creation and Intelligence, rests upon a much surer foundation if inferred from the uniformity . . . of causes'. Yet Bray also entertained an imaginative sense of the beauty of the Universe, and a pragmatic mysticism, for he argued that true religion was 'the love of the Invisible source of all that is good and beautiful, springing from the love of goodness and beauty that is visible; which spends not itself in idle admiration and adulation, but perpetually gains strength by efforts to make this earth still more good – still more beautiful'.[23] Bray's liberal Christianity fortified the impressions Marian Evans received from Carlyle and Coleridge. She spoke of Unitarianism as a 'beautiful, *refined* Christianity'. Two months after her refusal to go to church, she reflected 'the thoughts of the good and great are an inexhaustible world of delights, and the felt desire to be one in will and design with the Great Mind that has laid open to us these treasures is the sun that warms and fructifies it'. She retained her respect and affection for the Unitarians to the end of her life. In June 1980, Catherine Herford recalled 'My mother – living in Hampstead until her marriage in 1886 and brought up as a member of the Rosslyn Hill (Unitarian) Chapel – used to tell us that she remembered [George Eliot] attending the chapel more Sundays than not, and finding there a spiritual home denied in other recognised communities. Her circumstances were well known and by no means condoned, but it was felt that if Jesus could accept such friendship, it was wonderful company and by no means to be despised'.[24]

The *Philosophy of Necessity* often reads like a handbook of contemporary thought, and strays from its main theme into discussions of such varied subjects as technology, statistics, mesmerism and political economy. Yet Marian Evans would have recognised how Bray's wide reading precluded uncritical commitment to any single ideology. It was this scepticism which had prompted his attempt to merge opposed methods of inquiry and concepts. Yet Bray also attempted a synthesis of all types of knowledge, and the application of such a synthesis to ethics. The influences of Shelley's *Notes to Queen Mab*, which he read at an early age, and also of Bentham, were obvious in this aspect of the work, but Bray also extended Marian Evans's knowledge of the system of Saint-Simon, whose ideas she had first encountered in the work of Carlyle. Mary Hennell supplied an appendix on utopianism to the 1841 edition of *The Philosophy of Necessity*, and sixteen pages were devoted to Saint-Simon. The Appendix was published as a separate pamphlet in 1844. Bray noted that learning was 'useful according to the manner in which it is used', and considered it was 'only valuable as a source of happiness, and that happiness arises principally from the directions which knowledge gives of our feelings to their legitimate gratifications. . . . When time has blunted the feelings, when the objects of them no longer exist, knowledge is of little use as a means to happiness, unless it can be . . . infused into a new form'.[25] Bray's concept of the utility of knowledge co-existed, however, with a sense of its limitations, and Marian Evans had encountered in Carlyle and Coleridge a similar delimitation of the powers of intellect. Following Hume, Bray admitted the mysteriousness of causality, and emphasised that only sequence was perceivable, since man 'independently of a supernatural Revelation . . . can know neither the beginning nor the end of things, but can only observe what is. He can know in itself, neither the real nature of matter nor that of mind, but only the order in which one event follows another'.[26] Bray's empirical bias was new to Marian Evans, and crucial in paving the way for a later interest in Comte. But the neo-Idealists, Coleridge and Carlyle, had already taught her the value of philosophical eclecticism, and the need to relate ideas to life, whilst admitting their limitations, and the limitations of perception itself.

II

Although Marian Evans's marked copy of Hennell's *An Inquiry Concerning the Origin of Christianity* (1838) is inscribed 'Jany 1st 1842', she bought the book before she entered Bray's circle. She also read Strauss before she took over the translation from Rufa Brabant in 1844, for in July 1842 she returned to Francis Watts (Professor of Theology at Spring Hill College, Birmingham and a friend of the Sibrees) books which attacked *Das Leben Jesu*. There is even a remote possibility that she came across some reference to the Higher Criticism as early as 1840. When she was planning her chart of ecclesiastical history, she was eager to know 'the best authority for the date of the apostolical writings', and around this time, she also conceived the desire to learn German. Historical criticism of the Bible was to remain an interest: her library contained commentaries on Strauss's work published in the 1870s as well as Charles Hennell's[27] *Christian Theism* (1839) which was given to Marian Evans on 29 May 1846 by its author.

The initiative for the translation of Strauss came from a radical political source, as did the work on Strauss which had already appeared in England.[28] The translation was started by Rufa Brabant (later Hennell), who had already translated Baur. Rufa's father was a friend of Strauss and Paulus, and he had organised the celebrations in Devizes of the passing of the 1832 Reform Bill. The main sponsor of the project was Joseph Parkes, who, as a young man, had enjoyed close contact with the Unitarian community in Warwick. Samuel Parr, a latitudinarian clergyman, who insisted on precise scholarship and a well-informed religious tolerance, had been a crucial influence on his early thinking. Parkes's interest in the history of English Dissent, his knowledge of American republicanism, and reading of books by English Jacobins of the late eighteenth century, caused him to see politics as inextricably bound up with religion. An MP of idiosyncratic radical views, Parkes virtually shared the leadership of the Birmingham Political Union with Attwood: he thought that a translation of Strauss would aid the cause of political reform.[29] Marian Evans undertook the work as a labour of love. The translation took two years, and was an exacting task, for which she was paid a mere twenty pounds. It was brought out by John Chapman, whose purchase of the firm of John Green had led him to inherit a radical publishing policy. The translation was not a financial success, despite the praise bestowed upon Marian Evans's work. The edition sold out, but some of the guarantors forgot their pledge of financial aid.[30]

Marian Evans's interest in the Higher Criticism in the early 1840s placed her in an avant-garde minority of English thinkers, an unusual position for a future Victorian novelist. Interest in the historical criticism of the Bible was confined to isolated individuals, and to the Dissenting Academies, especially those with a Unitarian connection.[31] Some of the methods and conclusions of the Germans had been anticipated by English thinkers from the early eighteenth century onwards: Hume's views on miracles foreshadowed Strauss's ideas. Pusey and Milman had paid some attention to German scholarship in the 1820s, and Connop Thirlwall at Cambridge had translated Schleiermacher's *Essay on St. Luke* (1825). But the ancient universities usually voiced ignorant disapproval of the subject: Thirlwall noted 'the knowledge of German subjected a divine to . . . suspicion of heterodoxy'. The Higher Criticism was to be ignored well into the century. The parson whom Kingsley's Alton Locke met in prison 'had never read Strauss – hardly even heard of him'. In 1852, Marian Evans described her translation as 'fitted for the few rather than for the many'. Mark Pattison said that, as late as 1857, German theology was regarded as 'wild and lawless', 'bearing no relation to religion', 'antichristian'. Yet he paid tribute to the fertility of German thinking on religion, for 'it is now in Germany alone that the vital questions of Religion are discussed with the full and free application of all the resources of learning and criticism which our age has at its command. It is not that better books are produced in Germany than elsewhere; it is, that theological inquiry and research are alive there as they are not elsewhere'. This reaction was to be echoed by Mrs Ward's hero, David Grieve, who came from that artisan class which, according to Engels, read Strauss eagerly.[32]

Strauss's work constituted a watershed in nineteenth-century theology. It was produced in a stormy political atmosphere in Germany, in which the preservation of religious orthodoxy was bound up with the survival of the state: it came out at a time when government suppression of the *Rheinische Zeitung* led to the deflection of the radical attack from politics to religion. Strauss defied religious and political authorities alike in his search for truth, and invited social and academic ostracism by publication of the work.[33] From Brabant, Marian Evans probably heard of the storm the work had caused, and Strauss's willingness to suffer for his views doubtless struck a chord in the soul of the young woman who had refused to go to church, and had incurred the wrath of her family. The view that *Das Leben Jesu* was a work of totally negative character would have surprised Strauss. His investigative method originated in the researches of sixteenth- and seventeenth-century scholars, of whom Spinoza was the most famous, and was initiated as a systematic mode of analysis by Eichhorn's *Introduction to the New Testament* (1783). Strauss's Biblical commentary emulated this quasi-scientific method of historiography which sought to establish irrefutable truths. Strauss also drew upon the Idealist philosophy, whose kinship with the Romantic movement made it concerned with a reassessment and reinstatement of Christianity, rather than with destruction of belief. Strauss, like Hegel, was 'conscious of the substance of the Christian religion as identical with the highest philosophical truth'. He had heard Hegel lecture when he was a student, and was friendly with the Hegelians. At Tübingen, he saw himself as one of Hegel's disciples, when he lectured on logic in 1832. In 1833, he remarked 'In my theology, philosophy occupies such a predominant position that my theological view can only be worked out to completeness by means of a thorough study of philosophy'.[34]

Hennell's work also drew upon a mode of thought which vindicated Christianity, but promoted freedom of inquiry. Hennell's sister, Cara, was the wife of Charles Bray, who had distressed his bride on their honeymoon by expounding unorthodox religious views. Cara Bray discussed her husband's ideas with her brother, and the result was the *Inquiry*. The work was rooted in that Unitarian tradition in which the Hennells had been reared; Charles Hennell was seen, in 1840, as one of a group of especially progressive Unitarians, populist in tendency, interested in phrenology, emphasising the psychological basis of belief.[35] Unitarianism came into being after the Reformation, when the supreme authority of the scriptures, and the individual interpretation of them, were much emphasised. In its early form, it had much in common with eighteenth-century deism. The sect based its faith upon 'an underlying reverence for reason, a feeling that the Bible must be interpreted rationally, and a faith that the Bible must be capable of rational exposition because it came from God, and God was rational'.[36] In the nineteenth century, the sect was often a half-way house to secularism: as such, it held an irresistible attraction for puzzled thinkers such as Hazlitt, Leigh Hunt, or Mrs Ward's fictional hero, Robert Elsmere. It also appealed to intellectuals such as Coleridge, J. S. Mill and Marian Evans. Unitarians opposed dogmatic creeds because they were said to 'imply finality, because they interfere with the free working of the mind in its search for truth'. Channing propounded doctrines which recalled the Idealism which inspired the Higher Criticism, for his teaching, 'while derived from the Bible and dependent on the Bible, yet appealed to an inward light and an inward experience which was independent of the Bible'. The Unitarians' liberal doctrinal stance was reflected by their academies, which pioneered innovative curricula, characterised by an attention to continental thought. The social position of many Unitarians, as well as their intellectual position, had political implications. They often came from the new élite of the commercial classes; they were the only sect able to provide 'fearless investigators and earnest reformers in morals and religion'. Yet discrimination against dissenters deprived them of certain civil rights. They therefore worked for greater religious tolerance, and identified politically with social groups they felt to be similarly oppressed.[37]

Both Hennell and Strauss made clear the standpoints from which they derived their views. Hennell referred to Unitarian writings; Strauss opened and closed his work with expositions of Kant, Schelling and Hegel. Strauss distinguished himself from both the 'naturalistic theologian' and the 'free thinker' for he was 'filled with veneration for every religion, and especially for the substance of the sublimest of all religions, the Christian, which he perceives to be identical with the deepest philosophical truth'.[38] The similarities in intent of the *Inquiry* and *Das Leben Jesu* were noted by Philip Harwood, who lectured on Strauss at Finsbury Chapel in 1841, and by Strauss himself in the Preface he wrote for Marian Evans's translation. Strauss and Hennel did not see their work proceeding from, or encouraging, an atheistic viewpoint. Hennell wrote his book for 'the real service of Christianity', and Strauss asserted that he offered no threat to the essential spirit of Christianity, although he conceded that his readers might find themselves questioning specific doctrines they had hitherto taken for granted. Strauss conceded the valid existence of religion 'if the assumption is granted that the feeling of dependence, of selfsurrender, of inner freedom, which has sprung from the pantheistic world-view, can be called religion'.[39]

Both writers suggested a *via media* between, on the one hand, sectarianism and belief in divine revelation, and, on the other hand, an abandonment of the Christian faith. Strauss's Hegelianism enabled him to avoid the extremes of both mysticism and rationalism. His early work established the lack of historical veracity and God-given truth in the gospels. Yet in *Das Leben Jesu für das deutsche Volk bearbeitet* (1864), he stressed the positive aspects of his teaching, and the Preface to the English translation of this work reiterated the summaries of Idealist thought found in *Das Leben Jesu*. Hennell found a constructive argument within a Unitarian framework. He argued that denial of the historical truth and supernatural inspiration of the Bible could exist alongside affirmation of the essential truths of Christianity. Strauss distinguished the 'essence' from the 'husk', and Hennel noted 'The philosophizing tone adopted by many of the most distinguished advocates of religion renders the transition easy from Christianity as a divine revelation to Christianity as the purest form yet existing of natural religion'. Both writers also vindicated Christianity by reference to its conformity to psychological truth; Hennell predicted that faith would survive if it rested 'its claims on an evidence clearer, simpler, and always at hand, – the thoughts and feelings of the human mind itself'.[40] Strauss and Hennell also employed similar methods of analysis, whereby the supposedly irrefutable truths of the scriptures were tested against the other truths of the historical moment, the very nature of human existence, and the precise meaning of words. Both writers gave weight to political factors, and the influence of other Jewish writings, on the composition of the Gospels, and on Christ's behaviour.[41] Strauss argued that invariable sequence, the operative principle of existence, precluded divine intervention but, like Bray, modified this necessitarian notion to admit the possibility of human freedom. Hennell stated a similar, less carefully modified, viewpoint. Strauss deployed the argument from psychology more flexibly than Hennell, and also possessed knowledge, such as that of optics and astronomy, which was not apparent in the *Inquiry*.[42] In their knowledge of the language of the gospels, Strauss was the professional scholar and Hennell the talented amateur, yet both used such knowledge in a similarly critical fashion.[43]

Both Strauss and Hennell ultimately admitted that the Gospels contained an important kind of truth. They saw them as literature, as subjective records made by men impressed by the personality of Christ. From the beauty of the records, they inferred the objective truth of Christ's nobility. From Strauss's deployment of the Hegelian dialectic came his term *mythus*, which indicated the way in which subjective perception transformed objective facts into literature. Strauss defined genuine religion as 'the perception of truth, not in the form of an idea, which is the philosophical perception, but invested with imagery'. The description of the calling of Matthew followed 'the procedure of legend and poetry, which loves contrasts and effective scenes, which aim to give a graphic conception of man's exit from an old sphere of life, and his entrance into a new one'. Harwood stressed that Strauss was not hostile to the ethical ideals of Christianity, and in 1860, Strauss spoke of his reverence for the figure of Christ.[44] In Christ, Strauss saw a miracle of a precisely defined nature, a man rooted in

historical time, yet timeless in his moral excellence. Christ, like
Moses, was a product of history, but 'attained perfect freedom, in
relation to the one point by which each man was destined to
contribute to the advancement of mankind'. Hennell saw the
gospels as a form of poetry, and, in this respect, both he and
Strauss echoed the views of Horst.[45] Hennell and Strauss suggested that it was *qua* literature that the gospels were able to
inspire men to moral excellence: the lack of historical and scientific
accuracy in the sacred writings became an argument for their
importance. After retelling the Christ story, Hennell commented
that the 'indistinctness of the image allows it to become the
gathering centre for all those highly exalted ideas of excellence
which a more closely defined delineation might have prevented
from resting upon it'.[46]

Hennell and Strauss did not bring about a sudden revolution in
Marian Evans's attitude towards Christianity. In the works of
Carlyle and Coleridge, she had already encountered an eclectic
literary Idealism providing a basis for a vindication of Christianity.
In Strauss's Hegelianism, and Hennell's modified rationalism, she
met with unfamiliar philosophical positions, but their theories of
perception were like those of Carlyle and Coleridge, in that they
attempted to bridge the gap between objective and subjective.
Hennell and Strauss were not willing to regard the Bible as sacro-
sanct. They considered that its veracity as an historical record, and
also its validity as a teacher of universal spiritual truths, could be
tested by reference to truths which were irrefutable. This technique embodied a principle of the freedom of sceptical historical
inquiry which Marian Evans had encountered, in a less scholarly
and scientific form, in the novels of Scott. Both writers, however,
laid themselves open to controversy, and their views found a
favourable reception only from an enlightened minority. The positive intellectual aspects of their work were seen to have negative,
often politically radical, implications. German Idealism was long
mistrusted in England; Hennell's rationalist bias smacked of the
discredited philosophy of revolutionary France. Freedom of inquiry was seen as a threat to the stability of society. In her
enthusiasm for their works, Marian Evans acclaimed writers who
linked philosophies embodying eclectic logical methods to live
issues, but who also advocated a creative and controversial scepticism. It was an attitude she was to admire in other writers, and to
articulate in her own reflections upon the uses of speculation and
the nature of truth.

III

After the church-going crisis had died down, and before Maria‹
Evans became absorbed in the translation of Strauss, there was ‹
period punctuated by activities which show the tightening of he‹
connection with the Rosehill circle. On 1 November 1843, sh‹
attended Rufa Brabant's marriage to Charles Hennell at the Fins‹
bury chapel where Harwood had delivered his discourses o‹
Strauss. After the wedding, she visited Rufa's father in Devizes‹
but her stay ended abruptly when Mrs Brabant became jealous o‹
the flirtatious attention her husband lavished on their visitor. I‹
the same year, there were trips to Worcestershire and Wales wit‹
the Brays and Hennells. Her main interest, in the wake of the 184‹
crisis, was the religious question. Her desire to see all sides of th‹
question continued. She re-read the Bible carefully; she considere‹
Joseph Butler's *The Analogy of Religion* (1736) which dealt with th‹
arguments against both deism and revealed religion. In 1843‹
Newman left St. Mary's. This event may have spurred Maria‹
Evans to read books on Catholicism, and she commended th‹
Catholic Allesandro Manzoni's distinction between Moral Philo‹
sophy and Theology.[47] Her interest in the Higher Criticism was no‹
confined to *Das Leben Jesu*. She read the work of F. A. F. Tholuc‹
and Carl Ullmann's *Historisch oder Mythisch*? Ullmann adhered t‹
the Kantian views of Schleiermacher, and encouraged her to stud‹
Kant. In 1843, she borrowed from Francis Watts J. C. C. C‹
Kiesewetter's *Grundriss einer allgemeinen Logik nach Kantische*‹
Grundsätzen. She returned to Coleridge and Carlyle, who had firs‹
made her aware of Kant's work. She read books which explore‹
the connection between religion, and political and speculativ‹
freedom. She referred to Guizot, and in December 1842 propose‹
translating the work of Rodolphe A. Vinet.[48]

   Perhaps influenced by Charles Bray's enthusiasm for his work‹
she first read Spinoza in January 1843, and she started to translat‹
Tractatus Theologico-Politicus (1670). After many years of neglect‹
Spinoza was beginning to attract attention. He was read eagerly b‹
Lessing, Goethe and Heine, and his 'vision of the way in which th‹
finite subject fitted into a universal current of life' was an import‹
ant influence on Hegel. Coleridge had stimulated interest in th‹
subject by his discussion of it in *Biographia Literaria*, althoug‹
Lewes, who, like Marian Evans, became interested in Spinoza i‹
the 1840s, noted that in England, in the mid-1830s, Spinoza's wor‹

was often denounced or misrepresented.[49] Spinoza's writings pioneered a method of Biblical criticism to which German commentators like Strauss were heavily indebted. He approached the Scriptures with scientific impartiality, and brought to his examination of them knowledge of ancient languages, history and textual transmission.[50] It was also, once more, a thinker who tried to reconcile opposing modes of inquiry who attracted Marian Evans's attention. At the heart of Spinoza's system was a theory of perception which delineated three levels of knowledge: confused sensations, ordered sensations or scientific knowledge, and *scientia intuitiva*, which simultaneously grasped isolated specifics and the totality of existence. Spinoza also reconciled seemingly opposed concepts. J. A. Froude commented that Spinoza's system accepted 'with equal welcome the extremes of materialism and of spiritualism'. His central notion of Substance, *Deus sive Natura*, showed the influence of both Cartesianism and Judaic monism. All finite beings were seen as modifications of this prior reality; Substance might be viewed under the attribute of thought (minds), or extension (bodies).

Spinoza disputed the claim that the Bible was 'in every passage true and divine', but wished to sift out what was worthy of consideration. Like other writers Marian Evans read during this period, he was concerned to establish a rational basis for Christianity. He demonstrated that the miracles of the Bible were inconceivable: God could not intervene in Nature for, according to the doctrine of Substance, God and Nature were one. By Philosophy, Spinoza understood knowledge of the laws of Substance attainable by the operation of scientific knowledge and *scientia intuitiva*. To understand the laws was to understand God. The scientific investigator was superior to 'the common herd of believers because . . . he possesses . . . a true and distinct conception'.[51] Spinoza scrutinised not only the world-view of the Bible, but also its moral teachings. The prophets were seen not as rational or divinely-inspired men but as imaginative, historically conditioned writers. God has 'revealed through his prophets that the covenant of God is no longer written in ink, or on tablets of stone, but with the Spirit of God in the fleshy tablets of the heart'. Yet Spinoza asserted that their moral teachings were commendable because they could be 'apprehended by the natural faculties of all'; they came 'within the sphere of reason'.[52]

The *Tractatus Theologico-Politicus* was also a pioneer statement about

the link between religion and politics. The concept of Substance
suggested that all men partook of the same reality, but also sough
to fulfil their own nature: Spinoza thus advocated democracy as a
via media between anarchic individualism and state control. He also
entered a powerful plea for the state to tolerate freedom of conscience and speculation as necessary to 'piety and public peace'
Religion, he said, asked not whether doctrines were true, bu
whether they were conducive to piety. It allowed men 'to think
what we like about anything . . . only condemning . . . those who
teach opinions which tend to produce obstinacy, hatred, strife
or anger'. Men were to be judged by their actions, not their
opinions.[53] Spinoza also defended freedom of thought, which was
'man's natural right which he cannot abdicate even with his own
consent'. Love of God encouraged scientific enquiry, for Substance
included both God and nature. Spinoza thus contrasted man-made
religious laws, which need not be obeyed, to the need to acknowledge the eternal, scientifically-ascertained laws of God. Christianity
should admit God's existence, and the value of charity, obedience
and repentance. But blessedness could not be enforced by man-
made laws, but only by 'brotherly admonition, sound education,
and, above all, free use of the individual judgment'.[54]

IV

Spinoza, Lewes commented, was 'a mystic whose mind moved in
geometrical processes',[55] and Spinoza's reconciliation of seemingly
opposed modes of apprehension suggests how the reading of the
Tractatus was congruent with Marian Evans's other interests.
Bray's modified Benthamism, Strauss's Hegelianism, Hennell's
Unitarianism, Spinoza's blend of Cartesianism and Judaism were
linked by the fact that all four writers merged antithetical ways of
analysing phenomena. From this eclectic method stemmed a duality of perception. The world was seen rationally, but reason itself
often prompted the emotion of wonder. The limitations of reason
were also stated or implied; imagination and the religious consciousness were seen to discern important truths. Reality was also
viewed in terms of an awareness of a dimension in reality beyond
the merely material. The sceptical rejection of mutually exclusive
logical methods and concepts also led all four writers to champion
the principle of freedom of inquiry. They also put their method of

analysis to constructive use in relation to the linked issues of religion and politics. Yet, since the logical methods of these writers were reconciliatory, their views on specific issues were moderate. That Marian Evans was fascinated by such eclectic philosophies is suggested by the desire she expressed at Foleshill to live to 'reconcile the philosophy of Locke and Kant'.[56] In August 1842, she wrote to Watts, perhaps echoing the eclectic tendency 'I am in much the same mental condition as Henry IV when he said of opposite pleaders, "*Il me semble que tous les deux ont raison*"'. She forswore the sectarianism of unorthodoxy, noting in 1843 'It is the quackery of infidelity to suppose that it has a nostrum for all mankind, and to say to all and singular, "Swallow my opinions, and you shall be whole"'. She had no desire to proselytise, and remained open to all viewpoints. She significantly invoked *Sartor Resartus* when she assured Mrs Pears 'Do not fear that I will become a stagnant pool by self-sufficient determination only to listen to my own echo; to read the yea, yea, on my side, and be most comfortably deaf to the nay, nay'.[57]

During these early days at Foleshill, the broad Christianity she had commended in Scott, Carlyle and Coleridge was reinforced by Bray's ideas and those of the Biblical commentators, who salvaged truths from Christianity. She regretted her flamboyant action of refusing to go to Church, attributing it to her 'ignorance of life' and 'narrowness of . . . intellectual superiority'. There was intellectual justification for her decision to resume attendance at the Sunday services, for Strauss had argued that speculative theologians should remain within the Church. In dealing with the Scriptures, such thinkers should 'exhibit their spiritual significance, which . . . constitutes their sole truth, and thus prepare – though such a result is only to be thought of as an unending process – the resolution of those forms into their original ideas in the consciousness of the Church also'.[58] Marian Evans also described her sense of the divine within the natural in the terminology of a philosophical Christianity, noting 'the only heaven here or hereafter is to be found in conformity with the will of the Supreme; a continual aiming at the attainment of that perfect ideal, the true Logos that dwells in the bosom of One Father'. She told Sara Hennell 'Assuredly this earth is not the home of the spirit – it will rest only in the bosom of the Infinite'. She still admired 'much of what I believe to have been the moral teaching of Jesus himself'.[59]

The reading of these writers also provided a theoretical basis for, and encouraged a new intensity in, Marian Evan's scepticism, which

expressed itself mainly in relation to religious questions. Her
doubts had arisen before she settled in Foleshill: Mary Sibree, who
knew her at this time, reported that Marian Evans did not need
anyone else to 'put doubts into her head'. In some respects, her
scepticism was negative. The reading of the Biblical critics left her
unable to believe in the literal truth of the scriptures; they sharp-
pened that quality of her disbelief which was 'historical . . .
but . . . of the most sincere and absolute kind'. She also did not see
the Bible as divine revelation, and reiterated this view when she
read Renan's *Vie de Jésus* in 1863. She rejected the doctrine of
salvation. Yet her scepticism also had positive results. She found
herself able to tolerate religious beliefs which she found intellectually untenable: beliefs were an integral part of character, a prerequisite of its vitality, and she was reluctant to 'root up tares where
we must inevitably gather all the wheat with them'. She was,
anyway, critical of the intellect, contrasting its weakness to the
strength of the emotions, seeing *'truth of feeling'* as 'the only
universal bond of union'.[60] She also started to show a zeal for the
process of inquiry akin to that which had animated Mill and
Carlyle as they extricated themselves from the sectarianism of
philosophical debate. She responded positively to Hennell's work
because it was fired by 'a pure love of truth' and was 'the outcome
of a perfectly unbiassed examination'. She spoke of her intoxica-
tion with ideas, and her belief in the final ascendancy of truth.[61]
Before reading the Higher Criticism, she told Miss Lewis 'my only
desire is to know the truth, my only fear to cling to error'. The
search for truth took on the religious connotations which firm belief
once possessed for her. She saw fear of ideas as 'an intellectual and
moral palsy' and commented 'the best proof of a real love of truth,
– that freshest stamp of divinity – is a calm confidence in its
intrinsic power to secure its own high destiny – that of universal
empire'.[62] After 1843 she was to search for truth with such calm
confidence in an ever-increasing variety of areas.

10

Marian Evans (1844–1850) Foster and Rousseau

Reason is all very well in its own province; but there are things which transcend it, and thereon it must be silent.

With the different systems of philosophy . . . she was completely acquainted.[1]

To describe Marian Evans's life, to chart her intellectual development, during the period after she had absorbed the ideas of those writers who influenced the growth of her scepticism, and before she became established as a writer in London, is no easy task. At Foleshill, there was little time to write letters, for she was nursing her father and translating Strauss. There was also little need; the Brays were close at hand, and her friendship with Miss Lewis ended in December 1846. She was a reasonably prolific correspondent after she settled abroad in the autumn of 1849, but even then, her letters spoke little of herself. She was, initially, very unhappy, and then turned to describing a new country and the people she met. Some documents have simply vanished. M. d'Albert Durade destroyed the letters she wrote to him; Cross tore out that portion of her Journal which started with her stay in Switzerland in 1849, and ended with her departure for Germany with Lewes in 1854. Such evidence as does exist points to a busy life during the five and a half years before she left for Europe. She participated in the social life at Rosehill; she went with the Brays to London, Birmingham and Stratford. In 1844, she visited the Lake District, and Manchester, that city which many saw as a mysterious foreshadowing of a new age.[2] In October 1845, she was in Scotland, touring places associated with Scott; in the early summer of 1846, she visited the Hennells in Clapton. Her life was not without emotional upheavals. In March 1845, she was briefly engaged, and at Christmas 1846, she ended her friendship with Maria Lewis when her old teacher tried to entice her back to Christianity.[3] Her father's failing health prompted sojourns with him at Dover in the summer of 1846, on the Isle of Wight in autumn 1847, in Sussex in the late spring of 1848. She managed to reconcile daughterly duties and personal aspirations. In November 1846, she started to contribute reviews to Bray's newspaper and, although she advised against translating as a job, she was working on Spinoza in March 1849. The death of her father in May 1849 left her with a memory she was always to revere, but brought a way of life to a close. Robert Evans's will made only modest provision for his unmarried child and Isaac, like many married brothers, as Mary Wollstonecraft bitterly noted, proved a grudging provider.[4] Marian Evans left for Europe with the Brays in June 1849, stayed on there alone and returned to England the following March. From October 1849 she settled in Geneva, a city she was later to use for the setting of *The Lifted Veil*. The Durades, with whom she lodged, remained lifelong friends. M. Durade had trained to be an evangelical minister but, at the age of twenty-two, had abandoned this calling to become a painter. Mme. Durade became, as George Eliot recalled in 1871, 'one of the sweet memories of my life'.[5] The stay in Switzerland marked the onset of a rootless phase in Marian Evans life which ended only with her decision to live with Lewes. The ten months between her return to England, and her final move to London, found her making Rosehill, if anywhere, her home. Her own family provided nowhere for her to live.

Neither the quietly industrious period in Coventry, nor the period of unrest after her father's death however, militated, against continuing intellectual development. Her reading of certain authors extended her knowledge of the sceptically eclectic and pragmatic mode of philosophical thinking. This tradition was characterised by its critique of rationalism, and Marian Evans's letters were sprinkled with references to the English romantic writers, and also to those German Romantic writers who had been commended by Carlyle and Coleridge. After 1847, although she re-read Hennell's *Inquiry* with renewed admiration, her interest in Biblical criticism waned. The bias of her mind was increasingly affirmative, and she turned to religious biographies which showed questing minds retaining their Christian faith. She praised Blanco White's progress from Catholic to Anglican to Unitarian as exhibiting 'earnestness and love of truth' . She found *The Life and Correspondence of John Foster* (2 vols, 1846) 'deeply interesting' because it enabled her to 'study the life of a genius under circumstances amid which genius is so seldom to be found'.[6] Foster typified the liberal, well-informed Dissenter whose existence encouraged Marian Evans's tolerance of Christianity; born into a Baptist family, Foster ended up in the Universalist Church which had many affinities with Unitarianism.

Foster reconciled freedom of inquiry with Christian belief, noting in 1792 'It is delightful to feel one's mind enlarging, to contemplate an endless succession of new objects, to extend our conquests in the regions of intellect and fancy, and to be perpetually aspiring to the sublimities of knowledge and piety'. He considered that Dissent would gain ground 'in whatever proportion true religion and free thinking shall do so', and argued for an openness of debate which echoed the mood of Rosehill, asserting 'all subjects whatever are considered as free for discusion . . . all systems, institutions, and practices, as being merely of human authority, are fully open to the exercise of human reason'.[7] Foster also based his faith on insights culled from non-theological sources. He envisaged a merging of philosophy and religion which would illuminate reality. His belief in God rested partly upon a romantic sense of the sublime, an enthusiasm inculcated by his reading of Schiller, Mrs Radcliffe, Rousseau, and, especially, Coleridge.[8] Foster also insisted that Christian ideas must be applied to life. He proposed an active Christianity, contrasting this to theological speculation, which led to the 'neglect of practical, personal piety'. He urged political reform. His early republicanism waned, but he was impressed by Cobbett, opposed to privilege, and disillusioned by the 1832 Reform Bill. He emphasised the need to educate men for democracy, and eloquently pleaded that the amelioration of the lot of the urban poor was a Christian duty.[9]

Foster's championing of the principle of sceptical inquiry derived partly from his reading of Rousseau, and Rousseau's work was at this period of her life, Marian Evans's 'great passion'. William Hale White and Emerson both recalled this enthusiasm.[10] Rousseau was a solitary and unfashionable interest; because of their moral and political views, his works were suspect in the early nineteenth century, and a Victorian translation of *Les confessions* did not appear until 1861. In settling in Geneva, Marian Evans was opting to stay in Rousseau's birthplace. It was *Les confessions* which most impressed her; she told White 'it was worth while to undertake all the labour of learning to read French if it resulted in nothing more than reading one book – Rousseau's Confessions'.

Charles Lewes withdrew the copy of *Les confessions* from the collection of books he presented to Dr Williams' Library, presumably because it had special significance for George Eliot, for Lewes was very critical of Rousseau.[11] Marian Evans also probably read the defensive postscript to *Les confessions, Les rêveries du promeneur solitaire,* as well as *Emile* and *La nouvelle Héloise.*

Both White and Emerson associated her scepticism with her reading of Rousseau. Rousseau offered a radical critique of the eighteenth-century rationalism with which he had been associated, but to which he was temperamentally opposed. He was centrally concerned with perception, but was sceptical about the theories of the Encyclopaedists. He criticised the limited vision of educated men, for 'no-one seeks to see things as they are, but only as they fit into their system'. He praised, instead, the insight of children, artisans, provincials, country-dwellers.[12] His own views sprang from solitary self-contemplation, which he distinguished from egoism, for it was not concerned with self-elevation, but with an awareness of individuality. Initially in agony because of his isolation, he transformed this negative state, and began to nourish his heart 'with its own substance, and to seek its nourishment within the self'. In solitude, he inspected his own consciousness, and found there interdependent and flexible modes of perception. His visionary sense rested upon an apprehension of concrete details; his perception shifted easily from particular to general, from outer to inner. The solitary relish of individuality led to an awareness of others; the aloneness of grief bound together disparate personalities; a solitary contemplation of nature reminded man, via sensation, of the existence of the outside world.[13]

Rousseau's criticism of reason also led him to contemplate the nature of feeling. His only attempt to define feeling in a conventional philosophical fashion occurred in his discussion of the term *sensation,* which leant heavily on Locke. He considered feeling to be complex in nature, and spoke of the incapacity of language to describe emotions. He thus allowed a definition of feeling to emerge from his description of feeling in action, and, in the course of this description, recurringly deployed such terms as *sentiment, affections, coeur, conscience.*[14] Rousseau vindicated feeling in forensic fashion, insisting, for instance, that no true love could exist without enthusiasm. He also linked feeling to a superior mode of perception; he saw the wisdom of the heart as superior to the arid complications of contemporary metaphysics. He explored the possibility of linking reason and feeling within perception. He suggested that ideas were linked to feelings because both originated in sensation. He noted 'In certain respects ideas are feelings and feelings are ideas. The two terms are suitable for all perceptions which concern us, both as regards the object of our perception, and as regards ourselves who are influenced by the object'.[15]

Rousseau was sceptical about the Encyclopaedist view of perception because such theories were at odds with his observation of his own mental cast. This crucial insight led him to forge a revolutionary new form of philosophical discourse, which embodied, by its very method, his radical scepticism. The structure of his works often embodied an anti-rational stance, for the exposition of ideas was frequently unsystematic. His works attempted to present the reality of self and world in fiction, or in memoirs; his writing was concerned with solitary self-communing and self-analysis. Rousseau suggested that truth was conveyed by such description, rather than by a philosophical and theoretical analysis of reality. His sensuous relish of the outer world led him to reflect upon the meaninglessness of philosophical distinctions between appearance and reality. He considered that observing reality was more useful than reading about it, and that history should be studied via scrutiny of the individual.[16]

A sceptical view of the Encyclopaedist theory of perception, and a method which embodied a reaction against schematic theorising led to writings whose aim was didactic only in an idiosyncratic fashion. The existence of an audience for his self-communing was, for Rousseau, incidental. He did not try to inculcate opinions; in his autobiography, he did not try to justify himself. He wished rather to promote individual examination of ideas and to present his life for contemplation.[17] In three important areas Rousseau did, however, apply his re-evaluation of rationalism to specific issues. In the field of ethics, he insisted that feeling, not reason, motivated desirable actions. On a political level, he suggested that *rêverie*, the polar opposite of rational activity, produced the inspiring vision of an ideal world. His reaction against the Encyclopaedists made him reassess the religious truths which they had disputed, and feeling provided the basis of his religious views. He avoided the extremes of atheism and belief. He painted the horrors of religious doubt, but criticised sectarian division. The philosophical spirit, he said, 'in attaching me to the essential nature of religion, detached me from that mass of rubbish made up of the little formulas with which men have obscured religion itself'. The Savoyard Priest who instructs the narrator of *Emile* with a lengthy recitation of his creed recommended 'theism of natural religion which Christians pretend to confuse with atheism of irreligion which is the directly opposite doctrine'. Rousseau based his faith upon his distrust of intellect for 'impenetrable mysteries surround us on all sides; they lie beneath that life the senses may perceive; to penetrate into these mysteries, we believe we only need to have reason, but all we can really use is the imagination'. God, said Rousseau, could be seen in the world, but not described; true religion expressed itself in silent reverence before God's creation. Religion, he insisted, articulated essential truths about the natural world and man's perception of it, as well as necessary moral truths.[18]

Marian Evans paid a glowing tribute to Rousseau. She wrote to Sara Hennell on 9 February 1849,

> I wish you thoroughly to understand that the writers who have most profoundly influenced me – who have rolled away the waters from their bed raised new mountains and spread delicious valleys for me – are not in the least oracles to me. It is just possible that I may not embrace one of their opinions, that I may wish my life to be shaped quite differently from theirs. For instance it would signify nothing to me if a very wise person were to stun me with proofs that Rousseau's view of life, religion and government are miserably erroneous – that he was guilty of some of the worst basenesses that have degraded civilized man. I might admit all this – and it would be not less true that Rousseau's genius has sent that electric thrill through my intellectual and moral frame which has awakened me to new perception, which has made man and nature a fresh world of thought and feeling to me – and this not by teaching me any new belief. It is simply that the rushing mighty wind of his inspiration has so quickened my faculties that I have been able to shape more definitely for myself ideas which had previously dwelt as dim 'ahnungen' in my soul – the fire of his genius has so fired together old thoughts and prejudices that I have been ready to make new combinations.[19]

In pondering upon the nature of perception, Rousseau arbitrated critically between the claims of intellect and feeling as truth-yielding faculties. The debate had been familiar to Marian Evans since her reading of Carlyle and Coleridge, but her enthusiasm for Rousseau sharpened her consideration of the question, and ef- fected a further shift in emphasis towards feeling. She thought that feeling could transform reason and morality, so that 'Creation is the superadded life of the intellect: sympathy, all-embracing love, the superadded moral life'. She saw love and thought in interac- tion as 'in themselves a more intense and extended participation of a divine existence – as they grow the highest species of faith grows too – and "all things are possible"'. Rousseau's plea for a positive emotional affirmativeness was also echoed. She praised John Sibree's enthusiasm for 'what is actually great and beautiful without putting forth any cold reservations and incredulities to save . . . credit for wisdom'. Writers she had read earlier had suggested a judicious blending of thought and feeling, but Rous- seau's plea for emotional intensity struck in Marian Evans the chord which had earlier responded to the anti-intellectual aspects of evangelical Anglicanism. 'Vitality' became a key term to express her approbation. Discussing her tendency to depression, she noted 'This conscious kind of false life that is ever and anon endeavouring to form itself within us and eat away our true life will be overcome by continuing accession of vitality'.[20]

Rousseau's anti-didactic method seemed to be invoked by Mar- ian Evans in her praise of the French writer, for she echoed the Savoyard Priest's injunctions to Emile, 'seek the truth for yourself', and his comment that 'I do not wish to philosophise with you, but to help you consult your own heart'.[21] Rousseau's presentation of a complex reality left its mark upon Marian Evans's thought. Her sense of the existence of a non-material dimension in the natural world had been nurtured by her reading of Carlyle and the English Romantic poets, and Rousseau encouraged such a world-view. She responded fervently to manifestations of the sublime, and shocked M. Durade with her pantheistic views as they took walks together. For Marian Evans, as for Rousseau, appreciation of the wonders of the natural world underpinned the sense of the poetry of religion, which she distinguished from Christian mythology, history and doctrine. She also possessed a general sense of the poetry of all existence. She spoke with sympathy for those who woke to find 'all the poetry in which the world was bathed only the evening before utterly gone – the hard angular world of chairs and tables and looking-glasses staring at them in all its naked prose'.[22] Rous- seau also encouraged in her a fascinated and tolerant scrunity of the particular which was most obvious in her contemplation of human character. She commented, 'We may satirise character and qualities in the abstract without injury to our moral nature, but persons hardly ever'. She was especially interested in that inner life whose workings Rousseau's writings had described. She enjoyed reading an old journal which contained 'the simplest record of events and feelings', an occupation she would previously have found 'insupportable'. 'Individuals', she remarked in 1848 'are precious to me in proportion as they unfold to me their intimate selves.' The character sketches in her letters from Switzerland show her guessing, for instance, at the inner life of Mlle de Phaison, or turning a quizzical glance upon new acquaintances. At once impressionistic and precise, concerned with the inner and outer life, such descriptions revealed a flexible mode of perception, a shifting from details to total effect, which recalled Rousseau's mode of vision as he strove to present a truthful picture of reality. She also found, as had Rousseau, that contemplation of the individual led to a sense of man's common destiny: when acquaintances confessed their troubles to her, she realised 'all the old commonplaces about the equality of human destinies' were true.[23]

Rousseau's discriminating appraisal of Christianity also reinforced her views on religion. She wrote to John Sibree Jnr. of 'the miserable etiquette (it deserves no better or more spiritual name) of sectarianism'. She urged upon him a Rousseauesque ideal of self-aware, individualistic belief when she supported him in his decision to leave the ministry, an episode which, once more, found her beliefs leading her into a difficult situation, for Sibree's father suspected her of being a bad influence on his children. She remained, however, vitally interested in religion, and in Switzerland went out of her way to learn about the country's different sects. Rousseau's broadly-based Christianity further encouraged her tolerance of sincerely held religious beliefs. She abandoned, in 1847, her plans to write a book on 'The superiority of the consolations of philosophy to those of (so-called) religion'. Liberal cultured Christians, such as George Dawson and the Durades, won her approval.[24]

Rousseau's notion of feeling had underpinned his Christian beliefs, and Marian Evans, once more like Rousseau, saw that feeling had an important ethical role to play in human relationships, enforcing sympathy rather than division. She felt that the Durades 'without entering into or even knowing the greater part of my views . . . understand my character, and have a real interest in

me'. Her 'heresies' were no bar to friendship; the kindness of the
Baronness de Ludwigsdorff showed that 'heaven sends kind souls,
though they are by no means kindred ones'. She discovered that
she could, in 1849, be interested in a Miss Forbes, despite the fact
that she was 'very evangelical'.[25]

Rousseau's application of his newly-evolved view of perception
to religion and ethics was similar in broad intent to the pragmatic
tradition represented by those writers Marian Evans read between
1840 and 1844. Yet the genesis of his critique of rationalism strikingly differentiated him from the writers she had read earlier.
Bray, Hennell, Strauss and Spinoza sought to reconcile established, opposed intellectual traditions. Rousseau was more revolutionary, for he based his sceptical eclecticism upon observation of
self and the world. The reality of the workings of his own consciousness and of the outside world confirmed the paradoxes
which philosophers misrepresented as they exposed and tried to
resolve them. It was *Les confessions* which had first 'wakened'
Carlyle to 'deep reflection' as Emerson told Marian Evans. Carlyle
asserted that speculation only found 'any centre to revolve around' via 'a felt indubitable certainty of experience'. Rousseau's
shifting of the initial premiss of inquiry to experience necessitated,
as it had for Carlyle, a turning away from conventional modes of
philosophical discourse. Truth was not conveyed through didactic, intellectualised theory, but via representational description of a
complex reality, eclectically perceived. With hindsight, Marian
Evans criticised the over-theoretical quality of Strauss's work: he
was sometimes wrong, she commented, 'as every man must be in
working out into detail an idea which has general truth, but is only
one element in a perfect theory'.[26] Rousseau and Carlyle asserted
the importance of observed and felt truth as a weapon against the
sterilities of doctrinaire philosophical positions; they foreshadowed the Arnoldian ideal of 'simply trying to see things as they
are'.[27]

Marian Evans's enthusiasm for Rousseau suggests her adoption
of an intellectual position increasingly removed from rationalism.
Rousseau's critical view of intellect directed her to three other
attacks on the logical problem. The fact that all three critiques came
from outside England indicated her increasing dissatisfaction with
the timidity of English thinkers, and cast her in the role of European intellectual. She turned first to the French tradition represented by Voltaire, Saint-Simon and Comte, and, secondly, to

Hegel's idealism. She then considered the idiosyncratic novels of George Sand, which were much influenced by Rousseau in both form and content. Her interest in a form of fiction which engaged in dialogue with the philosophers was a crucial signpost towards her own future role.

11

Philosophy, Politics and History

I. PRELUDE TO POSITIVISM

Around 1848, Marian Evans appears to have read Voltaire's *Dictionnaire philosophique* (1764).[1] Into the second half of the nineteenth century, the book was associated with unorthodox intellectual stances: the schoolboy Coleridge was flogged for reading it, and in 1842 one of Holyoake's friends tried to smuggle a copy into Gloucester gaol for the leader of English secularism to read as he awaited trial. In England, the work was quite widely translated from the 1760s to the 1840s, and helped promote a spirit of free inquiry.[2] Voltaire's work was framed to furnish wide-ranging reflection and was aimed, not at philosophers,but at thinking men. Its method was such as to appeal to the ever-curious Marian Evans, for Voltaire deployed his knowledge of such diverse topics as psychology, physiology, Oriental and classical history. Voltaire's standpoint was historicist and tolerant; his moral pragmatism, with its elements of anti-intellectualism, foreshadowed Rousseau's views, and he also meditated critically upon the ethical implications of the solitude Rousseau was to exalt.[3]

Voltaire's religious views were unorthodox. He considered that religion should teach 'a good deal about ethics and very little about dogma' and his *Catéchisme de curé* presented the ideal of a liberal clergyman, which recalled that set forth in *Emile*, a work published two years previously. Whilst Voltaire considered religious enthusiasm an obstacle to perception, he also suggested that poets had shown themselves capable of fusing enthusiasm with reason. His method of Biblical criticism had much in common with Spinoza, and anticipated the analytical technique of the Higher Criticism.[4] The work was partly informed by a philosophical position similar to Locke's. Voltaire refuted Berkeley with considerable wit. He insisted upon the scientifically ascertainable truths of mathematics, and spoke of the origin of knowledge in sensation. Yet he modified

109

his rationalist stance to acknowledge the possible existence of deity. He was willing to admit a faith based on reason, for 'un-philosophical geometricians have rejected the idea of final causes, but true philosophers admit their existence and a cathechist announces God's existence to children, and Newton demonstrates it to wise men'.[5]

Marian Evans also turned to Saint-Simon and Comte as commentators upon the empirical tradition. Her enthusiasm for Rousseau helped inspire this interest, but other factors were crucial in encouraging her reading of French writers. The political implications of a philosophical position had been explored by Carlyle and Bray, but Marian Evans was unimpressed by most English writers who attempted to link philosophy and politics. Bray was enthusiastic about Owenism, but she was caustically critical.[6] Mill and Carlyle in the late 1830s had both exposed the inadequacy of the philosophical basis of English radicalism; in 1849, the poverty of English political thought again struck Mill after he read French Socialist writings. Those thinkers who were in revolt against the superficialities of eighteenth-century rationalism often entertained an enthusiasm for French theories of radicalism. Ridiculous though Saint-Simon's and Comte's schemes for social regeneration often were, they appealed to the English avant-garde during a time of mental and social confusion because of their intellectual and political coherence. Faced with the 'pinched, methodistical England' Mill saw in 1848, imaginative minds also despairingly echoed, by their enthusiasm for such theories, the speaker in Tennyson's *The Princess*, who reflected, ' . . . ourselves are full/Of social wrong; and maybe wildest dreams/Are but the needful preludes of the truth'. The disturbing events of the 1840s also accounted for an intensification of Marian Evans's interest in political theory. She turned to Comte for reasons similar to those which had prompted Mill and Carlyle, in the unrest of the two previous decades, to turn to Saint-Simon. England seemed once more to be in a potentially revolutionary situation. The rejection of the Chartist petition in 1839 had repercussions throughout the ensuing decade: Chartism and the Anti-Corn Law League continued to flourish. In 1842, corn prices rose as wages plummeted, and in Staffordshire originated a coal miners' strike which spread to the cotton towns, South Wales and the northern countries. In 1848, the Young Ireland Party prepared to resist the government with force; the Chartists organised a massive demonstration in London, and troops were drafted into the capital. Such events were accompanied by changes in the intellectual climate. A growing disillusion with sectarian disputes led to an increase in secularism as the anti-clericalism of Michelet, George Sand and Strauss, and the theological views of Strauss and Feuerbach, which were often linked to a radical political viewpoint, gained a wider audience. In 1849, Mill remarked upon the number of Communist papers being published in London. Events and ideas conspired to increase the atmosphere of panic.[7]

Marian Evans's Midlands did not go undisturbed. Birmingham was notable for its low level of participation in the Anti-Corn Law League, and for the relatively good standard of living enjoyed by its workshop-based, artisan working-class, who did not engage in capital/labour struggles as did the Manchester workers. In Coventry, however, Marian Evans witnessed the efforts of a reforming corporation, and the co-operative experiments of Cash and Bray which were aimed at improving the working-class lot. Similar experiments interested her in later years; letters written in 1865 speak of communes and co-operative enterprises.[8] In 1846, she dutifully went to the Mechanics' Institute to listen to lectures on 'Self Educated Men' and 'The Improvement of Society', although she described them patronisingly as 'very simple food'. She went to Coventry to hear O'Connell speak on his way to prison in London; she inspected the worst parts of Manchester to see if they confirmed the views of statisticians, and conceived an admiration for the still-radical Harriet Martineau. One of her earliest articles was a satirical political squib, about the involvement of John Vice, Coventry's Chief Constable, in a scandal concerning the city's butchers: it was published in Bray's newspaper on 26 February 1847.[9] She recalled in 1864 that she was 'in . . . revolutionary mood' when she stayed in Switzerland.She took a keen interest in the political views of those she met, and also in the local political scene.[10]

The revolutionary events of 1848 in Europe, and specifically in France, especially spurred her political interests. She followed the course of events closely. In Switzerland in 1849, she was quick to note the effects of the 1848 revolutions, and was enthusiastic about the Nonconformist minister, George Dawson, once said to be the 'first man in Birmingham to study and to understand foreign politics'.[11] The revolutions were not only unexpected; the ideas they embodied were those of middle-class intellectuals,'imbued with the idealism of a generation that had grown up in a romantic atmosphere'. In France, the government supported social experiments, particularly in the field of the organization of labour, and these radical attempts to translate thought into action opened the minds of Marian Evans's generation to new political ideas. Her reading of Voltaire and Rousseau helped pave the way for a favourable reception of the writings of the French theorists of radicalism, for the French Socialists themselves had returned with interest to the writings of these two reluctant sceptics. The library she and Lewes later shared was well-stocked with books by such writers as Lamartine and Blanc, and works relating to the history of this period in France.[12] The letters she wrote at this time revealed a familiarity with contemporary French theories. She cited works by the earlier revolutionary, Saint-Simon, and she referred to Lamartine, who was active in the 1848 events. She mentioned Louis Blanc's *L'organisation du travail* (1848) which provided one of the revolution's slogans, and which inspired the setting-up of the National Workshops, closed amidst savage scenes in 1848. She read Blanc's *L'histoire de dix ans* (1841), an account of the years following the 1830 revolution, and Etienne Cabet's *Voyage en Icarie* (1840), which described a Socialist utopia. It was probably also at this juncture that she acquired an interest in Proudhon: she retained her interest in this subject for, in 1866, she urged Barbara Bodichon to read Saint-Beuve's papers on his work in the *Revue contemporaine*.[13]

Her interest in Comte emerged from her existence within a revolutionary Europe, and from her particular interest in French radical thinking. Yet Comte's synthesis would not have been unfamiliar to Marian Evans, for she had already encountered the ideas of Saint-Simon. Carlyle had meditated upon Saint-Simonianism in both *Chartism* and *Sartor Resartus*, and Bray's *The Philosophy of Necessity* contained a concise outline of the theories of the French sect. In 1842, she discussed Fourier's ideas with the Rosehill circle when she first read Bray's book, which suggests that she read its Appendix on utopianism with some care. Saint-Simon's importance lay partly in the fact that he created an imaginative myth of a new society, inherited from the legend of the first French revolution. Like other early utopian Socialists, he saw social and economic change as more important than constitutional and political reform. It was to a visionary and fundamentalist political theory that Marian Evans responded. She was still quoting Saint-Simon's ideas in the late 1860s, and in *Middlemarch* she pinpointed the arrogance of the young Lydgate by relating how, when he was a student in Paris, he considered joining the sect, 'to turn them against some of their own doctrines'.[14] From this period between 1844 and 1850 dated Marian Evans's knowledge of Positivism. The first article she contributed to the *Westminster Review* in 1851 evinced a long-standing familiarity with Comte's ideas. Mill now exerted influence on her development. She was familiar with the work of Bray who sought to modify empiricism, and with the work of the neo-Idealists, Carlyle and Coleridge, who derived creative impetus from a reaction against rationalism. She now turned to Mill's *A System of Logic*. The work dealt with a theme which had long interested her, the reconciliation of the idealistic and experimental logics. The work also applied the new logic to specific issues: Book 6 dealt with liberty and necessity in a section which Mill considered the best chapter of the work.[15] The *Logic* also popularised Comte in England; in 1852, Marian Evans described Mill as 'at present the chief English interpreter of Comte'. If she followed her reading of the *Logic* with Mill's *Political Economy* (1848), she would have found in the latter work a critical discussion of Saint-Simon.[16]

Her earlier contact with Saint-Simonianism prepared her for a receptive interest in Comte for Comte derived his most important notions from Saint-Simon. The closeness in view was established when Comte worked as Saint-Simon's assistant; it was noted in an 1838 article in the *Dublin Review* and also by Mill.[17] Comte based the third *cashier* of the *Catéchisme des industriels* (1823–4) which outlined his 'système de politique positive' upon Saint-Simon's *Mémoire sur la science de l'homme*. Saint-Simon disputed the originality of the 'systeme' and this led to the severing of the connection between the two men. The *Mémoir* was not published, however, until 1859, and this fact was one of many which helped conceal Comte's indebtedness to his mentor. Although the link between the two philosophical movements was obscured, Comte learnt from the Saint-Simonians throughout his career. In 1826 he started the lectures which were to form the basis of the *Cours de philosophie positive*. In 1829 Bazard was delivering the addresses to which Carlyle referred in *Sartor Resartus* and which gave the Saint-Simonian doctrines an integrated form. Comte probably drew upon this material. By 1830, however, when the first volume of the *Cours*, the work which started to establish Comte's reputation as a systematic thinker, was published, the Saint-Simonians were, under Enfantin's ascendancy, degenerating into scandalous

excesses. Comte's debt to Saint-Simon's *Nouveau Christianisme* (1825) was also not apparent because of a lapse of time:
Comte only elaborated his plans for a new religion after the
death of his mistress in 1846. The importance of the Saint-
Simonian influence on Marian Evans has been overlooked, and it
stems partly from the fact that the link between the two philosophers themselves has been ignored. After the 1830s, the Saint-
Simonians were discredited; Comte himself denounced Saint-
Simon as 'a superficial and depraved cheat'. The Chapman household, in the 1850s, was notorious for being 'penetrated for the most
part with strongly scientific tendencies and especially with the
philosophy of the Comtist school'.[18] As a novelist, George Eliot
had her name linked, by Victorian critics, to the Positivist movement; she was connected by friendship to Comte's interpreters, to
Spencer, Lewes, Harrison and Congreve.[19]

Marian Evans's early acquaintance with the work of Saint-Simon
and Comte was variously important. Mill valued Comte's work for
its contribution to logical method, and it introduced Marian Evans
to one of the more radical attacks on a problem which fascinated
her as much as it had fascinated Carlyle, Coleridge and Bray. Her
interest in Comte in the 1840s also located her, as did her interest
in the Higher Criticism, in an avant-garde minority. Despite Sir
David Brewster's claim that Comte was widely appreciated in
England in 1838, Mill, in 1843, thought that the reverse was true.
Morell detected a surge of interest in Positivism in 1848, but in
1849, Frederic Harrison said that Comte's work was still 'almost
unknown'.[20] Books by Lewes and Harriet Martineau appeared in
1853, and helped to bring Comte's name before a wider audience;
in 1854, a writer in the *British Quarterly Review* said that Comte's
work was gaining recognition in England. Yet it never attracted
great assent. It aided the growth of Holyoake's secularist movement, and Taine, in the 1860s, saw Positivism as one of the forces
capable of 'opening doors' but not breaking 'any windows'. It
became widely known only in the 1880s, when there was a revived
interest in political theories, intimately linked with a growing
awareness of the results of monopolistic capitalism. Comte was
read but denounced with cheerful abandon by Beatrice Webb's
sister, Margaret, as the women tramped through the rain-drenched
Westmoreland countryside; one of Kipling's characters expressed
what was doubtless a typical English reaction: 'It was not much
of a creed. It only proved that men had no souls, and

there was no God and no hereafter, and that you must worry along somehow for the good of humanity'.[21] Whether Positivism deserved such an apathetic or critical reaction or not, it was to fascinate Marian Evans for a host of reasons, and for much of her life.

II. COMTE

The differences between Saint-Simon and Comte resided in the tones of their work, and the relative degrees of tightness in their syntheses. Saint-Simon was termed 'transcendental' and accused of mysticism,[22] but Comte produced an austerely intellectual system. An eclectic pragmatism, however, linked not only Saint-Simon and Comte, but also linked them to the writers who had already attracted Marian Evans's interest. Comte's work resembled Saint-Simon's in many respects. Both assumed that over the centuries the methods by which knowledge was gained had shown themselves capable of improvement. Comte produced a theory of the process of knowledge which fused opposite logical methods, which utilised both intellect and emotions. The new logic enabled Comte to lay claim to knowledge more certain than that hitherto attained. Comte also reorganised disciplines into a hierarchical synthesis. He finally demonstrated how knowledge obtained by valid methods determined man's view of the world, but also prompted an emotional response to that world, and prescribed how men should act within it.

Comte's system was divided into three closely-linked sections, defined by the Positivist slogan 'to think, to love, to act'. His theory of knowledge *(dogme)* was concerned to avoid mere intellectualism. In discussing logical method, Comte suggested that the intellect alone could not discover truth, for 'the heart is necessary to prompt the chief inspirations of the intellect, and it must also be put to service to understand the results of intellectual inquiry'. The eclectic method linked all disciplines together because all shared objective and subjective methods in varying proportions. The method of Positivism however, had practical implications. Comte rejected the outmoded theological and metaphysical search for final causes. His view of the universe was necessitarian, for all phenomena were subject to 'unvarying relationships': laws governed the physical world and the inner life, and 'the external world simultaneously nourishes, stimulates and governs us'. Although separate areas of inquiry focused upon specific kinds of phenomena, *'the noblest phenomena are in every case subordinated to the most ignoble phenomena'*. Positivism studied such laws 'in order to predict what will come about so that things may be improved as much as possible'. Comte's hierarchy of disciplines sought to show how understanding culminated in morally correct behaviour which served humanity. This linking of ethical and intellectual modes of action was seen by Comte to avert the negative scepticism of philosophical and scientific effort. Comte divided the sciences into those of the *external order* (mathematics and physics) and those of the *human order* (biology, sociology and ethics): he indicated how insight into the laws of the universe, which science provided, encouraged submission to those laws, upon which was founded personal freedom.He emphasised the superiority of ethics to all other forms of knowledge, because it merged reason and emotions, and also partook of all other disciplines. Positivism's originality stemmed from its systematisation of moral insights by the application of scientific principles: thereby it endowed such insights with validity, and provided a sure guide to behaviour.[23]

Comte connected his view of the emotional life (*culte*) to *dogme*, for he hoped to annul the mutual exclusivity of 'poetic education and philosophical study', which he saw as one of the consequences of contemporary mental anarchy. He insisted upon the connection of opposites. On a broad scale, he saw Positivism mediating between 'the Catholic impulse and the Voltairian tendency, between mysticism and empiricism'.[24] He also demonstrated how, for the individual, intellect and emotions were interdependent. Men could not help responding with feeling to the world-view presented by philosophy; sensibility was educated by 'a precise appreciation of the nature of reality'. He showed how reverential emotions stemmed from an accurate observation of reality, and how the inner life was strengthened by absorption in the outer world[25]. Comte eventually claimed the status of a religion for Positivism. To enforce his view of the importance of the emotions, he formulated a schematic scale of human relationships, which culminated in love for humanity. Months were allocated in the year to celebrate certain relationships with ceremonies and festivals which were often farcical, and rarely taken seriously by his English admirers.[26]

In dealing with his recommendations to the individual and society (*regime*) Comte emphasised how these emerged from the theory of the intellect and emotions:

> All study of Positivist dogma leads to the conclusion that our true unity consists most of all in living for others. Positivist religion is mainly destined to develop the feelings which necessarily lead to such a disposition. Upon this dual basis, the regime must now cause directly to prevail in practical existence, that unique principle of universal harmony.

Within Comte's new society the individual's life would be subject to a series of counterbalancing influences. Male intellect would act as a check upon female emotion; industry and politics would improve man's outer life, whilst religion ameliorated the inner life. A new priesthood of positivist priests would act as a force which entertained both progressive and conservative sentiments and views. The priesthood would also check the influence of the temporal power: the former would be theoretical in tendency, concerned with history and the inner life, whilst the latter would be concerned with action, the present and the external life.[27] Comte envisaged a new political system in which the emphasis would be shifted from the notion of rights to the notion of obligation. Democracy would be replaced by the rule of an élite group of Positivist philosophers, for social harmony could be brought about only by making the Positivist philosophy prevail. Comte envisaged the establishment of a two-class society to clarify and enforce the concept of human obligation, and a redivision of nations to foster a waning of nationalism and a love of humanity.[28]

Comte's concern to redefine the method whereby valid knowledge might be obtained aligned him with the tendency in nineteenth-century philosophy to concentrate upon the process of knowing. Like other writers Marian Evans read, he envisaged a fusion of hitherto separate methods: 'If every valid theory necessarily rests upon observed facts, it is equally certain that every acceptable observation demands a theory of some sort'.[29] In utilising this concept of method to link all disciplines, he also gave coherence to the wide body of knowledge which Marian Evans, like many of the other English polymaths who admired Comte, had at her command. Comte's emphasis upon the ethical relevance of both his logical method and his reorganisation of disciplines also elicited a favourable response from Marian Evans. Her religious experience had prepared her for an interest in this aspect of Comte's work. A distrust of mere intellect accompanied many modes of nineteenth-century religious enthusiasm. It was endemic in the evangelical Anglicanism to which she had been a youthful adherent, and also in the Oxford Movement, in which she had once been deeply interested. Isaac Williams learnt from Keble 'a strong depreciation of mere intellect' and Newman saw rationalism as 'the great evil of the day'.[30] Thomas à Kempis's *Imitation of Christ*, to which Marian Evans was devoted, spoke of the primacy of goodness over intellect, and of action over learning.[31] Comte also expounded, in his linking of *dogme* and *culte*, a solution to the conflict between head and heart which was often suggested by Coleridge and Carlyle as they explored the psychological repercussions of the philosophical debate. Comte suggested that intellectual insights were both prompted and only fully grasped by the emotions, and that they demanded an emotional response.

During the crises of the 1830s, both Mill and Carlyle saw the political failures of radical movements as stemming from the inadequacy of their philosophical basis, and both had critically scrutinised empiricism. Comte similarly viewed his evolution of a new theory of knowledge as of political importance. Only Positivism was capable of saving the western world from the universal and melancholy anarchy into which it was sinking.[32] It was in this respect that Comte was heavily indebted to Saint-Simon, who had argued in *L'industrie*, 'Every social regime is an application of a philosophic system and consequently it is impossible to institute a new regime without having previously established the new philosophic system to which it must correspond'.[33] Both writers were responding to a turbulent social context, Saint-Simon to a France coming to terms with the horrors of the 1789 revolution, Comte to the aftermath of the deposition of Charles X. Both produced syntheses which started with logic, suggested the reorganisation of knowledge, and culminated in proposals for new political and religious systems. The political systems they proposed were aimed at decreasing nationalism and fostering a love of humanity; both drew upon the religious experimentation of the 1789 revolution. Their differences were, however, obvious. Comte's work was motivated by a more intense sense of social and personal urgency than Saint-Simon's, which seemed to prompt, simultaneously, a greater clarity of analysis as well as a more dogmatic note. The tonal variation was apparent in the contrast between Comte's exegesis of his history of religion, which was subtle, clear, marvellously orchestrated, and Saint-Simon's laboured attempts at universal history, which recall those of Condorcet.[34] Comte's religious proposals were couched in the language of the dogmatic and the fanatic, as Mill noted, whereas Saint-Simon's *Nouveau Christianisme* was imaginatively innovative and suggestive. Within the *synthèses*, Comte established tight links between *dogme, culte,* and *régime* which distinguished his work from Saint-Simon's looser system. Saint-Simon's consideration of the logical problem was also more detailed than Comte's, and also more detached from the rest of his system. Saint-Simon's political and religious views were also more liberal than Comte's. Saint-Simon came to terms with the emergence of a new industrial working-class; Comte suggested a return to a static proletariat, dependent upon an aristocracy. Saint-Simon's new faith merged Christian and Socialist notions of fraternity; Comte, as Mill remarked, proposed a form of 'spiritual . . . despotism'.[35]

The pragmatic application of a new theory of knowledge to social issues by Comte and Saint-Simon spoke to Marian Evans's general sense of the relevance of ideas to live issues, but also specifically to her concern for the political situation in France in the 1840s. Both Saint-Simon and Comte offered explanations of social change in terms of human beliefs. Scott's novels had early stimulated her interest in the notion of change; in a notebook she kept in the 1870s, she was still pondering the subject.[36] Like Mill's, Marian Evans's reading in French revolutionary theory fostered a disillusion with the intellectual insubstantiality of English political thought. Coherent political philosophies resting upon a philosophical basis issued from the left in the 1840s: in 1847, the London-based Communist League commissioned Marx and Engels to compose a manifesto. This, like Comte's 1852 statement, and similar documents aimed at the proletariat, appeared in the form of a systematic catechism.[37] Yet, after the 1848 revolutions, the writings of the French Socialists were discredited after their authors had failed to convert theory into practice. The English experience of the revolutionary 1840s had also proved that revolution was not inevitable. George Eliot commented upon this fact in *Theophrastus Such*; it was remarked upon in speeches at the 1851 Great Exhibition.[38] By enfranchising the middle-class, the 1832 Reform Bill had prevented its union with the workers as an instrument of change: the reverse was the case in Germany, Austria and France. Marian Evans's interest in Comte was in line with an increasingly unsympathetic attitude towards radical views which started to emerge in England towards the end of the decade. Comte, like the French Socialists, rested his proposals for social reform upon a philosophical basis, but his proposals were as much conservative as radical. He was opposed to egalitarianism and spoke of duties, not rights. Positivism also claimed aloofness from, and incompatibility with, party allegiances: on such grounds did Frederic Harrison turn down a Commons seat in the 1860s.[39]

Comte's application of his eclectic logical method to the reorganisation of knowledge and to the questions of personal and social evolution resembled in many respects the non-sectarian and pragmatic tradition with which Marian Evans had been made familiar by the works of writers she had read earlier. As such, Comte's work attracted both her interest ahd her enthusiasm. Fascinated though she was by systems, she ultimately, however, felt the repugnance of a sceptic for them.[40] She steadfastly refused to be identified with the English Positivists. Her eclecticism was manifested in the reading which accompanied her introduction to Positivism. Comte's system, albeit critical of it, was biassed towards the empirical logic, and, as such, it won the approval of J. S. Mill. Marian Evans had also read, however, the more radical critiques of empiricism to be found in the neo-Idealists, Carlyle and Coleridge. It was characteristic of her eclecticism that, during the period when she was reading Comte, she also turned to the works of Hegel, who, like Comte, explored the link between a new logic and the historical process, but from a very different viewpoint.

III HEGEL AND HISTORIOGRAPHY

Marian Evans's interest in Hegel in the 1840s placed her once more within a progressive minority. During this period, Kant's name was becoming familiar in England. Yet, despite the fact that, in Germany, the Hegelian philosophy was already on the wane, Hegel had been given scant attention in England. Hegel was discussed by J. D. Morrell in *A Historical and Critical View of the Speculative Philosophy of Europe in the Nineteenth Century* (2 vols,1846) and Lewes wrote an article on Hegel for *The British and Foreign Review* in 1842. However, in *A Biographical History of Philosophy* (1845–6),Lewes noted, at the end of his fairly dispassionate account of Hegel, that few translations were available.[41] Carlyle initially prompted Marian Evans's interest in Idealism; contact with Coventry radicals furthered her interest in the subject. The *Lectures on the Philosophy of History* were translated by her neighbour, John Sibree Jnr. John Sibree's father had come as minister to the Vicar Lane Independent Chapel in 1819. He wrote works on education and the corn laws, and his chapel provided a forum for progressive views. In February 1842, he chaired a meeting between the Anti-Corn Law League and Chartists and in 1843 the schoolroom was used by the Complete Suffrage Movement. Marian Evans was friendly with his son because of a mutual enthusiasm for German writers. In rendering readable Hegel's arcane terminology, Sibree was motivated by a propagandist's sense that Hegel offered solutions to questions which vexed English thinkers. Ignorance of the German achievement was often seen to lead to wasted effort. John Sibree Jnr. had spent a year at Halle University, and Marian Evans taught German to his sister, Mary, from October 1844 until 1846. As Sibree followed in Marian Evans's footsteps as a translator of the Germans, their friendship flourished. She was discussing Hegel with him in 1848. She retained her respect for Sibree: in 1856, on her advice, Lewes sounded him out as a possible tutor for his three sons. In later years, she reported compliments paid to his translation, and, when Lewes was rewriting his history of philosophy in 1870 and 1871, she was especially interested in the revision of the section on Hegel.[42]

'The most important and most characteristic thing about many a great author is the diversity, the often latently discordant diversity, of the ideas to which his mind is responsive'.[43] Marian Evans's reading of Comte, whose work modified a tradition of scientific empiricism, occurred during the same period as her reading of Hegel, who developed the Idealist tradition of Kant. In any intellectual progress, as Marian Evans's idol George Sand commented, 'intellectual transformations come about imperceptibly, and without it being possible to distinguish the exact boundaries of each of their phases'.[44] Marian Evans's sceptical eclecticism led her to read works representing seemingly opposed viewpoints; she also returned to writers who had interested her in earlier periods. Her reading assumed a web-like pattern: the focal points of her interest were distinct, often ostensibly disparate, but her reading was also connected into a coherent whole because of filaments which linked together the writers she read. Those writers often modified empiricism within different traditions; they also revealed similar preoccupations and reached similar conclusions on specific topics. Hegel and Comte both attempted to construct all-inclusive systems: Hegel and Rousseau both attacked the aridity of metaphysics and yearned for a totality of vision. A focus upon fact marked the thought of both writers: even in the egocentric state of *rêverie* Rousseau's mind 'only freely took flight if it initially rested itself upon objects or concrete forms'. Both thought that the study of self illuminated society, and vice versa.[45] The Idealist notion of history as process which Carlyle also entertained was reiterated by Comte's suggestion of the merging of historical phases. Saint-Simon considered that the process of history was on the side of revolution, a Hegelian notion to which Marx was to give prominence.[46]

In 1846, Morrell considered that 'the mechanical tendency of the age is fast wearing itself out'.[47] Comte and Hegel were united by their suggestion of a non-material dimension in reality, and Comte acknowledged this link when he suggested that Hegel should be celebrated at Positivist festivals. By excluding certain areas of experience from analysis, Comte drew attention to forbidden fields: the notion of the unknowable was self-defeating, for 'there mingles subtly with the conception the feeling of the *Unknown*, the not yet known, the vast unexplored possibilities of the universe; and thus the notion is half redeemed in spite of itself'.[48] The romantic literature which Marian Evans was still reading in the 1840s corroborated the philosophical reaction against rationalism: A. W. von Schlegel considered 'What is usually called Enlightenment should . . . rather be called Darkening, because it means the extinction of the inner light of man'. Marian Evans's sense of the mystery of existence was evident in her attraction to impressionistic language, expressed as early as 1841, and this attraction may have conditioned a favourable response to the enigmatic Hegelian terminology. Her interest in the stylistic innovations of Carlyle reflected this tendency. Although Carlyle and Coleridge paved the way for her favourable reception of the German philosophy, many intellectuals became aware of the inadequacies of literary Idealism, and turned to the original sources. In 1841, when Marian Evans read Henry Hallam's *Introduction to the Literature of Europe*, she would have come across references to the German Idealist philosophers, and Hallam's book was written in the spirit of Hegel's universal history.[49] Marian Evans's reading during the period of the church-going crisis also fostered an interest in Hegel. Hegel had helped reinstate Spinoza's thought in the mainstream of European thought. Strauss also acknowledged his debt to Hegel.

like his mentor, he was fascinated by religious history, and wished to justify the Christian faith by recourse to Hegelian views. Hegel had profoundly influenced Strauss, for Hegel saw philosophy as offering a defence of Christianity, saving it from the outer attacks of rationalism, the inner corruptions of sentimentalism, mysticism and superstition. Sibree grasped the way in which Hegel avoided mysticism and empiricism: he managed to 'intellectualize Romanticism and to spiritualize Enlightenment'.[50] The view that religion afforded a corrective to the notion of a material, mechanistic reality united disparate thinkers in their reaction against empiricism. Hegel suggested that religion was 'everywhere idealism' because it was 'the denial or correction of the crass realism of the workaday consciousness, the restoring of things to their true proportions by setting them in the light of the eternal and the Whole'. Marian Evans's vision of reality was crucially indebted not only to literary romanticism, but also to her early religious experiences. She may well have viewed Hegel as an antidote to materialistic views. She had commented, in her early praise of Carlyle, that she disliked the vision whose 'baleful touch has the same effect as would a uniformity in the rays of light – it turns all objects to pale lead colour'.[51]

'In Germany', said Hegel, 'the eclaircissement was conducted in the interest of theology; in France it immediately took up a position of hostility to the church': Sibree noted that Hegel's insistence that philosophy should not be separated from theology made him unlike English thinkers. Philosophy, according to Hegel, should heed the truths of religion, for both disciplines 'have the Divine as their common object'. He associated reason not only with divine providence but also with the historical process, for 'what was *intended* by eternal wisdom, is actually *accomplished* in the domain of existent, active Spirit, as well as in that of mere nature. Our mode of treating the subject is, in this aspect, a Theodicea – a justification of the ways of God'.[52] Religion and philosophy were also linked because Hegel saw both of them as holding opposites in balance and synthesis by their deployment of the Hegelian dialectic; history reflected a similar process. The Universal Idea existed as 'the substantial totality of things on one side' and as 'the abstract essence of free volition on the other side', and metaphysics was concerned to comprehend 'the absolute connection of this antithesis'. Hegel considered that Christianity synthesised self and the world, and that the reconciliation of subjective and objective informed the evolution of the state. Hegel's crucial term *Geist*, which Sibree usually translated as 'Spirit' referred to both Intelligence and Will. Spirit, as self-consciousness, was free, and was contrasted to Matter, which was determined by the laws of gravity: Spirit was dependent on nothing outside itself, and was concerned only to know and realise its own nature. Man was free only when engaged in thought, for otherwise 'he sustains a relation to the world around him as to another, an alien form of being'. Spirit, as Will, allowed men to 'pursue a certain course of action in spite of all inducements, sensuous or emotional, to deviate from it.'[53]

Hegel defined history as both written records of past action (*historia rerum gestarum*) and as past action (*res gestae*) for both illuminated the workings of Spirit as Intelligence or Will. Both definitions showed Hegel's reaction against the supposed abstraction of Encyclopaedist thought. Words became a form of action, for written history, 'present[s] a people with their own image in a condition which thereby becomes objective to them. Without History their existence in time is blindly self-involved, – the recurring play of arbitrary volition in manifold forms'. Yet philosophic truth is 'not only Truth in and for itself . . ., but also Truth in its living form as exhibited in the world'. Hegel envisaged *res gestae* as including reference to interdependent mental and physical action. He described many aspects of a given society; the book opened with a deeply-felt picture of man's suffering through the ages. Whilst he included philosophical argument, he considered that the raw material of fact was also of supreme importance: 'Two elements . . . enter into the object of our investigation; the first the Idea, the second the complex of human passions; the one the warp, the other the woof of the vast arras-web of Universal History'.[54] Hegel's theory of historical development fused many notions current at the time. His 'enormous historical sense', his being 'the first who attempted to show an evolution, and inner coherence, in history', were praised by Engels.[55] In his description of the dialectical process, Hegel employed the verb *aufheben*, meaning both to cancel and to preserve, which enabled him to mediate between historicism and progressivism by demonstrating that 'the present form of Spirit comprehends within it all earlier steps . . . . The grades which Spirit seems to have left behind it, it still possesses in the depths of the present'. Hegel pointed to the 'strict correspondence' between the 'mental and moral conditions of individuals and their social and religious conditions', but also showed human progress, wherein the mind continually moved

owards perfect self-consciousness, and became aware of the interconnection of self and world. This synthesis was then imaged in all
areas of society. Each nation was seen as one of the 'grades of
progress' in a cosmic struggle. Change in history exhibited an
often agonising struggle towards perfection and freedom, unlike
change in nature, which was a peaceful 'self-repeating cycle'.
Upheaval and resolution were inbuilt in the historical condition,
yet destruction also preluded a new form of life. Hegel's description of world-history traced the interaction of developments in
philosophy, religion and institutions, and indicated the extent to
which these revealed the adjustment of man to the world. He
noted particularly those periods in which there was a revolution in
religious sensibility, such as the change from Judaism to Christianity which had preoccupied him in his early theological writings. In the Reformation, and particularly in the writings of
Luther, he detected his own notion of truth as 'not a finished and
completed thing'.[56]

As religion and the historical process embodied the merging of
objective and subjective, the state, likewise, manifested the workings of the spirit as intelligence and will. The growing 'harmoniza-
tion or reconciliation of Objective and Subjective intelligence' was
the index of the growth of rational freedom within the state. Hegel
viewed secular existence as 'the definite manifestation, the phenom-
enal existence of the Divine Essence. On this account it is that the
State rests on religion'. The process displayed in history 'is only
the manifestation of Religion as Human Reason – the production of
the religious principle which dwells in the heart of man, under the
form of Secular Freedom. Thus the discord between the inner life
of the heart and the actual world is removed'. Consequently, there
could be '[no] Revolution without a Reformation'. Progress was
seen in terms of 'the kingdom of *Will* manifesting itself in outward
existence'.[57] Hegel also dwelt upon the relationship between morality and the state, for 'only as a moral entity, can the state
demand morality of its citizens'. He distinguished between *Sittlich-
keit*, or conventional morality, and *Moralität*, the morality of the
heart and conscience. Ideally, individual and collective morality
were synchronous: in a civilised society, the individual consciousness submitted to the law because it recognised the state as an
embodiment of reason. The state thus became embodied synthesis, and 'Society and the State are the very conditions in which
Freedom is realised'.[58]

The definition of knowledge was at the heart of Hegel's system.

The quest for truth was endless, for all truths were conditioned and incomplete, but historically necessary at the time they were formulated. Hegel also pointed to the limitations of Understanding, whereby thought was 'abstract and general, stripped naked of the richness of sense'. In knowledge as process, thinker and subject remained discrete, yet 'in order to interpret any level of spirit, the philosopher must (1) be able to experience at that level and be able, as it were, to speak authoritatively for the subject which is at that level; and he must also (2) have raised himself to the higher level of philosophic experience'.[59] This was to suggest a process, and resultant vision, which combined the empathy of feeling-based romanticism with the detached accuracy of science. Hegel also suggested the cancelling of the distinction between reality and thought, for both were united in the Absolute. His dialectic gave play to his sense of the richness of the world, for he wished to show that clarity of thought promoted a sense of the world's unity. He thus produced 'a logic not only of knowledge . . . but also of Being, Existence, and Reality . . .. The objects of logic are concepts. But these concepts are not what a psychological logic might mean by concepts, merely subjective ideas. They are form and content at the same time. They express the nature of things, and that nature is thought in them'. Hegel insisted that history was both historiography and past events. The historical writer's task was to deploy the dialectic which mirrored the world's movement towards synthesis of self and world. By his emphasis upon thought as a mirror of the processes of reality, Hegel presented not merely a new logic. The Hegelian dialectic boldly 'establishes the kingdom of its truth on the grave of the intellect'.[60] Hegel's logic did not merely make possible the fusion of the tormenting opposites of freedom and necessity, detachment and subjectivity, finite and infinite, self and world. Its very method shattered the *a priori/a posteriori* distinction to suggest that Mind, as a manifestation of *Geist*, partook of, and could apprehend directly, a complex reality.

In the *Lectures on the Philosophy of History*, Hegel categorised the types and problems of historical narrative. In her reading which accompanied and also followed the reading of Hegel, Marian Evans turned to historical narratives, which, significantly, often had much in common with fiction. Historiography was, in the first half of the nineteenth century, largely the preserve of amateurs, and concern with it was a Victorian phenomenon. History books oomed large in the reading of the educated working-class and historians resembled novelists in their imaginative interpretation of events. Ideas of evolution informed historical works long before they appeared in scientific treatises, and historical evolutionism, as much as Darwinism, fostered middle-class heterodoxy. The concern with political events which Marian Evans showed in the late 1840s also directed her towards the past in order to understand the present, a response she shared with Mrs Gaskell and Frederic Harrison during the same troubled period.[61] Marian Evans's interest in history showed her as a product of her age, but her interest was crucially reinforced by the reading of continental thinkers to whom few English readers had access. The reading of Hegel continued a trend in her intellectual development evinced by her earlier enthusiasm for Scott and her study of the Bible as an historical document. Mill and Carlyle had also explored the implications of logical method for the historical process in the 1830s. Comte's *Bibliothèque du Prolétaire* included sixty-seven historical works out of a total of one hundred and fifty.[62] Marian Evans turned to Gibbon's *Autobiography*, a work written with Rousseauesque frankness and which suggested the universal appeal of historical writing, and its affinity with the novel.[63] In 1849, she also read the first two volumes of Macaulay's *History of England*, the progressivism of which aroused great admiration in Marian Evans, as it did in many of her generation, although Mill criticised Macaulay's intellectual shallowness and parochialism. The work commented obliquely on the 1848 events, for Macaulay emphasised how social reform in England came about by 'gradual development, not . . . demolition and reconstruction'. He showed partial eradication, partial continuation, of problems such as those of Ireland and child labour.[64] In 1816, the youthful Macaulay defended the reading of novels in the *Christian Observer* and his own writings were readable best-sellers, which broke down the distinction between fiction and formal history. Scott's novels helped to create an audience for Macaulay, and Macaulay's meticulous attention to detail recalled a quality the two writers shared, an 'omnivorous and disinterested craving for information'.[65] The effortless flow of Macaulay's narrative stemmed, however, from a theoretical basis which contributed to the debate on historiography. He argued that attention to detail precluded the writing of partisan history; his tolerant historicism caused him to inveigh, as had Hegel, against Pragmatical History, which saw lessons for the present in the past.[66] It was richness of

detail, rooted in intellectual scepticism, which was possessed by
the novelists Marian Evans admired during this period. They were
also novelists who dealt, as did Saint-Simon, Comte and Hegel,
with religious experience and the historical process. They were
also writers who were crucially indebted to Rousseau.

12

Philosophy and the Novel (1844–1850)

The leaves of the Diderot and Rousseau tree have produced this goodly fruit.[1]

I. THE ENGLISH TRADITION

In the eighteenth century, philosophy's rejection of universals, the Newtonian emphasis on space and time, aided the English novel's emphasis upon the quality of the particular.[2] In turning from philosophy to the novel, which implicitly celebrated life's resistance to theory, Marian Evans tacitly acknowledged this dialogue between speculation and fiction. It was, however, a pointer to her intellectuality that the novelists she admired during this period utilised philosophical ideas in their fictions, and tested them against notions of life's complicated unfathomability. Marian Evans commented little upon the important English novels published during the 1840s. *Martin Chuzzlewit* was published in 1844, in 1847 appeared *Agnes Gray*, *Jane Eyre*, *Wuthering Heights* and *Vanity Fair*, in 1848, *Mary Barton*, *Dombey and Son* and *The Tenant of Wildfell Hall*, and, in 1849, *Shirley*. She spoke scathingly of Charlotte Brontë, but re-read Scott and praised Richardson, whose resemblance to Rousseau was hinted at by Diderot. She entertained hopes for Disraeli, although they were disappointed, and, in later years, when her sympathy for the Jewish cause led her to estimate his works more highly, she still felt that her true affinity was with Scott. She praised Disraeli's political sentiments, rather than his artistic expression of them, perhaps because she sensed the connection *Sybil* had with *Chartism* and *Past and Present*, and because she saw in his work echoes of her own interest in Scott, the English romantic writers and the Oxford Movement.[3] Yet Marian Evans seemed to have sensed that Disraeli, like other English thinkers, paid heavily for his political maturity with the shallowness of his ideas. The political ideas in his novels lacked the

129

visionary impetus and clarity of exposition found in the French
political theorists she was reading, and in the novels of George
Sand. The Parliamentary system, Chartism, evolutionism and German Idealism were treated superficially.[4] Disraeli's sense of the
links between character, environment and belief was also weak if
compared to that of Scott and George Sand. He failed effectively to
relate individual growth to social change. *Coningsby* did not explore the hero's development in relation to the growing disillusion
with the 1832 Reform Bill; *Tancred* degenerated into a travelogue
cum adventure story. The historical setting was not realised in
concrete detail as in Macaulay's *History*. Marian Evans considered
that there was a thinness of historical detail, especially in *Tancred*,
and she was critical of Disraeli's hostility to French novelists.[5]

The English novelist who did arouse her enthusiasm was J. A.
Froude, whose book *The Nemesis of Faith* (1849) she reviewed for
the *Coventry Herald* on 16 March 1849. The novel caused a scandal
and Froude was widely attacked in the press. Marian Evans's
enthusiasm was prompted by her inclination to embrace controversial causes, but also by the circumstances in which she came to
review the book, and by her response to its author. John Chapman
despatched a complimentary copy, at Froude's request, to the
anonymous translator of Strauss, for Strauss's ideas had had some
influence on the novel. Marian Evans replied with a note to
Froude, who wrote back, 'naively and prettily requesting her to
reveal herself'.[6] Flattered by this attention, she met Froude on
7 June 1849. Robert Evans had been buried the day before, and
Froude excused himself from joining the Brays and Marian Evans
on the trip to France because of his engagement to Charles Kingsley's sister-in-law, Charlotte Grenfell, a strict Puseyite, who had
planned to enter a convent when Froude went to Oxford. The
eminently sensible Elizabeth Gaskell noticed Froude's 'Magical,
magnetic, glamour-like influence', and confessed, 'I stand just
without the circle of his influence; resisting with all my might, but
feeling and seeing the attraction'.[7] The younger Marian Evans,
depressed and vulnerable, may well have been less resistant to his
charm.

Marian Evans responded to the novel not only because of its
affinities with Goethe, as expounded by Carlyle, but also because
Froude was one of Rousseau's heirs.[8] Froude, like Rousseau,
intensified her perception of reality, so that 'life, both outward and
inward, presents itself to us in higher relief, in colours brightened

and deepened', and she felt herself 'in companionship with a spirit . . . transfusing himself into our souls and . . . vitalizing them by his superior energy'.[9] Rousseau was quoted admiringly in *The Nemesis of Faith*. Debts to the French writer were revealed structurally in the shapeless narrative which allowed the scrutiny of introspection. The central section of the novel, 'Confessions of a Sceptic', recalled both Goethe and *Les Confessions*. The attempt to reveal life's complications by aiming 'only at being true to human life' echoed Rousseau's non-didactic stance.[10] The evolution of the plot was indebted to *Les confessions*, for the central figure's erratic emotions, actions and intellectual development were explained by reference to an exaggerated version of Rousseau's notion of individuality, and the isolation of the sensitive soul. Froude also outlined the Rousseauesque adaptation of Locke, whereby environment was seen to have a crucial effect upon character. Rousseau's ideas of pastoral retreat and patriarchal service were shown when the hero, Sutherland, dwelt on the shores of Lake Como as a dreamy solitary, helping the peasants, playing music, and responding to nature. The idyllic love affair between the hero and Mrs Leonard also owed something to Rousseau's description of his affair with Mme de Warens.[11] In his portrayal of Sutherland, however Froude, modified Rousseau's ideas, as did George Sand. Sutherland's happy love affair was shattered by the death of his mistress's child, upon which author and characters alike moralised. The hero's nostalgia for his childhood was described with a low-key sociological detail, absent in Rousseau, and also with reference to Wordsworth's *Ode: Intimations of Immortality*.[12]

Froude also dramatised the apparent opposition of thought and feeling, and its influence upon action, in a fashion reminiscent of Rousseau's analysis of his own consciousness. Froude noted 'the union of clear intellect and even generous feeling with an entire absence of active power is too frequent in life to be false in art'. The union of feeling and intellect was presupposed when the hero saw that 'each step gained in knowledge is but one more nerve summoned out into consciousness of pain'. Sutherland read a wide variety of authors, and their influence upon his emotions and actions was described. But Froude, like Rousseau, insisted upon feeling as a prime reality. The division between feeling and intellect determined Froude's concept of tragic sexuality: like Rousseau and Comte, he saw women as notable for their emotional, not their intellectual capacity.[13]

The moral of the novel was that ideas alone worked no salvation, for Sutherland failed to find peace within any intellectual system. Faith was his nemesis, because man could only 'live and act manfully in this world, not in the strength of opinions, not according to what he thinks, but according to what he *is*'. His views brought disharmony to his family and doubt and remorse to himself. Froude suggested, as had Carlyle and Rousseau, that valid religion was based upon the heart. He criticised the Hebrew mythology from an emotional and moral standpoint, as 'insulting to the pure majesty of God . . . injurious in its direct effects to those who are brought to believe it'. Froude avoided extremes of belief, and dramatised the evils of sectarianism. True Christianity was also contrasted to destructive, intellectual theology and metaphysics.[14] Yet an internalised religion, because it was based upon the flux of consciousness, was seen as prone to fall victim to the self's anarchic tendencies, for 'religion, reduced to a sentiment resting only on internal emotion, is like a dissolving view, which will change its image as the passions shift their focal distances . . . unrealized in some constant external form, obeying inclination, not controlling it, it is but a dreamy phantom of painted shadow, and vanishes before temptation'. Such a view would have challenged what Marian Evans had salvaged from her own reorientation of belief after the church-going crisis. Froude argued that, ultimately, reality eluded the formulas of theologians and philosophers. Just as the nature of consciousness was evanescent, and thus provided a dangerous foundation for faith, so life was a 'farce tragedy', and 'neither so high nor so low as the Church would have it; chequered over with its wild light shadows, I could love it and all the children of it, more dearly, perhaps, because it was not all light'.[15] The art of the reverential sceptic was also to be encountered by Marian Evans in the novels of George Sand who, like Froude, drew inspiration from Rousseau.

II. GEORGE SAND

Exeter College, Oxford, of which Froude was a Fellow, denounced and burned *The Nemesis of Faith*: George Sand's novels were likewise widely censured. By the late 1830s, her work was beginning to gain acceptance in England, but doubts lingered about her moral influence. Thackeray, in 1840, suspected her novels because of the scandals surrounding her life, and singled out *Lélia* as 'a regular topsyturfication of morality, a thieves' and prostitutes' apotheosis'. In 1874, Margaret Oliphant, writing in *Blackwood's*, compared *Romola* to *Consuelo*, and decided that French novels were 'not so safe for general reading as English'. George Sand's novels were thought to encourage female rebellion, and they opened the mind of Mrs Ward's hero, David Grieve, to unconventional views of marriage.[16] For Marian Evans, however, as for the central figure in Hawthorne's *The Blithedale Romance*, they seem to have been like 'the cry of some solitary sentinel, whose station was on the outposts of the advance-guard of human progression'.[17] Visitors to the Priory, and Victorian writers like Mathilde Blind and Eliza Linton, often made comparisons between George Eliot and George Sand. Both emerged from the provinces to make their names as writers in a metropolis, and progressed from notoriety to middle-aged respectability.[18] Her enthusiasm for George Sand was at its height from 1844 into the early 1850s, and continued into the 1870s. To the youthful Marian Evans, the French novelist was 'my divinity' against whom she would hear 'no blasphemies'. Her enthusiasm was not shared by her friends. In 1847 she failed to interest Sara Hennell in the French writer's works and Cara Bray actively disliked some of George Sand's novels. The solitary nature of this interest suggests that George Sand, as well as discussing subjects such as Spinoza, physiology and phrenology, which Marian Evans also debated with the Rosehill circle, also spoke to the more idiosyncratic tendencies and preoccupations of Marian Evans's mind.[19]

Marian Evans was also aware that there was a link between Rousseau and George Sand. After speaking of Rousseau as a crucial influence on her thought, she went on to discuss George Sand in a way which suggested that she associated the two writers not just because both had influenced her, but because she grasped the qualities they had in common. She remarked upon George Sand's lack of didacticism, saying that her novels were not to be read 'as a text-book'; she sensed that her formlessness was controversial and deliberate, and linked to an intellectual viewpoint. She admired George Sand's capacity to strive for faithful, detailed representation, and yet also to shadow forth general truths. She valued George Sand, as she valued Rousseau, not because she imbibed from her novels specific notions, but because George Sand heightened her perception of reality, thus compensating for the inevitable incompleteness of 'one's own dull faculties'. Marian Evans's reading of *Lettres d'un voyageur* prompted her to echo the presentation of passionate, shifting sensibility which she found in both Rousseau and George Sand.[20] Moreover, if Marian Evans read the French theorists of Radicalism as a continuation of her interest in Rousseau, the same was true of George Sand's interest in the same writers. Both women shared a knowledge of provincial society, which Rousseau recommended as an index of national character; both had been in touch with provincial reformers at early stages in their careers. Whilst Marian Evans read the works of Saint-Simon and other intellectual radicals, she also read George Sand's critical meditations upon their ideas. Once more, there emerged a coherent pattern in her reading, which also suggested a desire constantly to reassess truths. Like Hegel, she saw truth as residing in the very process of the quest for it; like Mill, she seemed to feel it a duty to 'admit always a devil's advocate into the presence of your dearest, most sacred truths'.[21]

George Sand was of that generation of French artists whose imagination was fertilised by the atmosphere of France after the 1830 revolution, which bore certain resemblances to the England of the 1840s. Like Marian Evans, she was also crucially indebted to the literary reassessment of rationalism. The fevered imagination manifested in her early work responded to the flamboyant aspects of English romanticism, finding inspiration in Mrs Radcliffe for the Gothic elements in *Consuelo* and drawing upon the popular image of Lord Byron in *Jacques*. It was Rousseau, however, whose works she read in the early 1820s, who, she said, revolutionised her thought. In England, his influence upon her work was noted as early as 1834; Mathilde Blind described her as his 'spiritual daughter'. Rousseau's name was often invoked in her novels, and the heroine of *Mauprat*, growing up in solitude, 'had kindled her vast intelligence with the burning declamations of Jean-Jacques'.[22]

Rousseau's example exerted an influence upon the unpatterned structure of her novels: George Sand apologised for *Consuelo's* apparent absence of form, noting her 'habitual weakness: the absence of an overall design'. This was partially motivated by her mode of composition, for she wrote swiftly in order to make money and to seek refuge from her emotional problems, telling Flaubert in 1867, 'When I see the anguish you go through when you are working on a novel, I am disconcerted by my own facility and tell myself that my work is slipshod'.[23] Yet, as in Rousseau's case, the shapelessness of George Sand's novels is organically connected to her intellectual premises. Like Rousseau, she chose the loosest, most personal forms of narrative: the confessional reminiscence in *Mauprat*, the epistolary in *Jacques* and *Lélia*, the autobiographical in *Lettres d'un voyageur*. She saw her art as that of a sceptic; her unshaped narratives reflected her doubt, her sense of the complexity of reality. In 1832, she confessed herself to be too 'conscientious to conceal doubts, but too timid to raise them into certainties'. The melancholy unbelief of *Lélia* was obliquely didactic, akin to the 'Confessions of a Savoyard Priest' in *Emile*, for the reader, ultimately, 'must feel the need to find his way towards truth with more passion and more courage'. She denied that her novels advocated specific ideas, for she saw absorption in ideas, especially metaphysical ones, as less fertile than outward-looking scepticism.[24] Her art was Rousseauesque for it originated in the play of *rêverie* upon fact, and was suggestive rather than informative, for 'Art is not an invincible demonstrator and feeling is not always satisfied by the best of definitions'. Her stand against dogmatism was associated with her refusal to pattern narrative. Of *Indiana*, she said 'I created it without any preconceived design, without any theory of art or of philosophy'; she linked the undisciplined structure of *Lélia* to her portrayal of inner turmoil, which was, in its turn, 'a right without which faith would be neither a victory nor a virtue'.[25]

Her method was, however, intellectual, in that she made use of ideas. Like Marian Evans, she read widely, and Thackeray noted her 'philosophical friskiness'.[26] She commented, 'My nature is that of a poet, not a legislator, a fighter, if need be, but never a parliamentarian', but she tried to see whether concepts could interpret reality. Yet she rarely committed herself to any one doctrine. She employed the notion that environment conditioned personality in the depiction of Delmare in *Indiana* or influenced belief in *Jacques* and *Spiridion*, and she used this view as a basis for the plea for compassion in *Mauprat*. Yet she also asserted a doctrine of individualism in *Mauprat*, a novel indebted to Rousseau's treatment of education in *Emile*, for she showed how the hero rose above the hereditary and social conditioning of his feudal background. Yet events were shown to influence the development of tendencies which were innate; the essence of personality could be directed, but not changed. Her characters, likewise, aired theories, but saw themselves as dreamers and poets.[27]

Not only did her structure and sceptical deployment of concepts reflect Rousseau's influence: her very themes were Rousseau-esque, although she often responded critically to his conclusions. She dealt with the opposition of intellect and emotions. She attacked the intellectuality of German Idealism: she was morally pragmatic, and claimed that 'Learning without goodness is folly'. In line with Rousseau's adaptation of Locke, she also insisted that feeling was the central reality, uniting mind and body, for 'between *knowledge* and *sensation*, the link is *feeling*'. Yet her common sense disdained the distinction between heart and head, for 'the same blood . . . beats . . . beneath the breast and in the temple'. She demonstrated how tragedy sprang from a decision to base life exclusively upon either feeling or mind. Lélia's sorrow was 'produced by the misuse of thought'; Lamarche in *Mauprat*, and Ramière in *Indiana* found their intellectualised philanthropy at odds with their feelings of privilege. In *Spiridion*, the central characters saw their dilemmas springing from a conflict between impulse and reason. The ideal of balance was set forth when the foundling's employer in *François le champi* remarked 'that which pleases me about you is that your heart is as good as your head and your hand'.[28]

Rousseau's liberal Christianity also influenced the way in which George Sand showed how her characters evolved from scepticism to a non-sectarian, humanitarian religion. Edmée remarked 'within poetic souls, mysticism and doubt reign together. Of this, Jean-Jacques was a striking and magnificent example'. Faith must satisfy 'all the needs . . . and faculties of the soul'. George Sand rejected unfeeling, priestly precepts, and championed an imaginative faith, inspired by the examples of Christ and the early Church, 'a hope offered to free souls, and not a yoke imposed by the powerful and the rich'. Lélia, in the midst of a crisis of belief, still adored Christ as an image of 'human suffering relieved by divine hope; resignation . . . acceptance of human life; redemption . . . calm amidst agony and hope in death'. Alexis abandoned sectarian Christianity, but retained from it a sense of justice and 'love of the good and the need for truth'; he suggested that the mysteries as expounded by Platonic, Christian and Pythagorean doctrines were 'the same doctrine continued and modified, and the essence of this doctrine seems the basis of eternal truth'.[29]

In *La nouvelle Héloise*, Rousseau used his own experience as the basis for fiction, and George Sand's novels contained 'the history of her soul's life'.[30] She was concerned with the movement of consciousness in which ideas and feelings were entangled, and the *Lettres d'un voyageur*, written as a frank observation of her own heart, closely resembled *Les confessions*. She dealt prominently with Rousseauesque notions of isolation. Her characters were placed in remote locations, on large estates, in castles, mountainous regions, monasteries, on an island. This, and their prosperity, allowed them to cultivate the inner life. In *Mauprat*, Bernard dealt briefly with his experience in the American War of Independence, noting: 'in telling you of my adventures, I isolate my existence from historical facts'.[31] George Sand supplemented, however, Rousseau's notion of isolation with her desire to explore the reasons for alienation, which was often seen, in her novels, as necessitated by circumstances. Ralph in *Indiana* withdrew from life after experience of loveless relationships; Indiana, Consuelo and Edmée lose their mothers at an early age. George Sand also assessed the value of isolation. The wandering of her characters was an apt correlative of their questing scepticism; she noted: 'A voyage for me is just a course in psychology and physiology and I am the *subject* of it'. The pain of introspection tempered *ennui*, and Ralph, Indiana, Consuelo and Anzolete chose isolation because freedom, innocence and beauty were unattainable in society. Ralph saw solitude as indicating superior sensitivity; Patience in *Mauprat*, Zdenko and Albert in *Consuelo* derived magical powers from their solitude. Yet she also showed that sensitivity fostered self-absorption, producing mental and physical malaise in Indiana, Jacques, Marcelle in *Le Meunier d'Angibault* and Madaleine in *François le champi*. The closed worlds of the monasteries in *Mauprat* and *Spiridion*, the musical circles in *Consuelo*, were open to corruption. She also showed that isolation was always short-lived, for man was necessarily bound up with a reality outside self. Following the way in which Rousseau, especially in *La nouvelle Héloise*, had emphasised the influence of environment upon character, George Sand created characters who shared her own immense and detailed 'love of nature'. Yet she realised, as Lamenais suggested, that 'man is not made to live with trees, stones, the clear sky, the azure sea, flowers and mountains, but with his fellow man . . . if we cannot live in peace with our fellow-men, neither romantic raptures nor aesthetic enjoyment will ever fill the abyss gaping at the bottom of our heart.[32] In *Lettres d'un voyageur*, she felt compelled to define her attitude not only towards nature, but also towards politics. Because man existed in time, he was bound to the destiny of all men. She often dealt with the period prior to, and during, the 1789 revolution because, in times of social change, men could not overlook their collective destiny. The Mauprats abandoned their feudal life because of social changes; Consuelo, the least political of the heroines, relinquished her art when she was offered patronage by the despotic Frederick the Great of Prussia. In *Spiridion*, the monastic community suffered upheaval because of revolution; economic factors influenced the love affairs in *Le Meunier d'Angibault* and *François le champi*.

Yet George Sand saw adjustment to society as painful. Alexis noted: 'The life of this age is wearying, the life in solitary places exasperates'. Contact with the world disillusioned the sensitive soul, and led George Sand herself to the unhappy solitude of creativity. Society's decadence defeated and misinterpreted the heroism of Ralph and Indiana; Alexis and Angel were persecuted by the other monks; Stenio's intelligence was 'crushed by a reality which lacks poetry and grandeur', an experience which he shared with Sylvia.[33] The harmonising of self and world haunted George Sand as it had haunted Rousseau and Hegel, and her concentration upon the themes of love (established as a serious topic in *La nouvelle Héloise*) and education was related to her sense of the solitary's need to come to terms with a reality outside self. She admitted that her early novels were obsessed with the way in which 'the very existence of society leads to the poor relationship between the sexes'.[34] Repressive social forces conditioned the experiences of Edmée, Ramière, Delmare and M. Blanchet. Evanescent, self-regarding passion was contrasted to loving friendship in *Indiana*, *Jacques* and *Consuelo*, a theme Rousseau had touched upon in his descriptions of his affair with Mme de Warens and Emile's marriage to Sophie. In *Le Meunier d'Angibault* and *François le champi*, she presented the ideal of a secluded rural education, which owed much to *Emile*. Yet in *Jacques*, Sylvia, who received such an education, experienced only disillusion in maturity. *Mauprat* showed how education must take into account both individualism and common humanity; the narrative focused also upon a series of encounters, in which love, or its absence, crucially influenced the hero.

George Sand also shared with Rousseau two seemingly contradictory tendencies. As non-didactic writers, both were concerned to capture the qualities of emotions and places, but both also longed to discover remedies for the problems such scrutiny of the particular revealed. She returned constantly to the themes of the distinction between heart and head, of religion and of isolation. She suggested that, in this respect, her work was inspired by the implications of the logical debate: she wrote *Indiana* 'by a process of following my artistic powers, analysing life in order to find therein a synthesis'. After outlining her theory of individuality, she added, 'but there is a general view which may be extracted by looking at the destinies of all men, and the thousand details which make up diversity may be adapted to that general view'.[35] Matthew Arnold detected in George Sand's works 'the cry of agony and revolt . . . the aspiration towards a purged and renewed human society'. In her treatment of political questions, her scepticism and her yearning for general truths were tellingly revealed. English critics noted her progressive views, and Mazzini hailed her as an 'apostle of religious democracy'.[36] George Sand first encountered Socialist ideas when she was sixteen. Casimir canvassed for the Berry Republicans in 1827, and George Sand maintained contact with the group when she moved to Paris. When she visited Majorca with Chopin in 1838, and viewed the backwardness of the peasantry, she spoke of France as the country which could 'bestow . . . the baptism of true liberty' on oppressed nations.[37] When the 1848 revolution occurred, she rushed to Paris. Edmée had praised Rousseau's fusion of doubt and mysticism, and George Sand turned, for a while, as other reluctant sceptics, such as Mill, Carlyle and Marian Evans turned, to the Saint-Simonians, whose scientism and idealistic aspirations had much in common with Rousseau's duality of mood. Lélia spoke enthusiastically of 'these beautiful poetic dreams which we hear proclaimed by the new sects, and which rise like mysterious perfumes above this age of doubt, a strange mixture of arrogant negations and tender hopes'.[38] Thackeray bracketed George Sand's name with that of the Saint-Simonians, and *Indiana*, published when the movement was the subject of much scandal, was censured because 'Saint-simonianism was blamed for everything'.[39] George Sand's criticism of metaphysical generalising, her linking of heart and head, her view of the relationships between the sexes, owed something to Saint-Simonianism, as did her religious views. Her education had been free from religious bias; her religious sense rested upon 'a certain respect for the divine art that directs the eternal creation of things'. The search for new religions was a prominent feature of

Frech life in the 1830s, and *Spiridion* was described as a 'religious manifesto'. Alexis echoed the Saint-Simonian synthesis which culminated in religion when he stated that man had duties to the outside world, by extending scientific knowledge, to himself, by perfecting his inner life in relation to a divine ideal, and to mankind, via respect for democratic institutions.[40]

Yet George Sand's works were inspired not merely by Saint-Simonianism, but by a broadly progressive stance which drew upon an eclectic variety of thinkers. Lewes spoke of how 'the humanitarian doctrine with its revolutionary consequences had seized upon her soul. It was felt in her novels'.[41] She saw her views as comparable not just to those of Saint-Simon, but also of Benjamin Franklin, Jesus Christ and George Washington. Up to 1848, when she was most interested in political ideas, she came into contact with a number of progressive ideologies, akin to Saint-Simonianism in their radicalism, but differing in their details. Her scepticism led her to doubt the efficacy of any single system. She discussed Socialism in the mid-1830s with Louis Michel, a Berry lawyer who had been imprisoned for his revolutionary activities. She met Abbé Féli and Lamenais, who had formulated theories of Christian Socialism, and the latter's views interested her for some time. Such thinkers, and the aftermath of the 1832 trial of Enfantin and two of his followers, led her to be critical of the sect. In March 1831, she had written to Casimir of one Saint-Simonian meeting 'There is a female Pope who is only there to show off her dress of sky-blue velvet and swansdown boa'.[42] In Switzerland, she discussed 'Fourier's system and the mediocrity of Father Enfantin'. And, when she needed a political mentor, she met Pierre Leroux, a leading exponent of romantically visionary Socialist ideas, in 1835. Thackeray and Ferra associated her name with Leroux's doctrines; by 1837, she was studying his works, and she dedicated *Spiridion* (1838–9) to him. Marian Evans was to meet Leroux in London in January 1852: they discussed George Sand and the political theorists of the 1830s and 1840s.[43] George Sand echoed the ideas of the Christian Socialists, Leroux and Lammenais. Love was seen as a force for social good; Albert states, in *Consuelo*, that 'equality is sacred . . . it is the intention of the father of mankind, and . . . men's duty is to seek to establish equality amongst themselves'. The political ideas in George Sand's novels also stemmed from a rationalisation of her own experience. The depiction of Indiana's respect for the peasants derived as much from George Sand's love of the Berry country folk as from any egalitarian theories.

Moreover, despite attention to such political theories, George Sand withheld assent from them. Just as she embroidered upon, and implicitly criticised, aspects of Rousseau's thought, so she turned a sceptical eye upon utopianism. It was her union of scepticism, and a search for certainty of solution and interpretation, which led her to such theories, for, in them, she found a counterpart of her own intellectual position. These critical and affirmative tendencies were reiterated in her consideration of philosophical writings. She seized upon the generalities of theory, but finally criticised them by referring them to that sense of the particular which stemmed from her Rousseauesque scepticism, and inspired her novelistic concern with the specifics of place, event and personality. Marcelle longed for a philosophy which would reconcile her duties towards individuals and mankind, meditated upon Fourier and Saint-Simon, and admitted their partial validity, but concluded, 'I am repelled by them because I have a foreboding that they are a new trap offered to human simplicity'.[44] In *Lettres d'un voyageur*, a work to which Marian Evans often referred, appeared a sustained critique of the theories which interested both women. Michel's Socialism was seen as joyless, antipathetic to individualism. Although she praised their Rousseauesque qualities of warmth and love as superior to logical thought, George Sand saw Enfantin's and Abbé Saint-Pierre's philosophies as mingling truth and error. She commended Saint-Simon and Fourier for their Rousseauesque retreats, but criticised their dogmatic theorising, their underestimation of the importance of the individual, which stemmed from the aloofness of their contemplation of humanity.[45]

In her consideration of political and religious ideas, George Sand was often seen as a propagandist, who wrote novels which imaged her own progress from 'doubt and the unquiet tossings of a soul in trouble' to 'hope and faith'.[46] This view, however, overlooked the complexity of the art which issued from her scepticism. She brought the particular qualities of a place, a person or a society into contact with theories, to reveal the partial validity of the theories, because of the supremacy of complicated and intransigent facts. Saint-Beuve complained that there was no resolution of her characters' crises: to Marian Evans, who increasingly saw truth as intellectual quest, not system, this would have been proof of those characters' humanity, an argument for their capacity to interest. In George Sand's art, scepticism and mysticism met in novels which found their inspiration in, and meditated upon, the writings of philosophers, who themselves related speculative issues to the nature and problems of existence. Yet she tested the conclusions of the pragmatic philosophers with due sceptical severity against the complexities of character, history and place. Her novels were determinedly not *romans à thèse*. She conceded that life raised the problems which the logical debate had suggested, and that art partook of the implications that debate had for the nature of the imagination. But she concluded that theories alone could not describe life or afford solutions to its problems, nor could they define the complicated way in which life was apprehended. Her art was thus philosophical, but in a distinctive sense.

Both Lewes and Marian Evans conceived an enthusiasm for Comte and Spinoza at approximately the same dates: mental sympathy existed before their lives converged. Long before he met Marian Evans, Lewes was also defending the works of George Sand. It was symptomatic of the way in which progressive mid-Victorian thinkers revealed a similarity of interests that the two became interested in George Sand around the same time. In 1842, Lewes defined how, in George Sand's case, speculation and art merged, for he argued that her readers 'will find abundance of doctrine illustrated in every possible manner – but this is *implied*, not *expressed*. She is a poet, and as a poet must have a philosophy, and from that philosophy must her poetry spring; but a scientific accuracy of statement is not the poet's object – not his task. If the reader, therefore, sees in a tale of her's [sic] nothing but a novel, he must not be disappointed. It was meant for a novel'.[47] In the works of Carlyle, to which she returned during this period, and in her letters, Marian Evans was likewise to consider the relevance of ideas to both life and artistic creations.

13

The Relevance of Ideas (1844–1850)

not all art is alike remote from the world of thought.[1]

I

In many of the works Marian Evans read during this period there was a political dimension. Foster's presentation of the dissenting consciousness, and the exegeses of the theories of perception in Rousseau, Saint-Simon, Comte and Hegel, extended beyond an analysis of the thought process to explore the implications of that analysis for a view of society. Macaulay offered lessons for the present, as well as pictures of past ages; Disraeli and George Sand meditated upon political philosophies. Yet George Sand's testing of the validity of ideas as a means of interpreting existence, and her pondering upon the efficacy of political ideologies, stemmed from a radically sceptical stance. The environment of the 1840s presented Marian Evans with conflicting evidence about the extent to which political philosophies could be transformed into effective social solutions. The new revolutionary Europe lasted only from April 1848 to the following summer after which, although elements of liberalism remained, a conservative reaction set in. In 1848, Marian Evans's interest in radicalism led her to watch with fascination the unfolding of events in France. On 10 December 1848, the presidential election returned to power Napoleon's nephew, backed by a Conservative ministry. On 13 June 1849, the failure of a *coup de force* of democratic politicians led to more repression, and the flight of the leaders of that *coup*. In England, there was a widespread belief that the Chartists would use physical force, but although progressive thinkers often supported revolution abroad, after 1845 they favoured peaceful action at home. By the 1850s, the millenarium aspect of secularism had waned, probably in the light of the 1848 failures in Europe. In Coventry itself, Marian Evans witnessed radical ideas meeting with a mixture of success and

143

failure. The city's ribbon industry linked it to the silk-weaving trade of Manchester, and the ideological tradition of Manchester's labour relations permeated the Coventry trade in the 1840s as labour/capital conflicts increased. Between 1844 and 1848, Marian Evans saw the reforming corporation improve the city's water supply, and establish a local Board of Health; technological progress came with the introduction of steam power which reached even the Foleshill cottages. From the late 1820s onwards, some successful attempts were made to provide education for lower-class adults. Efforts in this direction were inspired by Christian sentiments and were undertaken by middle-class Anglicans or members of dissenting chapel congregations. The secular Mechanics' Institute Movement started in 1828. Yet at close quarters Marian Evans observed the failure of some of Bray's plans to improve the cultural lot of the working class.[2]

In returning again to the work of Carlyle, Marian Evans found a writer who was preoccupied with the relationship between ideology, reality and action. Her enthusiasm for Carlyle persisted and, in later years, it was his early writings to which she returned: she loyally defended the later works, but often privately disliked them. She described *Past and Present* (1843) as 'that thrilling book'.[3] The work drew together views she had encountered elsewhere; it contained, as had Hegel's *Lectures on the Philosophy of History*, criticism of contemporary historiography. Carlyle often conceptualised the historical process for didactic ends. He saw the study of history as elucidating contemporary problems and, like other English social critics, he found political solutions in an idealised English past, rather than in contemporary social models. He suggested that history revealed human interdependence and the impossibility of isolation.[4] In describing the historical process, he merged concepts. He reconciled notions of continuity and change and showed how the Ideal operated in the context of the real, so that context must be studied to understand how that Ideal was modified. Yet Carlyle retained the sceptic's sense, so evident in *The French Revolution*, that reality eluded total explanation. Jocelin of Brokeland was 'as in all History, and indeed in all Nature . . . at once inscrutable and certain; so dim, yet so indubitable; exciting us to endless considerations'.[5] Carlyle had concluded that only that mode of vision which was not slavishly bound to the implications of any single logic could truly interpret reality and prompt correct action. He criticised Methodists, Utilitarians and Encyclopaedists for their partial vision; he praised the spirit, not the form of political endeavours, commenting 'Jacobinism unfolded into Saint-Simonism bodes innumerable blessed things; but the thing itself might draw tears from a Stoic!'[6] The non-sectarian political attitude of Carlyle's early years in London continued. Carlyle based his opinion on specific topics on the philosophical stance which had informed his view of the historical process. His notion that history embodied continuity as well as change led him to distrust philosophers who spoke only of epochs; he was sceptical about the transforming power of revolution or legislation, although he conceded that the latter might act as a check upon anarchy. He also shifted the political argument towards redefinition of fundamental concepts; like Hegel, he defined liberty in apolitical terms.[7] Because of its radical scepticism, *Past and Present* contained few prescriptive statements. Carlyle praised those aspects of society which echoed his notions about the nature of reality: an aristocracy, for instance, embodied the concept of the continuity of time. He saw politics and religion as having failed correctly to interpret reality and guide conduct. These tasks were now to fall to writers, who were to become 'an actual instead of a virtual Priesthood'.[8] Like Saint-Simon and Comte, Carlyle argued that social reform was to be based upon the reorientation of perception which the writer would bring about. Hegel had argued that *historia rerum gestarum* was as important to human destiny as *res gestae*: in elevating the writer to priest, Carlyle demonstrated his affinity with Hegel, and endowed art with a social function.

This assigning of a social purpose to the writer justified, on a theoretical basis, Carlyle's excursion into the periodical press in 1848. Marian Evans felt that Carlyle's view of the 1848 revolutions was, along with John Sibree's, the only response she could praise, for both men could 'glory in what is actually great and beautiful without putting forth any cold reservations and incredulities to save their credit for wisdom'.[9] Carlyle saw these revolutions, as he had seen the 1789 revolution, as fulfilling his contentions about the inadequacy of the Encyclopaedist philosophy. He brought to his commentary upon current events, as had Mill in the articles he wrote between 1834 and 1840, a carefully formulated attitude towards philosophy, upon which he based his political views. His view of the 1848 revolutions repeated the interpretation of events he had put forth in *The French Revolution*: reality demonstrated the invalidity of a sectarian philosophical viewpoint. Carlyle presented a complex reality by creating a picture of human experience during the revolution; he showed the corruption of the monarchy, the suffering of the workers. He felt pity for individuals, disgust for the system they represented.[10] In his articles on Ireland, he applied the ideas he had evolved in *Past and Present* to a contemporary problem. He noted the inutility of theorists such as Robert Owen, Fourier and Blanc. He spoke of the irrelevance of legislation and the failure of the teaching class of priests.[11] In Carlyle's works, Marian Evans rediscovered the existence, in England, of a type of writing which flourished in vital relationship to philosophy, and she contemplated an innovative narrative form which she had hitherto found mainly in France in the works of Rousseau and George Sand. The thematic preoccupations evident in the works of these writers were forcible reminders to her that the eclectic philosophical tradition did not rest content with speculation about logical method, but explored the implications of the merging of logics in the areas of politics, history and religion. The form of such works showed that an interest in philosophy had nourished non-philosophical forms of narrative which, in testing philosophical truths against an intuitively apprehended reality, made a contribution to philosophical debate. This opened up for Marian Evans a wider field of endeavour in which her ambition to write could realise itself. An interest in philosophy did not consign a writer's activity to the confines of the speculative discipline.

II

Marian Evans's letters during the period from 1844 to 1850 indicated the lines of her intellectual development, despite their irregularity, despite the fact that, although she encouraged confessions from her friends, she made few herself.[12] Her development can be discerned partly from the pattern which emerged in her reading, and from her response to the books she read. By 1850, Marian Evans was familiar with the issues of the philosophical debate, and had started to emerge from provincial obscurity to be recognised as a thinker of some repute. During the latter half of the 1840s, she, like George Sand, manifested 'a high intelligence matured amid storms, and eminently progressive'.[13] Maria Bury, who was to marry Richard Congreve, the Positivist and friend of George Eliot in later years, was the daughter of the surgeon who attended Robert Evans in his last illness, and she recalled being greatly impressed by Marian Evans when she met her at that time.[14] This impressive personality shines through in her correspondence with John Sibree, which she described as 'purely moral and intellectual carried on for the sake of ghostly edification, . . . each party has to put salt on the tails of all sorts of ideas on all sorts of subjects'.[15] These letters revealed an enthusiastically speculative mind; they incorporated ideas from a wide variety of sources, and showed a passionate involvement with them, and a tendency to merge ideas from disparate sources to describe phenomena. Her letters from Switzerland were written with an eagerness to convey the quality of an unfamiliar reality, and, in their treatment of character and setting, foreshadowed something of the future novelist's gifts. It was, however, the casual turn of phrase, often in conjunction with a passing reference to what she was reading, which hinted at Marian Evans's intellectual presuppositions and preoccupations which were frequently evolved out of her interest in the philosophical debate. Her stand against dehumanised speculation showed her participation in the tradition of the post-Bentham thinkers in England, the post-Enlightenment movement in France and Germany. Marian Evans's generation in England, along with Coleridge, Mill and Carlyle, often exaggerated the extent to which Bentham propounded merely abstract views, but this forensic distortion fruitfully sanctioned their own humanitarianism. Philosophical issues, for Marian Evans, had implications for human issues. The writers she read explored the relationship between speculative method and religion, politics and history. Marian Evans sought out the views of her friends in Coventry on such topics, and discussed them eagerly with new acquaintances, like the Chevalier du Berray.[16]

Her letters expressed a religious heterodoxy which avoided both materialistic atheism and supernaturalistic Christianity. She criticised any sectarian viewpoint which simplified life's complexity. Strauss was censured for his onesidedness, as well as believers who 'see everything so clearly and with so little trouble, but at the price of sad self-mutilation'. She praised a sceptical questing for truth in terms which recalled Mill's praise of de Vigny and de Tocqueville, and commented that the 'highest inspiration of the purest, noblest human soul is the nearest expression of the truth'. She saw herself, perhaps, as experiencing 'the hardships of new Protestantism'; she praised Christ as a 'Jewish philosopher'. She equated the sense of the poetry of existence with religion, contrasting this to the scientific view, which saw the self as 'a miserable agglomeration of atoms . . . that mathematical abstraction, a point'.[17] She was also alert to the political implications of the philosophical debate, and this alertness expressed itself in a radicalism which declined in later years. Her discriminating tolerance of Christianity stemmed partly from the fact that some of the writers she admired viewed Christianity as a source of democratic ideas. Marian Evans spoke scathingly about the British monarchy and the fear of change, and wrote tirades against materialism.[18] Yet she was little interested in legislative or party issues, but considered political questions in relation to the spiritual state of society as Rousseau had recommended. She entertained visionary hopes for a total regeneration of society which she articulated in quasi-religious terminology, reminiscent of the imaginative schemes of Rousseau, Saint-Simon and George Sand, and, to some extent, of Foster's politicised Dissent. She hoped society would attain 'a more perfect idea and exhibition of Paul's exhortation – Let the same mind be in you which was also in Christ Jesus'. Viewing European anarchy, she longed for a state where 'all is subdued into a universal kingdom over which the Ancient of Days presides – the spirit of love – the Catholicism of the Universe'.[19] Yet the anti-democratic notions of Comte also permeated her letters. She considered true perception was associated with, and consequent upon, a transformed social organisation; she referred to Comte's ideas on mental hygiene, on education, on the stages of progress, and on the religion of humanity.[20] Comte, as well as Hegel, sharpened her historical sense. She was acutely aware of change and progress in her own life, and in the world which conditioned that life. She possessed a sense of the complex medium in which ideas operated which was revealed in her analysis of the situation in England in 1848. She concluded, as had Mill and Macaulay, that reforms would come in England by evolution, not revolution, and looked wistfully to France where 'the *mind* of the people is highly electrified – they are full of ideas on social subjects – they really desire social *reform* – not merely an acting-out of Sancho Panza's favourite proverb 'Yesterday for you, today for me'.[21]

At the heart of the effort of the post-Enlightenment generations was a methodological attempt to formulate a logic which would avoid the partial view of reality consequent upon the exclusive application of either the *a priori* or *a posteriori* method; this effort prompted the search to define and articulate new modes of perception. Notebooks Marian Evans kept after she had established herself as a novelist show her continuing concern with the 'reconciliation of the objective and subjective methods'.[22] Her letters during the period from 1844 to 1850 revealed an awareness of the perceptual issue raised by the move to merge rival logics. A desire eclectically to synthesise opposed concepts, and thereby to perceive the complexity of reality, informed her mental cast. She demanded that her friends describe both their inner and outer life; she played with the idea of a contrast between the spirit and the form of life. Notions of the general and the particular informed the way in which she viewed phenomena. Her description of Alum Bay on the Isle of Wight was Rousseauesque in method, moving from detailed, quasi-scientific analysis, to an impressionistic, panoramic vision, expressed in her comment 'It seems an enchanted land where the earth is of more delicate, refined materials than this dingy planet of ours is wrought out of'. In the Gospels or in Disraeli's novels, she attended to both the significance of an event which may be conceptualised, and also to the way in which the author conveyed the event's unstructured reality. She asked Sara Hennell whether she thought *Tancred* contained 'any lofty meaning . . . or any true picturing of life'. She requested self-revelation on a Rousseauesque basis, and used the information she received to speculate on issues which Rousseau had also considered. In her contemplation of personality, she was aware, as Rousseau was, of common humanity and individualism. The confessions of the wealthy led her to feel 'all the old commonplaces about the equality of human destinies, always excepting those spiritual differences which are apart not only from poverty and riches but from individual affections'.[23]

She was also aware that many writers dramatised the debate about logical method into a delineation of the conflict between intellect and emotions, and its possible resolution. The terms 'objective' and 'subjective' were used by Marian Evans as intellectual shorthand; their perceptual and psychological references were blended, and often expressed in Comtean terminology. She wrote to the Brays in 1849 'I assure you my letters are subjectively true – the falsehood, if there be any, is in my manner of seeing things. But to satisfy Cara, I will give you some "verités positives"'. The balance between thought and feeling was posited as an attainable ideal, both in the psychological and perceptual sense. When she speculated upon the forces governing existence, she did so in terms of a *rapprochement* between emotions and intellect, and added an emphasis upon the supreme importance of ethics, akin to that found in Comte's synthesis.[24] Her analysis of feeling was discriminating, and, in this respect especially, she learnt much from Rousseau. She distinguished feeling from excess subjectivity; enthusiasm was a prerequisite of life, but feeling was also potentially 'but egotism and mental idleness'. True understanding was difficult because men saw 'through all sorts of mists raised by their own passions and preoccupations'. Her experience taught her, however, that feeling could be a positive influence upon behaviour. It could unite those whose beliefs were at variance. She admired the inspirational power of emotional energy, confessing: 'I am beginning to lose respect for the petty acumen that sees difficulties. I love the souls that rush along to their goal with a full stream of sentiment, that have too much of the positive to be harassed by the perpetual negatives'.[25] Some of her comments also show her meditating upon the link between emotions and vision as had Mill after the 1826 crisis. She sensed that deep feeling intensified perception: sorrow 'is after all only a deepened gaze into life, like the sight of the darker blue and the thickening host of stars when the hazy effect of twilight is gone'. She envisaged an emotion which connected love of self to love of humanity, and was above selfishness and sentimentality: 'Egotism apart, another's greatness, beauty or bliss is our own – and let us sing a Magnificat when we are conscious that this power of expansion and sympathy is growing just in proportion as the individual satisfactions are lessening'. Just as feeling shifted perception from others to self, so the movement was reversed, and she reflected 'who is not proud to be loved? For there is a beautiful kind of pride at which no one need frown – I may call it a sort of impersonal pride – a thrill of exultation at all that is good and lovely and joyous as a possession of our human nature'.[26]

The stand against the remoteness of thought from life, and the critique of sectarian logic assumed revolutionary form in the works of Hegel and Carlyle. Their works had implications for the status of the artist, for they explored the relationship between speculation and human issues, and proposed a mode of perceiving reality which operated outside the confines of a single logical method. This was to sanction indirectly the artist who focused upon the particular and exercised the imagination. Both writers suggested that the antithesis between word and action was false. Hegel saw thought and deed as manifestations of *Geist*; Carlyle considered writers to be 'an actual instead of a virtual Priesthood'.[27] Both writers viewed words as a form of action, and Marian Evans had seen the furore created by works which she had championed, such as *Das Leben Jesu* and *The Nemesis of Faith*. The attack on speculation culminated in the reinstatement of a new mode of philosophical thought, which was preoccupied with human issues and claimed enlarged powers for perception. The new philosophy also annexed to itself the quasi-religious capacity to interpret existence and to offer consolation in the form of political and ethical recommendations. Moreover, as Carlyle, Rousseau and George Sand had shown, this new form of intellectual effort need not be confined to the form of conventional philosophical discourse.

Marian Evans discussed art in relation to the examples and preoccupations of the writers she read at this juncture. Her definition of art centred upon the idiosyncratic mode of perception art articulated and the way in which the imagination focused upon, and connected to, life. She saw art as voicing general truths, but expressing those truths in a way which fostered heightened perception of them, a view of art which encouraged strenuous attention to form and technical experimentation. She saw the words used as crucially important and affirmed Herder's notion that the content of thought was inseparable from the medium of expression or, on those grounds, she abandoned her translation of Spinoza.[28] She emphasised the way in which the imagination blended subjective perception and objective attention to fact: 'Painting and sculpture are but an idealizing of our actual existence. Music arches over this existence with another and a diviner'. She defined artistic power as

an intuitive perception of the varied states of which the human mind is susceptible with ability to give them out anew in intensified expression. It is true that the older the world gets, originality becomes less possible. Great subjects are used up, and civilization tends evermore to repress individual predominance, highly-wrought agony or ecstatic joy. But all the gentler emotions will ever be new – ever wrought up into more and more lovely combinations and genius will probably take their direction.[29]

The raw material of art possessed the familiarity of irrefutable truths, but the form of art expressed the artist's vision and was organically linked to it, and thus rendered that reality interesting and comprehensible. In 1858 she commented that 'the soul of art lies in its treatment and not in its subject'. That concepts of objective and subjective underpinned her view of art was suggested by the fact that her comment on painting preceded a passage in praise of Hegel. Hegel's writings on aesthetics were carefully annotated by Lewes, who was also to explore the artistic implications of the merging of logics.[30] George Sand had commented that 'All that is needed . . . is to look and to feel . . . the greatest poet is . . . he who invents least'. George Eliot's own novels aspired to be 'not studies of life, but life interpreted by the poet's vision'.[31] The imagination operated in terms of a reconciliation of subjective vision and a faithful recognition of life's complexities; the imaginative process whereby art was evolved refuted sectarian philosophical theories about the nature of mind. By speaking of art as presenting pictures given out 'anew in intensified perception', Marian Evans hints at Carlyle's notion of the quasi-religious function of art whereby it could both interpret and console. Her emphasis upon the imagination's 'intuitive perception' led her, however, to reject the dogmatic interpretations of *tranche de vie* naturalist theory, or the sectarian *nostra* of propagandist consolation. She suggested that art taught by non-didactic revelation. Art did not propose a single truth about life, but sceptically pondered a plurality of truths via the heightened perception of the artist. Implicit in her views was the attitude Lewes pinpointed in George Sand and Balzac when he commented that 'Life is a problem to perplex the deepest thinkers. The greatest seem to have arrived only at a profound and reverential scepticism', and Lewes quoted Hegel's comment on didactic art in relation to George Sand in the same article.[32]

Not only did Marian Evans's letters show that she defined the imaginative process and the kind of pictures it produced in relation to the philosophical preoccupations of the writers she read; her mind was also turning towards the possibilities of fiction. She was searching for some useful role, and even aspired temporarily to Comtean female self-abnegation. In September 1846 Sara Hennell thought that Marian Evans was happy because she had started writing a novel, and there were attempts at fiction in letters to the Rosehill circle. She conceived of the creative task as a strenuous ne. She spoke of the difficulty of conveying original insight: all perception was idiosyncratic for 'No mind that has any *real* life is a mere echo of another'. The problem of expression was described in terms of profound personal struggle, which recalled Carlyle's meditation upon the problem of form and language in *The French Revolution* and, in tone, Mill's notion of the arduousness of the quest for truth. She noted that it is 'scarcely possible for a man simply to give out his true inspiration – the real profound conviction which he has won by hard wrestling or the few and far between pearls of imagination – he must go on talking or writing by rote or he must starve'. She also affirmed her belief in the importance of expression, her fascination with the power of words. In a letter to John Sibree she seemed to evoke Hegel's insistence upon the equal importance of *historia rerum gestarum* and *res gestae* when she confessed: 'It is necessary to me, not simply to *be* but to *utter*'. She suggested a quasi-sacred role for literature and writers: 'What is anything worth until it is uttered? Is not the Universe one great utterance? Utterance there must be in word and deed to make life of any worth. Every true pentecost is a gift of utterance'.[33]

Language, Marian Evans realised, recorded the personal vision, and a definition of perception which gave due weight to subjectivity was at the heart of the work of the post-Enlightenment thinkers in England, France and Germany. The new notions of perception tried not just to solve the problems of logical method. The reinterpretation of the act of knowing could suggest the necessary connection of heart and head, self and world, whose seeming opposition gave birth to many of the dilemmas, psychological, religious and social, which troubled nineteenth-century thinkers. By emphasising the subjective element in perception, the philosophers also vindicated the imaginative method and visions of the artist, and became willing to learn from him. Carlyle found salvation in German literature; Mill found consolation in Wordsworth's poetry during the 1826 crisis, and he wrote enthusiastically about de Vigny. Saint-Simon respected artists, and Hegel spoke of the importance of representational narrative. If, as philosophers suggested, a new way of seeing was a new way of knowing, art was a species of knowledge. Knowledge was seen by philosophers as a force for social reform; art, consequently, could be a social act. Comte suggested that the regeneration of civilisation would be effected by 'an exact appreciation of the nature of reality'.[34] The post-Encyclopaedist attack on rationalism's arid intellectualism ultimately enlarged the view of the nature and power of thought. By suggesting that feeling must supplement intellect, Marian Evans and others of her generation came to see recourse to, and consideration of, non-philosophical forms of perceptual experience and expression as imperative. Philosophy, they realised, could learn from religion and literature: Carlyle, for instance, retained respect for the vision of reality implicit in the Dissent of his parents. Such a view broke down distinctions of genre, and suggested a community of effort between all who laboured within a tradition of sceptical eclecticism and intellectual pragmatism. George Sand commented: 'every road leads to the truth the mind which is animated by purity of intention and unblinded by pride'.[35] In her years in London, Marian Evans was to receive more indications that, for her, a valid road to truth could best be found in fiction. Her certainty was, however, to be reinforced by further contact with thinkers who laboured within the post-rationalist philosophical tradition.

14
London (1851–1854)

When do we hear of women who, starting out of obscurity, boldly claim respect on account of their great abilities or daring virtues? Where are they to be found?[1]

I. 'THE PROGRESS OF THE INTELLECT'

To reconstruct a picture of Marian Evans's early years in London is a task hampered by her reticence. She confessed: 'I cannot write about myself save to one or two people in the world'. Lack of candour also marked her close relationships; to Fanny Houghton, the most sympathetic member of her family, she wrote apologetically in 1851: 'I always feel that out interviews are unsatisfactory, because I don't like to talk of myself and my affairs and you may think that I have no sisterly confidence'.[2] Her work, however, spoke for her, and her article on Mackay indicated her intellectual position in 1850. Her friendship with Bray presented her with the opportunity to make her début in a metropolitan publication. In October 1850, John Chapman visited Rosehill with Robert Mackay, who was the assistant editor of the *Westminster Review*. Chapman had just published Mackay's *The Progress of the Intellect as exemplified in the Religious Development of the Greeks and Hebrews* (2 vols, 1850). The book was strongly attacked in the *British Quarterly Review* in November 1850, but was defended in the *Inquirer* a year later by Dr Brabant, a move which Marian Evans warmly welcomed.[3] Chapman, with a characteristic mixture of commercial enterprise and liberal zeal, suggested to Miss Evans, whose translation of the controversial *Das Leben Jesu* he had published, that she write an article on Mackay's book for the *Westminster Review* which was edited by the Unitarian Henry James Slack and owned by W. E. Hickson. At the outset of her career as a London writer, she placed herself on the side of the progressive cause, welcoming the work as 'the nearest approach in our language to a satisfactory natural history of religion'.[4]

155

The article echoed the views of the writers she read between 1844 and 1850. Allusions to Comte revealed long-standing familiarity with his theory of progress, and she adhered to his notion that polytheism gave way to monotheism, whereas Mackay had argued the coexistence of the two attitudes. She singled out Positivist methods and themes in Mackay's book. She praised the way he set the development of Hebraism in the world-historical context. Mackay emphasised that 'undeviating law' prevailed not only in the physical world, but also in 'our social organization, our ethics and our religion', and this vision promoted the recommendation that 'human duty is comprised in the earnest study of the law and patient obedience to its teaching'. Her awareness of the debate about logical method to which Comte had contributed was also obvious. She spoke of the 'dilemma of sensuousness and sentimentalism', and envisaged a union of methods whereby a 'correct generalization gives significance to the smallest detail'.[5] Marian Evans also followed in the footsteps of Coleridge and Carlyle, as well as her Coventry friend, John Sibree, as a propagandist for German scholarship. She spoke of the way in which the Germans had pioneered the study of the Bible as *mythus*, and lamented, as she did in a letter she wrote in August 1851, the English 'backwardness in critical science'.[6] She viewed the Bible as containing historical facts, yet the recording of the facts was subjective because of 'the mental state in which they originated'. A similar view had been expounded by Strauss, Hennell and Spinoza, and encapsulated an historicism and a neo-Hegelian notion of the balanced coalescence of subjective and objective. She criticised Mackay for his insensitivity to the poetry of the Bible, and, in the spirit of Hegel's and Comte's historical relativism, suggested that the new 'more liberal views of Biblical criticism' provided a defence of Christianity as 'corresponding to the wants and culture of the age'.[7]

Her concept of the nature of knowledge was defined in relation to the historian's task. She criticised a Christian faith which was motivated by a 'morbid eagerness for a cheap and easy solution of the mysteries of existence', and equated 'the worse forms of atheism' with the denial of 'the ultimately beneficial tendency of inquiry'. It was inquiry which she vindicated. Previously, she noted, with an allusion to Utilitarian views, knowledge had been seen as profitable, but 'we are beginning to find out that it is moral, and shall at last discover it to be religious'. Historical studies morally benefited the individual, for 'mastering a remote form of thought' provided 'a perception which resembles an expansion of one's own being, a pre-existence in the past', and the greatest fruits of knowledge were 'those disinterested gratifications which minister to the highest want of the highest faculties'. Such study also benefited man in his social role. A study of past ages revealed how all truths were conditioned, for 'each age, and each race had a faith and symbolism suited to its need'. By studying the past, man might isolate anachronistic forms which were barriers to present progress 'which have allied themselves, on the one hand with men's better sentiments, and on the other with institutions in whose defence are arrayed the passions and the interests of the dominant classes'. In viewing the past, 'every mistake, every absurdity into which poor human nature has fallen, may be looked on as an experiment of which we may reap the benefit'. She thus praised Mackay's 'high appreciation of the genius of antiquity', for relativism encouraged that sympathetic understanding of the past, the quest for which she thought improved the individual, but she commended also his 'profound belief in the progressive character of human development', which was fostered by historical studies.[8]

In vindicating knowledge, she also argued, as had Comte, that all disciplines were connected because all were humanistic in intent. Defining genius in 1852, she reflected that 'All discovery must be the discovery either of a *fact* or of a *relation*'.[9] Science, religion and philosophy all revealed the operation of the law of consequences, upon which public and private ethics were to be based. She quoted Mackay's view that 'Religion and science are inseparable . . . the known and the unknown are intimately connected and correlative. A superstructure of faith can be securely built only on the foundations of the known. Philosophy and religion have one common aim; they are but different forms of answer to the same great question – that of man and his destination'. Faith, like science, was 'a legitimate result of the calculation of probabilities; it may transcend experience, but can never absolutely contradict it'.[10] When she defined the ideal process of knowledge, she suggested the combining of seemingly opposed virtues. In the German writers, she found a succumbing to the dangers of either pedantry of detail, or over-theoretical vision. Coleridge had sought to merge logical methods and apply them to psychological, religious and political questions; Carlyle had tested schematised analyses against the yardstick of an intuitively apprehended reality. Marian Evans considered, probably looking to their examples, that 'the greater solidity and directness of the English mind ensure a superiority of treatment'. She praised the passages in Mackay's book, 'into which are absorbed the finest rays of intelligence and feeling'. The ideal mind would combine 'the faculty for amassing minute erudition with the largeness of view necessary to give it a practical bearing'. Knowledge must not lack 'warmth of moral sympathy . . . fertility and grandeur of perception'.[11] Also crucial to her ideal of knowledge was her definition of the 'truly philosophical culture' as residing in an open-minded scepticism, characterised by 'flexibility . . . ready sympathy . . . tolerance . . . susceptibility to the pleasure of changing its point of view', and yet able to reach conclusions, for it perceived 'identity of nature under variety of manifestation'. She praised the Germans' attention to non-Christian religions, for general truths could only emerge from wide-ranging analysis. The notion of truth as positive process, coupled with an admission of the provisional nature of its conclusions, dominated the article. She quoted approvingly Mackay's comment that the 'true religious philosophy of an imperfect being is not a system or creed, but, as Socrates thought, an inifinite search or approximation. Finality is but another name for bewilderment or defeat, the common affectation of indolence and superstition, a temporary suspension of the mind's health arising from prejudice, and especially from the old error of clinging too closely to notions found instrumental in assisting it after they have ceased to be serviceable, and striving rather to defend and retain them, than to make them more correct'.[12] The notion of truth as quest aligned her not only with Hegel, but also with J. S. Mill who had found the Platonic Dialogues a source of inspiration in initiating his emancipation from the sterile certainties of Benthamite sectarianism.

II. LONDON

The article on Mackay marked the start of her involvement with the *Westminster Review*, and the man who was to purchase the periodical soon after her article appeared in it – John Chapman. If Marian Evans's life in London extended her knowledge of the philosophical debate because of her contact with advanced thinkers, her friendship with Chapman in particular deepened her sense of the difficulties attendant upon articulating the progressive stance which the debate about logic often prompted. On 8 January 1851, Marian Evans went to live at 142 Strand. At this address,

Chapman lived and ran both his publishing business and a boarding-house patronised by visitors of advanced views and literary interests, from foreign countries and the English provinces. Emerson had stayed at Chapman's in 1848 and two to three hundred people attended his farewell party. When Marian Evans moved to 142 Strand, the house was especially busy, for it was the year of the Great Exhibition. Chapman, when he lived in Clapton, had instituted regular literary parties and he continued this custom when he moved to central London. His house became a gathering-point for radical intellectuals who shared a general interest in science, and a particular interest in Positivism. His assemblies brought together rising and established intellectuals, such as David Brewster, one of the early commentators on Comte, and Louis Blanc, the French Socialist.[13] The world of the provincial *avant-garde* was not without its narrowness, and within the wider scope of the London literary scene, Marian Evans was stimulated by unfamiliar minds, and the presence of a greater number of people supporting the radical causes in which she was interested lent a tone of assurance to her pronouncements. Yet the metropolitan scene was also a claustrophobic one in which critics, authors, publishers and readers constantly met and mingled. When Marian Evans was in London, she came to see its close-knit nature, qualities dramatised in such novels as Lewes's *Ranthorpe* (1847) and Gissing's *New Grub Street* (1891). When she went to Germany with Lewes, she discovered its penchant for vicious gossip.

Marian Evans moved into Chapman's orbit for a number of reasons. Upon her return from Switzerland in March 1850, she used Rosehill as a base, but, despite her close friendship with the Brays, there was no suggestion that they were willing to provide her with a permanent home. Her own family offered no help: Charles Bray told George Combe in 1854 that they had 'never noticed her – never appreciated her'.[14] Relations with Isaac were strained; Chrissey Clarke was not wealthy, and had five children to care for. The more compatible Fanny Houghton did not seem to think of inviting her half-sister to live with her. Marian Evans also had to earn money, and, having rejected the idea of becoming a governess during the panic over her refusal to go to church, writing seemed the only alternative. With articles for Bray's newspaper, and one for the *Westminster Review*, and her translation of Strauss, she had already made a modest start. Coventry offered little scope for regular journalistic assignments, but London did. Between 1821 and 1830, a hundred new periodicals had been established in the capital, and, for the hard-working writer, there was an income potentially available. With the coming of the railways, the regional identities of provincial areas waned; London became increasingly the centre of English literary activity, and attracted ambitious writers like a magnet. To the metropolis came those products of regional dissent who were to vitalise the capital's literary scene. Carlyle moved to London in the 1830s. Spencer arrived in London from Derby; Harriet Martineau came from Norwich. That Marian Evans settled at 142 Strand was not surprising. Sara Hennell had lived close to Chapman in Clapton, and visited him there, and Marian Evans had probably met him when staying with Sara in 1846. He had been to Rosehill, and was on friendly terms with the Brays and Marian Evans had seen him in London when she was en route for Switzerland after her father's death.

Chapman, like the Brays, came from that Midlands intelligentsia of progressive views, often found within the class of textile manufacturers. Such men evolved their liberal stance from the education offered by the Dissenting Academies and Working Men's Institutes, and from contact with the Unitarian Church. As an apprentice watchmaker, learning a trade which had links with Coventry, Chapman attended the Worksop Pestalozzian Institute, where lectures were given by Robert Owen and John Bowring. While still an apprentice, he ran away to Australia. Upon his return to England, he married Susanne Brewitt, fourteen years his senior, who possessed some fortune from her lace-manufacturing family, who opposed the match. During his years in the provinces, Chapman was associated with the *Christian Teacher*, which fostered the most advanced trends in Unitarian thought.[15] He visited John Green, the publisher of the *Christian Teacher*, in an attempt to sell him his book, ambitiously entitled *Human Nature*, and ended up buying Green's publishing business instead. The man who was to be a close intellectual associate of Marian Evans, and also, for a time, the focus of her confused emotions, was a paradoxical personality. He was a strikingly handsome womaniser, and, according to J. S. Mill, capable of betraying his vulgarity even in a short note. George Combe, during the period Marian Evans worked on the *Westminster Review*, became increasingly irritated by Chapman. He dismissed him as a 'dreamer and a schemer', 'deficient in business talent, in conscientiousness, and in real depth of intellect'. Chapman was usually beset by personal and financial problems, often of his own making, yet he possessed a genuine desire to promote free thought. Even Combe acknowledged his 'great ambition, Benevolence, and a sympathy with liberal views', even if he added 'but transcendentally, rather than practically'. Chapman's unfortunate wife, who had every reason to be critical of her husband, told Combe defensively that Chapman worked hard, rising at five in the morning, and retiring to bed at ten in the evening.[16]

In the middle of the nineteenth century, book-publishing entailed a heavy financial risk. Despite the revolution in printing techniques which took place during the 1830s and 1840s, with the introduction of steam-powered presses, a wider use of stereotypes, and cheaper binding methods and materials, books were still beyond the pockets of most people. Publishers also fixed the price beneath which no book could be sold, a practice Chapman campaigned against in the 1850s. Chapman compounded such inbuilt financial problems by paying high wages and indulging his preference for expensive materials.[17] He also chose to publish books which appealed to a limited section of an already small market. In buying Green's business, Chapman inherited a liberal publishing policy which was in accordance with his own predilections. The major publishing houses of the early nineteenth century were headed by bright young men with new ideas, and when Chapman, at the age of twenty-five, published the translation of *Das Leben Jesu*, his firm was becoming well-known as the outstanding London outlet for books expressing a liberal viewpoint. 'Persecution', noted Lewes, 'is the mother of heresy.'[18] Chapman published books which were frowned upon, and unbought, by all but an enlightened élite. He brought out few novels, choosing to concentrate on progressive religious and philosophical works. Chapman's policies defiantly flew in the face of an adverse intellectual climate, which only strengthened his resolve to pursue them. The late 1840s and early 1850s did not favour works expressing progressive views. The events of the late 1840s led to a widespread fear of radicalism. James Martineau's comment of 1846 that 'It is a dishonourable characteristic of the present age that on its most marked intellectual tendencies is impressed a character of *Fear*. While its great practical agitations exhibit a progress towards some positive and attainable good, all its conspicuous movements of thought seem to be mere retreats from some apprehended evil',[19] held good for the early 1850s. In 1848, philosophical Christianity and scientific theology were seen as a greater threat to orthodoxy than outright atheism. By the end of the 1840s, Socialist societies had declined, and the 1851 Great Exhibition was cited as proof of England's political stability. Holyoake, in 1851, launched the Secularist movement, which tried to present free thought as moderate and respectable, but in the provinces even such a temperate movement had little success. The 1854 census, which showed that 30 per cent of the population went to Anglican churches, and that 50 per cent went to nonconformist places of worship, and one-fifth of the population to neither church nor chapel, offered little reassurance to orthodox opinion.[20] Victorian best-sellers did not come out of the 'Liberalisms, "Extinct Socinianisms"', which Carlyle found on Chapman's list. Chapman knew that his ideas were seen as a threat to private morality and public peace. Intellectual nonconformity was linked in the public mind with moral baseness, and Chapman attempted to preserve an image of respectability in sensitive areas. He and Marian Evans visited Eliza Lynn on 12 January 1851, and tried to persuade her to cancel passages in her novel which 'excited the sensual nature', for, Chapman recorded in his diary, 'As I am the publisher of works notable for the [ir] intellectual freedom it behoves me to be exceedingly careful of the *moral* tendency of all I issue'.[21]

The market for the *Westminster Review* was also limited. Radical journalism enjoyed a period of hectic growth and prosperity during the troubled first three decades of the nineteenth century. Widely-circulating newspapers published lurid exposés of social conditions, accompanied by indignant comment, a policy both lucrative and satisfying to the editorial conscience. This kind of journalism was seen by conservatives and liberals alike as a threat to the nation's peace, and the general periodicals were founded to counterbalance such politicised journalism. Fiscal measures provided a weapon against the radical press; the newspaper tax priced such papers out of the range of the working class and was not abolished until 1855. Paper duty was not removed until 1861. If the radical daily and weekly press was subject to government disapproval and financial restraint, the problems of a radical quarterly were greater still. The quarterlies were expensive, and sold mainly to reading-rooms, to which access was gained by annual subscription. The aims of subsequent editors of the *Westminster Review* exacerbated its problems: those would could afford to buy it, disliked its radical stance, whereas many of those who favoured its progressivism were too poor to buy it, or to subscribe to a reading-room.[22] It had originated as a 'Radical organ to make head against the Edinburgh and Quarterly' but from its first number under Bowring's editorship in 1824 pleased neither Benthamites nor Tories. By 1828, the review was in financial trouble, and the Mills severed their links with it. It then became a broadly-based liberal quarterly, but its distinguished Benthamite origins influenced its future development. J. S. Mill returned to edit it with distinction from 1837 until 1840, and used it as a medium to express his modified utilitarian views. Under Hickson's editorship from 1840 onwards, it was still potentially powerful, and its liberal stance was shown by its being a consistent champion of George Sand between 1840 and 1844. Hickson himself worked for the repeal of the taxes on knowledge. It also continued in a financially precarious state: in 1844, Edward Flower, the Unitarian brewer from Stratford, who was a friend of the Brays, donated money to help it through a difficult period.[23]

Chapman bought the *Westminster Review* from Hickson in May 1851 for £300, and thus purchased a set of problems. He had plans to intensify the quarterly's liberalism. He hoped it would be 'the organ of the ablest and most liberal thinkers of the time'. The Prospectus, which Marian Evans wrote in June 1851, announced that it would 'exhibit that untemporizing expression of opinion, and that fearlessness of investigation and criticism which are the results of a consistent faith in the ultimate prevalence of truth'. It was to be 'the bold and uncompromising exponent of the most advanced and philosophical views'.[24] This was a brave clarion call to the progressive and the unorthodox. The magazine did become a mouthpiece for contemporary philosophical and scientific thought, and appealed to a serious-minded and radical élite, especially to those who were interested in Positivism, a philosophy it did much to promote. In 1854 Mill said that it allowed him to speak freely on most topics, although on another occasion he complained that Chapman would not allow him to speak of Comte's atheism, and Chapman's policies were certainly too tame for some progressives; some radicals saw his policies as timid. Others, of a more orthodox persuasion, were censorious for contrary reasons. Some libraries banned the *Westminster Review* altogether. Combe realised it was seen as 'the organ of infidelity', and the *Critic* in October 1852 said it promoted both 'infidelity in religion and radicalism in politics'. Herbert Spencer recalled 'its genuine liberalism' under

Mill and Molesworth, and noted that Chapman willingly continued the policy of criticising 'the excesses of Government
meddling'.[25] Disliked by some Radicals, and all conservatives, its
audience was a limited one, and Combe saw Chapman's problems
as stemming not just from financial incompetence, but from his
pursuit of a valuable progressive policy. Financial problems
dogged Chapman's footsteps. The Prospectus asked for temporary
financial aid for the magazine, and from the outset it was subsi-
dised by Edward Lombe, a moneyed landowner who lived abroad
but supported liberal publications in England. In 1852, Marian
Evans was discussing Chapman's financial problems with Combe;
in July that same year Susanna Chapman wrote tersely 'The Westminster is at present a loss rather than a gain'. Combe estimated
that the quarterly was losing £400 a year. By July 1854 Joseph
Parkes was telling his daughter Bessie that the magazine was in a
'barely-paying' state and that Chapman's debts were 'about
£9000'.[26]

When Marian Evans's association with the *Westminster Review*
started, the atmosphere at 142 Strand was one of excitement and
hope. It was not merely the resilience of Chapman's myopic
optimism which sustained her throughout these years. As her
Prospectus for it later indicated, she saw the *Westminster Review* as
performing a necessary function in disseminating advanced ideas,
and acting as a forum for free inquiry. Her loyalty to the cause kept
her at 142 Strand, working in conditions which often had little to
recommend them. She settled at Chapman's on 8 January 1851 but
left on 24 March because of the jealousy of Chapman's wife, and of
the family governess, Elizabeth Tilley, who was Chapman's mistress. She returned on 29 September 1851, after working on Chapman's Analytical Catalogue of his publications by correspondence
between Coventry and London, a task which she executed amidst
an atmosphere of emotional *sturm und drang*, involving Chapman
and all the three women. The omens upon return, given Chapman's undoubted talents for complicated and embroiled sexual
allegiances, hardly prognosticated domestic peace. Moreover,
when she was surrounded by noisy, chaotic and squalid London,
she missed the country. She made forays in search of rural peace.
In October 1852, she visited Edinburgh and Ambleside, and said
she 'never had a journey which did me as much good as this'. At
Tunbridge Wells in July 1853 she disliked the crowds of fashionable visitors but rejoiced in 'the large, free beauty nature has all

round here'. She was usually depressed upon returning to the city. The changing seasons filled her with nostalgia: the 'autumnal freshness of the mornings' made her 'dream of mellowing woods and gossamer threads', and in March 1852 she longed to see 'the budding hedgerows and all the other delights of Spring'. Even her health, she decided in July 1852, was better in Broadstairs than in London with 'its dingy restless life', yet she was only able to stay away 'as long as the business of the Review will let me'.[27] The move from Coventry had established her independence from her unresponsive family. She could not escape from their problems, though her commitment to the *Westminster Review* kept her in London. She felt how much she had changed, and charged herself with selfishness, but the old ties could not assume priority, nor did she return to the Midlands. In a family crisis, her main feeling was one of powerlessness. At the close of 1852, she quarrelled with Isaac. She worried about her impoverished, newly-widowed sister, Chrissey, and her brood of children, towards whom Isaac was less than sympathetic, and she made time to visit Chrissey even though work on the *Westminster Review* was especially pressing.[28] The move to London also did little to ease her financial problems. Years later, she was to reflect that an author 'must keep his expenditure low – he must make for himself no dire necessity to earn sums in order to pay bills'. In 1851 she tried, and failed, to procure commissions for articles; she wrote only one short review for the *Leader* in 1851, a short piece on Carlyle's *Life of Sterling* in 1852. She agreed to produce an abridged version of *Das Leben Jesu* for a paltry £100, but the project never materialised.[29]

She found some compensation, over and above her loyalty to the *Westminster Review*, in the freer atmosphere of London. Progressive circles in the capital were inclined to treat women as equals. In the 1830s, articles in the *Westminster Review* and the *Monthly Repository* proposed that women were sexual, independent creatures, and the small circles of Socialist sympathisers were especially notable for such views. Those who entertained ideas about the reorganisation of society often embraced, and put into practice, unconventional theories about relationships between the sexes. During the 1830s, a feminist group, centred around Harriet Taylor, could be found at Fox's South Place Chapel. Women's rights were to the fore in the discussions of free-thinkers in the 1840s and, towards the end of the same decade, moves were made towards improving women's education and legal position. Mill's article on the enfranchisement of women appeared in the *Westminster Review* in 1851. In the relatively permissive circles in which she moved, Marian Evans found herself accepted as men's equal, and she led a life which, for a mid-Victorian spinster, was unusually free of the restrictions imposed upon women by middle-class notions of propriety.[30] Not all of those who met Marian Evans were favourably impressed. Miss Lynn, who encountered her at Chapman's, knew of her reputation for being 'learned, industrious, thoughtful, noteworthy', but considered her 'essentially under-bred and provincial', and scorned her physical clumsiness, poor taste in clothes, and 'tone of superiority'.[31] But Miss Lynn was in a minority. The appreciation she received from new acquaintances must have cheered her as she contemplated the less satisfactory aspects of her new life. Members of the London avant-garde corroborated the opinion of Marian Evans's Coventry friends that she was exceptional: such people did not regard women who were 'logical, philosophical, scientific' as abnormal.[32] George Combe's admiration was constant until she eloped with Lewes. He saw her as the outstanding member of the Rosehill set, noted the analytic power of her mind, and her 'instinctive soundness of judgment'. He talked to her about 'religion, political economy, and political events', and found her combination of strong intellect, and femininity 'very interesting'.[33] Bessie Parkes found Marian Evans's presence both intangibly and tangibly impressive. She too noted her femininity and thought her 'astonishing'. She was struck by her honesty, industrious development of her talents, and her courage. She recalled how Marian Evans's 'great weight of intellect told in all circles', and how 'real, deep thought and quiet wit' characterised her conversation. Notwithstanding this daunting array of virtues, Miss Evans was kind and polite, with an appealingly vulnerable 'air of resigned fatigue'. She was also, despite Miss Lynn's acerbic comments, not without beauty: Miss Parkes was fascinated by 'her extraordinary quantity of beautiful brown hair . . . her kind blue eyes'. Joseph Parkes, Bessie's father, who was a Radical MP and who had sponsored the translation of Strauss, would ask Miss Evans to dinner to meet famous politicians and authors. She and Mrs Parkes would be the only women present: Miss Evans would, unusually for a spinster, attire herself in black velvet for the occasion. Miss Parkes thought Strauss's translator could easily have risen in society circles in the capital.[34] The Miss Evans who knew seven languages in her early thirties was asked by Mackay what books he should read before writing about the development of Protestantism; a Miss Lupton consulted her about the art of translation. She was sometimes seen as a dangerous influence on other young women because of her independent mind and way of life, but she was also considered unusual and admirable. Bessie Parkes spoke of her 'large, unprejudiced mind, her complete superiority to other women' and of her critical yet compassionate nature, for 'She never spares, but expresses every opinion, good or bad, with the most unflinching plainness and yet she seems able to see faults without losing tenderness'. She anticipated great achievements, commenting that 'Large angels take a long time unfolding their wings; but when they do, soar out of sight. Miss Evans either has no wings, or, which I think is the case, they are coming, budding'.[35]

The friendships Marian Evans formed during this period afforded her new stimulation and corroborated her liberal principles. Ties of gratitude and long-standing affection still bound her to her Coventry friends. She took a keen interest in the campaign for secular education which concerned Charles Bray, and discussed with him the recommendations of the Commissioners on Divorce. She enjoyed meeting Edward Neale, a legal adviser to co-operative societies whom she encountered at a party at Mackay's house. In Edinburgh, in October 1852, she was introduced to Robert Cox, former editor of the *Phrenological Journal*, and W. Matthieu William, headmaster of the Williams Secular School.[36] She confessed to Sara that in London, 'the male friends always eclipse the female', yet she did come to know women she found sympathetic.[37] Barbara Smith, who was to marry Dr Eugene Bodichon, became a lifelong friend. They met for the first time in 1852: Barbara, like Marian Evans, attracted Chapman's attentions. Barbara's grandfather had been an ally of Wilberforce's; her father was a Unitarian merchant and, later, Radical MP for Norwich. He gave his daughter a good education and financial independence, and Barbara devoted time and money at various stages of her life, to writing a sensational tract on women and property laws which appeared in 1854, to founding an inter-denominational school which admitted the children of freethinkers, to opening up the life classes of the Royal Academy to women, and to founding Girton College. After his wife's death, Cross wrote to Barbara: 'Amongst all her intimate friends I know there was none she valued more or who was more to her than yourself'.[38] Marian Evans continued to be friendly with Bessie Parkes, who had connections with liberal Unitarianism via both parents. Her mother was the daughter of Joseph Priestley and the Parkes family had been closely involved in the agitation for the Reform Bill. She also met Barbara Smith's first cousin, Florence Nightingale, and might even have been related to her via her Methodist aunt, Elizabeth Evans. In 1850, Florence wrote in her diary, 'I might have been a literary woman, or a married woman, or a hospital sister'. By 1852 she had decided upon nursing and in 1853 went to prepare further for that career in Paris, before landing at Scutari Base Hospital in 1854. It is interesting to speculate whether the two women discussed the problems of spinsterhood: Florence, years later, reviewed *Middlemarch* for *Fraser's*, and deplored what she saw as the book's pessimistic treatment of the theme.[39] Marian Evans also met literary women such as Frederika Bremer, the Swedish novelist. Her admiration for the eccentric Harriet Martineau blossomed, although she was unenthusiastic about her when they first met. Harriet's father had lost the family fortune, which freed his daughter to pursue her career as a writer. Marian Evans praised Harriet's *Letters on the Laws of Man's Nature and Development* (1851) as 'certainly the boldest I have ever seen in the English language'. She decided that Harriet was 'an admirable woman worth twenty of the people who are sniffing at her' and, after reading the article on Niebuhr which she contributed to the *Westminster Review* in July 1852, described her as 'the only English woman that thoroughly possessed the art of writing'. In the autumn of 1852 she visited Harriet at Ambleside, and inspected the progress of her co-operative scheme for the construction of workmen's cottages, which she considered to be a heartening example of Harriet's 'practical goodness'. In *Middlemarch*, Dorothea's plans to rehouse the poor of Tipton were, constrastingly, never to get beyond the planning stage.[40]

Contact with the progressive tradition of the *Westminster Review*, with Chapman, and with the advanced thinkers who gathered round him intensified Marian Evans's liberal stance. Her interest in continental Radicalism was sustained by contact with the revolutionaries who had fled to London after the events of 1848, for England, albeit its inhabitants were xenophobic where ideas of revolution were concerned, provided an open door to those fleeing from repressive régimes. In the early 1850s, secularists associated themselves with such refugees, for Republicanism frequently went hand in hand with free thought, and the liberals' struggles often revolved around theological issues. Funds were set up for foreign radicals, although middle-class support went mainly to moderates, such as Mazzini and Kossuth, rather than to Socialists such as Louis Blanc. London Socialists cheerfully applauded revolutionary actions abroad, whilst paying scant attention to homegrown populist movements such as Chartism and the Anti-Corn Law League, which had originated in the English provinces. Marian Evans continued to express her dislike of English political thinkers, such as Robert Owen or Disraeli, but continental radicals in exile attracted her attention.[41] In 1851, she considered asking Ferdinand Freiligrath, the poet and revolutionary who had been expelled from Prussia, to contribute to the *Westminster Review*. She reverenced Mazzini and thought of him as another potential recruit for the magazine. She probably admired his commendations of George Sand and Carlyle, his emphasis on man's duty 'to serve his fellows by political action in the sight of God', and his onslaught upon negative scepticism in philosophy and literature. Lewes and J. A. Froude were on the Committee of the Society of the Friends of Italy, which was founded in 1851, and Marian Evans went to some of the meetings, at one of which Mazzini denounced the papacy. In 1853, she regretted having to turn down an invitation from Sir James Clark to meet the Hungarian, Aurelius Pulszky, who was a friend of Kossuth who had attracted huge crowds when he visited Manchester and Birmingham in 1851.[42] It was, however, the political thought and destiny of France which most interested her, as it had interested Mill and Carlyle. The 1848 revolutions had exhausted that rationalist ideology of change which originated in the first French Revolution, and the establishment of the Second Empire under Napoleon III showed the start of a conservative reaction in France which was echoed in England.[43] Marian Evans was critical of the new order, and continued to study those French theorists who, in the late 1840s, had contributed to the debate about the political implications of revised theories of perception. She appears to have re-read the Appendix on utopianism in Bray's *The Philosophy of Necessity*; at one of Chapman's gatherings, she met Louis Blanc.[44]

She was enthusiastic about her meeting in January 1852 with Pierre Leroux when she spent two hours 'talking and listening' to the 'dreamy genius', and sympathising with his early struggles to live by writing. Leroux had been a member of the French Constitutional Assembly in 1848, and of the Legislative Assembly in 1851. He fled from France in December 1851, when many progressive intellectuals were being arrested, and the courts were passing severe sentences upon them. Her fascination with Leroux probably stemmed partly from the fact that she could hear at first hand his reminiscences of the events she had followed eagerly in the English press. She noted his association with the Saint-Simonian paper, the *Globe*, and his disagreements with Saint-Simon. Leroux was also a friend of George Sand, and, with her, had run the short-lived *Revue Indépendante* in 1841, which had been founded to inform the masses and to spread the message of social equality. Marian Evans summarised for Sara Hennell her conversation with Leroux:

> He belongs neither to the school of Proudhon which represents Liberty only, nor to that of Louis Blanc which represents Equality only, nor to that of Cabet which represents Fraternity. Pierre Leroux' système is the 'synthèse' which combines all three. He has found the true 'pont' which is to unite the love of self with the love of one's neighbour . . . George Sand has dedicated some of her books to him. He dilated on his views of the origins of Christianity – Strauss deficient because he has not shewn the *identity of the teaching of Jesus* with that of the *Essenes*. This is Leroux' favourite idea. I told him of your brother. He moreover traces Essenism back to Egypt and thence to India, the cradle of all religions . . . . 'Est-ce que nous sommes faits pour chercher le bonheur? Est-ce là votre idée? dîtes-moi.' 'Mais non – nous sommes faites . . . pour nous développer le plus que possible.' 'Ah! c'est ca'.[45]

The conversation suggested, as did the Mackay article, the fruits of the years in Coventry. Her familiarity with the different French versions of radicalism, and their relationship to the sloganising ideals of the 1789 revolution was evident, and the casual remarks in French hinted that she discussed with Leroux the contribution the French thinkers had made to a modification of utilitarian theory. She was interested in the synthetic cast of Leroux's views, as she had been in a similar quality in the work of Comte and Saint-Simon. She associated with both Leroux and George Sand the theme of the connection of the self to other men (also to be explored by Feuerbach, whose work she was to translate) which George Sand had first found in Rousseau's works. Leroux seems to have discussed religion in the light of the new Biblical criticism, and as illuminating moral and social ideas. The way in which the conversation skipped from politics to philosophy, religion and literature suggested the breadth of her interests; the interlinking of the various fields of inquiry had, however, also been characteristic of the writers she had admired in the late 1840s, and had been considered in her article on Mackay. The juxtaposition of, and easy transitions between, disciplines suggested that both Leroux and Marian Evans saw a necessary connection between the various ways of interpreting the world. At the heart of all disciplines was the problem of philosophical method; the methods and conclusions of any one discipline could inform those of other disciplines. That had been the conclusion reached by the sceptical questing of, amongst others, Mill and Carlyle.

15

Dogmatism and Truth (1851–1854)

Marian Evans's conversation with Leroux indicated her awareness of the implications of the debate about logic. That debate raised the issue of the nature of truth. Many thinkers who focused intently upon the process of knowing came to see truth as residing in the very quest for it: such 'truths' as were discovered were inevitably partial, and invited modification. Opposed to this neo-Hegelian emphasis upon process were those thinkers who evolved dogmatic pronouncements about logical method, and ultimately, life, often cast in the shape of elaborate systems. Marian Evans's friendship with Herbert Spencer was important for a number of reasons, not the least of which was that it shed light on the intellectual preoccupations of the circles in which she moved, for Spencer made his own contribution to the debate about logic and the nature of truth. Marian Evans's reaction to that contribution helped to define her own stance. Spencer, with Chapman, and later, Lewes, provided her with the male companionship she needed. He had met Sara Hennell at Chapman's in the 1840s, and encountered Marian Evans in August 1851 when she was visiting the Great Exhibition. When she moved to London, the friendship burgeoned. In February 1852, she wrote to Charles Bray that she wanted to introduce Spencer to him, and relayed the news that Sara Hennell, who was staying with her, was reading Spencer's *Social Statics* (1850). During the spring of the same year, Spencer helped her with Chapman's campaign against the Booksellers' Association, and they made frequent visits to the theatre.[1] Spencer later expressed himself forcibly on the subject of women. In *Education* (1861), he noted 'men care very little for erudition in women; but very much for physical beauty', and in *Principles of Ethics* (1892–3), he argued that women had a duty to marry, in order to perpetuate the race and stave off the evils associated with celibacy.[2] It soon became apparent to Marian Evans, however, that the 'tremendous glacier' she knew as Herbert Spencer was unmeltable, and felt no such duty to be incumbent upon himself. Seven months after their initial meeting, she announced to the Brays, possibly parodying Spencer's rational approach to emotional matters, 'We have agreed that we are not in love with each other, and that there is no reason why we should not have as much of each other's society as we like'. By May 1852, she was referring to their 'deliciously calm *new* friendship' and reported 'We see each other every day and have a delightful *camaraderie* in everything'. He may have been calm as regards their friendship, but she was not. The crisis came when she was resting at Broadstairs during the July and August of 1852. Both were depressed by Spencer's inability to fall in love with the well-educated (but unbeautiful) Miss Evans, and her passionate, imploring letters, which followed his rejection of her, did not elicit the offer of marriage she desperately desired. Their friendship survived this episode. He visited her the same evening she returned from Ambleside and Coventry in November 1852, but by the end of that year her involvement with Lewes, whom she first met on 6 October 1851, was becoming serious. All three were to remain friends for the rest of their lives; Marian Evans retained an affectionate interest in Spencer's work and reputation.[3]

Spencer's early life had much in common with Marian Evans's. He attributed his intellectual unorthodoxy to his dissenting background, saying that members of his family were characterised by their 'independence, self-asserting judgment, the tendency to non-conformity, and the unrestrained display of their sentiments and opinions; more especially in respect of political, social, religious, and ethical matters'. Before his move to London, he worked in the Derby area as an engineer, but his life, even then, was dominated by writing about, and studying, miscellaneous subjects. Having rejected Christianity at an early age, Spencer immersed himself in topics which interested other non-believers. Like Charles Bray, he turned to phrenology, the pseudo-science which advocated freedom of religious opinion; during its heyday between 1820 and 1840, he contributed articles to the *Phrenological Journal* and the *Zoist*. In the 1840s, a decade which also stimulated Marian Evans's interest in public affairs, Spencer was active in politics, spurred on by a family tradition which manifested itself in

an interest in 'principles and measures' not 'ministries and men'.
He emerged from the Midlands to establish himself, in the late
1840s, as a well-known figure in metropolitan circles. When Marian Evans met him, he was a sub-editor on the *Economist*, a position
he resigned in 1853, to lead the precarious life of a free-lance writer
of books and articles on serious subjects.[4] Like Marian Evans,
Spencer had contemplated contemporary German thought. He
was enthusiastic about *Das Leben Jesu*, which must have endeared
him to its translator but, for the most part, Spencer showed that
indifference or ill-informed hostility towards the German achievement which Marian Evans lamented. His thought remained deliberately resistant to foreign influences. In 1844, when he read a
newly-published translation of Kant's *Critique of Pure Reason*, he
immediately rejected the ideas it expounded. He gave little praise
to the disseminators of Idealism. Emerson's work, and *Sartor
Resartus*, which he read in 1843, provoked in Spencer a profound
mental indifference, although he conceded that others had experienced 'revolutions in their state of mind' after reading Carlyle.
Coleridge was commended but, significantly, not for his massive
attempt to domesticate Idealism, or for his demonstration of the
relevance of its new logic to private and public dilemmas. Rather,
Spencer isolated and praised the exposition, in *The Idea of Life*, of
Schelling's notion that 'life is the tendency to individuation', a
theme he himself was to elaborate in relation to sociology and
biology. In 1854, he over-simplified Hegel's views and criticised his
classification of the sciences; his use of the term 'transcendental'
blithely ignored the word's complex connotations within Idealist
tradition.[5]

Spencer's reactions to Idealism exemplified his tendency to
reject ideas which did not confirm his own views. He scorned any
education which inculcated '*submissive receptivity* instead of *independent activity*'. This ideal of intellectual independence, which was
admirable as an adumbration of the critical spirit exhibited by Mill,
Carlyle and Marian Evans, was carried by Spencer to ludicrous
excess. He consistently ignored insights afforded by other writers
and retreated into the isolation of egocentric dogmatism. Spencer
linked this trait to the fact that, from an early age, he was unable to
read for any length of time, so that the 'tendency then, as afterwards, towards independent thought, was relatively so dominant
that I soon became impatient with the process of taking in ideas set

before me'. As a youth, he also possessed 'a faculty of seizing cardinal truths rather than of accumulating detailed information. The implications of phenomena were . . . always, more interesting to me than the phenomena themselves'. Spencer's remoteness from the tangled, concrete detail of a complex world, and the over-theoretical nature of his mind, were especially obvious to those to whom reverent contemplation of phenomena was habitual. The scientist T. H. Huxley remarked that 'Spencer's idea of a tragedy is a deduction killed by a fact'.[6] In 1884, Beatrice Webb, the patient accumulator of statistics, noted 'something pathetic in the isolation of his mind, a sort of spider-like existence; sitting alone in the centre of his theoretical web, catching facts, and weaving them again into theory'. Her father felt a similar compassion: Spencer's intellect, he told his daughter, was 'like a machine racing along without raw material'.[7] Spencer's ignoring of the need to base theory on facts, and the lack of intellectual humility this implied, called forth from Marian Evans annoyance and baffled amusement. Spencer himself reported how she once asked him why his brow was so unwrinkled: '"I suppose it is because I am never puzzled," I said. This called forth the exclamation – "O! that's the most arrogant thing I ever heard uttered"'. Spencer's idea of a 'scientific expedition', she explained, was to go *'proof-hunting'* at Kew, and 'if the flowers didn't correspond to the theories, we said *"tant pis pour les fleurs"*'. When Spencer was visiting the Brays, she sympathetically hoped that they were 'likely to survive the heavy dose of theories'.[8]

Spencer was, nevertheless, concerned to reconcile the *a priori* and *a posteriori* logical methods, and his interest in the question placed him firmly in the mainstream of the philosophical movement which interested Marian Evans. His effort was, however, foredoomed to limited success. His intellectual inviolability made him unable to appreciate the efforts of other thinkers, whether they wished to reconcile the two methods, or to advocate one of them; his penchant for theorising in particular blunted his appreciation of the empirical accumulation of evidence from which conclusions could be drawn. He also considered that his detached temperament, which placed personal above impersonal considerations, uniquely fitted him for the task. This viewpoint was in marked contrast to that of the post-Enlightenment thinkers whose works Marian Evans admired. For them, the question of logical method involved crucial issues, such as religion, politics, morality and aesthetics. Carlyle, said Spencer, was no philosopher because he 'thought in a passion'. Ironically, it was this quality which allowed Carlyle, as it allowed Coleridge, to exert an influence over other thinkers denied to Spencer's bloodless cerebration. Marian Evans considered that Spencer's 'excès de *raison*' was much more debilitating than Carlyle's emotionalism.[9] The desire to modify and reconcile the rival philosophical schools was, nevertheless, the moving force behind much of Spencer's work. He noted: 'Leaving a truth in an inductive form is, in a sense, leaving its parts with loose ends; and the bringing it to a deductive form is, in a sense, uniting its facts as all parts of the one fact'. His emphasis was, however, anti-empirical. *Social Statics* was framed as a critique of utilitarianism. Spencer argued that hypothesis was necessary to, and implicit in, all perception. In his writings for the *Westminster Review* in 1854, as in *Principles of Biology* (1864–7), 'General truths . . . served as keys to the more special truths, and caused these to fall into coherent order'. Just as Spencer misunderstood, and thus easily domesticated the notion of transcendental, so, in relation to scientific studies, he diluted the complications of the *a priori* logic. He sometimes distinguished between legitimate and illegitimate uses of the *a priori* method, to suggest a merging of methods: 'The progress of science is duplex: it is at once from the special to the general, and from the general to the special; it is analytical and synthetical at the same time'. Yet Spencer often interpreted the *a priori* method simply as the scientist's working hypothesis: it also degenerated into the theory into which he fitted his facts.[10]

Spencer was also aware that neither empiricists nor Idealists believed that reason alone could explain the world, and that some had argued that the exercise of that faculty's limited powers only served to confirm the world's mystery. As a child of his time, Spencer inherited the awareness which he shared with Marian Evans that the 'clear, thin light of reason, concentrated on one object, left whatever surrounded the luminous point in too profound a darkness, which involuntarily attracted attention. Mystery, which had been driven out of the human mind, took its revenge'.[11] He argued that an awareness of the poetry of existence could coexist with a scientific view of the universe, citing Goethe and Professor Tyndall as examples. Discussing *First Principles* (1862), Spencer conceded that 'our ideas of matter and motion are but symbols of that which transcends the possibilities of knowledge: and . . . any explanation of the *order* of the changes which the Cosmos exhibits, still leaves unexplained the *nature* and *origin* of them'. Partly in deference to the contemporary re-evaluation of reason, partly, perhaps, to counterbalance his intellectual self-sufficiency, Spencer evolved the concept of the Unknown. If he was not temperamentally equipped to explore the profound darkness, Spencer nevertheless often returned to his idea of the Unknown from the time he first expounded it in a letter to his father in 1849. In 'Progress: Its Law and Cause' (1857), he asserted 'the littleness of human intellect . . . absolute knowledge is impossible . . . under all things there lies an impenetrable mystery'. He argued that evolution showed a progress from simple to complex, but the cause of this movement could not be ascertained for 'To do this could be to solve that ultimate mystery which must ever transcend experience'. Inquiry, by demonstrating the limitations of the intellect, and the mystery of existence, could form the foundation for religious belief. Inquiry was also, as Marian Evans had argued in her review of Mackay, a duty, and Spencer castigated the Christian fear of it as 'the profoundest of all infidelity – the fear lest the truth be bad'.[12]

Spencer's main interest was in science, and scientific ideas permeated his uninspired discussion of literary questions. In 1852, 'The Philosophy of Style' appeared in the *Westminster Review*, and its argument for a link between science and literature was in line with the periodical's bias.[13] This interest in science helped direct him towards Comte's work. His youthful enthusiasm for phrenology may have introduced him to Positivist ideas, for *The Zoist* had a Comtean strain in its prospectus. He also read Mill's *A System of Logic* as soon as it was published. Marian Evans urged him to read Comte in 1852, but in 1854 she reported that Spencer had not read Comte's work in French, although he had praised Harriet Martineau's summarising of it in *The Positive Philosophy of Auguste Comte*.[14] Spencer's *Autobiography* revealed the extent to which Positivism was discussed in the Chapman circle and how, as the interest in Comte's work increased, Marian Evans and Lewes were in the vanguard of the movement. Spencer recorded discussing the French philosophy with Lewes but Spencer, for whom a sceptical consideration of other men's ideas was a rare experience, attributed to Lewes and Marian Evans an uncomplicated attitude towards Comte which their writings did not bear out. Marian Evans, he said, was 'anxious that I should accept Positivist doctrines', and she and Lewes were 'in large measure adherents of Comte's views'.[15] His own comments on Comte demonstrated how Spencer reacted to other men's ideas. In 1863, 1867 and 1895, he issued public denials of his allegiance to Positivism, and he devoted much of his energy to refuting Comte. In January and February of 1854, he was 'getting up a very formidable case against him'.[16] From this spate of activity came 'The Genesis of Science', and Marian Evans's praise of this partially censorious article refuted Spencer's view of her as an uncritical disciple of Comte. Spencer considered critically the classifications of the sciences devised by Oken, Hegel and Comte, and suggested the cross-influence between the sciences, a view at odds with Comte's hierarchical *échelle*. Yet Spencer was less antagonistic to Comte than his later statements suggested. Whilst dissenting from certain Positivist views, he praised Comte's 'largeness of . . . views . . . clearness of reasoning', and spoke of 'the value of his speculations as contributing to intellectual progress'.[17] Also in 1854, Spencer contributed to the *British Quarterly Review* 'Auguste Comte – His Religion and Philosophy'. The article reviewed eight books by Comte and his French disciples, and the commentaries by Lewes and Harriet Martineau. Intellectual antagonism, Spencer's own preoccupations and judicial assessment were strangely mixed. The overall tone was contemptuous; the main focus was, once more, on the classification of the sciences, and Comte's scheme was again compared to Hegel's. Yet Spencer treated all aspects of Comte's work fairly. He considered his association with the Saint-Simonian school, the reception of his work in England, his life, the outlining of a new religion, the theory of progress, and Comte's aesthetic and political views. The article also suggested that Spencer was open-minded enough to draw upon his discussions of Comte with Lewes and Marian Evans. Spencer had met Lewes at Chapman's house in 1850, and in 1851 and 1852 they went on walking trips to Kent and the Thames Valley and discussed philosophy together. Lewes also gave Spencer an introduction to Littré. In his article, Spencer commented upon Lewes's intellectual development, and his 'fondness for metaphysics', which Spencer saw as at odds with allegiance to Positivism. Spencer also compared Comte's concept of Humanity to that found in the work of Feuerbach. Spencer, however, dismissed the ethical and religious aspects of Positivism, which had some appeal to the more imaginative Lewes and Marian Evans. He praised the *Cours*, with revealing adjectives, as 'the steady, calm, passionless productions of a great philosopher'.[18]

The 'passionless, tone which Spencer admired in Comte distinguished those articles in which Spencer dealt with topics Comte had also considered. Comte's implicit materialism assumed an exaggerated form when Spencer traced laughter and tears to physical causes, such as the circulation of the blood in the brain. Like Comte, he considered belief historically, but showed little sensitivity to the beauties of past creeds. The question of belief was, in Comte's writings, linked to a general notion of development, and Spencer outlined his rival theory in 'Progress: Its Law and Cause' (1857). He argued that change was always from simple to complex, and that progress in one field of inquiry led to progress in others. He also offered his own modification to the theory of causation, suggesting that a cause is always less complex than its results, and stated axiomatically *'Every active cause produces more than one change – every cause produces more than one effect'*.[19] It was, however, as a writer on those scientific subjects upon which Comte based his philosophy that Marian Evans commended Spencer. She discussed with him *Principles of Psychology* (1855) in a way which he found useful. Marian Evans hoped the book would help establish the study of character as a respectable science. Spencer also gave impetus to the new science of sociology which Saint-Simon and Comte had pioneered, a science which was man-centred, and was praised by Marian Evans as providing a method and conclusions which the imaginative artist could utilise.[20] She particularly admired 'The Genesis of Science' which focused upon the nature and uses of scientific knowledge. Spencer noted that, although science was distinctively concerned with prevision and prediction, it was not, otherwise, different from other forms of knowledge. He saw both science and art as applied knowledge, and suggested that all disciplines could learn from each other. Science provided art with valid generalisations, and art supplied science with 'better materials, and more perfect instruments'.[21]

Frederic Harrison, speaking of Comte's earlier works, explained to Ruskin, 'With him [Comte] it [the term "positive"] always means that which is laid down as the conclusion drawn by logical methods from the best obtainable evidence. He never uses *positive* for absolute truth, or absolute knowledge. The distinctive mark of his teaching is, that all our ideas are *relative*'. It was this aspect of Comte's teaching, which implied the idea of truth as quest, which appealed to the sceptical, critical minds of Marian Evans, Lewes and Mill. Spencer certainly manifested a critical scepticism in his attitude towards Positivism. Although aware of the entirety of

Comte's system, he, like many English thinkers, gave close attention and praise only to selected aspects of it, singling out Comte's
classification of the sciences and his sociology. Yet Spencer, like
Comte, and many of Comte's English admirers, was a polymath,
and his aspiration to a comprehensive synthesis of his own was
Comtean in spirit. Spencer, unlike Mill, Carlyle and Marian Evans,
did not suspect the very validity of system-building. 'Progress: Its
Law and Cause' employed the method of the historian of civilisation, which had been utilised by such system-makers as Condorcet
and Saint-Simon, whose heir Comte was. It was Spencer's all-
inclusiveness which appealed to Frederic Harrison, who echoed
his terminology when defining the ideal way of studying Greek
poetry: Harrison, who was to help lead the English Positivist
movement, hinted at the affinity between Comte and his English
critic.[22] The older Comte and Spencer also possessed a common
talent for a dogmatism based upon intellectual unreceptiveness
which alienated their more open-minded contemporaries. Just as
Spencer could not assimilate other men's ideas, so Comte flaunted
his 'cerebral hygiene', to which Marian Evans referred in the 1840s.
In 1853 Comte told Sir Erskine Perry: 'I am ambitious, for I wish to
found a school, like Aristotle or St. Paul, and one that will probably
be more important than both of those two joined together I
never read; reading interrupts thinking; it is necessary to begin
with reading, but now I have given it up, and don't even read
scientific works'.[23] The Spencer who acknowledged 'the greatness
and the littleness of human intellect', and who suggested that
'under all things lies an impenetrable mystery',[24] could sometimes
assent to the concept of relative truth, and use the concept as the
basis for a critical evaluation of Positivism. Yet the dogmatism of
Comte also offended Spencer who, in the 1850s, was already
manifesting signs of the isolated, theoretical mind which Beatrice
Webb saw in the old man. In 1854, he ironically dismissed the
Système as 'the dreams of a theorist'.[25] Spencer did not question the
validity of system-building, but he rejected in cavalier fashion
systems constructed by anyone other than himself. Incipient dog-
matisms confronted each other when Spencer read Comte in the
1850s. Spencer's own version of cerebral hygiene prevailed, and
his brow remained unwrinkled, a reaction which Marian Evans
could neither sympathise with nor share. His certainties were a foil
to her dearly-bought scepticism.

II. FEUERBACH

Marian Evans's critical reaction to Spencer's unreceptive dogmatism contrasted to her enthusiasm for the work of Ludwig Feuerbach. It is difficult to determine when she first read *Das Wesen des Christenthums* (1841). Upon her death, she possessed other works by the same writer, and a copy of her own translation. Francis Watts, with whom she discussed religious questions in 1842, might have mentioned Feuerbach's name, for Watts was well-versed in German theology. There might be a reference to Feuerbach in a letter Marian Evans wrote to Cara Bray in June 1844, or John Sibree might have told her of this development of Hegelianism. In 1851, she came across Feuerbach's *Das Wesen der Religion*, and Robert Noel's visit to Rosehill in July of the same year might have given her the idea of a translation. In 1853, she agreed to translated *Das Wesen des Christenthums*: it was to be published by John Chapman in a quarterly series. The book had gone through three editions in seven years in Germany; Chapman, pursuing his policy of supporting radical thinkers, but also pressed for money, probably hoped for large sales in England.[26] Marian Evans was pressed for time, for she was editing the *Westminster Review*, possibly writing articles for Lewes, and drafting *The Idea of a Future Life*. She told the Brays of the assignment in February 1853, and the translation was advertised on 18 June of the same year. By 3 June 1854, she was correcting the penultimate sheet of proofs. Despite her anxiety about the reception of the translation, and about phraseology and the minutiae of printing, she entertained none of the reservations which marred her experience of translating *Das Leben Jesu*.[27] Her unwavering commitment to a difficult task argued enthusiasm, and the book did, in fact, reflect some of Marian Evans's main preoccupations. Feuerbach was the most revolutionary of the German writers who had found inspiration in the Idealist philosophy. His critique of the over-cerebral qualities of Idealism and his materialistic humanism, paved the way for Marxism and echoed Marian Evans's recoil from the over-theoretical cast of Positivism, and from Spencer's ignoring of the concrete complexity of life. Feuerbach's difficulties would also have provoked Marian Evans's sympathy as she reflected upon how the German authorities had attempted to obstruct the freedom of inquiry which she considered vital to the health of society. Strauss had considered Germany's power and greatness sprang from its liberal speculative tradition, which was untrammelled by clerical influence upon Germany's laws or intellectual life. But, with the accession of Frederick William IV in 1840, the atmosphere became unsympathetic to new ideas. Feuerbach's progress repeated a pattern familiar to the post-Romantic radicals in England; he confessed in *Philosophical Fragments*, 'God was my first thought; Reason my second; Man my third and last thought'.[28] He was born in 1804, the son of a distinguished jurist who was well-known for his progressive social views, and interest in the Kantian philosophy. Feuerbach studied theology at Heidelberg, lectured on Descartes and Spinoza at Erlangen, where he failed to obtain promotion because his early publications were deemed irreligious, and then retired, in 1837, to a secluded castle in Bruckberg. In Berlin, he was harassed by the police, because he was thought to be a member of a secret organisation. For a decade after the publication of *Wesen*, he was a celebrated figure in radical circles. He was offered a post in the short-lived Radical government of 1848; his Heidelberg lectures of 1848–9 were given at the request of the students, and attracted a large number of the public.[29] In choosing to translated *Wesen*, Marian Evans was, as in her championing of Strauss and Mackay, embracing the cause of a controversialist. The book's initial publication had caused 'clamour' and she noted that in Germany it was considered '*the* book of the age'. She chose, moreover, to translate the second edition, in which Feuerbach had toned down the Hegelianism, and strengthened and clarified his argument, so as to produce a more radical book with more popular appeal.[30] Feuerbach's prose style was unlike that usually found in works of philosophy. Engels contrasted its 'literary . . . even high flown style', which Marian Evans's translation reproduced, to the abstract, abstruse style of Hegel. From Carlyle, Marian Evans had learnt how a new language must be forged to express a new mode of perception. The forensic note in Feuerbach's prose was dictated by the fact that he considered the effects of religion upon the individual and society to be of urgent concern. He aimed the work at 'every cultivated and thinking man' and tried to abstain from 'the ostentation of philosophy'. Aphorisms and antitheses delineated striking paradoxes, and repetitions and rhetorical addresses arrested the reader's attention. The aim of clarity was abandoned by Feuerbach as key terms were repeated, rather than defined.[31]

Marian Evans was drawn, once more, to a revolutionary attack upon the problem of logical method. The structure of the work imaged its radical revision of the Hegelian dialectic which Marian Evans had encountered in its purest form in the *Lectures on the Philosophy of History*. The core of Feuerbach's book consisted of two sections, 'The True or Anthropological Essence of Religion' and 'The False or Theological Essence of Religion'. Feuerbach noted of the two parts 'the first is . . . *positive*, the second . . . not wholly but in the main, *negative*; in both, however, the same positions are proved, only in a different or rather opposite manner. The first exhibits religion in its *essence*, its *truth*, the second exhibits it in its *contradictions*; the first is development, the second polemic'. The second part's 'only aim' was 'to show that the sense in which religion was interpreted in the previous part of the work *must* be the true one, because the contrary is absurd'. In the Hegelian dialectic, thesis and antithesis were reconciled in synthesis, and all truths were compounded of opposites. Feuerbach argued that thesis and antithesis proved the same point in different ways.[32] Where Hegel described Christ in terms of synthesis, as uniting 'visible and invisible, reality and spirit', Feuerbach pointed to the contradiction in such a view, and argued that man's image of Christ reflected back on the reality of man, for it 'expresses the necessity of the imagination, the necessity of affirming the imagination as a divine power. The Son is the reflected splendour of the imagination'. In religion, Feuerbach noted, man 'separates himself from himself, but only to return always to the same point from which he set out. Man negatives himself, but only to posit himself again, and that in a glorified form'. Object and subject were identified: 'The *absolute* to man is his own nature'.[33] Man in his psychological complexity replaced Mind as the central philosophical concern.

Feuerbach concentrated upon the psychology of vision, an aspect of the logical debate to which Marian Evans had been introduced by the works of Coleridge. Feuerbach's revision of method was linked to his distinction between two types of perception; he denied that the concrete and the abstract were constituents of reality, and argued that they suggested 'not . . . two different materials, but . . . different principles, i.e. empirical *activity* and speculative *activity*'. Feuerbach's ideas were conclusions 'drawn from premises which are not themselves mere ideas, but objective facts either actual or historical', founded on 'materials which can be appropriated only through the activity of the senses'. He rejected the *a priori* logic, because it was overly cerebral, drawing its materials 'from within'. Feuerbach thus suggested a link between two psychological processes, whereas Hegel, in seeing the task of metaphysics as the attempt to 'comprehend the absolute connection' between 'the substantial totality of things on one side' and 'the abstract essence of free volition on the other side', had linked two kinds of co-existent reality.[34] Feuerbach distinguished between scientific and imaginative conceptions, the ideas of Reason and Faith. The former were true, because derived from an objective recognition of outer reality: the latter told man nothing in themselves but, as the product of psychological needs, obliquely revealed much about human nature. Religious conceptions indicated the need for 'the imagination as a middle term between the abstract and concrete': thus, 'the task of philosophy, in investigating this subject, is to comprehend the relation of the imagination to the reason, – the genesis of the image by means of which an object of thought becomes an object of sense, of feeling'.[35]

In his analysis of religious concepts, Feuerbach showed how the ideas of faith told truths not just about the workings of perception, but also more general truths about human nature. He converted the images of religion into statements about mankind, for religion was 'a dream, in which our own conceptions and emotions appear to us as separate existences, beings out of ourselves. The religious mind does not distinguish between subjective and objective'. Theological doctrines were thus of psychological interest, for 'in the being of God it is only thy own being which is an object to thee, and what presents itself *before* the consciousness is simply what lies *behind* it'. Feuerbach saw in the argument from Design the 'self-affirmation of the calculated activity of the understanding'; the image of the suffering God expressed the idea that suffering for others was of ethical value. George Eliot echoed these notions in a notebook she kept in the 1870s, but the idea was one she had already seen suggested by Scott and George Sand, who demonstrated a connection between temperament and belief.[36] Feuerbach's book expounded a view of human nature via an analysis of religion, and his discussion of religion was detailed, for religion expressed the entire self; it was 'human nature reflected, mirrored in itself . . . God is the mirror of man'. In so far as descriptive analysis of human personality assumed a central position in the

Essence, Feuerbach reiterated the emphases of other writers Marian Evans had read. Phrenologists saw man as the apex of creation, and they viewed religion as a phenomenon which stemmed from human sentiments and feelings, rather than from mysteries, miracles and subjectively narrated historical records. The science and religion of Positivism were also man-centred. During this period, as her articles on Mackay and Greg showed, Marian Evans was still vitally interested in German Biblical scholarship and Feuerbach, by stressing that man and nature were the prime realities, purported to resolve the debate in the higher criticism as to 'whether, in world history, "substance" or "self-consciousness" was the decisive driving force'.[37]

Feuerbach rejected Hegel's synthesis of opposites as a principle of logical method, and the Hegelian contention that synthesis was congruent with the nature of reality, but the synthetic tendency of Hegelianism was still apparent in his thought. He suggested the notion of a universal human nature. He argued that ethical judgments enshrined in religious conceptions were not idiosyncratic, as most creeds sanctified 'love, wisdom, justice'. All men possessed 'the inward conviction of the irreversible reality of morals'; the value of benevolence and man's faith in 'the infinitude and truth of his own nature' were truths unaffected by time.[38] Yet Feuerbach also spoke of the mysterious idiosyncracy of character. He noted that the 'characteristic of real personality is precisely exclusiveness, – the Leibnitzian principle of distinction, namely, that no one existence is exactly like another', and he showed how individualism was revealed by the variety of religious belief. Individuality was also reinforced by man's existence within time: 'Each man is a new predicate, a new phasis of humanity. As many as are the men, so many are the powers, the properties of humanity. It is true that there are the same elements in every individual, but under such various conditions and modifications that they appear new and peculiar. The mystery of the inexhaustible fulness of the divine predicates is therefore nothing else than the mystery of human nature'.[39] Yet for Feuerbach to speak of man's individuality was to pose the question which haunted both Rousseau and George Sand: how could the isolated self relate to other men and the world? Feuerbach insisted that the individual derived his vitality and humanity from the species yet, like Carlyle, he questioned the motivational efficacy of an abstract concept of humanity. He argued that relationship was essential not just for

man's vitality, but also in his role as a perceiving creature. Feuerbach attempted to span the chasm between particular and general
humanity by his psychological theory that consciousness of self
was 'essentially united to . . . consciousness of another'. The mind
was initially engulfed in subjectivity, for the feelings suggested
that individual powers were limitless, and coloured the world to
make it conform to the individual's desires. Yet to define the
desires of self necessitated referring them to the desires of others:
this process simultaneously affirmed the ego, and suggested a
limitation in its powers. Thus the 'ego . . . attains to consciousness
of the world through consciousness of the *thou*'. The doctrine that
God created the world was 'the mystic paraphrase of a psychological process' exhibiting 'the unity of consciousness and self-consciousness'. Philosophy and religion, in so far as they formulated
subjective dogmas without reference to other men, were seen as
obstacles to true perception. Feuerbach's work thus sanctioned the
stand against philosophical sectarianism made by Mill and Carlyle
in the 1830s; like Carlyle, Feuerbach had little respect for formulas
which were at odds with reality.[40]

Feuerbach also argued that those factors which defined man's
isolation, his innate individualism, and his existence in time,
inevitably led to relationship and promoted an awareness of
human unity. The sexual relationship, which was celebrated by
Feuerbach, at once pointed up difference, included reference to
another, and connected man to the species. A sense of personal,
historically determined limitation, promoted the contrasting sense
of mankind's unlimited capacity. The concept of the infinitude of
God was an image of the boundless power of humanity throughout time, and this notion underpinned Feuerbach's view of history
as 'a continuous and progressive conquest of limits'. He distinguished his view of humanity from that of Idealists saying, 'The
"Idea" is to me only faith in the historical future, in the triumph of
truth and virtue; it has for me only a political and moral significance'. Man's reaction against 'the disconsolate feeling of a void'
was embodied in the doctrine of the Trinity, which showed 'a God
in whom there is society, a union of beings fervently loving each
other'.[41] Feuerbach also considered man's relationship to the universe in terms of the psychology of consciousness. The self-
involved religious perception tailored its picture of the world to the
demands of subjective feelings. Reason, unlike religion, proposed
an objective vision of the world, and 'embraces with equal interest

he whole universe . . .. Reason is . . . the all-embracing, all-
ompassionate being, the love of the universe to itself'. In defining
larkness as 'the mother of religion', Feuerbach's metaphor was a
eminder that the debate about perception originated in Enlighten-
nent philosophy. The strenuous process of rational perception
inited man to the universe, whereas religion separated him from it.
'euerbach argued that notions of miracle and providence concealed
rom mankind the workings of nature. Religion 'knows nothing of
he joys of the thinker, of the investigator of Nature, of the artist'.
)nly obliquely did religion give clues to the wonder of the uni-
rerse. Feuerbach saw the sacraments as a celebration of natural
iubstances, and man's power to transform them; the after-life was
the present embellished, contemplated through the imagination'.
Reason, contrastingly, celebrated the world, for, to reason, 'The
)bject of the senses is in itself indifferent – independent of the
lisposition or of the judgment; but the object of religion . . .
:ssentially presupposes a critical judgment'. Reason and reverence
went hand in hand, for 'Contemplation and worship are not
:ssentially distinguished' and, in the act of scrutiny, man conse-
:rated to the universe 'my noblest possession, my heart, my
ntelligence'.[42]

Feuerbach's revision of logical method had important practical
ramifications. He emphasised the dangers of religious perception
oecause it alienated man from his own, and from humanity's,
richly diverse potential, by locating all human qualities in God.
Feuerbach also extended Strauss's rational arguments against miracle and providence to show how belief in miracle and providence
separated man from the universe. Theology reinforced these gulfs.
Feuerbach's theory of consciousness, with its emphasis upon the
inevitability of relationship, and his exaltation of objective perception, were meant to heal man's triple alienation. His argument that
man and the universe were the primary realities had political
implications. He wished to redirect human effort. In his 1848
Heidelberg lectures, he announced that he longed to change 'the
friends of God into friends of man, believers into thinkers, wor-
shippers into workers, candidates for the other world into students
of this world'. Marx was to extend this argument in his eleventh
thesis on Feuerbach, commenting that the 'philosophers have only
interpreted the world in various ways; the point however is to
change it'. Feuerbach suggested that men worshipped humanity
anyway, although they erroneously termed it God. The notion of

God as unlimited understanding was an expression of the reason'
capacity to unite all men. The Father and Son of the Trinit
expressed the heart's need for society and love.[43] Feuerbach'
argument also had moral implications. Reason promoted a sense o
common humanity which induced compassion, and was a necess
ary concomitant of the moral sense, for 'Depravity of understand
ing is always depravity of heart'. In a rational being, feeling migh
unite with reason to aid perception, but Marian Evans carefull
distinguished in her note between '*Herz*, or feeling directed towar
real objects, and therefore practically sympathetic; and *Gemüth*, o
feeling directed towards imaginary objects, and therefore practi
cally unsympathetic, self-absorbed'. Central to Feuerbach's foren
sic work was the advocating of a clear-sighted love of the actual
whether of self, other men, or the world, which led to correct socia
and moral behaviour: 'If human nature is the highest nature t
man, then practically also the highest and first law must be th
love of man to man. *Homo homini deus est*: – this is the grea
practical principle: – this is the axis on which revolves the histor
of the world'.[44]

Marian Evans gained little money from the translation of Feuer
bach. Chapman paid her two shillings a page; the lists she kept of he
earnings, which dated from 1855, recorded no further income from
the work. Trübner reissued it in 1881, the year after her death. Th
work received only guarded acclaim. Her skill as a translator wa
praised, but the *Spectator* damned the book as a work of 'ranl
Atheism' and even the *Westminster Review* saw it as of 'quit
secondary philosophical repute in its own country'. Her enthusiasn
for Feuerbach was a somewhat solitary one and was shared onl
with Sara Hennell. Lewes showed little interest; the *Leader* an
nounced the book's appearance, but never reviewed it. In 1860
George Eliot and Lewes seemed to be at odds over Sara's interpret
ation of Feuerbach in *Thoughts in Aid of Faith*. Marian Evans's
enthusiasm was also kindled when Feuerbach's work had ceased t
be fashionable. After his period of notoriety in the 1840s, Feuerbach's
works were little read, although his views strengthened the trenc
towards scientific materialism, and he contributed importantly t
the foundations of Marxist theory.[45] To Sara, Marian Evans wrote
'With the ideas of Feuerbach I everywhere agree, but of course
should, of myself, alter the phraseology considerably'. He clarifiec
ideas she had already encountered, and, if his exposition of these
ideas was sometimes chaotic and unclear, the book probably ap

>ealed to her because it was, after her contact with system-builders,
efreshingly undogmatic. Feuerbach's theory of consciousness,
vhich showed the impossibility of isolation, echoed a similar
heme considered by Rousseau and George Sand. His concerned
reatment of Christianity placed him in that line of post-Enlighten-
nent thinkers who were inclined to re-evaluate Christianity, rather
han to dismiss it. His political views also linked him to general
rends in the radical thought of the 1840s. He saw dogmatic
Christianity as an anachronism in the modern world. His stance
vould have struck a chord in the mind of the reviewer of *The
Progress of the Intellect* who had argued for balancing a sympathy for
>ast beliefs with an embracing of progressive tendencies. Yet, as
Marian Evans noted, 'Germany and England are *two* countries'.[46]
The aspects of Feuerbach's thought which Marx developed, his
:ationalism, his materialism, and his revolutionary political views
:ound no place in her later work. Such dogmatic ideologies were at
>dds with the sceptical English tradition, embodied in the works of
Mill and Carlyle, and Marian Evans's scepticism had been reinforced
>y those writers, such as George Sand and Rousseau, whom she
had read in the 1840s. After 1854, she did not discuss Feuerbach's
ideas, although they seem to inform her fictional treatment of
religion, isolation and the developing consciousness.[47]

Feuerbach was concerned with advocating a method of investigation, and suggesting those areas of concern in which that
method of investigation should be utilised. Unlike Spencer, he
proposed a way of viewing reality which was reverent in the face
of facts. He criticised intellectual theorising as the product of
egoism, and attacked philosophers and religious thinkers whose
interpretations of reality derived from a self-involved consciousness. He advocated objective observation, and placed the concrete
realities of man and the world at the centre of his philosophy.
Marian Evans's consideration of Feuerbach's critique of conventional philosophy as occupation was significant at this stage in her
career. Mill and Carlyle had progressed from suggesting a merging
of logical methods to the notion that the mind should confront
reality directly in a way which acknowledged, by its abandonment
of schematising logic, the world's rich complexity. Feuerbach, in
rejecting the subjectivity of religious and philosophical systems,
echoed this trend: like many young Hegelians who rejected religion, he had partial recourse to what Engels termed 'Anglo-
French materialism'.[48] But although Feuerbach entered a plea for

scientific rationalism, he tempered the over-cerebral implication
of empiricism. In *The Essence of Christianity*, he admitted the el
ement of wonder in vision, praised artists, and suggested that
carefully-defined mode of outward-directed feeling could aid rationa
perception.[49] He thus corroborated the view that perception wa
complex as a psychological faculty, and in its *modus operandi*, and i
was this view which was central to the philosophical works whick
Marian Evans admired, and which was embodied in the art she
praised. From an early stage, Marian Evans had also been convers
ant with, and thought within, a tradition which saw the debate
about logical method as involving urgent human issues. In hi
argument that, in philosophy and religion, man unconsciously
contemplated himself, Feuerbach entered a plea for the abandon
ment of philosophy, and a turning towards those disciplines which
deliberately scrutinised man and the world, such as sociology and
science. Marx and Engels, under Feuerbach's influence, aban
doned philosophical speculation, and analysed human *praxis* via
the disciplines of history, economics and sociology.[50] Feuerbach
criticised the limited perception embodied in philosophical and
theological systems, and redefined the legitimate areas and func
tion of inquiry. Rousseau, George Sand and Carlyle had showr
Marian Evans that innovative literary forms could best embody a
complex mode of perception, and thereby could enter into a critica
dialogue with philosophical sectarianism. Novelists, who tradition
ally contemplated man and the world, also focused upon those
areas of concern which Comte and Feuerbach had proposed as the
most important. The experience of translating Feuerbach's work
may well have been one more factor which helped direct Mariar
Evans's attention away from philosophical speculation as occupa
tion.

III. THE CONTINUING DEBATE

Despite her adverse reaction to his dogmatism, Spencer's remi
niscences of Marian Evans in the 1850s contained glowing tributes
to her intelligence and spoke of the pleasure he derived from thei
companionship. He may well have been fascinated by her scepti
cism, so different was it from his own mental cast. Her intellectual
alertness and openness were shown in her discussion of the debate
about logical method, and its application to the issues of life. As
Spencer considered the topic in the periodical press, so Mariar

,vans touched upon it in her letters, mentioned it in the articles
he wrote, and put into practice its implications in her work for the
Westminster Review. She was aware of the methodology of the
debate, and complained about an article which showed 'a miser-
ble confusion of the universal with the particular'. The psycho-
ogical implications attracted her attention, for she had encoun-
ered at Griff and Foleshill Carlyle's and Coleridge's dramatic
reatments of the heart/head dilemma. Feuerbach emphasised the
psychology of perception, and she often referred to the new
cience of psychology which Spencer helped to pioneer. She con-
rasted her own inner and outer senses, her instinct and experi-
nce. After reading Margaret Fuller's autobiography, she reflected
How inexpressibly touching that passage from her journal – "I
hall always reign through the intellect, but the life! the life! O my
God! shall that never be sweet"'.[51] She also considered the notion
f human isolation. The writers she read in the 1840s had been
much preoccupied with this theme, to which Marian Evans re-
ponded sympathetically for she herself had been isolated from
espectable society during the church-going crisis. Alone in London, she translated Feuerbach and her experience and her reading
einforced each other's conclusions. She wrote to Charles Bray:
We never make enough allowance for the difference between the
points of view of different people'. She embroidered upon the
heme in a letter to Cara:

When I spoke of myself as an island, I did not mean that I was so
exceptionally. We are all islands –

'Each in his hidden sphere of joy or woe,
Our hermit spirit dwells and roams apart' –

and this seclusion is sometimes the most intensely felt at the
very moment your friend is caressing you or consoling you. But
this gradually becomes a source of satisfaction instead of repin-
ing. When we are young we think our trouble a mighty business
– that the world is spread out expressly as a stage for the
particular drama of our lives and that we have a right to rant and
foam at the mouth if we are crossed. I have done enough of that
in my time. But we begin to understand that these things are
important only to one's own consciousness, which is but as a
globule of dew on a rose-leaf that at mid-day there will be no
trace of. This is no high-flown sentimentality, but a simple
reflection which I find useful to me every day.[52]

She pinpointed the paradox expounded in different ways by Rousseau and Feuerbach that a sense of individuality was bound up with relationship. She also constructed an argument about subjectivity, which extended to moral criticism of that tendency. The image of the littleness of the consciousness, compared with the world, recalled Feuerbach's attempt to deflect attention away from the self and to an outer reality. The picture of the consciousness as a 'globule of dew', iridescent and susceptible to change, evoked reference to a Rousseauesque notion of the flux of the emotions.

The writers she read in the 1840s who dealt with the human implications of the philosophical debate still attracted her interest. She remained faithful to her enthusiasm for Carlyle. She met Neuberg, who had helped Carlyle with his work on Frederick the Great and, in letters to Sara, she included anecdotes about Carlyle's behaviour and opinions.[53] Her review of *The Life of Sterling* was a public tribute to one of the most important influences upon her intellectual development. She spoke of how eagerly she looked forward to new books by Carlyle. She favoured autobiography as a genre in the 1840s, admiring especially Rousseau's *Confessions*. The subject of Carlyle's book pleased her, for it showed 'the struggle of a restless aspiring soul', to whom poetry and philosophy were 'an end in themselves', but she valued the book as much for its picture of Carlyle and his intellectual milieu as for its depiction of Sterling. She particularly admired Carlyle's method, and compared his impartial treatment of his subject to the clerically biased account provided by Hare, which had omitted discussion of Sterling's reading of Strauss. She also approved of the way in which Carlyle viewed his subjects. She commended the truthful perception which yet evidenced 'a loving and poetic nature which sees the beauty and the depth of familiar things', for 'comparatively tame scenes and incidents gather picturesqueness and interest under the rich lights of Carlyle's mind'. She praised his mingling of satire and veneration.[54] Carlyle seemed to conform to the definition of art which she articulated in the 1840s, when she noted that art expressed heightened, individualistic perception and that it used old subjects, but gave 'them out anew in intensified expression'.[55] Such art was obliquely didactic. She disliked the dogmatism of *Latter Day Pamphlets* (1850) compared to the scepticism of *Sartor Resartus* and noted that Carlyle, in *The Life of Sterling*, showed 'the meaning which his [Sterling's] experience has for his fellows'. Carlyle also manifested the 'love of the good and beautiful in character, which is, after all, the essence of piety', a comment recalling Feuerbach's humanistic revision of Christianity. The portrayal of the friendship between Sterling and Carlyle instructed the reader in the mysterious workings of feeling, for the reader was 'gladdened with a perception of the affinity that exists between noble souls, in spite of diversity of ideas'.[56]

Her enthusiasm for Comte was also evident in her letters. She quoted his ethical injunction, 'Notre vie se compose de résignation et d'activité' [Our life is made up of resignation and activity]: embracing this principle would, she told Mary Sibree in 1851, lead to 'divine unselfish love and from this again light'. She quoted the same Positivist aphorism to both Sara Hennell and Mrs Houghton in the winter of 1853 as she agonised about her relationship with Lewes, who also drew comfort in a crisis from Positivism. In Marian Evans's mind, as in the Comtist system, a mode of intellectual vision and ethics were inextricably linked. In the light of a progressivist historicism learnt from Comte as well as Feuerbach, she pronounced Holman Hunt's 'The Light of the World' as 'too medieval and pietistic to be rejoiced in as a product of the present age', and she told Chapman in July 1852 of her belief that 'the thought which is to mould the Future has for its root a belief in necessity, that a nobler presentation of humanity has yet to be given in resignation to individual nothingness, than could ever be shewn of a being who believes in the phantasmagoria of hope unsustained by reason'.[57] Her contact with Positivist sympathisers at 142 Strand strengthened her interest in Comte's work, and they, in their turn, were often concerned with other topics linked to the logical debate. She met David Brewster, who had written on Comte as early as 1838, and William John Birch, who was one of the first to subscribe to the *Westminster Review* under its new editorship. Birch supported free inquiry: in 1850, he pledged ten shillings a week to the new *Reasoner*, which was to deal solely with theological matters. A year later he chaired the first Free Discussion Festival at the City Road Hall of Science and, in 1852, contributed to Lewes's fund for Comte and became a member of the newly-founded Central Council of Secular Societies.[58]

Marian Evans also met Mill, whom Chapman recruited as a contributor. Her reactions to his articles were not consistently favourable, but she re-read those works which Mill had written in the 1840s which had introduced Comte's name to the English public. In October 1851, she asked Charles Bray to send her *A*

System of Logic, saying she would be 'glad to have it by me for reference'. In 1852, Spencer was reading her copy of the *Logic* when he visited her at Broadstairs, and she may have tried to get him to consider the work as an alternative treatment of the logical problem. In November of the same year, she read *Principles of Political Economy*.[59] She also came to know both Harriet Martineau and Lewes who published books on Comte in 1853. From the outset, Chapman kept Marian Evans in touch with his plans to bring out an abridgement of Comte, and in 1852 she became joint trustee with Mr Atkinson, Harriet's collaborator, of a fund set up to publish *The Positive Philosophy of Auguste Comte*. She defended Lewes's book when it was attacked by T. H. Huxley, and, because of her admiration for both works on Comte, tried to sort out the author's disagreements over their rival publications.[60]

Her interest in science, religion and politics, the analysis of whose interconnections was an integral part of Comte's system, was also evident. Her relationships with Lewes and Spencer sustained her interest in science. In 1851, soon after settling in London, she started to attend Faraday's lectures at the Royal Society, and commented that they were 'as fashionable as the opera'. The same winter she went to Francis Newman's lectures on geometry.[61] Her interest in religion also remained constant. Her comments upon orthodox Christians and the Established Church became sarcastically outspoken, a tone probably encouraged by the atmosphere of 142 Strand. Reporting her safe arrival in London to Cara in January 1852, she told her, "When I saw a coated animal getting into my carriage, I thought of all the horrible stories of madmen in railways, but his white neck-cloth and thin mincing voice soon convinced me that he was one of those exceedingly tame brutes, the clergy'. Echoing the reservations of William Blake in his 'Holy Thursday' poems, she said that a visit to St Paul's Cathedral to hear the charity children sing, had been 'worth doing once especially as we got out before the sermon'. Yet although she showed no signs of orthodox Christian belief, she retained a respect for those who held liberal religious views. She enjoyed meeting the Unitarian, Samuel Sharpe, during her visit to Broadstairs, and was interested in the views of Lord John Russell who argued against an education which inculcated sectarian religious beliefs. She spoke warmly of Richard Dawes, the Dean of Hereford, who established schools for working-class children, and voted for the admission of dissenters to the University of Cambridge. Books and articles on religion continued to attract her interest. In 1851, she read articles by the Unitarian Ebenezer Symes, Hickson's thoughts on life and immortality, and Newman's work on the present position of Catholics in England. She commended Conybeare's analytical article on church parties, and told Sara Hennell that she 'must read' James Martineau's 'On the Unity of Logical and Intuitive in the ultimate grounds of religious belief'.[62]

Her apostasy was underpinned by her championing of rigorous inquiry into the historical veracity of the Bible, and she explored the ethical implications of such efforts. She was interested in Ewald's *History of Israel*, to which she referred in 1853. She re-read Strauss and possibly Schleiermacher.[63] Her article on Greg's *The Creed of Christendom*, a book which Chapman published, showed her support for the higher criticism. She defended it against charges of being a negative attack upon Christianity; she argued that whilst Protestantism was effete 'in its ecclesiastical and sectarian forms', it had promoted the growth of 'free religious inquiry amongst earnest men'. The new criticism was inspired by 'the impulse of candour . . . by an interest in the spiritual well-being of society'. She proposed the value of a judicial assessment of Christianity, noting the blending of 'candour and reverence' in Greg and also in the work of her old acquaintance, Charles Hennell, and she especially commended the latter's 'rare combination of analytic acumen with breadth of conception'. Yet she asserted that these new speculators were not 'enamoured of theory, and careless of its practical results' nor were they 'anti-religious zealots who identify all faith with superstition'. She saw them as wishing to establish a less imperfect religion, because their intellect and their moral sense promoted antagonism to Christianity in its present form. There was a progressivist bias to the article, for it promoted a rationalist stance, picking up Greg's echoing of Comtist notions of monotheism, and tracing his treatment of miracles back to Locke. She saw the respectful reception of his work, compared to the hostility which greeted editions of Hennell's *Inquiry* in 1838 and 1845, as evidence of the general 'advancement, either in plain thinking or in liberality of religious views'. She was also open-minded enough to praise the insights of Greg's 'earnest, cultivated mind' even though she noted his ignorance of recent scholarship.[64]

Writing of Christianity in her review of Greg's book, she commented that 'If Christianity be no longer regarded as a revelation, but as the conception of a fallible though transcendently gifted mind, it follows that only so much of it is to be accepted as harmonizes with the reason and conscience: Christianity becomes "Christian Eclecticism"'. Marian Evans, like many serious thinkers in the first half of the nineteenth century, tried to understand and appreciate the essential elements of religion. She approved the view that Christianity was 'a set of symbols' expressing a philosophic creed and admired Leigh Hunt's *The Religion of the Heart* which was also praised by the secularist, W. J. Holyoake.[65] Her attitude towards Christianity was in line with the views expressed in the Prospectus to the *Westminster Review* which she had written. The Prospectus promised that the magazine would undertake 'an uncompromising pursuit of truth'. It would examine fearlessly the 'elements of ecclesiastical authority and of dogma' and discuss 'without reservation', 'the results of the most advanced Biblical criticism'. The Editors pledged themselves 'not [to] shrink from the expression of what they believe to be sound negative views'. Yet freedom of inquiry was to form the basis for improved creeds, for it would be united with 'a spirit of reverential sympathy for the cherished associations of pure and elevated minds'. The editors were convinced that (and the sentiment recalled Feuerbach's views) 'religion has its foundation in man's nature, and will only discard an old form to assume and vitalize one more expressive of its essence'. They also promised to 'bear in mind the pre-eminent importance of a constructive religious philosophy, as connected with the development and activity of the moral nature, and of those poetic and emotional elements, out of which proceed our noblest aspirations and the essential beauty of life'. In commissioning articles, Marian Evans remained faithful to these principles. She asked James Martineau to make 'impartial inquiry' into the morality of the early Christians, but said that his article should 'do full justice to the positive side and endeavour clearly to define what we really owe to Christianity as a stage in the religious development of the race'.[66]

Under Marian Evans's editorship, each number of the *Westminster Review* contained at least one article on the cause of reform in England, and one on foreign politics, which were treated from a radical point of view. Her reassessment of Christianity informed her political views. Much criticism of the Anglican Church stemmed from the fact that it seemed inhumanly to sanction the terrible fate of the poor. Marian Evans charged Christianity not only with being opposed to 'the culture of the intellect and taste', but also with a 'passivity towards political and social abuses'. She had a strong sense of the inequalities of wealth, confessing 'half the things I have are "le superflu" for the majority of mankind'. After Chapman had visited Dickens, she reported ironically to Charles Bray: 'Splendid library, of course, with soft carpet, couches etc such as become a sympathizer with the suffering classes. How can we sufficiently pity the needy unless we know fully the blessings of plenty?' She read W. J. Fox's *Lectures Addressed Chiefly to the Working Classes* (4 vols, 1845–9) but, as in the 1840s, she was scathing about English political theorists, such as Robert Owen, Cobden, and Lord Brougham. Prompted, perhaps, by Barbara Smith's interest in the subject, she read John J. S. Wharton's book on the laws of England as they affected women.[67]

Most of her time was devoted to the *Westminster Review*, and she identified herself with that periodical's attempt to be a voice of radical, constructive and sceptical eclecticism. In composing the Prospectus, she toned down a note of crude radicalism which existed in the original draft, which led James Martineau to say that the editors were pandering to the mob; Greg and Haldane were to admire the rewritten statement of intent. The first number under her sub-editorship appeared on 1 January 1852, and the Prospectus defined her own intellectual stance, when it stated, 'Convinced that the same fundamental truths are apprehended under a variety of forms, and that, therefore, opposing systems may in the end prove complements of each other, the Editors will endeavour to institute such a radical and comprehensive treatment of those controverted questions which are practically momentous, as may aid in the conciliation of divergent views'. The emphasis upon synthesis and the relationship between intellectual controversy and human issues aligned the magazine's aims with the efforts of such thinkers as Mill and Carlyle. Mill himself was initially to criticise the Prospectus as insufficiently radical but, in the 1860s, was retrospectively to praise the magazine's stance. Eclectic tolerance was the keynote of Chapman and Marian Evans's policy, and in this the magazine echoed Mill's position in the late 1830s. The motto on the title page of the new *Westminster Review* was taken from Goethe: translated, it read 'Love of truth shown in this: that one know how to find good everywhere and to treasure it'.[68]

Marian Evans's degree of commitment to this intellectual crusade in its early and exciting days was demonstrated by her hard work to promote the periodical. One of her first tasks was to assemble a team of suitable contributors. Marian Evans, as the translator of Strauss, and Chapman, as a publisher of works expressing radical viewpoints, were only too aware of how reviewers could set up 'a mound of stupidity and unconscientiousness between every really new book and the public'. They recruited those who were sympathetic to the periodical's progressive policies, and contact with such minds doubtless helped to strengthen Marian Evans's confidence in her own opinions. Carlyle, J. S. Mill, Leigh Hunt and R. W. Mackay were approached. Harriet Martineau became a regular contributor; J. A. Froude, whose novel Marian Evans had enthusiastically reviewed in the 1840s, was also sounded out. Lewes's services were enlisted, although she remarked: 'Defective as his articles are, they are the best we can get *of the kind*'. One of his articles appeared in nearly every number she edited. Pioneer articles were published, such as John Oxenford's study of Schopenhauer. Her team of writers included many who were to become the most eminent minds of the age, and they helped the *Westminster Review* to regain its former illustrious reputation. It became, arguably, the most distinguished voice of advanced opinion in the mid-Victorian period. Combe thought it 'the most important means of enlightenment of a literary nature in existence', and Marian Evans wrote to Chapman of their contributors, with a justifiable pride, 'These men can write more openly in the Westminster than anywhere else. They are amongst the world's vanguard, though not all in the foremost line; it is good for the world, therefore, that they should have every facility for speaking out'.[69]

In the service of the cause, her work involved much more than the pleasant task of seeking out talented writers. From Broadstairs in 1852, she wrote Chapman a letter which revealed the variety of tasks involved in her editorial duties. She dealt with letters from would-be contributors and from those already commissioned to write articles. She coped with unsolicited review copies and negotiated with writers, and with Chapman, about the space to be allocated to any one article. She consulted with Chapman about overall policy, made mistakes about stamping parcels, suggested topics for future articles and suitable writers of them. She kept an eye on what other magazines were doing, on current controversies and new publications. She meticulously scrutinised style. She was also well-placed to inspect the progress of the art of fiction. One of her first tasks at 142 Strand was to proofread Miss Lynn's *Realities*. She also had special responsibility for the Contemporary Literature section which appeared in each issue of the magazine. She continued to allude, in her letters of this time, to novelists who were her long-established favourites, to George Sand, Scott and Richardson, but the prolific references to contemporary writers, to Dickens, Hawthorne, Stowe, Thackeray, Gaskell and Charlotte Brontë were a new departure, and contrasted forcibly to the paucity of such references in the letters she wrote during the 1840s. References to Austen and Balzac probably indicated Lewes's influence. She had ample opportunity to see how English novelists were studying the humanity Feuerbach had seen as of primary concern for the trained mind. Her involvement with the native tradition of fiction was perhaps another clue as to the direction she was finally to take: Chapman had initially engaged her to write on foreign literature, which demonstrated his awareness of the former bias of her tastes and expertise.[70]

Robert Evans had left his youngest child between eighty and one hundred pounds a year for the rest of her life and this was her sole income. Chapman paid her nothing at all, and she told Combe that lack of money was the reason why she decided to give up the *Westminster Review*. Her work brought her no wide acclaim, for initially, her editorship was a secret. When she took on the task, she agreed to do anything 'really for the interest of the Review'. Infatuation with Chapman may have played a part in her initial decision to help him with his new venture but, when that had vanished, her defensive loyalty to him as an innovatory publisher remained, even though she was aware of his intellectual limitations. She associated herself with Chapman's disinterested zeal that truth should prevail: both she and Chapman considered that free inquiry and the reconciliation of divergent truths crucially benefitted mankind. This shared conviction motivated her to defend the *Westminster Review* and its owner amidst many difficulties. Financial support was given to the magazine by Birch in 1851, by Grote and Mill in 1852, yet money problems continued amidst criticism from Chapman's friends and associates. Marian Evans vindicated Chapman from the vantage point of her intimate knowledge of the difficulties attendant upon the review's mission. In the summer of 1852, she chided Combe and Charles Bray for their carping comments, and, in 1853, she told Bray that Chapman did 'his best in everything . . . I know no one who works harder or seeks fewer indulgences than he'.[71]

Her dedication to the aims of the *Westminster Review* which were furthered by her tasks as 'something less than half an editor' was demonstrated by the fact that she remained working on the magazine for as long as she did. Many factors encouraged her to resign. The work was arduous; it kept her in London, which she often hated. She was unpaid; the periodical was plagued with financial troubles; the atmosphere at 142 Strand was often electric with Chapman's emotional problems. She remained even when alternatives offered themselves. Chapman asked her to write a book on 'The Idea of a Future Life' and to translate Feuerbach. She started to contribute articles to the *Leader*. Her friendship with Lewes was deepening into love, and she contemplated a complete change in her way of life. On 22 January 1853 she decided to leave 142 Strand; in February of the same year, she spoke of giving up the editorship. On 17 October, she moved to 21 Cambridge Street, near Hyde Park, and from that time dated her serious commitment to Lewes. Yet she did not announce her decision to give up the editorship to Chapman until 24 November. The connection finally ended on 1 January 1854. Her reluctance was significant: in the pages of the *Westminster Review* was embodied the principle of free inquiry. She also found there a medium for articulating her ideas about the eclectic process whereby truth might be ascertained, and the periodical directed its attention to those problems which the debate about logical method raised. Despite pleas that she was 'out of spirits' with the task, and that the work was 'not satisfactory and I should be glad to run away from it altogether', she cared sufficiently about the periodical's aims to console herself for a long time with the fact that 'one thing is clear – that the Review would be a great deal worse if I were not here'.[72] Humdrum and unsung though most of her work was, in its promotion of an intellectual viewpoint it bore witness to that creative potential whose slow growth was seen by Bessie Parkes and Herbert Spencer as the keynote of Marian Evans's early years in London. Her relationship with Lewes, her exploration of the implications of the philosophical debate in articles for the periodical press, were both slowly to edge that burgeoning creativity further in the direction which transformed Marian Evans, translator, editor and journalist, into George Eliot, novelist.

16

George Henry Lewes to 1850

He knew little, and that not until late in life, of the subtle interweaving of habit with affection, which makes life saturated with love, and love itself become dignified through the serious aims of life. He knew little of the exquisite *companionship* of two souls striving in emulous spirit of loving rivalry to become better, to become wiser, teaching each other to soar.[1]

On 6 May 1880, George Eliot became Mrs John Cross. Reflecting upon the marriage four months later, Edith Simcox thought of Lewes, and opined flatly, 'she will miss the active intellectual companionship'.[2] The man Marian Evans lived with for twenty-four years without the legal tie of marriage spent his first three and a half decades in a fashion which was such as to engage Marian Evans's sympathy and interest when their paths finally crossed. Their preoccupations often ran mysteriously parallel in the years before they met. Lewes was born in 1817 and came from a theatrical family: his grandfather was a comic actor, and his father both actor and theatre manager. His education was unconventional and his intelligence, like that of Marian Evans and many progressive Victorians, conspired with his background to render him *declassé*. He was educated at private schools in Boulogne, Brittany and St Helier, which gave him a good command of the French language and, as George Sand observed, a character, 'more French than English'.[3] He left his last school in Greenwich in 1833, and was subsequently employed as a clerk in a notary's office and in the counting-room of a Russian merchant. For a time he studied medicine, which left him with a permanent interest in the life sciences. In 1837 he described himself as 'a student living a quiet life'. During this period, he spent a good deal of time at the theatre, and his interest in philosophy commenced. He discussed philosophy with William Bell Scott, and he acquired Carlyle, the inspirer of George Eliot's youthful scepticism, as an unofficial teacher. Visits to a club in Holborn gave Lewes insight into the world of educated artisans, and his early political radicalism originated in his vision of the 'pinching poverty' of the Jewish watchmaker, Cohen, whom he met there. Marian Evans, during her church-going crisis, had turned to the *Tractatus Theologico-Politicus*, and the young Lewes also identified with Spinoza, to whose works Cohen had introduced him, because he felt that he, like Spinoza, was 'suffering the social persecution which embitters all departure from accepted creeds'. The club discussions fostered Lewes's intellectual radicalism for most of the members were 'anti-mystics', and Lewes boldly described Spinoza's thought as 'the grandest and most religious of all philosophies'. Spinoza's ideas on the subjectivity of the concept of evil, the noble example of his life, which showed that morality was distinct from adherence to orthodox Christian doctrines, encouraged Lewes's ethical heterodoxy. Spinoza's eclectic blending of seemingly disparate logical methods and doctrines was profoundly influential upon Lewes as it was upon Marian Evans. Lewes started a translation of the *Ethics* in 1836, and wrote on Spinoza in the *Penny Cyclopaedia* in 1843. Marian Evans translated the *Tractatus* in the early 1840s, and the *Ethics* in 1855. Their joint library contained a host of editions of, and commentaries upon, his work.[4]

Lewes embarked early upon his literary career. In 1834, he wrote a short story and a poem which attracted the attention of the progressive journalist Leigh Hunt. Hunt, with Carlyle and later, John Stuart Mill, formed the triumvirate of Lewes's mentors and with Hunt's son, Thornton, Lewes's destiny became inextricably entwined. Radical Unitarianism was an element in the intellectual *milieu* of the young Lewes as it was in that of the young Marian Evans. Lewes contributed articles to the *Monthly Repository* which Leigh Hunt was co-editing with R. H. Horne and, via this connection, the twenty-year-old Lewes came to lecture at Finsbury Chapel in 1837: under William Fox's direction, the chapel was associated with freedom of inquiry, and controversial thinkers were invited to speak there.[5] Marian Evans met Fox at Rosehill, and, in 1843, was bridesmaid to Rufa Brabant when she married Charles Hennell in Finsbury Chapel. As Marian Evans, under Carlyle's influence, was conceiving a desire to learn German, Lewes too was becoming interested in German writing. He found in German writing that fusion of philosophy and literature which so aptly matched his own interests: Lewes, like Marian Evans, Carlyle and Mill, saw speculation as concerned with the practical problems of life itself as it had been in German literature. His early knowledge of the subject placed him, as it placed Marian Evans, within the intellectual progressive minority. After his death, Edith Simcox was shown a letter 'from a German who said how few writers either German or English understood equally the philosophy – or even the philosophical languages of the 2 countries as he did'.[6] Lewes had, before 1838, read Coleridge's works and echoed in his writings German ideas gleaned from secondary sources. In July 1838, he purchased a copy of *German Romance* and, inspired by a curiosity about German literature which Carlyle stimulated, and prompted by a wanderlust which never left him, he left for Germany that same year. Carlyle provided him with an introduction to Varnhagen von Ense, and Lewes learnt German and supported himself by teaching English and writing articles for English periodicals. He lived in Germany during the heyday of Hegelianism, and von Ense presented him with a copy of Hegel's *Aesthetik* which Lewes diligently annotated.[7] Lewes returned to England in 1839 and established himself as part of the progressive group centred around Leigh Hunt. He also met, and in 1841 married, Agnes Jervis. Four sons were born to them between 1842 and 1848. The marriage was, by Victorian standards, a liberated one. Agnes's inheritance, plus her translation and adaptation of articles from French and Spanish, augmented their income as Lewes settled down to the precarious existence of a freelance writer. Agnes also tolerated Lewes's absences. He went to France in 1842 and 1847, was in Berlin in 1845, where he heard Schelling lecture, and toured the north of England in 1849. These years were energetic and hopeful, even if not especially prosperous. Lewes was convinced of the importance of his chosen profession for he, like Marian Evans, had imbibed Carlyle's views about the serious role of the writer. In 1845, he wrote cheerfully of 'the aristocracy of intellect' replacing an aristocracy of birth. He saw intelligence as 'the great social power . . . in the only true sense – of directing the souls, and consequently the acts, of men', and he argued for the excitement to be gained from ideas. He criticised writers who lacked a sense of the dignity and importance of their 'mission', but he also emphasised the happiness to be gained from literary creation.[8] 'Those who draw their greatest enjoyments from within', he reflected, 'can readily dispense with luxury: and poverty is the stimulus to endeavour.' Lewes contemplated the decline of the English theatre, and soon became one of the most important Victorian critics of drama; his book, *The Spanish Drama*, appeared in 1846. He also adapted foreign plays. Yet, as he noted in 1847, writing for the theatre was very poorly paid, and he also returned to the family profession and acted in some of the plays he adapted. He appeared at the Whitehall Theatre in 1841, and turned to acting again after appearing with Dickens's amateur company in 1847 and 1848.[9]

The most important work Lewes produced during these years was *A Biographical History of Philosophy* (4 vols, 1845–6) which was based upon the lectures Lewes had given in 1837 at Finsbury Chapel. Although frowned upon by some academics, it was widely influential, even finding a degree of acceptance at Oxford and Cambridge. It was also a financial success. By 1856, 40,000 copies had been sold; a third edition appeared in 1867, and a fourth in 1871.[10] Lewes was well qualified to write such a work, for, like Marian Evans, he was, from an early age, conversant with the rival philosophical schools. His years in France, his connections with Cohen and the Unitarians, had given him contact with a tradition of speculation biased towards rationalism; his reading of Coleridge and his friendship with Carlyle, as well as his stay in Germany, had allowed him to consider both the critical disseminators of Idealism in England and Idealism's original exponents. However, in 1840 Lewes met Mill, with whom he discussed *A System of Logic*, the work which encapsulated Mill's eclectic stance. Mill introduced Lewes not only to his own anti-sectarian bias, but also, possibly as early as 1840, to the work of Auguste Comte. Marian Evans also encountered Comte's ideas in the early 1840s. Lewes met Comte in 1842. The influences of Mill and Comte gave Lewes's thought a bias which was evident in *A Biographical History of Philosophy*, for Lewes's friendship with Mill coincided with the period when Mill felt the most sympathy for Comte's views. Mill read and praised Lewes's manuscript as he worked on it although, in later years, Mill commented scathingly that he never expected anything 'profound either in philosophy or scholarship' from Lewes.[11] Lewes's section on Plato was reminiscent of Mill's articles on the same topic which appeared in the *Monthly Repository* in the 1830s. Lewes also inherited Mill's mantle as one of the earliest English critics of, and propagandists for, Comte, for he followed up the plea which Mill had entered for Comte in the *Logic*. Lewes wished to reach a wide audience with his Comtist propaganda, and *A Biographical History of Philosophy* appeared over a period of two years in volumes costing one shilling each in Knight's Weekly Volume Series. The lucid exposition of ideas and the style were tailored to a popular audience. The liveliness of Lewes's narrative prose was well exemplified, for instance, in his description of the life of Socrates, although this quality was criticised as 'hardly consistent with the grave discussion of philosophical question'.[12]

Lewes responded enthusiastically to Comte's work for various reasons. Like Comte, and many of his English admirers, such as Marian Evans, Lewes was a man of wide interests, and Comte's synthesis gave full play to, and explanation of, many of them. Lewes was to evolve the view that all disciplines contributed to an overall view of the world.[13] The 1840s were also a decade when, because of the turbulent political situation, social prophecy was much in vogue. Initially, and this was true of Marian Evans too, many of the early English Positivists were attracted to Comte's work because of his theory of history, which seemed to shed light on their own problematical context. Lewes was, however, like Marian Evans at a similar stage, and like his mentors, Mill and Carlyle, vitally concerned with the rival logical methods and the kind of truth each could attain: the focus of *A Biographical History of Philosophy* was upon the processes by which knowledge was sought, and the kinds of truth these processes yielded. The book made an impact because of its patently ideological standpoint, and in 1846, Lewes was termed 'a disciple of Comte' because he was 'an advocate of positive knowledge'.[14] Comte himself recognised the bias of the work by his inclusion of it, in 1851, in his *Bibliothèque Prolétaire*. Lewes did not aim at a comprehensive scope, but selectively dealt only with such thinkers 'as represent the various phases of progressive development; and only such opinions as were connected with those phases'. Nor did he claim to be impartial, for he envisaged the work as 'a contribution to the History of Humanity', and sought to show 'how and by what steps Philosophy became Positive Science; in other words, by what Methods the Human Mind was enabled to conquer for itself, in the long struggle of centuries, its present modicum of certain knowledge'.[15]

Comte's theory of progress, conceived in terms of humanity's intellectual development, pervaded the work. Lewes distinguished centrally between Metaphysics (Comte's second stage of knowledge) and Positive Science (Comte's third stage) which Lewes associated with a tradition of inductive reasoning and scientific inquiry. Lewes asserted that 'the Infinite cannot be known by the finite; man can only know phenomena'. Metaphysics aspired to know '*Essences* and *Causes*', and was criticised 'as an impossible attempt . . . it never has had any certitude, never can have any'. Its practitioners were 'too apt to argue without reference to the facts'. Progress in metaphysics was impossible. The survival of metaphysics in Germany was seen as a sign of backwardness in that nation; an anti-rational philosophy was, like religion and theology, an obstacle to science which, unlike metaphysics, provided more limited, but more certain knowledge. The large but empty claims of metaphysics were contrasted to positive science which was concerned with the 'knowledge of *Laws*' and showed a limitless capacity for 'slow and gradual developments'. Yet Lewes's advocacy of empirical scientism was crucially modified. Like the writers both he and Marian Evans read in the 1840s, Lewes wished to arbitrate between extremes: he yearned, as had Comte, for a synthesis of logical methods. Although Lewes conceded that life was ultimately an enigma, he suggested that 'in what ways, and under what conditions it manifests itself, may be discovered by proper investigations'. He defended the use of the *a priori* in science, for he was critical of the scientist who was a mere fact-collector.[16]

Lewes also agreed with Comte's view that metaphysics constituted an essential stage in 'the education of the human race'. Despite his proclaimed Comtist hostility to metaphysics, his fascination with it, acquired in the 1830s, led him to devote much space and some praise to the writers Coleridge and Carlyle had introduced to an English audience, and these were the same writers who had fascinated Marian Evans. This ambivalent attitude towards Idealism may be traced to the influence of both Carlyle and Mill. When Lewes met Carlyle, the older man was known as a propagandist for the Germans, but thought of himself as having moved beyond the period in which they had most influenced him. Mill, in the *Logic*, tempered empiricism by reference to the insights of writers within other traditions. Whilst noting wryly that 'Intelligibility is not the characteristic of German speculation', Lewes provided lucid accounts of Fichte and Schelling, and he considered the theological offshoots of Idealism in the work of Schleiermacher, Strauss and Feuerbach. He noted of Hegel that 'his ideas, if repugnant to what we regard as the truth are yet so coherent, so systematically developed, and the whole matter so obviously coming from matured meditation, that we have always risen from the perusal with a sense of the author's greatness'; and he spoke with interest of the *Geschichte der Philosophie* (Berlin 1833). He defended Kant against charges of mysticism, saying that he created 'a system of philosophy . . . which for rigour, clearness, and, above all, intelligibility, surpasses, by many degrees, systems hitherto considered easy enough of comprehension'. Marian Evans echoed this opinion in 1865.[17]

A professed antagonism to the methods and claims of metaphysical philosophy, coupled with a discriminatingly sympathetic treatment of some of its exponents, illuminates the central contradiction of Lewes's supposedly Comtist propaganda. Lewes's perception of the philosophical dilemma mirrored the experience of Marian Evans, as well as of Mill and Carlyle. The choice between truth as process and truth as system presented itself to Lewes in dramatic terms as between 'a yawning gulf of scepticism, or a baseless cloud-land of Idealism'. One aspect of his work extolled those philosophers who had been concerned to establish a method of inquiry. Lewes commended Bacon and spoke admiringly of Mill's *Logic* as having done 'more for the education of the scientific intellect' than the work of any other philosopher. The invention of a method was 'perhaps the greatest effort of philosophical genius, and the most deserving of the historian's attention. . . . Whoso discovers a path whereon mankind may travel in quest of truth, has done more towards the discovery of truth than thousands of men merely speculating'. He believed, as he stated in 1845, that a writer's task was 'to stimulate inquiry, not to prevent it; to make the reader think truly . . . to make him work by stimulating and assisting, not by doing all the work for him'.[18] In dealing with systems, Lewes claimed his scepticism would ensure impartiality, since 'believing no one system to be truer than another, though it may be more plausible, we can calmly appreciate the value of every one'. The scientific method suggested an open-ended quest for truth, yet Lewes had been sufficiently impressed by Hegelianism to see the value of systems. He was aware that systems had profound personal and social implications: after visiting Germany, he deplored the intellectual anarchy of the post-Hegelian school and its reduction of philosophy to a purely academic pursuit. Comte aimed at a comprehensive synthesis and geared it to practical ends.[19]

Lewes praised, as did others of his generation, those writers who mediated between extremes. In aesthetics, he was to discern the need for a resolution of 'the tension between empiricism and abstraction',[20] for he considered that truth should be sought by combining logical methods. He commended Anaxagoras for linking Sensationalism and Idealism. The eclectic method of merging opposed concepts was employed by Lewes: he noted that the cyclic view of history did not preclude a notion of linear progress, a view which he may well have imbibed from Carlyle's musings on historiography in the 1830s. Yet Lewes insisted that eclecticism could only be a '*subsidiary* process', and that the revision of method alone was no solution to intellectual and social anarchy. In this respect, his views differed from those evolved by Mill and Carlyle in the 1830s. Lewes discussed the systems of Leroux and Saint-Simon. He thought that the *Cours* was the '*opus magnum* of our age', and emphasised the unity of Comte's system. Between the scientist's concern for detail, and the metaphysician's generalities, Comte offered a middle way. He had solved the problem of logical method, and had built a system on this new basis which was 'destined to put an end to this anarchy, by presenting a doctrine *positive*, because elaborated from the sciences, and yet possessing all the desired *generality* of metaphysical doctrines, without possessing their vagueness, instability, and inapplicability'.[21] Scepticism, coupled with a yearning for general truths, and the sense of the practical implications of a philosophical position were to be feelings both Marian Evans and Lewes shared.

Ranthorpe, Lewes's first novel, was written in 1842 and dedicated affectionately to Agnes: it was published five years later. The autobiographical elements in the novel gave glimpses into the early years of Lewes's literary life. He described vividly the young author dreaming of fame, the world of London journalism, the disillusioning experiences of Ranthorpe in the theatre. The intoxicating romance of being a writer was obvious when Ranthorpe was a drama critic: 'the printing office, dirty, murky, and ill-ventilated, was a sacred spot to him. He rejoiced in the gaseous-heated atmosphere; he loved the smell of ink and damp paper'.[22] Lewes's inglorious career as a novelist was to stand him in good stead as the future companion of Marian Evans, the novelist-to-be. Writing novels gave him insight into the potential of fiction as a mode of expression.

The nineteenth-century novel offered virtually unlimited freedom of expression to the versatile mind, and for such reasons it was to be adopted by Marian Evans as a mode of expression. Lewes took full and undisciplined advantage of the genre's flexibility. The novel's thematic focus was extremely uncertain. In dealing with the maturing of the hero, the novel was indebted to *Wilhelm Meister*, and Lewes used the novel as a vehicle for ideas he culled from the works of both Goethe and Carlyle. He discussed the contrast between passion and intellect and preached the importance of will power. As the plot reached its climax, Ranthorpe reached the ideal Carlyle saw embodied in Goethe's life; he had 'walked up through mists, but has reached a certain height. The storms are below him'.[23] Lewes's plot was digressive and full of preposterous coincidences and melodramatic and sentimental incidents; its different strands were not closely interwoven, and its mood changed with startling abruptness.

In the 1840s, Marian Evans was tentatively expressing in her letters views which assigned elevated functions to the writer and to art. At the same time, Lewes was airing his idealistic notions about authorship. He spoke, as in the article he wrote for *Hood's* in 1845, of the author's serious 'mission', of the new aristocracy of intellect, and of the joy of literary creativity. In *Ranthorpe*, Lewes frequently defined the imaginative writer's role, as did Marian Evans, in terms which were reminiscent of Carlyle and, in Lewes's case, of Carlyle's exegesis of Goethe. Goethe was quoted at the start of the first three books, and Carlyle's translation of *Wilhelm Meister* was cited at the start of Chapter 10 of Book III. Lewes thought seriously about the function of literature. He saw art as opposed to utilitarian values, and genius as the power to transform sorrow into art, thus restoring the writer to happiness. Ranthorpe was rescued from despair by Thornton, an old man who was a friend of Goethe, and who was modelled on Carlyle. Ranthorpe's life at the end of the novel fulfilled 'the true ideal of an author's life', for it was 'one of activity and happiness'.[24]

In March 1848 Lewes finished writing his second novel, *Rose, Blanche and Violet* (1849). Part of it was read with little enthusiasm by Marian Evans when she was staying at Broadstairs in 1852.[25] The novel once more drew closely upon Lewes's personal experiences and preoccupations. The settings were often those he and Agnes must have come to know well, dingy suburban lodging-houses and London literary parties. Lewes digressed from his narrative to discuss the state of the drama, the English obsession with respectability, and the corruption of the English electoral system.[26] His technical ineptitude was once more apparent. He mixed epistolary and omniscient narratives for no useful reason; the plot lacked direction and was frequently melodramatic, especially when it made excursions into the seedy worlds of gambling and prostitution. In the novel, Lewes spoke once more of the importance of the writer's task, and the hard work it involved, and he saw his second novel as breaking new ground. Like Marian Evans in the letters she wrote in the latter half of the 1840s, he contemplated the relationship between art and reality, and contrasted a true view of reality to the falsified view presented by many novels.[27] Lewes linked his views on this topic to a consideration of literary didacticism, a subject raised by Marian Evans in her comments on Rousseau and George Sand. In line with a growing critical trend which condemned overt moralising, Lewes stated that he had been faced with 'a choice between truth of passion and character . . . and . . . didactic clearness. I could not hesitate in choosing the former', and he quoted Hegel in support of this view, an author Marian Evans had quoted in a similar discussion with John Sibree.[28]

Lewes attempted to embody life's complex truth in his portrayal of people. *Ranthorpe* had shown his penchant for aphoristic psychological analysis and the fascination with abnormal psychology which he shared with his friend Dickens. In *Rose, Blanche and Violet*, these trends became more pronounced. He asserted the mystery and complications of human nature, arguing that the mind was not 'like a mathematical problem', but was a 'bundle of motives, of prejudices, and of passions'. He focused upon the gambler's psychology, a theme George Eliot later explored more subtly in *Daniel Deronda*, just as in her portrayal of the Ladislaw/Casaubon/Dorothea triangle, she was to echo Lewes's portrayal of the relationship between Mr and Mrs Vyner and Marmaduke.[29] The concept of what distinguished male from female psychology had been floated in *Ranthorpe*, and was explored in greater depth in *Rose, Blanche and Violet*. Lewes distinguished between women as they really were, and the idealised pictures of women which appeared in novels, and spoke of the extent to which the male view of women was ignorant and prejudiced. The names of three women provided the novel's title, and Rose and Violet were types of the New Woman. Violet was 'exquisitely feminine', yet showed energy and enterprise, driving off a raging bull with a whip as her cowardly lover fled in fright. She had 'the virile energy and strength of will' usually possessed only by men. Rose was a 'lively girl' who showed 'masculine strength of mind' in the 'stoic courage' with which she faced the discovery that her lover was having an affair with her step-mother. Lewes also created the grotesque Mrs Vyner, a charismatic, golden-haired hunchback, as a specimen of female idiosyncracy.[30]

If *Ranthorpe* owed much of its inspiration to Goethe and Carlyle, it was two French novelists who inspired *Rose, Blanche and Violet*. German writers were still referred to, and Carlyle's terminology and ideas were echoed, but were subordinate to the influences of Balzac and, to a greater extent, George Sand. The portrayal of the passions existing beneath a surface of provincial calm owed something to Balzac's example. Lewes took, however, his title from George Sand's novel, *Rose et Blanche*, and it was George Sand who was frequently cited.[31] Marian Evans, in the 1840s, was fascinated by the complex method of George Sand's art which embodied a sceptical philosophical stance learnt from Rousseau, in the light of which the ideas of Rousseau and other French post-Enlightenment philosophers were considered. Lewes simply echoed in his novels the obvious and often potentially sensational themes of the French novelist. He utilised the setting of the isolated country house where the characters fell in and out of love; he brooded upon different types of love. George Sand's heroines inspired Lewes's ambivalent portrayal of the poetess, Hester Mason. He inveighed against learned women, and described Hester's salon and the unappealing literary women who surrounded her. His criticisms of the silliness of women writers anticipated Marian Evans's article, 'Silly Novels by Lady Novelists' (1856). Yet to some extent Hester was treated sympathetically. She echoed Lewes's and George Sand's radical sentiments, saying that man's mission was 'to place Man in majestic antagonism to Convention; to erect the Banner of Progress, and give the democratic Mind of Europe its unfettered sphere of action'. She emphasised that the reorganisation of society must lead to equal rights for women. She rebelled against the Christian and conservative views of women and marriage which she found in the provinces; she had a 'freedom of manner' which shocked respectable people. As a sop to his less liberal readers, Lewes had Hester's protector die as she was about to marry him, and she eventually turned to prostitution. Yet Lewes's attitude shifted again as he showed the prudish censoriousness of provincial society towards her when she was restored to her family. Ultimately, he assented to Hester's view that a double sexual standard existed; she noted 'Purity, which is supposed to be woman's greatest virtue, is never thought of in a man'.[32] Hester was a George Sand heroine as Saint-Simonian rebel, a theme Lewes returned to in *The Apprenticeship of Life*, and Lewes, the heterodox thinker, showed his sympathy for her as far as the strictures of conventional morality allowed.

First novels, Lewes noted, rarely paid.[33] As a novelist, Lewes was undoubtedly a failure, but his practice of the art gave him an insight into it which made him one of the most perceptive critics of the genre. He saw the writing of fiction as a serious activity, in no way inferior to seemingly more intellectual disciplines, and Marian Evans's articles in the *Westminster Review* in the 1850s were to echo his general view, as well as many of his specific notions about the aims of fiction. Lewes utterly denied a 'novel being a waste of time'. He urged high standards for fiction, and helped to pave the way for the high quality of English fiction in the latter half of the nineteenth century. He confessed his pleasure in reading good novels, for, with such, the genre 'rises into the first rank of literature'.[34] Lewes invoked a standard of truthfulness to life as a yardstick for excellence in fiction: he commented that 'incidents however wonderful, adventures however perilous, are almost as nought when compared with the deep and lasting interest excited by any thing like a correct representation of life. That, indeed, seems to us to be Art, and the only Art we care to applaud'. He criticised those elements in fiction whereby the novelist distorted reality. He castigated didacticism, melodrama and sensationalism, although his own novels often contained the last two elements.[35] In reviewing Balzac's *Le Cousin Pons*, he praised the 'Dutch painter in prose' of the first half of the novel, criticised the sensationalism of the latter half. Marian Evans spoke of the 'precocious justness of his appreciations' in his early criticism and, as a spotter of new talent, Lewes was acutely sensitive. He championed *Wuthering Heights* when it baffled others; he pleaded the cause of *Jane Eyre* in more than one review because 'Reality – deep significant reality – is the great characteristic of the book'.[36]

Lewes started to read George Sand's novels in 1839, and George Sand herself noted in 1846 that Lewes 'has my work by heart and knows the *Lettres d'un voyageur* much better than I do'.[37] In the mid-1840s, when the moral tendencies of French fiction were frowned upon, Marian Evans defended George Sand's novels to Cara Bray and Sara Hennell in Coventry as Lewes defended them in the metropolitan periodical press. Lewes pleaded her cause after the attack launched on her in 1836, claiming that she was 'the most remarkable writer of the present century'. To liken other novelists, such as Thornton Hunt and Charlotte Brontë, to George Sand was to pay them the highest compliment Lewes could devise.[38] In the 1840s, Marian Evans was drawn to the works of J. A. Froude and George Sand because they incorporated ideas into their fictions. As another disciple of Carlyle, Lewes likewise was interested in the interfusion of speculative notions into literature so evident in German writers. Like Carlyle, he also contemplated literature's capacity to offer spiritual solutions. On both counts, George Sand attracted his attention. He grasped, as did Marian Evans, the idiosyncratic fashion in which ideas entered into her novels, and his knowledge of French intellectual history enabled him to detect at work those influences of which Marian Evans had likewise been aware. He noted George Sand's response to the ideas of Saint-Simon, Leroux, Rousseau and Lamenais.[39] Moreover, although he deplored those of her novels such as *Lélia* which seemed exaggeratedly sceptical, he denied that she was an immoral novelist. Because of the very fashion in which she pondered ideas, he saw her fiction as deeply moral and obliquely didactic. Her novels were the expression of a search for truth, rather than a statement of solutions. Just as Marian Evans had quoted Hegel when defining her views on art, so Lewes noted in relation to George Sand: '"From every work of art", says Hegel, "a good moral is to be drawn; but then this is a *deduction*, and indeed entirely depends on *him that* draws it." No work is immoral which is true – all are when false'. He merged Hegel's views with a paraphrase of ideas George Sand expressed in, for instance, *François le champi* (1850), commenting that 'Although a *narrative* is not a *demonstration*, and cannot be made one; although . . . in the strict sense of the word, Art *proves* nothing; yet . . . the details of a narrative may be grouped so as to satisfy the mind like a sermon. It is an exhortation . . . not a demonstration, but it does not the less appeal to our moral sense'.[40] A later review further clarified Lewes's attitude. He criticised George Sand's hasty composition of the works she produced for newspapers, but continued to defend her moral influence. He also stated that he preferred her 'as an artist' to 'a philosopher', but other comments revealed an uncertainty behind this judgment. He commended her as a 'painter of passion and character' and noted that her portrayal of the Bricolins in *Le Meunier d'Angibault* was 'a Dutch painting for life-like effect'. He criticised the expression of Saint-Simonian ideas in *Isidora*. Yet representation alone was seen as insufficient. He commended the way in which she integrated discussion of philosophical ideas into her novel, and noted that the picture of the Bricolins had 'a deeper meaning than any Dutch painter ever cared for'.[41] Lewes had by no means resolved in his own mind the tension between impartial picture-making and the interpretative vision, and this was to be evident in his last, and unfinished, novel, *The Apprenticeship of Life*. Behind his contemplation of the problem lay his concern with the rival philosophical notions of particular and general truths; similar philosophical preoccupations informed Marian Evans's evaluation of George Sand and her later decision to write fiction.

Like Marian Evans, Lewes was a polymath, and versatility was to characterise his life's work. His journalism was prolific and appeared in a host of periodicals. He wrote on Italian and Greek, as well as Spanish and English drama, and on classical topics. He wrote about Shakespeare, Lamb, Goldsmith, Keats and Shelley, and about newer English authors such as Browning. Like Carlyle and Marian Evans, he pioneered the study of German writers in England, turning to good account his stay in Germany. He produced articles on Schlegel, Niebuhr, Hegel and Goethe, but, like Carlyle in the late 1830s and Marian Evans in the 1850s, he was capable of a detached assessment of German literature. He was critical of the abstract and obscure tendencies of German speculation, which showed a 'universal tendency towards whatever is most remote from human interest, – indeed, from human comprehension'. In Lessing, however, he found much that he admired: an erudition turned towards practical purposes, an oblique didacticism, a disassociation of religion and morality and an anti-sectarian tolerance of others' opinions. He commended, in a Comtean spirit, Lessing's stand against the futility of metaphysics. Marian Evans, Carlyle and Mill proposed, at various junctures, the notion of the relativity of truths, and saw the quest for truth as endless. Lewes praised Lessing's 'scepticism as to the possibility of man's ever attaining absolute truth; not scepticism as to the virtue of the endeavour. Truth can only be sought, not found . . . Lessing declares that if the choice were offered him, he should prefer the search after truth to the attainment of truth'.[42] Two years after Marian Evans's translation of Strauss appeared, Lewes saw the higher criticism as she saw it, as demonstrating truths about the progressive tendency of mankind's intellectual development, a concept eminently reconcilable with Comte's analysis. He praised Strauss's pamphlet criticising Frederick William IV's 'feeble ambition of arresting the course of modern development, by a restoration of the defunct spirit of the Middle Ages'.[43]

In 1847, at the age of thirty, Lewes laid claim to a cosmopolitan viewpoint when he confidently compared the condition of authors in France, England and Germany.[44] Like Marian Evans, Lewes inhabited a mental landscape which was indebted to the intellectual life of Germany and France, as well as to that of England. His early education in France, and subsequent visits there, fired an enthusiasm for French writers. He wrote about Sue and Dumas as well as George Sand. During the 1840s, he was reading the works of those French historians who sympathised with radical ideas, a taste which echoes Marian Evans's fascination with French radicalism at the same juncture. This interest was fostered by the progressive circles in which Lewes moved, but his 1849 article on Guizot suggested that the parlous state of Europe intensified his concern with French revolutionary thought. Lewes focused upon Guizot's countering of Socialist theories, and was critical of his failure to define democracy and to suggest clear alternatives to it. Lewes also produced articles on Mignet and Michelet, and on French historiography and moral philosophy. More specifically, Lewes's contact with Mill and Carlyle, who spent much of the 1830s evolving political views which were related to a philosophical stance, inspired Lewes's *Life of Robespierre*. His knowledge of French philosophy was evident in the ease with which he sketched in the intellectual background to Robespierre's life. He considered the views of Condorcet, and discussed at length the influence exerted upon French political thinking by Rousseau.[45] Rousseau was the great inspiration of Marian Evans when she was in her twenties, but Lewes dismissed him scathingly, saying his 'love of paradox was almost an idiosyncracy'. The list of sources Lewes used for *Robespierre* demonstrated his immersion in French history, and his radical contacts were evident when he acknowledged the loan of manuscripts from 'my friend M. Louis Blanc'.[46]

Carlyle's influence pervaded the biography, and Carlyle had

been encouraged in his study of the French Revolution by Lewes's other mentor, Mill. Lewes's use of italicisation, inverted syntax, French phrases and rhetorical questions imitated the style of *The French Revolution*. Carlyle's work was acknowledged in Lewes's list of sources, and was quoted in the course of the narrative; the descriptions of Mirabeau and the opening of the States General borrowed heavily from Carlyle. The idea of truthful representation Lewes proposed for fiction was echoed in *Robespierre*; he insisted, in emulation of Carlyle's *The French Revolution*, that he aimed merely to present an impartial picture.[47] The book was a hastily assembled compilation from secondary sources, yet Lewes's practice in the art of fiction enabled him to give the narrative a sprightly pace. He presented Robespierre as neither monster nor hero; he aimed to furnish only 'the data upon which a judgment . . . may be formed'.[48] Yet Lewes could not resist didactic interpretation of the events of the revolution and Robespierre's life; Carlyle had often based his biographies around an idea. The discrediting of the ideology of revolution in 1848 led Lewes to see, as Carlyle had seen, urgently instructive analogies between the 1789 revolution and Europe in the late 1840s. The book was dedicated, somewhat ironically, to Lewes's father-in-law, Swynfen Jervis, who was a Radical MP, part of a faction which Carlyle's *The French Revolution* had indirectly criticised. Lewes compared the first French revolution to that of 1848, and considered Robespierre's arguments vindicating insurrection to those 'used to justify our own revolution'.[49]

The attack upon a rational and schematised interpretation of reality which Carlyle had launched in *The French Revolution* was echoed by Lewes in his interpretative comments, as it was theoretically embodied in his objective method. He admired Mirabeau for rising above mere intellectuality; he agreed with Carlyle that the causes of the revolution were ultimately indecipherable. He attacked formulae which presented glib political solutions or stereotyped views of social groups.[50] Lewes also pondered, as had Carlyle, the gulf between mental notions which interpreted and patterned reality, and the complex nature of reality itself, and showed the danger of embodying a partial view of reality in doctrinaire political practice. Lewes admitted the motivational power of abstract ideas, for 'great periods in human development have been uniformly opened by a consideration of questions the most abstract, and apparently the most remote from immediate interests'. He emphasised that the complexity of reality rendered

ociety resistant to the execution of such ideas in revolutionary
practice, for 'living, as we do, amidst imperfect human beings, and
having to work out our ends by human means, abstract principles
of justice, irrespective all of human affections, never have, and
never will, command unmixed admiration'. Lewes noted that
forms of government which act so smoothly upon paper, become
very different things when we attempt to realize them, having as
our instruments ferocious and ignorant masses of hungry men'.
The theorist was hampered by his medium, for men are 'not
simple units in a calculation; they are complex beings, having
many wants, many passions, and much foolishness'.[51] The complications of life which Lewes the novelist attempted to reproduce
were brought to bear upon philosophical theory, and it was the
latter which was found to be wanting in truth.

Lewes considered that the gulf between rational notions and
complex reality 'furnishes us the key' to Robespierre's career, for
Robespierre endeavoured to 'shape society into order by means of
his convictions'. Robespierre's experience was a practical demonstration of the inefficacy of the theory upon which he based his
notions. Carlyle thought that in the act of perception 'the whole
man must coöperate'. Lewes showed how the incompleteness of
Robespierre's intellectual temperament vitiated his vision, and
how this limited perception initiated dangerous actions. Robespierre's theoretical philanthropy lacked sympathy for the individual. Whilst admiring his 'sincerity . . . singleness of purpose . . .
exalted aims . . . vigorous consistency', Lewes showed that his
intellectual confidence was perilous because it stemmed from
narrow-mindedness, want of feeling, of consideration and of
sympathy; unscrupulousness of means, pedantic wilfulness, and
relentless ferocity'. He saw in Robespierre 'Pride, assuming the
majestic aspect of the Love of Truth . . . intense dogmatism
coupled with a want of human sympathy, excusing the violence of
its acts, by the supposed purity of its designs. 'Lewes defended the
promulgation of what the individual saw as truth, but insisted that
this must be tempered by moral compassion, an awareness of
human fallibility and a sceptical tolerance of others' opinions. He
noted caustically, 'To go to the block for an opinion, is heroism; to
send others to the block because they differ from you, is
fanaticism'.[52] George Eliot, the novelist, in her handling of the
theme of fanaticism, was to imply anti-sectarian conclusions similar to those which Lewes propounded in this early biography.

Behind Lewes's conclusions about Robespierre lay a proposition about the nature of truth akin to that found in the letters and articles written by Marian Evans in the 1840s and 1850s, and to the views of Mill and Carlyle. Metaphysicians, like Robespierre, arrogantly trusted in their own intellect to interpret a reality which they misrepresented because they simplified it. They presented the truths evolved out of their own speculative efforts as absolute. In metaphysics, said Lewes, following Comte, 'instead of *examining the thing before us* to find out its properties, we studiously examine *the idea of that thing as it exists in our own minds*'. In line with the eclecticism of Mill and Carlyle, and with Comte's scientism, Lewes suggested that men should be humble enough to admit the limitations of the intellect, the complexity of reality, and the relativity of all truths. He proposed the value of the outward-looking scientific method, whereby 'A man wishing to know the structure and organic processes of plants, examines plants, and not his *idea* of a plant'.[53] Intellectual humility and reverence for the impalpable complexities of reality was an intellectual stance Lewes learned, as Marian Evans learned it, from Carlyle. It was this, amongst other things, they were to have in common when, two years after the *Life of Robespierre* was published, they met.

17

George Henry Lewes and Marian Evans (1850–1854)

the pleasantest companions are not always the most 'respectable'.

it is reputation, not chastity . . . that they are employed to keep free from spot.[1]

I

First impressions of Lewes's personality, Marian Evans's included, were often unfavourable. Superficiality was one charge, and coarseness was another; his after-dinner talk shocked men, and when he met women 'his way of shaking hands suggested the Divorce Court'. Yet even the hostile Mrs Linton admitted that 'wherever he went there was a patch of intellectual sunshine in the room', and she was struck by 'the wonderful expressiveness of his eyes'.[2] Spencer paid tribute to his amiability: 'As a companion Lewes was extremely attractive. Interested in, and well informed upon, a variety of subjects; full of various anecdote; and an admirable mimic; it was impossible to be dull in his company'. One acquaintance described him as 'a most kinly, genial, guileless person & with versatility & accomplishment that make him a miracle. All who really know him, like him and appreciate him highly'. After his death, the *Westminster Review* spoke of his 'many endearing qualities'; Morley revered him as 'one of the most vivid, helpful, and encouraging of our friends', and Lord Lytton remembered him as 'the last of the few friends wiser than myself, to whom from boyhood I have looked up'.[3] Pondering Marian Evans's relationship to Lewes, Mrs Belloc reflected that she 'evoked some better self than that perceived by the outer world', and Barbara Bodichon recalled for Edith Simcox how she had remarked to Marian Evans 'in the earlier days "I do not like Mr. Lewes" and was answered "You do not know him": but, she went on to me, he was not then as we knew him later, her influence, all agree, improved his character, though she must have seen in advance all that was to be – and was her justification'.[4]

By 1850, Lewes was well-known on the literary scene, especially in that section of it inhabited by semi-Bohemians of radical views. Versatility was the keynote of his reputation, and even Mrs Linton acknowledged his brilliance and his industry.[5] He had laid the foundations for a potentially eminent career. Holyoake in the *Reasoner* on 2 November 1853 listed Lewes alongside Carlyle as a writer who would 'shape this age and rule the next . . . bring lustrious contributions to the truths of the future'.[6] Yet, although his future as an author boded well, Lewes was deeply unhappy. Charlotte Brontë, who met him in London in the summer of 1850, saw no frivolity, and recorded how 'the aspect of Lewes's face almost moves me to tears; it is so wonderfully like Emily . . . whatever Lewes says, I believe I cannot hate him'.[7] Lewes had early experienced that loneliness which invaded the hearts of those whose ideas were at odds with respectable society, and this feeling had led to his youthful identification with Spinoza. It also probably contributed to his decision to seek out the freer atmospheres of France and Germany. Upon his return from Germany, he portrayed Shylock as 'the champion and avenger of a persecuted race'. His contacts in the literary world helped to assuage his feeling of alienation, yet Lewes recognised the inadequacy of purely intellectual companionship. 'Shut out from our family', he noted, 'we may seek a brotherhood of apostacy; but these new and precarious intellectual sympathies are no compensation for the loss of the emotive sympathies.'[8] It was a sentiment which Marian Evans, who often felt similarly lonely at 142 Strand, would have recognised only too well. Lewes's many friendships afforded him scant consolation when his marriage foundered in 1849 as he embarked on a lecturing and fund-raising tour in the north of England. Thornton Hunt, his wife Agnes's lover, was the son of the man who had befriended Lewes when he was an aspiring writer, and the Hunts and Leweses were the closest of friends. Liberal views on love and marriage, such as Marian Evans had encountered at Rosehill and 142 Strand, were prevalent amongst Lewes's friends. Lewes's mentor, Mill, presented Harriet Taylor with a written promise that he would not claim the superior legal rights marriage gave men over women; Herbert Spencer was similarly critical of the legal bond of marriage.[9] Lewes had been a hedonist in his youth, and to him and Hunt, 'Legal obligation [in marriage] was . . . the remnant of a foreign barbarism, and enforced permanency was unholy tyranny'. In *Rose, Blanche and Violet*, Lewes wrote in comic, risqué tones of the technique of seduction: after Thornton and Agnes had embarked upon their affair, and Lewes had become involved with Marian Evans, his review of *Ruth* considered the question of seduction and the allied one of illegitimacy more seriously, albeit still from a morally liberal viewpoint.[10] Agnes's entanglement with Thornton put Lewes's views to the test, as it forced him to cope emotionally with that which he was notorious for condoning on an intellectual level. For Lewes, the birth of Agnes's second child by Hunt in October 1851 marked the end of his marriage and the end of an important friendship. His intermittent feelings of intellectual isolation were compounded by estrangement from his wife and the son of his mentor: in 1859, he recalled that the years immediately prior to his meeting with Marian Evans were 'a very dreary *wasted* period of my life. I had given up all ambition whatever, lived from hand to mouth, and thought the evil of each day sufficient'.[11]

Lewes may have thought of the period as wasted because he was unhappy, but his unhappiness did not impede his productivity. In 1850 and 1851 he produced articles on Borrow's *Lavengro*, Spanish literature, *The Iliad* and French historians. He returned to writing plays. He continued his onslaught on the parochialism of English literary tastes, and between January 1852 and July 1853 wrote the summaries of French literature for the *Westminster Review* which Marian Evans was editing. He continued to meditate upon literature, and upon women and literature in particular. He once more championed Charlotte Brontë, although *Shirley* impressed him less than *Jane Eyre*. He reviewed the novel briefly, and somewhat negatively, for the *Westminster Review* in January 1850, and in more detail for the *Edinburgh Review* in the same month. He again applied his criterion of 'truth' as he was to apply it to *Ruth* and *Villette*.[12] He also spoke of the imagination in terms which recalled Marian Evans's comments in the 1840s, noting 'the coinage of imagination . . . is not accepted *because* it departs from the actual truth, but only because it presents the recognised attributes of our nature in new and striking combinations'. He singled out Charlotte's discourses upon the position of women in *Shirley* and, three months before Agnes was to give birth to her first child by Hunt, spoke of Mrs Pryor's rejection of her child as an unnatural manifestation of the maternal instinct. The grand female function was, he argued, maternity: it was woman's 'distinctive characteristic, and

most endearing charm . . . a high and holy office'. Whilst defending women's intellectual powers, and speaking of how society had
never given 'fair play to their capabilities', he noted, perhaps with
a glance at his once-literary wife, pregnant with her sixth child at
the age of twenty-eight, that maternity prevented 'steady and
unbroken application' of a kind necessary for the pursuit of other
noble activities. Well might Mrs Linton later speak of Agnes's
'dono fatale di belleza [fatal gift of beauty]'.[13]

During 1849 and 1850, Lewes's professional life was also bound
up with Thornton Hunt's. Lewes had worked with Thornton and
his father on the *Monthly Repository* in the 1830s; Lewes and
Thornton had weathered their period of *sturm und drang* together,
rebelling against the past, entertaining idealistic hopes for the
future; they shared a liberal stance on important issues. Lewes's
1849 trip north was motivated partly by a need to raise money for a
new weekly he and Hunt planned to co-edit. Lewes was to deal
with the literary sections, and Hunt was to concern himself with
politics and public affairs. The first number of the *Leader* appeared
on 30 March 1850; it was to enjoy a brief but impressive existence.[14]
Lewes's work on the *Leader* was animated, as was Marian Evans's
on the *Westminster Review*, by a sense of mission. In 1847, he had
seen periodical literature as 'a potent instrument for the education
of the people', and the *Leader* was populist in a way the *Westminster
Review* was not, and was read by the provincial working class as
well as the intelligentsia. The paper was more radical than the
Westminster Review, which it accused of political timidity. Spencer
insisted that his contributions be anonymous 'because I declined to
be identified with the socialist views' he saw the *Leader* to represent, and Carlyle was likewise suspicious of its political stance.
Like Marian Evans and his mentors Mill and Carlyle, Lewes had
been interested in the ideas of the Saint-Simonians, and he looked
to Europe for his political ideas. As did the *Westminster Review*, the
Leader opened its pages to the refugees from the 1848 revolutions.
It denounced the evils of competition, favoured co-operative
schemes, and envisaged itself as the defender of the working class
against an aristocratic government. Lewes wrote of communism as
an ideal which could inspire men with hope, and urged the
gradual transformation of society in the light of an utopian ideal,
although he forswore violent revolution.[15] Lewes and Hunt also
championed, as did Marian Evans and Chapman, the politically
suspect cause of free inquiry. Lewes met the future leader of the

Secularist movement after Holyoake had written a favourable review of *Robespierre*; Hunt, at the time, was trying to galvanise literary men into more open expression of radical and political opinions. Lewes courageously included Holyoake's name in the list of contributors to the *Leader* when Holyoake was an outcast from respectable society, and Holyoake became the paper's business manager as it tried to provide a forum for the most advanced opinions. The *Leader*, like the *Westminster Review*, and for similar political reasons, was beset with financial problems, which added to Lewes's worries. On 14 June 1851, Lewes and Hunt withdrew from the company which owned the paper, although both Lewes and Marian Evans contributed articles to it until well into the 1850s.[16]

In the *Leader* between 30 March and 8 June 1850 appeared ten episodes of Lewes's third, and unfinished novel, *The Apprenticeship of Life*, the last work he produced before he met Marian Evans. Lewes was still preoccupied with defining the function of the novel in terms of literature's relation to reality, a theme which was also dwelt upon by the *Westminster Review* under Marian Evans's editorship. Lewes termed the work 'a philosophical romance, and not a "thrilling story"', for he had often criticised unconvincing sensationalism in novels. Yet his own novel once more incorporated melodrama, coincidence and sentimentality. Echoing the Preface to *Rose, Blanche and Violet*, he said that he aimed to 'give expression to the *truth* . . . the morality I must leave for others to settle', but, as in *Robespierre*, he could not resist the lure of didacticism.[17] Lewes's concern with the paradigmatic maturing of his hero was reminiscent, as was a similar theme in *Ranthorpe*, of Goethe's *Wilhelm Meister*, and Goethe was quoted. The main inspiration of the novel was again, however, Lewes's and Marian Evans's idol, George Sand. Yet, where Marian Evans had been interested in George Sand's method, Lewes seized upon the French novelist's themes. Specific reminiscences of the Frenchwoman's novels occurred. Hortense, the model-estate owner, resembled George Sand herself; the military man, General Laboissière, recalled Ramière in *Indiana*. Armand's *rêverie* amidst nature drew upon the example of George Sand, rather than of Rousseau whom, unlike Marian Evans, Lewes disliked. The setting of the early episodes, a remote faded château, was close to that used in many George Sand novels. Discussions of the French revolutions of 1789 and 1830 revealed that fascination with French history which Lewes shared with Marian Evans and which had been shown in *Robespierre* and his journalism; his analysis of the intellectual evolution of his characters in relation to revolutionary events recalled *Mauprat* and *Spiridion*.

The politicised religions of post-revolutionary France which fascinated Marian Evans in the 1840s were discussed by Lewes with a mixture of scepticism and sympathy as they had been in George Sand's novels, and especially in *Lettres d'un voyageur*, the work Lewes knew so well and from which Marian Evans often quoted. Lewes's novel was concerned with varieties of belief and the analysis of the views of the infidel Baron, the devout Baronne, the questing Armand and the philosophical Frangipolo echoed George Sand's preoccupation with the inner life in *Lélia* and *Spiridion*. The pretentiousness of some French thinkers was criticised, for they 'give themselves airs of Prophets and Teachers upon the strength of a few vague formulas'.[18] Hortense and Armand debated the concept of Humanity, and Armand and Frangipolo formed a humanitarian revolutionary society. In the light of his domestic problems, Lewes also considered that aspect of French radicalism which concerned itself with the position of women and love. Hortense blamed her indolence on the fact that women lacked a useful social function. The flux of feelings, another Rousseauesque concept which Lewes picked up from George Sand, was seen to make constancy difficult. Hortense, like Hester in *Rose, Blanche and Violet*, 'proclaims the bond of love to be the only bond of marriage . . . it is an unsacred thing to force two human beings to live together as man and wife, after all affection has died out'. But whereas Lewes often satirised Hester for her principles, and showed how society made her suffer for them, Hortense retreated from the world, then made a conventional marriage with Armand, accepted his rejection of her when she lost her beauty, and planned to become a Sister of Charity. Hortense was a melancholy figure, unlike Hester, who was part-comic, part sensationally tragic, which may hint at how Lewes saw himself and Agnes at this stage of their lives. The acting-out of radical principles was not seen to bring unalloyed happiness: the Baronne, who read one of Marian Evans's favourite authors, à Kempis, and who lived a life of virtuous duty, provided a moral perspective on Saint-Simonianism, which she associated with 'the most dissolute and desperate of the outcasts of society'.[19]

Lewes, like George Sand, conceived of his characters' search for faith as operating in relation to the philosophical debate. Like Marian Evans, he had learnt from Coleridge and Carlyle of the personal relevance of that debate; like those two disseminators of Idealism, and also like Mill, Lewes made a stand against rationalism and philosophical sectarianism. The journalists in *Ranthorpe* saw scepticism and utilitarianism as the dominant notes of the age. Armand was reared in the bigoted rationalism of 'the followers of the Encyclopaedists', the 'thinkers to whom this universe was no mystery at all', who saw religion as 'supported only by the terrors and prejudices of the credulous, and not the spontaneous product of the human soul – the instinct imperiously moving the whole being of man'. Such philosophers, said Lewes, failed to understand the complexities of the soul, in which faculties other than reason existed. Armand also lamented sectarianism, commenting: 'It is an age of individualism and anarchy. Instead of *a* philosophy, we have *systems*; instead of a religion we have *sects*; instead of a nation we have *coteries*', a view which recalled Lewes's perspective on the aftermath of Hegelianism in Germany in *A Biographical History of Philosophy*.[20] Yet Armand echoed Lewes's comment in *Robespierre* when he admitted that men were moved by ideas, despite the difficulty presented to the realisation of ideals by human imperfection. In the depiction of Armand, Lewes imaged his own search for a belief, for the 'restless scepticism of youth will soon subside, for no true soul can be content to dwell amid ruins'. Wisdom was seen to come from heart and intellect combined. Lewes asserted the existence in all men of *'un fibre religieux'*: Frangipolo noted *'Religion is a Sentiment before it is a Belief*; – the intellectual part of it, the formula, will vary with the intelligence of mankind, but there is little variation in the sentiment'. Religion 'profoundly affects the whole nature of man; not his intellect alone'; the life of the Baronne showed that 'belief could be something more than an intellectual act . . . it could *beautify and fortify a life*'.[21] Frangipolo expounded a philosophical form of Christianity which Armand finally embraced and Lewes's portrayal of Frangipolo drew upon George Sand's portrayal of prophet/saviour figures, such as Trenmor in *Lélia*, Patience in *Mauprat*, or Spiridion.

Lewes praised *Ruth* because it had a 'moral carried in the story; not preached, but manifested'.[22] In *The Apprenticeship of Life* he explored once more the nature of fictional realism and didacticism.

These problems were to be discussed by Marian Evans and other reviewers of fiction in the *Westminster Review*, for they were bound up with the very status of the novel. Articles in the *Westminster Review* were to conclude that the fiction writer's sceptical scrutiny of life, and presentation of pictures, had much to teach the philosophers Lewes criticised in his novel, for the novelist could challenge the sectarian logical method and generalising dogmatism of metaphysical conclusions. Lewes and Marian Evans were, moreover, attracted to the work of George Sand because she corroborated their view that ideas could not be divorced from life. In his fictional theme of a search for faith, Lewes showed how ideas could explain existence, console man and direct action. His quest for a practical philosophy was to lead him once more to write about Auguste Comte.

II

Just over a year after *The Apprenticeship of Life* was left unfinished, Lewes met Marian Evans in Jeff's shop 'whose window' as Lewes had written in 1847, 'resplendent with green, blue, and yellow volumes, makes Burlington Arcade an expensively attractive spot to us'.[23] If Lewes was depressed because of the collapse of his marriage, Marian Evans was also far from happy. Lewes realised how precarious the life of women writers was, and settling in London had done little to give her financial stability. The pecuniary state of the *Westminster Review* was going from bad to worse. She also spoke of how her friends had been indifferent to her needs when she lived in London 'in privacy and loneliness'. Despite her commitment to the aims of the *Westminster Review*, she frequently experienced a feeling of uselessness, recalling in 1861 how, between 1849 and 1851, she felt 'moments of despair . . . that life would ever be made precious to me by the consciousness that I lived to some good purpose. It was the sort of despair that sucked away the sap of half the hours which might have been filled by energetic youthful activity'.[24] Her love for Lewes was of slow growth. She was fruitlessly involved with Spencer until the early months of 1853. She also heard the gossip surrounding Hunt's tangled domestic and financial situation; Lewes was implicated in these and she was probably and understandably wary. Lewes's and Marian Evans's work, however, threw them together. The

Leader offices were in Wellington Street round the corner from Chapman's house; Marian Evans visited them soon after her arrival in the capital, and Lewes asked her to write for the weekly in the autumn of 1852. He called on her as she worked on the *Westminster Review*. They also met at the theatre. As her involvement with Spencer diminished, that with Lewes increased. Lewes was soon showing interest in her old friends, inquiring after Sara Hennell, whom he had met and liked, and visiting the Brays. She hinted, early in 1853, that reasons other than those of health made her wish to move from the Strand, and references to Lewes subsequently became more frequent and more favourable. She told Sara that Lewes 'has quite won my liking, in spite of myself' and added, in a telling postscript, 'Of course, Mr. Bray highly approves the recommendations of the Commissioners on *Divorce*', a subject discussed in the *Leader* on 26 March 1853. A crisis between herself and Lewes in late March resolved itself. Initially she was discreet with the Brays, deleting from a letter written on 11 April 1853 a reference to Lewes having been 'quite a pleasant friend lately', and speaking of emigrating to Australia with Chrissey. On 16 April, however, she wrote to Cara that Lewes was 'especially . . . kind and attentive and has quite won my regard after having a good deal of my vituperation'. Defensively, she commented, 'he is much better than he seems – a man of heart and conscience wearing a mask of flippancy'. In June, she told her Coventry friends of a visit with him to the opera; in July, probably while she was resting at St Leonard's, Lewes poured out the story of his unhappy marriage. The following October, she moved to lodgings on her own, and nine months later, they left for Weimar.[25]

'Love', Lewes reflected, 'is an instinct, it remains a mystery, and defies all calculation. We are not "judicious" in love; we do not select those whom we "ought to love", but those whom we cannot help loving.'[26] Their decision to live together predictably created a scandal in polite circles. A submerged sexual activity, which led foreign visitors to remark upon the number of prostitutes on the London streets, was masked by a façade of public respectability. As the Parnell case showed, the public horror of divorce lasted well into the 1880s. Meredith's *The Ordeal of Richard Feverel* (1859) and Hardy's *Tess of the d'Urbervilles* (1891) were seen as morally offensive. The woman who was seduced acquired an immediate social stigma, and was seen to lose all her other virtues, and most Victorian novels castigated women's sexual misdemeanours far more severely than men's.[27] Gossip and censure pursued Marian Evans and Lewes for years. Mrs Gaskell always regretted their liaison. After her marriage to Cross in 1880, the old rumour, that she had started to live with Lewes after he had deserted his wife and children, was revived. Even the couple's supposedly en-lightened friends were shocked. Combe wondered whether there was insanity in Marian Evans's family; Bray regretted her actions as 'imprudent and laying herself open to evil report' (his own non-marital union was more discreet). Chapman blamed Lewes, and said that Marian Evans would be '*utterly* lost' if Lewes proved inconstant, an ironic comment, considering that Chapman's own womanising habits had extended in the direction of his assistant editor.[28] The earnest and learned Marian Evans was, as Mrs Belloc recalled, 'the very last woman in England of whom such a step could have been prophesied'. Marian Evans told her of the deci-sion during a long walk round Hyde Park; Mrs Belloc confessed that that 'conversation seems to me, after a lapse of nearly forty years, to be printed on the very stones of Park Lane'.[29] In the reactions of the progressive intelligentsia, it was not only a very English residual sexual hypocrisy and an insistence on discretion which were evident. Discussions of free love, in G. R. Drysdale's best-seller, *The Elements of Social Science* (1854) and in the circles in which Lewes and Marian Evans moved were fairly commonplace, but to transform theory into practice merely endangered the image of the progressive faction. Moral laxity was often seen by respect-able people as a consequence of radical ideas. Railway navvies were notorious, in middle-class eyes, for their Socialism and their sexual permissiveness, and the latter was seen as a result of the former. Progressive intellectuals had already discredited their cause by embracing sexual freedom; W. J. Fox had published articles in the *Monthly Repository* which criticised the institution of marriage, and in 1833 had been expelled from the Unitarian Church because of his immoral behaviour. Marian Evans and Lewes had, said Combe, 'inflicted a great injury on the cause of religious freedom'. Decades later, Holyoake felt it necessary to defend the decision taken by Lewes and Marian Evans in 1854.[30]

Lewes and Marian Evans knew that their decision would alien-ate them from respectable society and damage the causes for which they and their friends had so actively laboured. In these respects, their actions further intensified the loneliness both were experi-encing. Lewes had defended George Sand because 'she has never made adultery a jest; always a crime terrible in its consequences', and Marian Evans's nerves were only partly calmed by her move to Cambridge Street. Yet Lewes, in 1859, described his life after meeting Marian Evans as 'a new birth', saying, 'To her I owe all my prosperity and all my happiness'. The end result of the decision which caused them such agonising was to be what Chapman described enviously as 'a pattern marriage'. They saw their union as a true marriage, 'an alliance of a sacred kind, having a binding and permanent character', after a Tennysonian pattern: 'Self reverent each and reverencing each/Distinct in individualities'.[31] They found an emotional fulfilment which the network of friendships within the 'brotherhood of apostacy' could never have provided. Although their unorthodox arrangement isolated them from both society's mainstream and their progressive friends, such seclusion encouraged an intense interest in each other's work. It forced them, as Marian Evans confessed in 1879, 'to live for each other and in such complete independence of the outer world that the world could be nothing for them . . . it seemed a sort of dual egoism'.[32]

Lewes's experience and interests, before they met, had often run parallel to Marian Evans's. Both had been nurtured by a family context which rendered them *declassés*, and had received an unorthodox education. Both had experienced feelings of emotional and intellectual isolation. They had embraced the causes of political radicalism and freedom of inquiry. Radical Unitarianism played a part in their early intellectual developments. Both also operated in an intellectual landscape which was European, not English. Carlyle and Coleridge had introduced them to German thought: Lewes had written on Strauss and Marian Evans had translated *Das Leben Jesu*. Lewes learnt of the political and aesthetic developments of Idealism in Germany as Marian Evans discussed them with her friend, John Sibree. She translated *The Essence of Christianity*, and it might have been Lewes's overt radicalism which made her willing to work on so obviously political a book. The same French writers had also caught their attention. George Sand was the outstanding example, but Lewes's interest in the post-Encyclopaedist tradition of historiography and political philosophy found an echo in the books Marian Evans read in the late 1840s. Mill's work was important in introducing both to Comtism. Broadly speaking, both were well versed in a philosophical tradition of eclectic pragmatism, which forswore any single mode of inquiry and dogmatic and sectarian systems of interpretation, yet emphasised how speculation had implications for religion, ethics, politics and aesthetics. Books by Spinoza, Spencer, Comte and Mill were annotated by both Lewes and Marian Evans.[33]

In the early stages of their relationship, the kinship of their enthusiasms was apparent. Lewes described Carlyle, with whom he was on good terms, as 'a poet without music', as Marian Evans enthusiastically reviewed *The Life of Sterling*. Mill was also a friend of Lewes's, and Marian Evans re-read some of Mill's more important works. Lewes had met Spencer at 142 Strand in 1850; he encouraged him to become a freelance writer, and gave him contacts in the London literary world. Marian Evans's letters also contained references to Spinoza in whom Lewes was to have a lifelong interest.[34] From the outset, they were interested in each other's work. Lewes called on Chapman on 23 September 1851 to express approval of Marian Evans's review of Greg's *Creed of Christendom*. The caustic views on literary women expressed in *Rose, Blanche and Violet* were being modified. In 1852, he defended 'the right of Woman to citizenship in the Republic of Letters', adding, 'The man who would deny to woman the cultivation of her intellect, ought, for consistency, to shut her up in a harem'.[35] Marian Evans was also interested in Lewes's projects. She reported to Sara, with obvious pleasure, that Lewes had visited Cambridge, and had found 'a knot of devotees . . . who make his history of Philosophy a private text-book'. She re-read Goethe. Lewes increased her interest in the novel. She thought critically about *Villette* since he championed Charlotte Brontë. In June 1852, she asked the Brays to send her copies of *Sense and Sensibility* and George Sand's novels; Lewes discussed these in 'The Lady Novelists' which appeared in the *Westminster Review* a month later. She also gave him practical help, correcting proofs, and taking dictation of his articles. When he was ill in 1854, she probably wrote contributions to periodicals on his behalf.[36] Their common interests and involvement in each other's projects did not, however, submerge the critical faculty which both possessed to a marked degree. John Chapman remembered 'the originality, the fearlessness, the independence of her mind', and she insisted in later years that it was respect for the freedom of each other's opinion which formed the basis of their happiness. She contested, during this early period, his judgment of Harriet Martineau's article on Niebuhr, disagreed with aspects of his assessments of *Ruth* and

Villette, and of Francis Newman's *Phases of Faith.*[37] Emotional ties and intellectual affinities were never to weaken the critical spirit which characterised her mind, as it characterised Lewes's. Rather, they encouraged each other's spirit of scepticism; that spirit animated Lewes's second book on Comte, and was eventually to inspire Marian Evans's decision to write fiction.

III

On 3 April 1852 the first of eighteen instalments of *Auguste Comte's Philosophy of the Sciences* appeared in the *Leader.* Marian Evans's critical spirit showed itself in her initial reaction: the series, she said did 'not promise well, though he is understood to have applied himself very closely to the subject'. She was to change her view. She read the proofs after Lewes had revised the text for its publication in book form; she defended Lewes against Huxley, and generally promoted the work.[38] After the completion of *A Biographical History of Philosophy,* Lewes started a correspondence with Comte which lasted until 1853 and, from 1848 onwards, Comte considered Lewes had replaced Mill as the representative of Positivism in England. The *Leader* was well-known for its Comtist slant, which became obvious by the middle of 1851. In that year, Lewes helped set up a fund for Comte who had lost his job at the Ecole Polytechnique and the *Leader* published lists of those who had donated money to subsidise the founder of Positivism. Through his contact with the *Leader,* Holyoake encountered Comte's ideas which helped give him courage to found the secularist movement. Morell and Spencer both saw a Positivist bias in Lewes's work; Comte himself, however, detected a critical note in *Comte's Philosophy of the Sciences* and after 1852 his friendship with Lewes cooled.[39] The contrasting views of Morell, Spencer and Comte shed light upon Lewes's ambivalent attitude towards Positivism: like Marian Evans, Lewes found much to admire in Comte's philosophy, but that did not prevent him, as it did not prevent her, from being sceptical and critical of certain aspects of it.

Marian Evans's enthusiasm for Comte, which Bray considered to have lasted throughout her life,[40] may well have reinforced Lewes's favourable response. The ever-increasing diversity of Lewes's interests intensified his fascination with Positivism. Comte's synthesis of disciplines justified the mind of the polymath, whose virtues Lewes extolled, and which made Lewes one of the ablest of popularisers. Lewes lived before the emergence of widespread educational specialisation; Frederic Harrison, another enthusiast for Comte, contrasted the narrowness of an Oxford education to the broad culture of London society, and Comte often appealed to those who had had, or favoured, an unorthodox education. In the 1850s, one man could keep up with developments in a variety of fields, and disciplines existed in a state of cross-fertilisation.[41] Comte also proposed a solution to the rivalry between empiricism and intuitionism with which Lewes was preoccupied in the 1840s and 1850s. Lewes was interested in science, and contact with Spencer probably increased this tendency. By 1849, Lewes was deploring the mania for German philosophy. Yet he retained a sympathetic interest in metaphysics, and in a review of *Modern Painters* which appeared in the *Leader* on 13 April 1850, he said that Ruskin rightly showed that 'empiricism is as idle and pernicious in Art as in Philosophy'. Comte's philosophy was based on the sciences, yet it was not unalleviated in its empiricism.[42] Lewes had been much influenced by the notion that speculation had implications for human issues, and Comte's admirers often shared a distaste for purely academic knowledge. In 1850, Lewes lamented the fact that German metaphysics could not grapple with pressing social problems. From his revised philosophical method, Comte had evolved a new faith, and Lewes's search for belief had been reflected in *The Apprenticeship of Life*. In *Comte's Philosophy of the Sciences*, Lewes once more made a direct attempt to popularise Comte's views but, in contrast to *A Biographical History of Philosophy*, which had used Comtist views as a structural principle, Lewes now emphasised that his debt to Comte was as much emotional as intellectual.[43] He explicated Comte, as Carlyle had explicated German writings, for the benefit of those suffering spiritual crises. Lewes saw his own turmoil as a microcosm of a general dilemma, to which Comte provided a solution. He considered 'It is one of our noble human instincts that we cannot feel within us the glory and power of a real conviction without earnestly striving to make that conviction pass into other minds. All propaganda is religious; all steadfast preaching of the truth, such as our minds decree it, is a human duty, a social instinct'.[44]

Lewes saw the interconnection of the sciences as important for both 'doctrine' and 'method'. He singled out Comte's 'system which absorbs all intellectual activity' and brought order to all forms of knowledge as one of the most valuable aspects of Positivism. Lewes deplored specialisation as intellectually narrowing and socially divisive, and also suggested that it led to the exclusive pursuit of a single logical method. He noted: 'the thinking world happens, unfortunately, to be divided into two classes – men of science destitute of a philosophy, because incompetent for the most part to the thorough grasp of those generalities which form a philosophy; and metaphysicians, whose tendency towards generalities causes them to disdain the creeping specialities of physical science'.[45] Lewes echoed the implications of an eclectic logical method when describing his view of the universe. Well before the publication of *The Origin of Species* (1859) writers were trying to reconcile science and religion; Kingsley's popularising book on marine biology, *Glaucus* (1855) was tellingly subtitled 'The Wonders of the Shore'. Lewes was also probably aware of the Unitarian argument from design from his days on the *Monthly Repository*. His earlier comment, 'How unwise is this terror of science! In studying the facts of nature we study the thoughts of God, for in the world of realities fact is the direct speech of God', had echoed Carlyle's natural supernaturalism and recalled Mill's argument with Roebuck.[46] In *Comte's Philosophy of the Sciences*, Lewes reiterated his view of the futility of the metaphysician's attempt to 'penetrate inaccessible mysteries' of causation, yet he also expatiated upon the mystery of the actual, a quasi-religious concept associated with an Idealist tradition. He showed how an objective study of nature's laws inculcated a wondering and joyous reverence for life. When Comte explained that the biologist was concerned with life in its more complex forms, but that all forms of life were still interconnected, Lewes commented, 'No thinking man will imagine anything is *explained* by this. The great mystery of Life and Being remains as inaccessible as ever. But a grander conception of Nature as one Whole, and a more philosophic attitude of mind, in contemplating the varieties in that whole, will result from the restitution of the homogeneity of Nature, when we learn with Goethe, Schelling, and Coleridge, to see Life everywhere, and nowhere Death'. Lewes proposed that a religious sense of wonder could be based upon outward-looking scientism, and he focused upon Comte's attempt to construct a new religion, an aspect of Positivism which he had dealt with but briefly in *A Biographical History of Philosophy*. This emphasis showed the anguished, heterodox

Lewes searching for a new faith. As in his unfinished third novel, he also suggested the value of a non-sectarian religion which would satisfy man's intellectual and moral being.[47]

Lewes also dwelt upon Comte's analysis of the link between intellect, emotions and action. Comte's emphasis upon the importance of the emotions tempered, for Lewes, the cerebral rationalism he had criticised in *Robespierre*. It also, perhaps, afforded justification of his relationship with Marian Evans, for he was one of the few English commentators to consider sympathetically Comte's relationship to his mistress.[48] Lewes had imbibed enough Benthamite influence from Mill to insist upon a clear distinction between intellect and emotions. But whilst admitting that 'it is under intellectual direction that human progress has always been accomplished', Lewes said that no philosophy satisfied 'the demands of Humanity' unless it recognised that 'man is moved by his emotions, not by his ideas: using his Intellect only as an eye to *see the way* . . .. Intellect is the servant, not the lord of the Heart'. He argued that history showed the predominance of emotional over intellectual factors. He conceded the blindness of instinct, but saw rational powers as unable to stir men to action; intellect was a weak basis for religion, and 'I would rather worship Jupiter than the metaphysician's "Reason"'.[49]

Comte's sociology attracted the attention of Mill and Spencer; Marian Evans was to praise Riehl, the pioneer German sociologist.[50] As in his advocacy of psychology, Lewes also praised a new, man-centred science, and he composed the sections on this theme for the publication of his articles in book form. His plea for Comte's sociology was also allied to his discussion of the links between intellect, feeling and action. In life, Lewes noted that 'all our thought has an aim in Action', and Comte's social science united the scientific analysis of laws with the emotional and moral concerns of religion. Within Comte's *échelle*, sociology issued in ethics, for, as sociology blended intellect and emotions in theory, so ethics blended them in action. Lewes also saw ethical issues as linked to political factors; the individual's moral character determined his social value, and ethical issues were implicit in economic theory. Lewes considered that not only did sociology give a scientific basis to ethics; it also provided an intellectual basis for social reform. In the 1830s, Mill and Carlyle had tried to evolve a sound philosophical foundation for theories of reform, which might give direction to social change. Impatience with the pragmatic English approach to political questions characterised Lewes's thought as it had characterised Mill's and Carlyle's. He saw the English political dilemma as stemming from 'the increasing preponderance of the material and temporary view taken of political questions'. Because of his interest in French radicalism, Lewes had learnt, like Marian Evans, the appeal of utopian solutions which rested on a philosophical basis. Comte offered a comprehensive plan of reform which rested upon a reformed philosophical foundation, and Lewes saw this as the only solution to 'the present state of disorder which is essentially mental'. Comte's Social Dynamics could furnish 'the real theory of Progress to practical politics' because it codified man's instinctive historical sense and awareness of human interdependence.[51]

'Reverence', said Lewes, 'is not incompatible with independence', and his view of Comte was critical in certain respects. In 1853, Comte had given up the reading even of scientific works, and Lewes was vitally interested in the sciences' open-ended quest for truth. The longest section of the book was devoted to scientific themes, and contained, as well as exposition of Comte's views, 'criticism, illustration, new speculation and fact'. Lewes compared his own views on post-Newtonian physics to Comte's; he showed how Comte's theories about nutrition needed modification. He pointed out errors in Comte's writings on chemistry. He differed from Comte, and agreed with Mill, that psychology should be accorded the status of a separate science.[52] Lewes also disputed Comte's claim to originality of method. He saw him, as he had in *A Biographical History of Philosophy*, as the heir of Bacon and Descartes. Mrs Somerville's work on the interconnection of the sciences (which Marian Evans had read in the 1840s) and Herschel's were seen to foreshadow Comte. Lewes also pointed out Comte's indebtedness to Turgot, and to the pioneering of sociological method by Montesquieu and Condorcet. The original articles in the *Leader* had demonstrated Comte's connection to the Saint-Simonians. The views of other writers who dealt with sociological and scientific themes were also considered, and were compared to the handling of similar themes within the Positivist synthesis. Mill's work on logical method was praised; in Lewes's discussion of complex organisms, Spencer's *Social Statics* was quoted. Comte's cerebral theory was compared in some detail to that of the phrenologist, Gall.[53]

That sceptical tendency within Positivism which proposed the merging of methods and ideas, and the relativity of all truths appealed strongly to Lewes and informed his response to Comte's ideas. It was not only in relation to thinkers within a rational tradition that Lewes discussed Comte's ideas. He invoked views from an opposite philosophical tradition to provide a critical yard-stick. He dissented from Comte's view that the study of astronomy destroyed religion, and employed a Carlylean terminology to note that this view was true only for those who 'identify Religion with the *theologies* which from time to time obscure the true formula'. A similar distinction between religion and theology was made by Feuerbach. Also like Carlyle, Lewes distinguished between the unchanging religious emotion and its historical forms, and he echoed, as he had done in *Robespierre*, Carlyle's interpretation of the 1789 revolution. A host of influences converged when Lewes expounded his view of the natural world. Like Spinoza, he insisted upon 'the grand unity of Nature'. His criticism of Comte's Religion of Humanity eloquently invoked Spinoza's Substance and Spencer's Unknown, as he commented, 'There must still remain for us, outlying this terrestrial sphere, the other sphere named Infinite, into which our eager and aspiring thoughts *will* wander, carrying with them, as ever, the obedient emotions of love and awe. So that besides the Religion of Humanity, there must be a Religion of the Universe . . .we need the conception of a God as the Infinite Life, from whom the Universe proceeds, not in alien indifference – not in estranged subjection – but in the fulness of abounding Power as the incarnation of resistless Activity!' *Sartor Resartus*, which profoundly affected Lewes's generation, had fused a Dissenting perception of the divine within the material with a Saint-Simonian sense of the need to assert 'the fundamental ident-ity of all things', to deify 'temporal reality'. Bazard considered that religion must 'extend itself to all reality . . .consecrate equally the material and the spiritual . . .make this world its domain'.[54] Such a notion reinforced Carlyle's natural supernaturalism; Lewes, like Marian Evans, responded to the more imaginative cast of the system upon which Comtism so heavily relied, in so far as that system celebrated the glory of the universe.

Lewes's scepticism also manifested itself in relation to Comte's political views, and his critical stance was probably reinforced by his awareness of the dogmatism of Comte's *Système de politique positive* (Vols 1–2 (1852), Vol. 3 (1853)). Lewes was also alert to the fact that aspects of Comte's analysis were prompted by phenomena peculiar to the French system, and Lewes's sensitivity to the particular qualities of the English context fuelled his questioning response to Comte's supposedly universal truths. Carlyle and Mill, in their reaction to Saint-Simonianism in the 1830s, and Marian Evans, in her reading of the French theorists of the 1840s, had reacted similarly to imported political views. Lewes had grave doubts about Comte's plans for the reorganisation of soc;ety. He also reacted adversely to Comte's more idiosyncratic views. In the radical circles in which Lewes moved, a liberal view was taken of women's role, whereas Comte thought that female emancipation would lead to social anarchy. Lewes also tended to view Comtism in the light of his own political preoccupations. His interest in left-wing developments of Idealism led him to disagree with Comte, or to describe him inaccurately as a 'philosophic socialist'. Lewes also commented that the Whigs should unite, according to Comtist theory, the ideals of progress and order, yet he shared Mill's view that the Whigs' reputation as a party of progress was a hollow sham. The Whigs failed because they alternated 'between two systems instead of combining them; and Whigs are not inaptly styled "Tories in Opposition"'.[55]

Comte's Philosophy of the Sciences was favourably received. Huxley, although critical of Lewes's scientific knowledge, considered that the book would be attractive to the ordinary reader, describing it as 'in many respects exceedingly clever. As an exposition, it is clearness and lucidity itself, and every now and then it rises into genuine eloquence'.[56] Those aspects of Positivism which Lewes praised, the synthesis of disciplines, the merging of logics, the linking of an intellectual position to the emotions, and to ethical and political action, all appealed to Marian Evans as much as they did to Lewes. Like Lewes, she was a polymath and she turned to thinkers who urgently sought an exit from the *impasse* reached by the two rival logics, because logical method, as Bentham noted in the eighteenth century, had repercussions in many areas. In *Comte's Philosophy of the Sciences*, however, Lewes pinpointed two aspects of Positivism which he had not considered so fully or so sympathetically in *A Biographical History of Philosophy*. As in *The Apprenticeship of Life*, he dwelt upon the possibility of establishing a new faith once orthodox Christian belief had been relinquished. This was in tune with Marian Evans's preoccupations: in the 1840s, she had read critics of Christianity who attempted to base faith on new foundations, such as Strauss, Hennell and Spinoza, and her interest in the subject was still evident in her reviews of Mackay and Greg in the 1850s. She had been fascinated by the radical creeds of the 1848 revolutions. In his second book on Comte, Lewes also placed new emphasis upon the anti-rational aspects of Comte's thought. He spoke of his own debt to Comte as an emotional one, and emphasised Comte's exegesis of the power of the emotions. Yet Marian Evans would also have applauded Lewes's championing of the principle of inquiry in his criticisms of Comte, for she had championed it herself in her review of Mackay, her stand against Spencer's dogmatism and her willingness to translate Feuerbach. With Lewes, she could also have disputed Comte's originality, for she had read many of those writers Lewes cited as Comte's forerunners. In invoking the views of writers from a primarily non-rational tradition as a yardstick against which to measure Comte's views, Lewes not only referred to writers Marian Evans had praised. He also extended Comte's thesis of the limitations of the intellect to argue for a view of the universe which acknowledged its mysterious beauty. This general critique of rationalism, and Lewes's specific conclusions, echoed Marian Evans's intellectual position as she had outlined it in the letters she wrote in the 1840s and early 1850s. Lewes's criticisms of Comte's political views, and of other aspects of Comte's system which were presented dogmatically, owed much, ironically enough, to Comte's own concept of relative truth, which underpinned both Lewes's and Marian Evans's championing of free inquiry. The obverse of the advocating of the sceptical notion of truth as process was a distrust of the theoretical abstractions of philosophical thinking, however fascinating they might appear. Lewes and Marian Evans had been introduced to this view by Carlyle, and Lewes's method of criticising Comte owed much to Carlyle's method of criticising rationalism in *The French Revolution*, a method which Lewes had already employed in *Robespierre*. Lewes was aware that even Positivism, which culminated in a concern for human issues, was like all philosophical speculation in that it contained the seeds of a dangerous over-abstraction. He thus brought critically to bear upon Comte's truths insights he had culled by non-philosophical methods, and from disciplines which focused upon life's concrete and mysteriously intricate manifestations. Lewes the scientist spoke of new discoveries, and Lewes the radical spoke of the complicated political situation in England. As a novelist, Lewes expressed his disapproval when Comte ignored or underestimated the complexity of the human personality and the power of the imagination. As an alienated sufferer, he also protested when Comte played down the needs of the heart.

Comte's Philosophy of the Sciences shed light upon the extent to which Marian Evans and Lewes shared a common response to the philosophical debate. The mental sympathy which existed between the two of them enabled Marian Evans, in Germany, to assist Lewes in his research into the life and work of Goethe who was, like Comte and Lewes and Marian Evans, a polymath and an eclectic. That task was to take them back to the work of Carlyle whose views had influenced Lewes's second book on Comte. It was Carlyle who had initially suggested to Lewes and Marian Evans that, in England, literature could exist in dynamic relation to speculation, as it had in the heyday of German romanticism. The twin examples of Carlyle and Goethe (of whom Carlyle was one of the earliest advocates) were to raise once more for Marian Evans the question of how best to articulate the insights of a well-informed, eclectically perceptive mind. The stay in Germany was to mark another of her tentative steps in the direction of the novel.

18
Germany (1854–1855)

I

if there is any one action or relation of my life which is and always has been profoundly serious, it is my relation to Mr. Lewes . . .From the majority of persons . . .we never looked for anything but condemnation. We are leading no life of self-indulgence, except indeed, that being happy in each other, we find everything easy.

No society can be so intimate as that admirable primitive combination by which two natures become almost fused into one.[1]

The decision to go abroad was taken for many reasons. Lewes wished to avoid contact with Agnes, and Marian Evans hinted at circumstances in Lewes's relationship with his wife which made him determined to separate from her. Before they met, Lewes and Marian Evans each had lamented their sense of alienation from society; their liaison led to the circulation of rumours in literary circles, and this increased their feeling of being outcasts. Scandalous stories were widespread, as Combe told Bray in November 1854. Thomas Woolner wrote to Lewes's old friend, William Bell Scott, denouncing 'the filthy contaminations of these hideous satyrs and smirking moralists – these workers in the Agapemone – these Mormonites in another name – stink pots of humanity'. Lewes's friends, who were acquainted with his views on relations between the sexes, were inclined to view him as the blameworthy seducer, although they also felt that he was justified in leaving Agnes. Harriet Martineau told vicious tales about Marian Evans and Lewes, the first sign of a hostility which lasted for the rest of her life, despite Marian Evans's respect for her.[2] Absence from the scene of the rumours was perhaps contrived to give them a fresh perspective on the furore. Lewes reflected that foreign travel provided 'a new standing-point from which we can judge

240

ourselves and others'. Soon after they returned to England, Marian Evans wrote to Chapman, 'I have counted the cost of the step that I have taken and am prepared to bear, without irritation or bitterness, renunciation by all my friends'.[3] Their choice of destination was probably prompted by Lewes's enthusiastic familiarity with Germany. He considered that the German cost of living was lower than the English, and both he and Marian Evans were short of money. His visits to Germany in the 1830s and 1840s meant that he already knew some of the country's leading thinkers, and he had revelled in the intellectual stimulation he had derived from such trips. One of Lewes's projects also motivated their choice of country. Lewes, like Marian Evans, was one of Carlyle's heirs, and was a propagandist for the achievements of German literature and scholarship, and he wished to collect more material for his long-planned biography of Goethe.[4]

They stayed abroad for nearly eight months, leaving London on 20 July 1854, and returning to Dover on 14 March 1855. They arrived in Weimar on 2 August 1854, having travelled there via Brussels, Liège, Cologne, Coblenz, Mainz and Frankfurt. Marian Evans's Journal recorded her delight in the peacefulness of the small town as a respite from 'English unrest . . .that society of "eels in a jar" where each is trying to get his head above the other', and she came to love that 'Nature in her gentle aspects' which she found in Weimar and the surrounding countryside.[5] From Weimar, they went to Berlin, where they stayed from 3 November 1854 until 11 March 1855, and then they journeyed back to England via Cologne, Brussels and Calais. Berlin was very different from Weimar. Marian Evans still continued consciously to delight in the new life she was leading with Lewes, but she and her companion had reservations about the city itself. The Crimean War had started in 1853: in 1854 came the battles of Alma, Balaclava and Inkerman, and the troops suffered dreadfully during the severe winter. Marian Evans was distressed to see crowds of soldiers in the streets, and described to Chapman her sorrow at seeing the German 'nation's vitality going to feed 300,000 puppets in uniform. In the streets one's legs are in constant danger from officers' swords, and at tables d'hôte the most noise is always made by the officers'. Lewes found literary circles in Berlin less attractive than those in Weimar and London. In 1856 he recalled how 'much bad paper is dirtied there by muddy printer's ink, and . . .much dreary discussion goes on in academies, and select tea-parties, where sausage and grated ham are handed round on circles of bread and butter to shrivelled Hegelians and toothless poets'.[6]

The time in Germany was somewhat marred by circumstances over which they had no control. The news from England was often depressing. They heard of the malicious gossip about their liaison, of how, for instance, Harriet Martineau and George Combe felt somehow personally affronted by their actions. Cara Bray and Sara Hennell misunderstood the situation. Although she reassured Mrs Combe that nothing dreadful had happened to Marian Evans, Cara wrote but once to Marian herself to protest about her behaviour, and was then silent. Sara indulged in one angry letter, and then loyally maintained contact. In their last weeks in Weimar, they heard of the deaths of Chrissey's son and of one of Chapman's cousins. Lewes and Marian Evans were also facing a bleak financial situation. She was constantly worried about his health; for the first six weeks in Berlin, 'G's head would not allow him to sit very long at work'.[7] Mostly, however, they were happy, particularly in each other. Marian Evans was learning, as had Lewes, that happiness could be 'wholly independent of our worldly goods and chattels'. In her private recollections of Weimar, Marian noted: 'every incident is precious in the remembrance of being made bright by the sunshine of love'; she and Lewes were 'two loving, happy human beings'. His behaviour set the tone of tender consideration which was to characterise their union and he provided living proof of his own reflection that 'the wildest youths turn out the best men. Dissipation, though an evil, is an evil best got through in youth'. Returning from a solitary walk, he presented her with 'a bunch of berries from the mountain ash as a proof that he had thought of me by the way'. She recorded that when they had to wait for a train, Lewes 'beguiled the time by telling me of the fiasco he made with a lecture on Othello at Hackney'.[8] Both of them were also heartened by the support which came from some of their friends. To Chapman and his wife, Marian Evans had revealed Lewes's difficulties. Chapman saw her as sharing the responsibility with Lewes for their irregular situation, yet he was concerned for her, and his concern was reciprocated by her anxiety about him as his personal and financial problems increased. Charles Bray was the third person in whom she had confided. To the irascible Combe, Bray wrote in October 1854, 'Nothing that I have yet heard or know will make any difference in my conduct toward her' and he was constant to his later pledge that 'It would never be other than a *strong sense* of *public* duty to the highest interests that would separate me from her or her from my friendship'. As well as unswerving affection, he offered practical help, keeping open her lines of communication with Cara and Sara, contradicting rumours, and visiting her troublesome brother, Isaac. Moral support came from Bessie Parkes, despite her father's anger, and from Herbert Spencer. Carlyle, unexpectedly, sent what Marian and Lewes interpreted as an approving letter.[9]

Their happiness also stemmed from the pleasure they derived from the atmosphere in Germany, for there they found social mores more liberal than those of England. They noted that Adolf Stahr lived openly with the novelist Fanny Lewald, who campaigned for women's independence, and that Liszt, an old friend of Lewes's from his days in Vienna in 1839, made no attempt to conceal his liaison with the Princess Caroline Sayn-Wittgenstein. In Weimar, Marian Evans was pleased by the way women could go about without an escort. She also admired the German lack of materialism, and absence of the 'suspicion that happiness is a vice'. She liked the way in which the citizens of Weimar set time aside for the pursuit of pleasure.[10] Both Lewes and Marian were also delighted by the German intelligentsia, and Lewes's earlier visits to the country, and his wide interests, gave them access to widely differing circles. In Weimar, they were intimate with Liszt, and he provided them with more information about George Sand. They also became friendly with G. A. Schöll, Director of the Free Art Institute, which was a focal point for visiting intellectuals. Schöll, under Strauss's influence, had given up teaching theology at Halle; he had edited Goethe's essays and letters, and introduced Marian Evans and Lewes to other Goethe scholars. Lewes and his companion were even received by the Grand Duke and Duchess in Weimar. In Cologne, Marian Evans met Strauss, who was brought to call by Dr Brabant, and it may have been Strauss who referred her to A. H. Ewerboeck's work which included a synopsis, and free adaptation of, Feuerbach's views.[11] In Berlin, von Ense, to whom Carlyle had given Lewes an introduction in 1838, provided them with an entrée into the city's intellectual circles. Marian spoke warmly of von Ense himself as possessing 'that thorough liberalism, social religious and political which sets the mind at ease in conversation'. He took them to Fraulein von Solmar's salon; they met Otto Gruppe, whose work on logic Marian Evans was later to commend, Heinrich Magnus, the chemist, and other scientists, and Christian Rauch, the sculptor. Ludwig Dessoir, Berlin's leading actor, whose work Lewes had reviewed for the *Leader* in

1853, presented them with tickets for the theatre. The welcome they received forged a durable, affectionate link with Germany. During the Franco-Prussian war of 1870–1, Marian Evans was greatly distressed on Prussia's behalf, and she and Lewes sent a donation to the Stahrs to be passed on to the German casualties of the aggression. They were, said Lewes, 'specially bound by many a grateful thought to German friends and to the German people'. It was not only as disciples of Carlyle that they felt an intellectual debt to the Germans: Germany had been kind to them when England had been censorious.[12]

Their new-found joy in life acted as a mental stimulus. To John Chapman, Marian Evans confided in January 1855, 'The day seems too short for our happiness, and we both of us feel that we have begun life afresh – with new ambitions and new powers'. Their meeting with Liszt in Weimar aroused her interest in music and Berlin fostered her fascination for painting. One of their greatest pleasures was to visit 'the Raczinsky Gallery – a small but very choice collection of pictures, chiefly by modern artists'. She and Lewes would argue over the merits of the works. She recorded that one painting 'G. admired very much. To me it was too theatrical'. The tastes of the actor/dramatist/sensational novelist in Lewes were still near the surface. Her interest in the visual arts prompted the detailed analysis of both painting and landscape in her Journal: she also perused Knight's *History of Painting*.[13] She and Lewes read omnivorously. She recalled how, in the evenings, she had looked forward to retreating from the bitter cold of the Berlin streets to spend the rest of the day in their warm room, drinking coffee and reading. German writers figured prominently in the lists of the authors they read, not only Goethe, but also Heine and Lessing, and German writers were quoted in her Journal. They also read, however, French writers such as Sainte-Beuve, Pascal and George Sand. There were references to classic English authors, such as Milton, and Lewes's love of drama probably accounted for the inclusion in the lists of their reading of seventeen plays by Shakespeare and Moore's *Life of Sheridan*. Works by their contemporaries Carlyle and Macaulay also attracted their attention. Letter-writing became for Marian Evans, as it had been during her stay in Switzerland, an outlet for her newly-fired imagination. She sent her friends vivid characterisations of the places they visited, and of the people they met, such as the Princess Wittgenstein, Liszt and Professor Gruppe.[14]

She was also striving to establish herself as a journalist, partly to alleviate their financial difficulties which Chapman, judging by his tardiness in offering her work, did not seem fully to appreciate.[15] Two short articles show her evolving a view of art in relation to the issues raised by the philosophers she and Lewes read, and this process was to culminate in the spate of articles she wrote which considered that subject upon her return to England. 'The Romantic School of Music', which appeared in the *Leader* on 28 October 1854, was a triple collaboration whereby Lewes added comments to Marian's translated extracts of an article by Liszt on Wagner and Meyerbeer. Lewes and Marian had heard Wagner's operas in Weimar: tacitly, they assented to the view that the operas should be commended for their attention to human psychology, and for exhibiting the law of progress operating in the arts. This argument, with its emphasis upon the primacy of a human reality, revealed a Comtist and Feuerbachian bias, and it was in line with the progressive tendencies of the *Leader*.[16] Marian Evans's review of Stahr's book on ancient art commented that intellectual progress was facilitated by the relinquishment of *a priori* methods, and the growth of a 'truer spirit of investigation'. Conforming to the *Leader*'s discriminating attitude towards German literature, Marian Evans also praised Stahr's lack of pedantry and of obscurity of style, suggesting, as Lewes had in some of his earlier articles on German literature, that these qualities were too often present.[17]

From a Berlin acquaintance, Eduard Vehse, Marian borrowed the books she reviewed in 'Memoirs of the Court of Austria'. She wrote the article in Berlin, and it appeared in the *Westminster Review* in April 1855. The article was mainly a summary of Vehse's massive work; eleven of the twenty-eight volumes had appeared. The work contained an unflattering view of the aristocracy and diplomacy in Austria. It was widely read in its German edition and in 1856 its author received a six-month prison sentence. The skill of the potential novelist was evident in her article, for her translated extracts were arranged to form a smoothly-flowing narrative. Her interests were shown in the extracts she selected which dealt with the position of women and of intellectuals, and with religious issues. The nature of personality also concerned her. She saw in the characters a mixture of the ludicrous and the magnificent, and focused upon their environment. The influences of Carlyle and Macaulay were apparent as she unveiled the human face of monarchs, and praised biographies and memoirs which 'take the

reader behind the scenes of history'. She also assessed the particular strengths of those three literatures, English, French and German, with which she and Lewes were familiar. She noted how
France and England, unlike Germany, were rich in memoirs like
Vehse's; she praised the English tendency to produce works 'at
once solid and popular'. An ideal of truth as process also informed
her assessments. She denounced German censorship, and, whilst
she criticised Vehse's failure to organise his material, she did
commend his unbiased viewpoint.[18]

Chapman commissioned the article 'Woman in France' on 5
August 1854, and she despatched it from Weimar on 8 September.
Of the articles she wrote in Germany, this provided most insight
into her capabilities and views. The article showed once more the
extent to which she and Lewes shared common preoccupations.
The position of women and, in particular, of literary women,
interested both of them. Marian Evans commented on these topics
in her letters, and her attention was caught by the writings of her
friend, Bessie Parkes, on women's education.[19] Lewes had praised
Mrs Gaskell, Charlotte Brontë and Jane Austen, and had written
about a female poet in *Rose, Blanche and Violet*. Both had long
admired George Sand; in her article on Mme de Sablé, Marian
Evans noted the similarities between George Sand and Rousseau
upon which she and Lewes had commented independently in the
1840s.[20] The style of the article, and its mode of interpretation,
were sufficiently characteristic of Marian Evans for her friends in
Coventry to recognise her authorship easily. The novelist-to-be
could be seen consolidating the skills of her craft. The prose was
lucid, albeit syntactically complex. Although she only took just
over a month to write the article, it bore no signs of hasty composition; Lewes's journalistic expertise was available to her, and he
suggested various revisions, but she also drew upon her editing
experience on the *Westminster Review*.[21] The method was stringently analytical, and her erudition was brought to bear upon the
mystery of a human life, an approach suggestively implicit in
Comte's modified scientism and his *échelle*. The result was a richly
textured narrative, which rooted personality in a solidly-realised
social context, a technique she had learnt from novelists as well as
historians. Like Carlyle, she conveyed the quality of a life as much
by the analysis of accidentals as by consideration of essentials. Her
historicism underpinned a tolerant curiosity manifested in her
discussion of the enthusiasm of Port Royal; the same sensitivity to

cultural change led her to contemplate a complimentary article on the history of German women.[22] A broadly radical humanism, exemplified by Comte and Feuerbach, informed her notion that all individuals, however obscure, made an unproclaimed contribution to the progress of humanity. Mme de Sablé prefigured Dorothea Brooke in being 'chiefly valuable in what she stimulated others to do, rather than in what she did herself'.[23]

She also tentatively expressed her views upon art. The Hôtel de Rambouillet circle was praised for encouraging women to become 'intelligent observers of character and events'. Like Lewes and Carlyle, Marian Evans viewed the ideal perception as taking the form of unbiased, yet informed, contemplation. She emphasised that equal access to ideas for both sexes was essential not merely for the welfare of society, but also for art, which must draw upon learning, as well as upon personal experience. In proposing an art which utilised erudition, she sanctioned a mode of creativity wherein there was a dynamic interplay between a writer's sense of actuality and a response to concepts as in, for instance, George Sand's novels. Inspiration was not divorced from intellect. Her empirical bias existed, however, alongside a sense of the complex mystery of character: her delimitation of the powers of the mind restored wonder to the universe. Mme de Sablé, she noted, 'affects us by no special quality, but by her entire being'. La Rochefoucauld's maxims were 'false if taken as a representation of all the elements and possibilities of human nature'. She also saw art as a potent expression of a valuable subjectivity. There was one correct process in scientific enquiry, which 'has no sex; the mere knowing and reasoning faculties, if they act correctly, must go through the same process and arrive at the same result'. From Rousseau and Feuerbach, however, she had learnt doctrines of individualism. Individual perception might arrive at visions more comprehensive than the exclusive pursuit of the empirical method was capable of attaining. In art, she argued that there was engaged, "the action of the entire being, in which every fibre of nature is engaged, in which every peculiar modification of the individual makes itself felt'. The search for some method of inquiry and mode of expression, based on human wholeness, had likewise motivated the efforts of Coleridge, Carlyle and Mill. Marian Evans validated art as a mode of knowledge more broadly based in method that the *a posteriori* logic, a view that she had hinted at in her letter to John Sibree in the 1840s. However, in emphasising the difference between the sexes, she introduced a new dimension to her thought which she had learnt partly from Feuerbach and partly from Lewes, who had long been preoccupied with the distinctive features of the female psychology. Her suggestion that women had a special contribution to make to art by dint of their sexuality supplemented a Carlylean notion that creation was an expression of an integrated human personality.[24]

Upon returning to England, Marian Evans wrote two articles about Germany which rearranged material from her Journal, and omitted its overt references to herself and Lewes. These articles afforded insight into her preoccupations and habitual way of viewing reality. She again tentatively formulated a view of art. A progressivist cast to her thought was apparent. Intuitively, she was attracted to the melodic tradition of the old composers, but she tried to understand Wagner, seeing his work as the music of the future and conceding that any 'attempt at an innovation reveals a want that has not hitherto been met'. The intellect alone was once more seen as an imperfect source of inspiration; artists should not premeditate the meaning of a symbol, rather, the meaning must rush 'in on their imagination before their slower reflection has seized any abstract idea embodied in it'.[25] In her Berlin Journal she meditated upon the relationship between art and reality, and she focused upon how this was connected to the workings of the mind; this theme also figured in her articles. An allusion to *Les confessions* hinted that Rousseau's notion of the idiosyncracy of perception informed some of her comments. Since she considered that the whole being was exercised in the act of creation, she suggested 'how inevitably subjective art is, even when it professes to be purely imitative – how the most active perception gives us rather a reflex of what we think and feel, than the real sum of objects before us'. She was critical of art which only idealised, and praised a bust of Gluck which represented his flaws, as a reflection of nature. In such comments, she obliquely defined her view of reality. She argued also that nature contained dimensions of mystery and beauty, and praised the sculptor because 'he has done what, doubtless, Nature also did . . .made one feel in those coarsely-cut features the presence of the genius *qui divinise la laideur*'. The whole mind engaged in the act of creation thus glimpsed dimensions in reality which the analytical faculties overlooked, because they were doomed to simplify the object of their contemplation.[26] Her own mode of vision, in some repects, echoed this theory of art. Her erudition informed, but did not constrain, her vision. She compared Weimar to the cities of the ancient world, and to English provincial towns, but also observed it closely in its specificity. Her description of Bercka was a similar exercise in accurate observation of detail. Her concern for the complex truth of character was equally in line with her notion that reality was complicated. She praised Wagner's operas because 'feelings and situations spring out of *character*' and saw Liszt as a Carlylean hero, in whom there was 'baser metal mingled with fine gold', comparing her view of him to Scheffer's idealised portrait.[27] Simultaneous with such a comment was the notion that mental ideas perished on contact with that true knowledge which stemmed from an act of perception involving all aspects of personality. She showed how, as she came to know Liszt better, her view of him became more complicated. Weimar initially failed to correspond to her preconceived ideas; it was 'more like a market town than the precinct of a court', and she saw 'nothing but the most arid prosaism'. She then showed how her opinions changed. In informal fashion, the article recorded the dispelling of preconceived illusions via acquired knowledge and sympathy: her novels were to conduct the reader through a similar process.[28]

Chapman, despite the enthusiastic reception given to the article on Mme de Sablé, offered Marian Evans no more work. Financially pressed, she turned back to her trade as a translator, and set to work on Spinoza's *Ethics*. She worked on the text almost every day in Berlin and, by the time she and Lewes left for England, Part III was nearly finished.[29] Over and above her need to earn money, Marian Evans's translation of Spinoza was motivated by her long-standing interest in the subject. Spinoza was one of Bray's enthusiasms and at Foleshill, when she was so vitally concerned with questions of religious belief, she worked on the *Tractatus*. In 1852, she read Froude's article on Spinoza, and criticised its 'usual Froudian sentimentality and false veneration'.[30] Her desire to translate the *Ethics* was doubtless spurred on by Lewes's enthusiasm for the work. Spinoza's concept of the subjectivity of evil attracted Lewes's interest in the late 1830s. He started a translation of the *Ethics* in 1836 and during that period of anguished isolation closely identified with Spinoza. In *A Biographical History of Philosophy*. he remarked that little had been written on Spinoza in

England. He oddly overlooked Coleridge's pioneer remarks in *Biographia Literaria* (1817), but he did mention Hallam's comments in *Introduction to the Literature of Europe* (1837–9), which Marian Evans read in 1841. Lewes, Leigh Hunt and Marian Evans all heavily annotated Hallam's remarks: Lewes's notes defended Spinoza against Hallam's analysis of Spinoza's limitations, and also contrasted Spinoza's sternly logical analysis of the natural world to what Lewes viewed unfavourably as Carlyle's oscillation between Pantheism and Deism. Lewes subsequently contributed articles on Spinoza to the *Penny Cyclopaedia* in 1842. In his history of philosophy, he emphasised the romance of Spinoza's life, and rebutted the view of him as a 'bugbear of theologians . . . an atheist . . . a frigid logician', describing him as 'one of the immortal intellects whose labours cleared the way for the present state of things'. He pointed to his connections with German Idealism and the Higher Criticism, and quoted his own translation of the *Ethics*. Spinoza's ideas also permeated his view of the natural world in *Comte's Philosophy of the Sciences*.[31]

Bray had been enthusiastic about Spinoza because, in attempting to avoid the extremes of empiricism and intuitionism, Spinoza anticipated the philosophical trend which characterised so much of the intellectual effort of Marian Evans's generation, and which informed the articles Marian Evans wrote during this period. Spinoza's views on specific topics also avoided extremes. His stringent method of Biblical criticism was tempered by piety; the doctrine of Substance allowed for scientific scrutiny of phenomena as well as a joyous response to the natural world. He proposed freedom of thought and a theory of progress, yet eschewed a revolutionary viewpoint. Spinoza formulated a theory of the emotions which was akin to the project undertaken by Spencer, and which he discussed with Marian Evans. Spinoza wished to describe feelings from a scientific, non-moral viewpoint, 'as though I were concerned with lines, planes and solids'.[32] He argued that pleasure prompted love, and pain prompted hatred, and, from this premiss, evolved his definition of all other emotions. The nature of perception was central to his argument. Egocentric emotions, such as avarice, ambition or lust stemmed from a false perception of reality: pride was 'a species of madness wherein a man dreams with his eyes open, thinking that he can accomplish all things that fall within the scope of his perception'.[33] Spinoza, like Comte, also attempted to forge a link between a scientifically conceived theory of perception and ethics, and Lewes's work on both philosophers once more demonstrated the congruity of his interests and Marian Evans's. It also enabled him to advise her on her work. Spinoza outlined three types of knowledge as in the *Tractatus*, but emphasised more firmly the obstacles to perception. As Froude noted, the link was established between informed vision and action; 'The better we know the better we act, and the fallacy of all common arguments against necessitarianism lies in the assumption that it leaves no room for self-direction; whereas it merely insists on exact conformity with experience on the conditions under which self-determination is possible. Conduct, according to the necessitarian, depends on knowledge'. Spinoza argued that notions of good and evil were subjective because they originated in the senses, and that 'we deem a thing to be good because we strive for it, wish for it, long for it, or desire it'.[34]

Spinoza also linked his ideas about freedom and necessity to a theory of perception, and the contemplation of determinism had induced Carlyle's spiritual crisis, as described in *Sartor Resartus*, and had been the central theme of Bray's *The Philosophy of Necessity*. Spinoza denied the existence of will, and admitted only the existence of 'particular volitions'. With reference to his concept of Substance, he noted 'a mental decision and a bodily appetite, or determined state, are simultaneous, or rather are one and the same thing, which we call decision, when it is regarded under and explained through the attribute of thought, and a conditioned state, when it is regarded under the attribute of extension, and deduced from the laws of motion and rest'. Reason, that faculty which religious moralists often condemned, was thus transformed into the source of right action, for it recognised that man was a determined being who was part of nature, and that he had a limited capacity for independent action, and reason thus promoted a virtuous obedience to laws. The emotions, by contrast, encouraged anarchical and tyrannous behaviour.[35]

Spinoza's concern with the logical problem was, like Marian Evans's and Lewes's, a pragmatic one. He showed that the resolution of the debate about perception would give sure direction to religious belief, and private and social behaviour. Spiritual perfection was seen to reside in striving to know God through rational scrutiny of the laws of the universe, and ethical perfection was expressed in private and public acts which, deriving from this knowledge of Substance, obeyed the laws, and laboured for the good of others out of a reverence for life. Science provided a basis for religion; Spinoza spoke of the joy to be derived from the rational contemplation of inexorable laws, which allowed man to 'necessarily . . . participate of the divine nature'. The work proposed a modified stoicism as man viewed a universe governed by laws he could not influence. Man's understanding of the emotions also emancipated him from their tyranny, and enabled him to 'frame a system of right conduct, or fixed practical precepts . . . commit it to memory, and apply it forthwith to the particular circumstances which now and again meet us in life, so that our imagination may become fully imbued therewith'. This was to propound a doctrine of 'joyful activity within the limits of man's true sphere', akin to the Comtean notion that Marian Evans so often quoted, 'Notre vraie destinée se compose de résignation et d'activité'. From his phrase of rational perception stemmed a reiteration of the *Tractatus*'s political argument for tolerance and compassion.[36]

Marian Evans was clearly absorbed by her work on the *Ethics*. The task was performed with the meticulous care for her author's meaning which characterised her work on Strauss and Feuerbach; the manuscript shows how she spread out her text to leave room for prolific deletions and corrections. Had the translation been published, it would have been the first translation of the *Ethics* into English. Lewes delivered the manuscript to Bohn in London just before he left for Devon on 8 May 1856, but, after an exchange of angry letters between Lewes and the publisher, who had initially engaged Lewes himself to edit a translation of Spinoza, the project was dropped. On 15 June 1856, Lewes asked Bohn to return the manuscript.[37] A handful of articles, and the text of a translation which was never to be published, seem scant harvest for the time Marian Evans spent in Germany. Yet her work allowed her to contemplate the ramifications, aesthetic and otherwise, of the philosophical debate.

II

Hardly anything can be of greater value to a man of theory and speculation . . . than to carry on his speculations in the companionship, and under the criticism, of a really superior woman.[38]

Lewes's and Marian Evans's projects were complementary, for the theme of the rival logics, and its application to specific topics, which was evident in Spinoza's *Ethics*, was found also in Lewes's biography of Goethe. Spinoza had exerted some influence on Goethe, and those who were interested in Spinoza were often, like Adolf Stahr, interested in Goethe as well. In his annotation of Hallam, Lewes noted, 'Spinoza's Pantheism is in truth the grandest & most religious of all philosophies, and as such it is recognised by Göthe & the German philosophers who all embrace his creed'. Marian Evans read 'Goethe's wonderful observations on Spinoza' and was 'Particularly struck with the beautiful modesty of the passage in which he says he cannot presume to say that he thoroughly understands Spinoza'. Goethe's views on Spinoza probably influenced her own.[39]

Work on the biography dominated their days in Germany, although it was not Lewes's only project. On 15 October 1854, Marian Evans told Chapman that Lewes had 'given up the Leader' and by November 1854 Hunt also had relinquished his editorial duties. But Lewes still needed money to support Agnes. He wrote articles for the *Leader* which he dictated to Marian Evans, and he also adapted a French farce.[40] The *Ethics* was, to some extent, a joint project; the same was true of Lewes's biography of Goethe, for if Lewes was well-equipped to advise Marian Evans on Spinoza, she was his ideal assistant for his work on Goethe. German literature was one of her long-standing enthusiasms. As Lewes worked on the biography, she read German literature and works by Carlyle who had directed her attention to German literature when she was housekeeping for her father at Griff. She tried to improve her command of the German language. She translated the quotations Lewes used in the biography, and read and re-read the manuscript. The journal she kept in Germany, and the articles she based upon that journal, reveal how the places she and Lewes visited became inextricably associated in her mind with Goethe's life and writings. She and Lewes sought out such places, staying, for instance, near the house in which Goethe was born in Frankfurt, and visiting it twice. Between 1868 and 1869, when her career as a novelist was well-established, she recorded many quotations from Goethe in her notebooks.[41] Interest in Goethe had been stimulated by the *Monthly Repository*'s policy of promoting foreign literature, and Lewes, as a young man, had been associated with that periodical. Therein were published, between 1806 and 1826, various articles on Goethe. Lewes acknowledged his particular debt to Crabb Robinson, whose translations had been published in 1806. In May 1832 Robinson contributed a commemorative article, and between June 1832 and April 1833 a critical bibliography. In 1834 he reviewed Sarah Austin's *Characteristics of Goethe*, which was largely a translation from the German of J. D. Falk, and Lewes's *Life of Goethe* was also to acknowledge Austin's work.[42]

If his work on Comte demonstrated the influence of Mill on Lewes, the biography of Goethe showed him as the protegé of Carlyle. He dedicated the book 'To Thomas Carlyle, who first taught England to appreciate Goethe'; it was 'a Memorial of Gratitude' to Carlyle 'for Intellectual Guidance, and of Esteem for Noble Qualities'. Carlyle not only fostered Lewes's interest in Goethe; his view of Goethe's significance was profoundly to influence Lewes's interpretation of the German writer's life and writings. Carlyle's promotion of Goethe had started with his translation of *Wilhelm Meister* in 1824, a work he still spoke of admiringly in 1866; at the end of 1837, he told von Ense that his task as the advocate of the German cause was almost complete. Carlyle saw Goethe as a writer who had shown the way forward for a tormented generation, for he had evinced a capacity to evolve from, and beyond, the conflict between intellectualism and sentimentalism. He was 'learned not in the head only, but also in the heart . . . the grand characteristic of his writings' was 'not . . . knowledge, but wisdom'. Carlyle's later comments reiterated his view of Goethe as simultaneously representative of, and offering a solution to, contemporary spiritual dilemmas. His *Inaugural Address* (1866) spoke of his gratitude to Goethe, and he confessed in his *Reminiscences*, 'I . . . still feel, endlessly indebted to Goethe. . . . He, in his fashion, I perceived, had travelled the steep rocky road before me, the first of the moderns'.[43] Lewes had but recently looked to Positivism for similar consolation: it is significant, as regards Lewes's and Marian Evans's estimation of the function and value of literature that they turned to a writer who was acknowledged by Carlyle as affording, in his novels, plays and poems, illumination of crucial intellectual and spiritual problems greater than that yielded by philosophy. Lewes's other mentor Mill, in the late 1820s and early 1830s, during his period of intense dissatisfaction with philosophical sectarianism, and in the throes of his spiritual crisis, had likewise turned to Goethe's writings.[44]

Lewes had worked on the biography since about 1844, and his efforts to finish it may have been spurred on by Marian Evans's interest in both Carlyle and German literature. Lewes's early work revealed his interest in, and sometimes his association of, Goethe and Carlyle. In 1842 Mill noticed the influence of Carlyle in an article Lewes wrote on Goethe, and *Ranthorpe*, written in the same year, referred to Goethe and his Scottish exponent. Lewes, like Carlyle, pleaded Goethe's case. He considered the literary response to Idealism, as represented by Goethe, important enough to mention in his history of philosophy, and Goethe was often cited in articles written by Lewes in the 1840s. The *Leader* promoted a discriminating appreciation of German literature, and Lewes quoted Goethe in *The Apprenticeship of Life* which appeared in that periodical in 1850.[45] Carlyle and Lewes did not, however, always agree in their literary evaluations, and Lewes assessed Goethe independently, and often in the light of his own interests. Carlyle disliked Lewes's 1843 article which spoke of Goethe's coldness, and Lewes also compared Goethe to George Sand whom Carlyle detested. In 1852, Lewes was still comparing Goethe to George Sand,[46] but he also wrote an article which was unusual in considering 'Goethe as a Man of Science'. Lewes demonstrated his versatility by his command of scientific material, and his ability to explain scientific ideas in a lucid fashion. The article also outlined some of the ideas he was to incorporate into *The Life of Goethe*. Lewes concentrated upon Goethe's contribution to the invention of a method of inquiry; for similar reasons he had commended Bacon and Comte, with whom Goethe was compared.[47] In comparative anatomy, Goethe attacked the search for final causes, yet he 'does more than expose the poverty of the reigning Method, he substitutes a true one'. The cast of his mind was anti-metaphysical, in that he derived 'the terms of comparison – the data for his judgment – not from within his own mind, but from the circle of things he contemplates'. His scientific thought and his poetry were 'always inseparably connected with concrete realities'.[48] Goethe's writings were, in this respect, commended for their dissimilarity to the abstractions of a Robespierre, and Carlyle's critique of ideas which were evolved without reference to reality informed such comment. Yet Lewes saw Goethe not as a mere collector of facts, for his 'proper domain' was 'that of general ideas'. Goethe was described in terms of synthesis: he was 'fully penetrated by the spirit of positive philosophy'. Carlyle had seen Goethe as fusing opposites and Lewes agreed with this interpretation. His mode of inquiry combined the deductive and the inductive. As a thinker, he reconciled science and poetry. As a scientist, Goethe was important philosophically, for he vindicated a specific use of the *a priori* method, which was little understood by English thinkers. Lewes, like Goethe, only dismissed this method of scientific hypothesis when 'it rests contented with its own verdicts without seeking the verification of facts, or seeking only a partial hasty confrontation with facts'.[49]

The Life of Goethe broke new ground, as had Lewes's articles on George Sand, his history of philosophy and his book on Comte, for it was the first biography of Goethe in any language. He had some trouble finding a publisher, but the first edition was well-received, and Lewes and Marian Evans were delighted by the impact it made in Germany. It became the standard work on the subject, and Jowett termed it 'the second best biography in the English language'.[50] In Germany, Lewes was bringing to a climax years of work on Goethe. He had collected books on the subject, and wrote from Germany to his sons that they would know who Goethe was 'by the portraits and little bust in our house'. Lewes, wrote Marian Evans, had 'gained very valuable materials for his life of Goethe by staying [in Germany], and his heart and soul are in the work'. He and Marian Evans met German scholars and those who had known Goethe, and visited places associated with him. Lewes discussed Goethe with the Princess Wittgenstein, with J. P. Eckermann, Goethe's friend and literary executor, and with Adolf Stahr. Von Ense lent Lewes books he could not get at the public library. Lewes visited the *atelier* of Rauch, who had painted portraits of Goethe, and provided Lewes with various anecdotes. Marian Evans reported to Chapman that Lewes had met 'an old court lady who was a blooming girl of sixteen when Goethe first came to Weimar'. Contact with Goethe's family made the writer come alive. His daughter-in-law, Ottilie, allowed Lewes to see Goethe's study and bedroom which were not generally open to the public, and Lewes described these in detail in his book.[51] One of the biography's most valuable qualities is its conveying of a sense of intimate acquaintance with the writer and the places in which he had lived and worked. As Carlyle's disciple, Lewes had a due regard for facts, and he and Marian Evans diligently searched them out.

Carlyle exerted direct influence on the book's composition. Lewes discussed Carlyle's recent work with von Ense, although the latter was, by 1855, feeling 'terrible disappointment' in Carlyle.

Lewes reported progress back to Cheyne Row, and, when Carlyle
wrote to them in Germany, Lewes replied 'I sat at your feet when
my mind was first awakening; I have honoured and loved you ever
since both as teacher and friend'. Carlyle read the proofs, and
wrote words of praise to Lewes, although his opinion of the work
was, in actuality, somewhat mixed. Grateful and admiring references to Carlyle occured frequently in *The Life of Goethe*. Lewes
recalled the friendship between the Scottish writer and the subject
of his biography, and the discussions of Goethe he himself had
had with Carlyle.[52] Marian Evans's involvement in the project
possibly strengthened the pervasive influence of Carlyle, but at
certain points in the narrative the biography bore witness to the
similarity of Lewes's and Marian Evans's immediate preoccupations.
Lewes's ideal of love echoed her description of their happiness in
her Journal and letters. He noted the lack of freedom for women in
Weimar, criticised frivolous adultery and ill-informed gossip. He
also spoke of the sadness of estrangement from old friends. In
analysing *Elective Affinities*, he praised the delineation of the theme
of 'the collision of Passion and Duty, – of Impulse on the one hand,
and on the other, of Social Law'.[53] Goethe's varied interests appealed to Lewes and Marian Evans, for, like Comte and themselves,
Goethe was a polymath. Lewes defended Goethe's wide-ranging
concerns as a preparation for fruitful activity, and Lewes's research
into these concerns allowed him to exercise his own competence in
diverse disciplines. The 1852 article had suggested that Goethe's
'versatile nature demanded *varieties* of activity', and had expounded Goethe's view that the versatile talent was often under-
rated. Material from this article formed the basis for Chapter 10 of
Book 5, entitled 'The Poet as a Man of Science'. In Berlin, Marian
Evans and Lewes met scientists, as well as artists and writers, and
this doubtless fuelled anew Lewes's interest in this aspect of
Goethe's career.[54]

In reviewing Goethe's career, Lewes saw 'constancy underlying
all his versatility . . . unity animating the variety of his life'.
Goethe was seen by Lewes, as he and Marian Evans had seen
Spinoza and George Sand, as a writer whose creative impetus
often rested upon a sense that philosophical issues informed all
kinds of intellectual activity. A similar tradition was exemplified in
England by Lewes's mentors, Mill and Carlyle who, like Goethe,
responded with a sense of personal and social urgency to the

debate between intuitionism and empiricism. As a scientist, Goethe saw how the divisive 1830 argument between the syntheti- cal thought of St Hilaire and the analytical mode of Cuvier was of profound importance: his fascination with that controversy de- monstrated 'his sincere and absorbing love of great ideas; he knew that a whole revolution in thought, far deeper and far more important to Humanity than twenty July days in France, was germinating in that doctrine'.[55] Lewes analysed Goethe's interest in the synthetic system of Spinoza, which, as well as the Cuvier/St Hilaire debate, may well have prompted Goethe's 1830 remark which Lewes applauded, 'what is all intercourse with Nature, if we merely occupy ourselves with individual material parts'.[56] Mazzini remarked that the German writer was 'like a magnificent tree growing on the confines of two worlds', and Goethe's discriminat- ing assessment of the rival philosophical schools was analysed by Lewes.[57] He stressed Goethe's hostility to extreme versions of Idealism with their inquiry into causality, saying that Goethe sought rather impartially to 'know what *is*'. He also reiterated Goethe's guarded praise of the *a priori* method as working hypo- thesis. Goethe's sceptical response to the philosophy of the En- lightenment was also demonstrated. Lewes, the author of *Robes- pierre* and *The Apprenticeship of Life*, which had contemplated the ideas of the French revolutionists, considered at length Goethe's reaction to the French Revolution. He focused particularly upon Goethe's changing attitude towards cults of humanity, which varied from an aristocratic contempt for the masses to the incorpor- ation of Saint-Simonian ideas into *Elective Affinities*. In *Faust*, Lewes saw as implicit the notion that 'man lives for man, and . . . only in as far as he is working for Humanity can his efforts bring perma- nent happiness'.[58]

Carlyle's views exerted a crucial influence upon Lewes's inter- pretation of Goethe's character. Lewes saw Goethe, as Carlyle had often seen the subjects of his own biographies, as a flawed hero. Lewes stressed that 'a certain grandeur of soul' may exist amidst weakness and error, and refused to equate heroism with perfec- tion. Rather, sympathy should be extended to the interconnection of strength and frailty within character. He admired, as did Marian Evans, emotional energy, for, 'life without its generous errors might want its lasting enjoyments; and thus the very mistakes which arise from an imprudent, unreflecting career, are absolved by that instinct which suggests other aims for existence beyond prudential aims'. Carlyle had also seen his subjects as iconographic archetypes, whose lives shed light on contemporary dilemmas. Lewes had emulated this method in *Robespierre*, and pursued it again in *The Life of Goethe*. Carlyle was searching for inner peace and, like Coleridge, dramatised the debate between associationism and intuitionism into a psychological conflict between head and heart. Lewes praised Goethe, in terms which recall Carlyle's, as embodying a synthesis of emotions and intellect in his personality, actions and writings. Mazzini, by contrast, saw Goethe in precisely opposite terms as failing to accomplish such a synthesis, but it was indicative of the widespread nature of the influence of Carlyle and Coleridge upon the thought of the mid-Victorian period that Mazzini's interpretation, like Lewes's, operated within the framework delineated by Coleridge and Carlyle. Carlyle, in 1828, had described Goethe's works as 'the voice of whole harmonious manhood'. Lewes commented at the start of his biography that 'self-mastery . . . forms the keystone' of Goethe's character, a view he had already expounded in *Ranthorpe*. Lewes echoed Carlyle's concept of the balanced and integrated personality: Goethe, he stated, 'sought both to feel and to know. . . . Poetry was the melodious voice breathing from his entire manhood, not a profession, not an act of duty'.[59]

The notions of conflict between, and synthesis of, opposed concepts, were explored by Lewes in areas other than the psychological. Lewes contrasted French and German culture, which were often seen to embody the antithesis between rationalism and sentimentalism. Goethe's work embraced both science and poetry, as Spencer had remarked.[60] In religion, Goethe steered a middle course between atheism and Christian orthodoxy, and criticised both Encyclopaedists and sectarian Christians. He blended eclectically the ideas of 'Spinoza, Kant and the Grecian sages', praised the belief which benefited the believer, and opposed proselytism. He 'had deep religious sentiments, with complete scepticism on most religious doctrines. . . . He declared himself in the deepest sense of the word a Protestant, and as such claimed "the right of holding his inner being free from all prescribed dogma, the right of developing himself religiously!"' Marian Evans, in 1849, considered she was experiencing the 'hardships of the new Protestantism'. Goethe viewed Christ, as Marian Evans came to view him, as a symbol of moral excellence, and proposed a 'Christianity of feeling and action'.[61]

Three other themes dominated Lewes's biography, and they reveal how he confronted the notions engendered by the philosophical debate to forge his own theoretical viewpoints, often as they related to a definition of art. He also frequently evolved from those viewpoints a method of analysis which he himself could follow. The first of these themes related to Lewes's consideration of Goethe's context. The historicist viewpoint, an offshoot of philosophical determinism, was praised, and the theme of the interaction of organisms and their habitat, and the view that art was a social product, pervaded Lewes's writings. Lewes and Marian Evans researched the social and intellectual structure of Goethe's Weimar; Book IV, Chapter 1, 'Weimar in the Eighteenth Century', provided 'solid information' about Goethe's environment of a kind Lewes found lacking in most books on German literature.[62] Yet, philosophically, Lewes eschewed, as did Marian Evans and Carlyle, unalleviated determinism. He saw the evolution of personality as a complex movement, and described changes in character via metaphors referring to vast mysterious processes, such as the emergence of musical harmony, the 'gathering splendour of the dawn', the geological formation of mountain ranges. He combined the notion of an unchanging human nature with notions of historical determinism, noting in neo-Idealist terminology that man 'does not change: forms only change, the spirit remains . . . – it only manifests itself differently'. Comte's discussion of the biological relationship between organism and habitat was also merged with a Carlylean notion of the hero as one who did not bow to necessity: Lewes commented, 'Character is to outward circumstance what the Organism is to the outward world: living *in* it, but not specially determined *by* it. . . . Every Biologist knows that Circumstance has a *modifying* influence; but he also knows that these modifications are only possible within certain limits . . . it would be nearer the mark to say that Man is the architect of Circumstance. It is Character which builds an existence out of Circumstance. Our strength is measured by our plastic powers'.[63]

Subsequent editions of *The Life of Goethe* elaborated the contrast between the metaphysical and empirical methods, and showed how this contrast implied divergences between subjective and objective vision. This contrast prompted Lewes's second and third topics, romanticism and realism. Some crucial implications of the philosophical debate regarding the way in which perception operated were raised by those post-Enlightenment poets and novelists whose works Marian Evans and Lewes had read in their youth. Lewes, in writing of Goethe, turned to a general critique of romanticism, that literary movement which, like many of the philosophers Lewes and Marian Evans read, contemplated and embodied the limitations of rationalism. Lewes's telling appraisal of romanticism as a 'brilliant error'[64] encapsulated the ambiguous response of many mid-Victorians to the earlier nineteenth-century tradition. The commendatory adjective of Lewes's phrase suggested, however, that he was willing, like Mill and Carlyle, to acknowledge the value of literary forms as a vehicle for illuminating the philosophical issue of perception. Such had been Carlyle's conclusions in his analysis of German literature; such had been Lewes's and Marian Evans's assumptions in their enthusiasm for George Sand. Such a view was crucially to influence Marian Evans's decision to write novels. Lewes advocated a modified romanticism, and noted the influence Scott and Goethe, who laboured towards a like end, exerted upon each other. He discussed the link between romanticism and the questioning spirit of the revived Protestantism at the turn of the century, for Lewes welcomed the impulse to challenge established ideas. He deplored, however, the sanction romanticism gave to self-indulgent emotionalism and exaggerated individualism and in this he followed Carlyle. He also saw one of the errors of the movement as a metaphysical tendency to over-abstraction, a readiness to simplify nature by referring it to theory. Lewes urged that such subjective tendencies must be countered by an outward-turning vision, which was also essential for psychic health, saying, 'Turn your mind to realities, and the self-made phantoms which darken your soul will disappear like night at the approach of dawn'.[65]

The definition of realism concerned Marian Evans: her Berlin Journal, discussing the paintings she and Lewes viewed, contained comments which were informed by her contrasting of an idealising art with one which she associated with 'truth and nature'.[66] Goethe had evolved a complex doctrine of literary realism, and Lewes discussed this in detail, for he granted art a high status, seeing it as a means of interpreting the world, as a discipline as stringent as science, and as one productive of important knowledge. Implicit in the perceptual repercussions of the philosophical debate, which were explored by romanticism, were rival definitions of reality. There was an apparent opposition between Idealism, which emphasised an intangible reality, and the materialist bias of empiricism. Spinoza, whom Marian Evans was translating as Lewes worked on *The Life of Goethe*, had tried to reconcile such opposite views via his doctrine of Substance. Lewes had pondered the concept of realism in his novels and his criticism of the novel, and he defined the concept broadly to take into account different kinds of reality. He did not accept that there was a dichotomy between realism and idealism: Hegel, whose aesthetic writings he reviewed in 1842, saw art as bodying forth a reality which partook of the infinite, as manifesting 'the Idea in sensible form', and revealing 'the spiritual at every point on its surface'.[67] In *The Life of Goethe*, Lewes blended Goethe's views with his own to formulate a doctrine of art which refuted the classification of writers as either realist or idealist. He insisted in ostensibly empirical vein that art should be 'the expression of real experience'. In the second edition of *The Life of Goethe* (1864), he elaborated his criticism of metaphysical doctrines of art, noting how the 'desire to get deeper than Life itself led to a disdain of reality and the present'. To speak of art as reflecting the genuine experience of reality was, however, to beg the question as to what sort of reality, and what kind of perceptual experience, were being invoked. Lewes's appraisal of romanticism suggested that perception was neither wholly empirical nor totally intuitionist. He specifically rejected naturalistic criteria as they were to be enacted by, for instance, scientific materialists like Zola. Art stemmed from the experience of a reality more complex than that presupposed by empiricism, and Lewes criticised that art which staked a claim to realism because it dealt with the sordid and the ugly. Art dealt with a material reality which was everywhere interfused with the divine as Hegel had suggested: Goethe 'animated fact with divine life: he saw in Reality the incarnation of the Ideal' and 'strove above all things to understand fact, because fact was divine manifestation'. Poetry was 'the beautiful vesture of reality', and Lewes quoted Devrient's comment on the Weimar school that 'although it demanded of the artist "to produce something resembling nature", nevertheless set up a new standard of nobleness and beauty. . . . The tendency hitherto dominant had by no means neglected the beautiful, but it had sought only a *beautiful reality*, – now, with subtle distinction, *beautiful truth* was demanded from it'.[68]

Also implicit in Lewes's argument was the assumption that form in art was crucially important in conveying this vision of reality, and such had been Marian Evans's suggestion in a letter to John Sibree.[69] Aesthetic factors controlled the emotions which inspired art, so that art 'enshrines the great sadness of the world, but is itself not sad. . . . While pain is in its newness it is pain, and nothing else; it is not Art, but Feeling'. Art, *qua* art, related to outer reality in a complicated and special fashion. *Faust* was 'not a story to be credited as *fact*, but a story to be credited as *representative* of fact'. The peasants in *Hermann und Dorothea* were 'ideal characters in the best sense, viz., in the purity of nature'. Goethe's domestic scenes were far removed from documentary naturalism; episodes in *Werther*, Lewes noted, 'have excited the ridicule of some English critics, to whom poetry is a thing of pomp and classicality, not the beautiful vesture of reality. The beauty and art of Werther is not in the incident (a Dumas would shrug despairing shoulders over such invention), but in the representation'. Modern art must forge an aesthetic which would express and acknowledge the complexity of life. The artist should aspire to a faithful vision which simultaneously and necessarily acknowledged moral and aesthetic values. He should aim to 'deal with Life no longer by halves, but to work it out in its totality, beauty and goodness'. Art must not resort to simple answers to the problems life raised. Romantic sensationalism, as the reference to Dumas showed, was seen as a distortion of reality; Lewes also rejected what was often the aesthetic counterpart of naturalism, the *tranche de vie* structure. Lewes thus proposed an ideal art which should have no recourse to the simplifications of philosophical theorising or the misrepresentation of extravagant plot manipulation.[70]

An ideal art was thus proposed which articulated a flexible mode of perception, and was non-doctrinaire in its assumptions about reality. Such an art would be necessarily representational, and non-didactic. Lewes's 1853 article on *Ruth* and *Villette* outlined his views on didacticism, citing in support of his ideal of art as an indirect, aesthetic mode of instruction, the views of Hegel and George Sand, and pointing to *Faust* as a sublime example of non-moralising art.[71] He rejected overt didacticism because 'Life forgets in activity all moral verdict'. True art, like life, provoked questions, but when 'the Singer becomes a Demonstrator, he abdicates his proper office, to bungle in the performance of another', a statement which echoed George Sand's 'Art is not . . . an irrefutable lecturer'.[72] *Faust* was 'at once a problem and a picture', for Goethe 'was an Artist, not an Advocate; he painted a true picture, and because he painted it truly, he necessarily presented it in a form which would permit men to draw from it those opposite conclusions which the reality itself might permit'.[73] Thought and language might, as Hegel had asserted, reflect life and assume life's functions.

This view of art corresponded to the anti-dogmatic philosophical position of Mill and Carlyle. Fixed and general truths were rejected by post-rationalists: Lewes and Marian Evans, like Mill and Carlyle embraced, instead, the sceptic's notion of truth as process. Quoting from *In Memoriam*, Lewes dwelt upon Goethe's 'honest doubt'. He saw this anti-dogmatic stance underlying Goethe's view of art as unideological representation. Kestner commented that Goethe 'strives after truth, yet values the feeling of truth more than the demonstration'. Goethe's desire to seek out truth precluded partisanship in philosophical matters. Whilst noting his involvement in the intellectual movements of the age, Lewes stressed that, for Goethe, ideas were but aids to understanding. He showed how Goethe flourished within a sceptical tradition which prompted an overriding concern with the texture of existence. In 1852, he noted that Goethe's poetry was, like his scientific work, animated by an 'intense feeling for concrete reality'. His attention was not directed towards schematic interpretation because, for Goethe, 'human life is the end and aim; for him the primary object is character, which is . . . of a mingled woof'.[74] *The Life of Goethe*, like Lewes's biography of Robespierre, strove to be instructively interpretative, for Lewes saw Goethe, as Carlyle had seen him, as demonstrating a way in which to resolve many of the conflicts which issued from the rivalry between intellectualism and emotionalism. Yet Lewes also aimed at being sceptically presentational in *The Life of Goethe*, and his method was partially evolved in emulation of Goethe's anti-dogmatic, philosophically-based notion of literary objectivity. His method also had much in common with von Schlegel's *Characteristiken*, which were cited in the biography and admired by Carlyle. Lewes assessed Goethe's achievement, weighing up areas of success and failure. Lewes linked his presentational approach, as he had in *Robespierre*, to the scientific method of observation: 'so long as we judge an organism *ab extra*, according to the Idea, or according to *our* Ideas, and not according to *its* nature, we shall never rightly understand structure and function; and this is as true of poems as of animals'. As Carlyle had done in his pioneering articles on German literature in the 1820s, Lewes outlined plots, provided extracts in translation, and details of a work's genesis. His earnest desire to inquire into the truth of Goethe's life and work was grounded in an explicit theoretical rejection of the dogmatism of both method and vision which Mill and Carlyle had lamented as they contemplated the divisive philosophical debate of the early nineteenth century. In the Preface to the 1864 edition of *The Life of Goethe*, Lewes stated, 'I have been guided solely by the desire to get at the truth, not having any cause to serve, no partizanship to mislead me, or personal connexion to trammel my judgment'. He wished only to come to terms with 'the mingled yarn of life'. He aimed to describe, not to plead; he responded in an open-minded fashion to Goethe's many-sided achievement, and exalted sympathy and foreswore the polemics of criticism and didacticism.[75]

Behind Lewes's method which focused upon concrete reality lay a concern to define valid knowledge such as had permeated Marian Evans's thinking in the early 1850s. Like many of his generation, Lewes was disillusioned with rationalism because of its inflated pretensions and dire historical consequences; his scepticism about the general truths of the metaphysicians stemmed from his unwillingness to claim too much for the power of the intellect. In 1849 he acknowledged the wisdom of Goethe's view that 'man is not born to solve the mystery of existence; but he must nevertheless attempt it, in order that he may learn how to keep within the limits of the knowable'. In an article on the influence of science on literature, which appeared shortly after *The Life of Goethe*, he noted that science might destroy superstition, but 'The mystery of nature remains as dark as before – our only light is that which enables us to see how false was the light by which we once thought the mystery was explained'. Idealism, he considered, 'so far from having the superiority which it claims, is only more lofty in its *pretensions*; the realist, with more modest pretensions, achieves loftier results'.[76] Yet although he resigned himself to the ultimate unfathomability of existence, Lewes assigned great significance to such knowledge as was attainable. The quest for truth was endowed with poignancy and ethical significance: an acknowledgment of the limitations of the intellect culminated in a realisation of life's richness, and a sense of the importance of inquiry. In exploring this theme, Lewes exalted Goethe's, and indirectly his own, sceptical literary method as the embodiment of the most desirable philosophical stance. Invoking Comte's notion of positive truth, and linking an humanitarian ideal to Carlyle's doctrine of willed activity, Lewes eloquently summed up the thinker's role: 'Activity

and sincerity carry us far, if we begin by Renunciation, if we at the
outset content ourselves with the Knowable and Attainable, and
give up the wild impatience of desire for the Unknowable and
Unattainable. The mystery of existence is an awful problem, but it
is a mystery and placed beyond the boundaries of human faculty.
Recognize it as such, and renounce! Knowledge can only be relative, never absolute. But this relative knowledge is infinite, and to
us infinitely important: in that wide sphere let each work according
to ability. . . . The sphere of active Duty is wide, sufficing, en-
nobling to all who strenuously work in it. In the very sweat of
labour there is stimulus which gives energy to life; and a consciousness that our labour tends in some way to the lasting benefit
of others making the rolling years endurable'.[77]

Marian Evans's close involvement with the ideas of both the
subject and the writer of the biography would have once more
directed her mind, honed as it was on philosophical problems, to
literature as the most satisfactory form of intellectual activity by
which might be avoided the sectarian narrowness of the rival
philosophical modes of perception and their dogmatic interpretations of the world, both of which ignored the complexity of reality
and curtailed progressive inquiry. Comte and Feuerbach had
shown how individual intellectual and social progress were possible only after the relinquishment of the old modes of perception
embodied in philosophy and religion. They had also stated explicitly that which Mill and Carlyle had implied: speculation
should culminate in a concern for the affairs of men. Goethe,
however, had suggested that art could replace the old disciplines
of apprehension, and become 'a sister of Religion, by whose aid
the great world-scheme was wrought into reality'.[78] Carlyle trans-
mitted this view of the high function of art to his disciples. Yet,
despite the criticisms of philosophy's inadequacies, it still, as
Bentham and Coleridge had asserted, crucially influenced other
disciplines, for other disciplines were like philosophy, in that they
articulated modes of perception, pursued certain processes of
inquiry, and proposed interpretations of reality. Mazzini, another
of Carlyle's heirs, considered that the 'true European writer will be
a philosopher, but with the poet's lyre in his hands'. Lewes, even
when most critical of philosophy, yet insisted that all intellectual
activity was philosophical: science and literature reflected, and
contributed to, the philosophical debate, because they arrogated to
themselves philosophy's methods, themes and interpretative function. In studying Goethe's life and intellectual context, Marian

Evans would have seen how 'art was given a central role to play in the realization of human nature, in the fulfilment of man . . . art begins to take on a function analogous to religion, and to some extent replacing it'.[79] It was because he held such views on art that Goethe was seen by Lewes and Carlyle to have elevated the status of that comparatively new form, the novel, for the potential of which Lewes and Chapman were to plead. The theoretical justification for Marian Evans, the translator and journalist to turn novelist was provided during the eight months in Germany, contemplating the text of Lewes's biography, and the example of Goethe himself. Her contact with old friends upon the return to London was further to open her eyes to the potential importance of fiction as a mode of expression. Her subsequent writings for the periodical press also gave her the opportunity to formulate a theory of art which drew upon Lewes's exposition of art's value as performing the functions of philosophy better than philosophy itself, for art was able to express an eclectic mode of perception, to pursue a process of sceptical inquiry, and to reflect life's complexities.

19

Plans for a Novel
(1855–1856)

I. NEW ASPECTS OF THE NOVEL

The extraordinary thing is that I never discovered this
power in her – that she never should have written a line
till her 35th year. Our friends – Herbert Spencer – and
others used to say to me – Why doesn't she write a novel?
and I used to reply that she was without the creative
power. At last – we were very badly off . . . I said to her
'My dear – try your hand at something. Do not attempt a
novel – but try a story. We may get 20 guineas for it from
Blackwood and that will be something.'[1]

(George Henry Lewes)

On 22 September 1856, Marian Evans started to write 'The Sad
Fortunes of the Rev. Amos Barton'. That the erudite translator and
journalist turned to fiction came as a surprise to many who knew
her. Oscar Browning observed that her intellectual development
up to the age of thirty-five did not suggest that she would become
a novelist, and Mrs Belloc (née Parkes) recalled that, in the early
1850s, 'not a soul suspected [Marian Evans] of a tinge of imaginative power'.[2] Yet Marian Evans had intermittently cherished a
desire to write fiction. At Miss Franklins' school, she had composed the opening of a story set in 1650, which was inspired by
Scott and G. P. R. James. She revived plans to write a novel in the
autumn of 1846 after finishing the translation of Strauss.[3] For
various reasons these early attempts never came to fruition. She
was fascinated by more obviously serious kinds of writing, such as
philosophy, theology and history, and in the 1840s the status of
the novel was indeterminate. She manifested little interest in the
English tradition represented by Dickens, Mrs Gaskell and the
Brontës, and her enthusiasm for George Sand, whose art found
much of its inspiration in philosophy, was a solitary one. Froude

nd Disraeli held out some promise that George Sand's model of
iction might flourish in England, but Disraeli failed to measure up
o Marian Evans's expectations, and Froude turned to other kinds
)f endeavours. Her disappointed sense that English novelists were
inable to avail themselves of philosophical speculation, coupled
vith her rootlessness and unhappiness after her father's death in
849, conspired to undermine her ever-fragile confidence.

By 1855 the situation had changed. The life she and Lewes led
vas conducive to creative endeavour. Upon their return from
Germany, Marian Evans lived alone for five weeks in Dover; her
,tay there was probably prolonged due to her insistence that
Agnes agree to a separation from Lewes, and this was doubtless an
inxious period. She worked on the *Ethics*, caught a cold, took
olitary walks, and read Shakespeare in the evenings. Eventually,
;he took rooms in Bayswater. She and Lewes then moved to East
)heen, and finally settled in Richmond on 3 October 1855 where
hey were to remain for four years. The way of life they established
vas quiet and, for Marian Evans, secluded. To Sara she wrote on
L6 October 1855, 'life has no incidents, except such as take place in
)ur own brains and the occasional arrival of a longer letter than
isual'. On 22 March 1856, she told Bessie Parkes that she had been
o London only twice since the previous spring, although Lewes
vent up once a week on business. In their shared solitude, they
vere impressively industrious. Marian Evans outlined their aus-
ere régime to Charles Bray: 'We breakfast at 1/2 past 8, read to
)urselves till 10, write till 1/2 past 1, walk till nearly 4, and dine at
5', and they read aloud together for three hours each evening. She
;reeted with delight trips to Worthing in the autumn of 1855, and
o Ilfracombe and Tenby in the summer of 1856, which allowed
hem to 'resume our old habits of undisturbed companionship and
work'.[4] 'Love', Lewes once remarked, 'not only strengthens the
;oul, it enlarges and deepens its capacities.'[5] His devotion to
Marian Evans, despite the gloomy predictions of her friends, was
inwavering, and gave her a long-sought emotional equilibrium
which ushered in a courage for new endeavours. T. A. Trollope
recalled 'if any man could ever be said to have lived in another
person, Lewes in those days, and to the end of his life, lived in and
for George Eliot'.[6] To Charles Bray, to Sara Hennell, and to Bessie
Parkes, Marian Evans spoke glowingly of her happiness. Barbara
Leigh Smith, who visited the couple at Tenby in 1856, received a
highly favourable impression of their liaison. Echoes of Marian

Evans's contentment resounded throughout her journalism. She described feelingly Margaret Fuller's 'blossoming time', and noted Heine's devotion to the woman he never married. Conversely, she criticised Young's mercenary marriage.[7]

Their happiness prevailed in the face of various problems. Their anomalous situation isolated them: Lewes, in *The Life of Goethe*, had not included all the facts about Goethe's liaison with Frau von Stein 'because the British public would have gone into fits at the open avowal'. They were also beset by financial worries. Hunt's support for Agnes had dwindled and while Marian Evans remained in Dover, Lewes spent a large part of his time in London settling his wife's debts with borrowed money. His own and Marian Evans's earnings were to go partly to support Agnes. Penny-pinching became a necessary habit, depriving them of inexpensive pleasures, such as walks on the Tors in Ilfracombe. Their need for money forced them to take on a daunting host of literary commitments. Lewes marketed his plays, and contributed prolifically to the *Leader*. Chapman commissioned five long articles from Marian Evans, and she also wrote the 'Belles Lettres' sections of the *Westminster Review* for £50 a year. Each article reviewed twenty to thirty books, and she re-used some of the material in the thirty-one articles she composed for the *Leader*. She wrote for *Fraser's* and the *Saturday Review* and continued to translate Spinoza. Such arduous work did not bother her. In 1879, she reminisced about 'the time when they were poor' and how she had 'nothing but a very hard chair covered with moreen to sit on when her head ached badly'. Nevertheless, she and Lewes 'laughed at all their troubles . . which would have been quite intolerable . . but for the happy love'.[8] Difficulties with their families were also resolved, or borne with stoicism. Marian Evans settled her financial disputes with Isaac. Chrissey survived the loss of her son at sea, and she and Mrs Houghton welcomed Marian Evans warmly when she visited them at the end of 1855, although she did not tell them about her domestic situation. Lewes's problems with Agnes were to persist for years; he also had to bear the loss of his brother and arrange for the education of his sons, whom he settled in a school in Switzerland in August 1856. Strained relations with her friends were another source of friction for Marian Evans. She wrote every week to Charles Bray, but he had business worries and his visits to her and Lewes were not successful. She did not see Sara Hennell for over twelve months, and then was out when she called in September 1855. Cara Bray stayed away from the couple for over four years, and the letters Marian sent to explain her relationship with Lewes failed to reconcile Cara to her old friend's decision. Mr Noel, whom Lewes and Marian Evans had met on the boat to Belgium, had to be instructed to ask for Mrs Lewes when he visited them; Bessie Parkes would only receive letters via John Chapman.[9]

If Marian Evans's happiness, despite many adverse factors, contributed to her decision to write fiction, so did her continued contact with the three men who had provided the focal points of her life in the early 1850s. The view that the novel was an inferior genre lasted well into the 1870s. Poetry supposedly dealt with universal truths, whereas the novel merely mirrored transitory manners; the ceaseless demands of the circulating libraries encouraged the production of low-quality fiction. Yet Spencer, Chapman and Lewes considered that the novel was a potentially important form. Spencer remained steadfast in his idiosyncratic brand of affection for Marian Evans and Lewes, corresponding with them, and visiting them at Richmond. They worried about his illness which prevented him from reading for more than a quarter of an hour. Spencer was an enthusiastic reader of novels when he first moved to London, and in 1852 and 1856 had urged Marian Evans to turn her mind towards fiction. The three of them shared an interest in Comte's welfare and work, and Comte considered that speculation should culminate in a contemplation of humanity, the traditional concern of the novelist.[10] Lewes and Marian Evans were also interested in Spencer's *Principles of Psychology* (1855) which dealt with what was, at the time, a new science. A concern with modes of cognition, and a recoil from the notion of truth as system, were to inform Marian Evans's choice of the novel as a mode of expression. In his review of Spencer's book, Lewes praised its concern with the nature of perception. Spencer's book tried 'to settle the primary demand of all speculation – What criterion have we for the truth of any belief?' Lewes also commended Spencer's exegesis of the notion of truth as quest: he felt 'pleasure and a high moral influence in the contact with a mind so thoroughly earnest and sincere in the search after truth'.[11]

With John Chapman, Marian Evans and Lewes maintained close contact, for reasons of both friendship and business. He visited them at Richmond and, throughout 1855, they worried about his health, his new career in medicine, his separation from his wife,

and his affair with Barbara Smith, which reached its climax in th
summer of 1855 when it was ended by the intervention of Barbara'
father.[12] Chapman took the art of fiction seriously. In 1851 he ha
suggested that Lewes should write an article which would 'erect
standard of Criticism whereby to judge [novels] with a view o
elevating the productions of Novelists as works of Art and a
refining and moral influences. If more were claimed from th
Novelist the best of them would accord more'.[13] From 1852 to 1853
under the joint editorship of Chapman and Marian Evans, th
Westminster Review had consistently argued for the reform of fic
tion. 'The Progress of Fiction as an Art', which appeared in Octo
ber 1853, was permeated by Comtist notions. The 'chaos' in the ar
of fiction stemmed from society's 'critical' state, and both wer
products of the intellectual atmosphere. The lack of originality in
and commercial motive behind, 'aimless' novels were castigated
for high ideals were posited for the novelist. Richardson, whose
work Marian Evans admired, was praised for establishing fictio
'as an art' whereby 'the novelist puts in a claim to the chair of th
moralist and the philosopher'. Fiction's progress would be facili
tated by the growing ascendancy of positivist tendencies, whic
would influence its method, choice of subject matter, and view o
reality. Novelists were praised who adopted an analytical method
The coming of a 'scientific, and somewhat sceptical age' woul
encourage novelists to 'restrict themselves more and more to th
actual and the possible', and they would depict feelings which di
not 'contradict nature'. According to Comte, understanding of th
past was essential to comprehension of the present, and the
historical novel, in the hands of Scott and Lytton, was praise
because 'to be the interpreter for distant ages' was 'perhaps the
highest, as it is unquestionably the most difficult achievement o
fiction'. The article also commended Mme de Lafayette for detach
ing the novel from fantasy by dealing with 'the characters and
manners of her own time'. It was also argued that the novelist had
a duty to present an unbiased, and thus comprehensive, view o
reality. The writer of the article rejected the selectivity of the *roman
à thèse*: Kingsley's *Hypatia* was 'vitiated by the departure from
actual life, which the following up of any special theory of the
author's own is sure to occasion, if it be not founded on the closest
observation and deepest knowledge of human nature'. The narrow
'realism' which dwelt upon the sordid, and equated such a vision
with 'real life' was also criticised. The presentation of life's com-

plexity was not, however, sufficient to establish the novel as a
force for moral and social improvement. Perfection in the novelist's
art could be reached only by 'deep study and long preparation'.
The novelist must 'enlarge the domain of thought' but also, by an
attempt to enlarge the imaginative and moral sympathies, 'exalt
the motives of action'. In this respect, the aesthetic arrangement of
material rendered the novelist's work indirectly didactic; the highest type of writer was one who 'whilst drawing the picture,
chooses models that may elevate and improve, – who, whilst using
the highest art conceals it so thoroughly as to allow incidents to
arise out of the natural sequence of events, thus carrying the moral
effect . . . home to the heart'. The novelist's mission, the article
insisted, could thus be described as 'high and holy'.[14]

Between 1852 and 1853 the case argued by 'The Progress of
Fiction as an Art' was reiterated in the regular articles on contemporary literature, which were of composite authorship, but subject
to the editorial pens of Chapman and Marian Evans. These articles
advocated a philosophical position with reference to which a
system of literary values was defined. The periodical's Positivist
bias was readily obvious. Comte's name was invoked, and the
analysis of contemporary philosophy echoed his view that thinkers
were 'forsaking the barren heights of speculation for the rich fields
of positive science'. The articles stressed the importance and excitement of scientific discovery, and described the popularisation
of science as 'one of the great intellectual characteristics of the age'.
There were references to the new sciences of sociology and ethics.
Comtist ideals were implied when a book was recommended to
'every friend of progress and every lover of humanity'. The articles
considered religious questions from a non-sectarian viewpoint,
which rested on the historicism Comte had done much to encourage; attention to 'the mechanism and meaning of religious development in every or in any age' was seen as an important task,
requiring the highest intellectual powers. Polytheism and hero-
worship were discussed sympathetically because of 'the interest
which . . . belongs to them as exemplifications of psychological
laws'. The historical and psychological approach to religion was
echoed by the new German critics, and their works, and those of
their English disciples, were frequently cited. The *Westminster
Review* also commended writers of scientific or liberal tendencies,
such as Francis Newman and Theodore Parker, but only reviewed
sectarian works if they were 'such as bear the impress of individual

thought or philosophical power, and which . . . have a claim upon
our attention as appreciable contributions to the development of
theological science'.[15]

In the 'Contemporary Literature' section, as in 'The Progress of
Fiction as an Art', the low standards of contemporary fiction were
denounced. The articles proposed an ideal of truthful and unbiased representation, and suggested that fiction should apply
scientific observation to the complexities of human experience.
Overt didacticism was proscribed. Fiction should aim at 'faithfully
depicting life and leaving it to teach its own lesson, as the stars do
theirs'. The quality of 'quiet naturalness' was praised; novels
should 'dramatize *life*, not *opinion*'.[16] A heterodox desire to forestall
accusations of nihilism underpinned, however, the suggestion of a
need to express constructive ideals in all kinds of writing. Utopian
visions were defended as productive of practical results. Marian
Evans much admired Harriet Martineau's article on Niebuhr which
criticised the German historian's lack of interest in the present and
future; he was scathingly described as 'all one great negation' and
castigated for his 'want of hope and of aspiration'.[17] The insistence
on the importance of the freedom of speculation also surfaced in
these articles on literature. In line with the principles outlined in
the Prospectus, which Marian Evans had helped to draft, any
genuine search for truth was seen to contribute to the good of
humanity, and controversial works were welcomed 'which, if not
in themselves direct contributions to truth, are helpful to that
freedom of investigation, "by which truth was never yet
hindered"'.[18] The *Westminster Review* also welcomed the exploration of new or under-explored areas of interest; the pre-Raphaelites
were commended, and Martineau praised Niebuhr's concern for
the German people. Works which focused on, or derived from, the
neglected groups upon whom Comte had concentrated, were also
recommended. The articles regarded biography enthusiastically
because it could be employed in 'portraying the heroism of humble
life, and in elevating the aristocracy of Nature into permanent
power and enduring influence over mankind'. Comte's notion that
women were especially gifted in emotional power also justified in
theory the view that women were uniquely equipped to write
novels. The portrayal of character was 'essentially a womanly
faculty'; *Cranford* was 'such a series as no male creature could have
written, – only a woman of genius, quick of wit, and not less quick
of feeling'.[19]

The *Westminster Review* explained the origins of fiction by reference to Positivist notions, and defined its ideal method, subject
matter and aims by reference to an eclectic and pragmatic philosophical tradition. It argued that the novel was determined by the
intellectual state of society. The writers in the periodical were
biased in favour of an analytical method, but concurred with
Comte and other influential thinkers who rejected inflexible modes
of perception, and schematised interpretations of reality. The
novel ideally learnt from this epistemological trend; it should
produce a verbal counterpart of existence to suggest what Lewes
called life's 'totality, beauty, and goodness'.[20] The ideal of truthful
representation meant that the reality posited was neither the
squalid horror of 'realistic' novels, the glamourised dream of escapist fiction, nor the subjectively patterned world of the *roman à
thèse*. Carlyle, in *The French Revolution*, that monument to the
eclectic tendency, had suggested that if the writer should not teach
truths, he should educate the reader's perception, and the *Westminster Review* echoed this position. The novel was also seen to
possess the power of heightening the reader's intellectual awareness, and of fostering attention to moral loveliness. Comte had
also asserted what others had implied: the debate about logic
should culminate in a concern for human issues. The *Westminster
Review*'s promotion of Comtist views gave tacit assent to this
viewpoint, as did its championing of the Higher Criticism, which
merged rationalist and idealist logics in order to resolve the issue of
Christian belief. The novel not only learnt from the method of
philosophers; its traditional area of concern was theirs. In dealing
with humanity, fiction also learnt from other disciplines, such as
ethics, psychology and sociology. The eclectic trend in philosophy
also embraced the principle of open-ended inquiry, and the novel
contributed to this process. It added new material to the human
sciences from which it learnt, could increase understanding of
neglected areas of life, such as the condition of the working class,
and could direct the reader's attention to the beauty of the visible.
It helped the understanding of both past and present realities and,
in Comtist terms, the comprehension of the latter was dependent
upon the comprehension of the former. The novel thus learnt from
philosophical method, and arrogated to itself philosophical functions, thus enabling it to make a contribution to the intellectual,
social and moral progress of the age. In pursuing freedom of
inquiry, the diverse foci of its attention also broke down barriers

between specialised disciplines. Such a view was clearly attractive to Marian Evans because of her fascination with philosophy and wide-ranging interests. Her years of contact with the *Westminster Review* gave her ample opportunity to see how current fiction fulfilled such high ideals.

From an early stage Lewes, like Chapman, had envisaged an elevated role for the novelist. He described George Sand in 1842 as 'a poet in the high and religious sense . . . uttering the collective voice of her epoch'; Jane Austen was 'Moralist . . . Artist . . . Entertaining Writer'. He defined the intellectuality of the novel in various ways. The material and insights the novelist offered might contribute directly to other disciplines, such as psychology. Lewes's purchase, in 1838, of Carlyle's *German Romance*, gave him access, as did Carlyle's translation of *Wilhelm Meister* and George Sand's novels, to the notion that fiction might make use of philosophical ideas, and ideas informed Lewes's own novels. Lewes was opposed, however, to the narrow mode of vision and over-abstraction of much speculation, and championed Comte because of his suggestion that perception must avail itself of both inductive and deductive methods, and because he considered that speculation should culminate in a concern for humanity. That this philosophical viewpoint had literary implications was shown by articles in the *Westminster Review* to which Lewes contributed in the 1850s. Lewes considered that there was a dynamic interplay between philosophy and literature. In his criticism and practice of fiction, he outlined a theory of realism which was based upon a sceptical rejection of philosophical theorising about the workings of the mind and the nature of reality, such as had been expounded by both Mill and Carlyle. The biography of Robespierre castigated the narrow vision and intellectual dogmatism of a rationalist and showed their dangerous consequences; the life of Goethe expounded, once more, a complex doctrine or realism and praised the flexible and comprehensive vision of a poet, novelist and dramatist, and demonstrated the contribution Goethe's literary mind made to the philosophical debate. Lewes suggested analogies between Goethe and Comte as regards their rejection of any single method of inquiry; literature's concern for human reality echoed the Positivist emphasis. Comte had also suggested that individual and social salvation would come only from a reorientation of perception. In so far as Goethe contributed to this end, Lewes was inclined to see him, as Carlyle had seen him, as mentor to a troubled age. In showing how literature assumed the methods, themes and functions of philosophy, Lewes was in line with the arguments put forth in the *Westminster Review* during the period of Chapman's and Marian Evans's editorship.[21] Lewes's article 'The Lady Novelists' (1852) incorporated ideas about fiction which resembled the views propounded elsewhere in Chapman's periodical. Lewes suggested the affinity between fiction and other disciplines in intent and status. He noted 'Science is the expression of the forms and order of Nature; Literature is the expression of the forms and order of human life', which suggested a view of literature as akin to Comtean sociology. Literature also contributed to psychology, affording one of the 'avenues through which we reach the sacred adytum of Humanity, and learn better to understand our fellows and ourselves'. Lewes's championing of female novelists was based upon the Positivist view that women were dominated by the emotions. He saw literature as rooted in feeling, and the novel, which customarily dealt with love and domestic experience, as especially suitable for the expression of female creativity. Lewes also explained the doctrine of realism which he was to elaborate in *The Life of Goethe*. As Marian Evans was to concede in the articles which she wrote as he worked on the biography, Lewes saw that the vision art presented was conditioned by both time and subjectivity. He also insisted, as he was to insist in his 1853 discussion of Comte, that just as scientific observation did not preclude wonder, so experience, upon which the novel was based, corroborated the existence of a mysterious dimension in reality. He, like Marian Evans, was critical of the squalid naturalism of Eliza Lynn Linton's *Realities*.[22]

Lewes's projects upon his return to England were such as to encourage Marian Evans's decision to turn to fiction. He capitalised on his earlier endeavours by selling some of his plays. He was also studying the human sciences. He reconsidered the claims of phrenology, and Marian Evans took a lively interest in his arguments about phrenology with Bray in the columns of the *Leader*, and Willis, their doctor in East Sheen, was a close friend of Spurzheim. Together they read weighty tomes on physiology and psychology, and Lewes wrote articles on the latter topic.[23] He was revising his history of philosophy to give more space to medieval and modern writers, and this probably strengthened their joint interest in philosophical trends; Marian discussed Kant with Sara during this period. He was also correcting the proofs of *The Life of*

Goethe which was published on 1 November 1855. Marian Evans
participated in Lewes's biological expeditions to Worthing, Ilfra
combe and Tenby to collect material for *Sea Side Studies* (1858). The
work was based upon a method of meticulous observation such a
Marian Evans was to employ in the novel: Lewes incorporated
descriptions from her Journal into his book.[24] Their closeness had
its less appealing aspects. To some extent, their dependence upon
each other for intellectual stimulation was forced upon them by
their anomalous relationship. The scratching of Lewes's pen sorely
tested her nerves as they sat writing in the same room. Yet it was
psychological support, as Edith Simcox noted, which Lewes gave
her. The peaceful and busy life in which they shared genuinely
compatible interests provided the atmosphere in which the novel
ist could emerge.[25]

Spencer, Chapman and Lewes all held forth the ideal of a new
form of fiction which would adequately express a complex vision
of existence, attainable by the exercise of a stringently eclectic
mode of perception. The new novel's arduous quest for truthful
vision would be philosophical in spirit and in its perceptual
method which learnt from the blending of logical methods in the
work of thinkers such as Carlyle, Mill and Comte. As the eclectic
logic issued in a scepticism about formulaic interpretations of
reality, so the new novel would be undidactic. Fiction would,
however, like philosophy, utilise the insights of other disciplines,
and contribute to them. Carlyle, Mill and Comte had, moreover,
argued that, to reform society, it was first necessary to reform
man's perception of reality. The novelist's vision did not simply
utilise and transmit specific knowledge: the way in which that
vision was articulated had significant social consequences. In the
light of this ideal, most current fiction was found wanting. The
novel could, however, be vindicated according to the theories of
Spencer, Chapman and Lewes. They defined it as a form whose
potential was still barely realised.

II. THE NATURE OF KNOWLEDGE

Upon her return to England, Marian Evans made steady progress
with her translation of the *Ethics*. By 15 March 1855 she had
completed the Preface to Book 3; she started Part 4 on 13 June, and
the following month discussed Froude's articles on Spinoza with

Sara Hennell. On 6 January 1856, she began to revise Book 4; by 19 February 1856, she had corrected the entire manuscript.[26] In June, the plan to publish the work collapsed amidst much acrimony. The many hours of work were wasted in that the project brought her neither much needed money nor acclaim. However, in that the translation of Spinoza was accomplished alongside her journalistic endeavours, it kept to the forefront of her mind the epistemological problem which vexed her, Lewes, the friends they cherished and the writers they read. A many-faceted view of knowledge emerged from her journalism, and had crucial implications for her decision to write fiction. She pondered the problem of logical method, and looked at the ways in which non-philosophical modes of investigation operated. She considered various practical applications of logical methods; she contemplated whether truth resided in an ideological interpretation of reality, or within a representation of reality in all its complexity.

She was well-aware of the problems journalists faced: she knew about the hard work involved in writing for the press, and the financial difficulties liberal magazines were likely to encounter. In later years she was to denigrate journalism in general, and to play down the value of her own contributions to periodicals. She spoke of the reviewer's task as one which dulled the sensibilities, and said that 'people who write regularly for the Press are almost sure to be spoiled by it'. Slightly more positively, she described journalism in 1866 as 'a sort of writing which had no great glory belonging to it, but which I felt certain I could do faithfully and well'. As a journalist, she was prolific. Lewes tried to allay her dissatisfaction with her efforts, and rightly so, for her craftsmanship was impressive.[27] The sweep of the narrative in her articles on Young or the court of Austria owed something, perhaps, to her enthusiastic study of Macaulay. She coped equally well with an argument framed in abstract terminology as when in 'German Wit' she defined the difference between wit and humour. The variety of topics covered in Marian Evans's articles bore witness to the breadth of interest which characterised her intellectual temperament. She offered, however, theoretical justification for such polymathy, as had Comte, Lewes and Goethe, for she suggested that all disciplines were interconnected, and that knowledge enriched perception. She argued the value of the widely-cultured intellect, and noted Ruskin's view that the study of one subject necessarily led to the study of others.[28] She commended the sociologist Riehl, and the novelist Mrs Stowe, for considering phenomena from a variety of points of view. She saw wide-ranging erudition as enriching the study of a narrow topic. She praised Adolf Stahr, who prepared 'for a special study by thorough general culture'. She admired Menzel's 'widely philosophic and historical spirit' which made his work 'far more than a study of Mythology'.[29] It may have been in part her unwillingness to confine herself to any single discipline which encouraged her to try her hand at fiction; Lewes, in his novels, had taken advantage of the potential all-inclusiveness of the form. Chapman, as well as Lewes, saw the novel as particularly suited to the polymath, for fiction could learn from, and contribute to, other disciplines.

The meditation upon the origins of knowledge in perception in the works of French Writers, which in the period from 1844 to 1850 had captured her interest, still preoccupied her. She objected to Cumming's misrepresentation of Voltaire. She defended *Les confessions* against Brougham's criticisms, and her view that genius was often characterised by heightened sensibility owed something to that work. Her discussion of egoism and sympathy invoked the opening sentence of *Les confessions* as she argued that awareness of one's own pain promoted sympathy for the suffering of others.[30] George Sand, whose novels had critically pondered Rousseau's ideas, was still revered by Marian Evans, and she described in detail the Paris *milieu* just before the 1830 Revolution which had stimulated the work of Heine as well as of George Sand.[31] Like Lewes, Marian Evans had inherited Carlyle's mantle as an advocate of German culture, and her enthusiasm for the subject was doubtless increased by her visit to Germany and her collaboration with Lewes on *The Life of Goethe*. From afar, the country exerted its fascination on them; they kept in touch with German friends, and planned to return to Germany when *The Life of Goethe* and the *Ethics* had been through the press.[32] In her journalism, Marian Evans strove to represent the reality of Germany, attempting to give her readers an idea of what the country looked like, and how its citizens lived, for she realised that it was difficult to come across such simple information. Her travelogue articles also allowed her to consider the effectiveness of varying descriptive techniques.[33] She also wrote prolifically about German literature, for ignorance of this, despite the efforts of Carlyle and Lewes, persisted. In 1856 Alison's account of German literature in his *History of Europe* left Marian Evans and Lewes 'half laughing, half indignant' because of

its stupidity. Her concentration upon this literature was significant, for it had responded vitally to post-Enlightenment philosophy, and had been seen by Carlyle crucially to modify some of its
methods and conclusions. In Germany, literature had been assigned a quasi-philosophical status and function. She discussed
writings on aesthetics by von Schlegel and Lessing, which Lewes
had written about in the early 1840s, and which had profoundly
influenced Coleridge and Carlyle. She wrote four articles on
Heine, which included some of the earliest English translations of
his work. She corroborated the high claims Carlyle and Lewes had
made for Goethe in her articles on *Wilhelm Meister* and *The Life of
Goethe*. Goethe was often quoted, and used as a point of comparison for other writers. In her 'Belles Lettres' articles she drew
attention to specialist books on, and translations of, Goethe.[34] She
commended other German writers because they acknowledged the
notion of truth as endless quest. Germany, she noted – probably
recalling the problems Strauss and Feuerbach had encountered –
had 'fought the hardest fight for freedom' and had consequently
'produced the grandest inventions, [had] made magnificent contributions to science, [had] given us some of the divinest poetry, and
quite the divinest music, in the world'. Although she criticised
German style, in a way which recalled Lewes's views on the topic,
she considered that German scholarship had pioneered 'historical
research and criticism'; the Germans were 'the purveyors of the
raw material of learning for all Europe'. She reviewed Riehl's
sociological works, Menzel's writings on mythology, and books of
religious history by Gieseler and Kehnis. The Germans, she said,
'take us to many remote quarters which we could hardly reach
without their aid'. She valued the presentation of a living past
because Comte had shown how comprehension of the past was
essential to understanding of the present. She had also argued in
her review of *The Progress of the Intellect* that attempts to understand
the past enlarged the sympathetic imagination. The erudition of
the Germans issued in picture-making, an end result which recalled the anti-didactic aims of both Carlyle and Lewes.[35] The
European cast of her mind was evident; her 'Belles Lettres' articles
compared and contrasted French and German works. She manifested, in relation to national intellectual traditions, the critical
eclecticism to which Carlyle's writings had introduced her during
her days at Griff. She suggested that valid methods of inquiry and
true insights were not the exclusive possession of any one culture.

She commented that if French scholarship was often facile, German scholarship was frequently plodding, and she illuminated a discussion of Richter by comparing him to Voltaire. She also spoke of the trade in ideas, showing how the French had popularised the discoveries of German scholarship.[36]

She returned also to Scott, whose works had helped to inspire her juvenile attempt at fiction. In May 1855 she was planning an article on Scott, and asked Charles Bray to send her the Waverley Novels, and she read *Old Mortality* and *The Fair Maid of Perth* to Lewes when he was ill in bed the following September. Scott's life and works were used to provide points of comparison; she contrasted Goethe's Spartan dwelling to the luxury of Abbotsford, and she compared Shakespeare's treatment of women with that found in Scott's fiction. She noted that Ruskin and Margaret Fuller, two writers she admired, also admired Scott. She unreservedly described him as 'a genius', an opinion she was never to change.[37] She valued Scott's work for the resources he brought to his perception of the world. In Lockhart's biography, which Marian Evans read in 1839, Scott was quoted as saying that the imagination was inevitably limited, because it was 'circumscribed and contracted to a few favourite images' and he emphasised the value of outward-turning vision, for 'whoever copied what was before his eyes, would possess the same variety in his descriptions, and exhibit apparently an imagination as boundless as the range of nature in the scenes he recorded'. Scott also argued that a knowledge of history and legend enriched the novel.[38] She admired in Scott, as she admired in German scholarship, a capacity to reanimate the past, and this, she noted, was achieved not just by 'sympathetic divination' and 'creative vigour' but by the possession of 'accurate and minute knowledge'. Scott's example vindicated both erudition and Comtist scientism of observation as constituents of the creative process. His open-minded contemplation of humanity had done much to foster her early anti-sectarianism, and his lack of ideological partisanship now enabled Marian Evans to see him as an exemplar of the ideal of fiction for his novels presented their readers with a verbal representation of life's complexity. She described him as 'the unequalled model of historical romanticists', comparing his work to some Belgian historical novels which were written in 'the spirit of the apologue . . .the men and women speak and act in order to prove a moral . . . and not as a result of any natural combination of character with circumstance'.[39] Marian

Evans also considered that the presentation of such pictures as Scott produced performed an important moral function. Hegel had commented that writers must guard against 'allowing a character to lose individuality in the expression of abstract historical forces' but also 'against lapsing into merely private human psychology'.[40] Scott's modified historical determinism appealed to Marian Evans because his work, like Riehl's, suggested that generalisations could only appeal to 'a moral sentiment already in activity', but that a picture of human life in all its complexity 'surprises even the trivial and the selfish into that attention to what is apart from themselves, which may be called the raw material of moral sentiment'. She saw the presentation of the otherness of a society or person as morally beneficial, whether achieved by a sociologist like Riehl, a poet like Wordsworth, or novelists like Scott and Kingsley, and she sensed in their works a community of aim and effect. Reviewing *Dred*, she noted how Mrs Stowe, like Scott and Riehl, exhibited 'a national life in all its phases – popular and aristocratic, humorous and tragic, political and religious'.[41] Behind such comments lay the notion that writers should emulate philosophers, and withstand the temptation to present formulaic truths: the furtherance of the process of inquiry, by providing the mind of the audience with new material and/or a new mode of perception was, in itself, an act of oblique didacticism with moral consequences. This was a method Lewes and Marian Evans utilised. In *The Life of Goethe* and *Sea-Side Studies*, Lewes deployed a method based upon observation which he had learnt partly from the Comtist emphasis, in sociology and biology, upon the interaction between organism and habitat. He also provided in his article on lady novelists a comparison of literature and science. Marian Evans's article on Young noted at the outset 'The study of men, as they have appeared in different ages, and under various social conditions, may be considered as the natural history of the race', a comment which suggested that she was trying to deploy a sociological mode of inquiry, for it invoked the title of her article on Riehl.[42]

Her concern with the nature of knowledge was also evidenced by a continuing interest in philosophical works. She translated Spinoza; she considered Whewell's *History of the Inductive Sciences* and Baden Powell's *Essay on the Spirit of the Inductive Philosophy*. She admired Spencer's article on logical method, 'The Universal Postulate', which compared the work of Reed, Mill, Whewell, Berkeley,

Hume and H. L. Mansel, and Spencer found it useful to discuss philosophy with her. Her 'critical and analytic' speculative
faculty which Spencer praised was manifested when she pinpointed specious reasoning or philosophical emptiness in the
works of other writers.[43] She turned increasingly, however, to
those disciplines, and especially those which were related to
human experience, which had applied the methods of philosophical logic. In writing of these areas of inquiry, she acted as inter-
mediary, in Coleridgian and Carlylean fashion, between philosophers
and a wider public little interested in the esoteric technicalities of
abstract speculation. Such writers as Marian Evans were important, for they established the centrality of philosophical discussion
to all disciplines of which Bentham had spoken. As Mark Pattison
noted, with a disillusioned glance at the English universities, 'such
philosophical teaching as the nation has had, has come to it from
without in the profound silence of its proper teachers'.[44] Science
occupied Marian Evans's attention not just because it was one of
Lewes's interests, but because, with its emphasis upon observation, it echoed the anti- doctrinaire stance Marian Evans found
in the philosophers she read, and in writers as diverse as Scott,
Riehl and Wordsworth. She honoured the endless scientific quest
for facts, because scientific investigation, like good fiction or sociology, employed scepticism as a starting point for inquiry. She
cheerfully accompanied Lewes on his expeditions; she read with
him works on medical science, zoology, anatomy and marine
biology.[45]

In England, after 1850, the focus of political interest was over-
seas, and, without stirring events like those of the hungry forties to
spur her interest in new directions, Marian Evans remained content to reconsider the political writers she had read before she left
for Switzerland in 1849. Those radical political theories which were
often based upon a reaction against the rational revolutionism of
the Enlightenment continued to interest her. Spencer kept her in
touch with Louis Blanc; in her journalism, she referred to Fourier,
Freiligrath, Rousseau and the French Socialists. She welcomed Mrs
Browning's discussion, in *Aurora Leigh*, of the ideas of Fourier,
Comte and Cabet, hoping, perhaps, that here was an English
equivalent of George Sand, and she described Heine's involvement in the revolutionary movements of Paris in the 1820s and
1830s.[46] Her early interest in Saint-Simon, who was 'a "utopian"
precisely in the Marxist sense, in that he had not worked out

mechanisms adequate to the realization of his moral objectives' probably lay behind her faint interest in the legislative process.[47] She was associated with a broadly liberal position because of her relationship with Lewes, and because of her links with the *Leader* and the *Westminster Review*. The latter continued to champion causes such as secular education and colonial independence, which laid it open to the charge that the European *literati* were socially subversive. Marian Evans expressed her sympathy for oppressed nations. She also eagerly waited for news of Bray's campaigns in the Midlands, and cited the theories of Robert Owen which had interested Bray in his youth. In writing of literature, she considered the political views of its practitioners; she censured the pettiness of the social criticism in *Maud*, and distinguished between Brougham's efforts as a liberal politician and his failure as a writer.[48] When she expressed her own political views, she tried to steer a middle course between seemingly opposed concepts, an impulse which owed much to the method of the eclectic logic. After the 1789 French revolution, the revision of political theories based upon rationalism gave birth to conflicting theories about the nature of, and machinery necessary to achieve, progress: theories which were forged in the atmosphere of a Europe still frighteningly prey to revolutionary upheaval. With the quietening of the political atmosphere in the 1850s, Marian Evans contemplated the idea of progress with the calm of hindsight, and with her contemporary reality in mind. She saw progress as likely to come from the simultaneous improvement of institutions and individuals. She argued that egoism might prompt reforms of general benefit, but suggested that unless harmony was established between society's laws and individual needs, 'we shall never be able to attain a great right without also doing a wrong'. Paraphrasing Riehl, she expounded an anti-revolutionary argument for gradual change; she noted 'What had grown up historically can only die out historically, by the gradual observation of necessary laws. The external conditions which society has inherited from the past are but the manifestation of inherited internal conditions in the human beings who compose it; the internal conditions and the external are related to each other as organism and its medium, and development can take place only by the gradual consentaneous development of both'.[49] Her awareness of the context within which ideals operated also made her sceptical about doctrinal theories of reform. Lewes had manifested a similar attitude in *Robespierre*, when he saw reformers as defeated by the nature of their simplified world-view. Marian Evans praised Riehl for his analysis of the working class, for such an analysis acted as a check upon the generalising of social reformers. Human character, at once historically conditioned and innately idiosyncratic, acted as a caution to revolutionary dreams; she noted caustically: 'As a necessary preliminary to a purely rational society, you must obtain purely rational men'.[50] All theories, she implicitly contended in Carlylean fashion, must rest, or perish, upon an acknowledgement of the rich complexity of fact. She conceded the power of ideas, admiring Riehl's explanation of the way in which economic, political and intellectual forces affected the life of the German peasant, but she considered that ideas were transformed by the medium within which they operated. Theories of co-operation were modified by personal and social traditions and beliefs.[51]

In mid-Victorian England, religious questions were accessible to more people than the philosophical problems which concerned the intellectual élite to which Marian Evans belonged. Yet the philosophical debate had profound implications for religious questions. The Enlightenment rationalism, of which Marian Evans's generation was often critical, was opposed to Christianity because rationalists considered that the Christian faith promoted a view of the world which did not correspond to reality. The post-rationalist reaction, in which Marian Evans participated, was prepared, however, to re-evaluate the Christian form of perception which was viewed as an alternative to discredited reason. Such had been Carlyle's experience after the Rue de l'Enfer crisis; writers such as Hegel and Strauss in Germany, Saint-Simon, George Sand and Comte in France, wished to build a new faith on the foundations of a rewritten philosophical logic. Lewes, in 1857, commented, 'The age of doubt and vacillation has passed, and I want something solid, or seemingly solid whereon to stand and look about me'.[52] Marian Evans's interest in religion was congruous with her philosophical interest in the origins of knowledge; in considering religion, she was considering a mode of perception which many saw as yielding valid insights which corrected the methods and conclusions of philosophers working within the rational tradition. She listened with interest to a Mormon preacher at Tenby. In writing letters of advice to Sara Hennell about the latter's essay on faith and infidelity, she applied her analytical powers in a way which showed her command of the *a priori* and *a posteriori* methods.[53] She also continued to champion the Higher Criticism which merged a

rationalist historiography with an Idealist appreciation of Christianity. 'Introduction to Genesis' showed her mastery of the new
methods of Biblical criticism, and she criticised Cumming's ignorance of such developments. She echoed Strauss's crucial concept
of *mythus* which he had evolved by reference to the Hegelian logic.
She assessed the value of the truths yielded by Christianity. Her
scepticism had emerged partly in response to the ferocious religious disputes of the 1830s and 1840s, and she maintained a firm
opposition to sectarianism. Yet she was fascinated by the state of
religious belief in different ages, as shown in her articles 'History
of German Protestantism' and 'Church History of the Nineteenth
Century'. Such articles revealed her awareness of the contextual
conditioning of a world-view and suggested the relativity of all
truths. These concepts informed articles on Milton, Cumming,
Young and Heine, in which she explored the connections between
character, history and religious belief, and the method she used
owed something to the Carlylean biographical model which Lewes
also emulated.[54] She saw religious belief as expressive of the needs
of personality, but, in her contemplation of personality, she balanced notions of an unchanging humanity against notions of
historical conditioning, a view which prompted an ambivalence in
her appraisal of the validity of religious insights. Christianity
yielded knowledge at once universal and relative. She thus demonstrated the similarity between forms of Christianity in all
nations and ages; equally, she concentrated upon the way in which
belief was bound up with any age's political and literary trends.[55]
With a characteristically pragmatic emphasis, Marian Evans commented to Jowett in 1878, 'the really great and abiding interest of
philosophy is human motive'.[56] In her consideration of Christianity, she also focused upon the ethical and psychological repercussions of the Christian view of the world. She praised, regardless of
their form, religions which ennobled human character; she was
enthusiastic about Julia Kavanagh's novel, *Rachel Gray*, because it
revealed Christianity as 'a refining and consoling influence in that
most prosaic of human stratum, the small shopkeeping class'. She
defended radical revisions of Christianity if they were conducive to
moral improvement. She attacked the Christianity of Cumming
not solely because it was intellectually dishonest, but because it
failed to promote virtue. As did Feuerbach in *The Essence of Christianity*, she valued Christianity in so far as it subserved an idealistic
morality. She suggested that the 'idea of God is really moral in its
influence – it really cherishes all that is best and loveliest in man –

only when God is contemplated as sympathizing with the pure
elements of human feeling, as possessing infinitely all those attributes which we recognise to be moral in humanity'. She valued
goodness above logic: commending the tolerance of the Roman
Catholic writer, Kenelm Digby, she noted, 'If any one objects that
all this liberality is logically inconsistent with Catholicism, we can
only reply that we prefer illogical virtues to logical vices; and still
more to *il*logical vices, of which one of the commonest is Protestant
intolerance'.[57]

To the works of Comte and Carlyle, which attempted to reconcile logical methods and which offered so powerful a critique of
dehumanised speculation, she frequently returned. Lewes and
Marian Evans were once more in close contact with John Chapman
who had promoted Positivism in England. Marian Evans echoed
Comte's attitude towards logic when, for instance, she contrasted
genuine prediction to spurious prophecy. In an article concerned
directly with philosophy, she was critical of the *a priori* method, yet
she was also aware of the limitations of empiricism, and cited J. S.
Mill to show that the distinction between associationism and
intuitionism was no simple matter. She was interested in Gruppe's
notion that 'synthetical and analytical judgements' were not 'two
distinct classes', but that 'from the simple act of judgment we
ascend to the formation of ideas, to their modification, and their
generalisation'.[58] Marian Evans also echoed some of the ideas
which Comte had evolved as he applied his logical method in
various fields of inquiry, such as his advocacy of scientific education and classification of the sciences. Comte, building upon the
efforts of Condorcet and Saint-Simon, consolidated the new
science of man and society, which evolved its ideas by a detached
observation of human and social phenomena, and issued in an
unbiased presentation of facts. Marian Evans focused especially
upon Comte's analysis of history and society, echoing his concept
of humanity and its three stages of progress. Her sense of the link
between past and present, of the connection between will and
determinism, shows her desire to evolve a coherent philosophy of
history, and, as both journalist and novelist, she may be categorised as, in an informal fashion, a thoughtful exponent of sociological principles.[59] Her interest in these subjects was at one with her
admiration of anti-didactic representation, and the humanitarian
focus of her thought. She praised writers who adopted a sociological method; to Riehl she devoted a lengthy article, carefully anno-

tating three volumes of his work in preparation for the task. Riehl's view that social groups were 'not only distinguished externally by their vocation, but essentially by their mental character' won her assent.[60] Comte saw social change stemming from a modification of man's perception of the world as much as from change in external institutions. The Riehl/Comte analysis spoke forcibly to the generation who were the heirs of Bentham and Coleridge, who had seen the crisis of the age in mental, not material, terms and had thus focused their attention upon epistemological problems. Just as Marian Evans explored the influence of the Christian world-view upon behaviour, so she contemplated the moral scheme which Comte rested upon a philosophical basis. Her reaction to Comtean ethics mingled criticism and appreciation. Post-rationalist thinkers, and Rousseau in particular, had taught her the value of feeling, and she was sceptical about intellectual theories of ethics, insisting upon the importance of 'sympathetic emotion'. In a passage which was deleted in the 1884 edition of her essays, she argued for a merging of head and heart in the moral process. She also stressed the contribution which knowledge coming from personal experience could make to ethics, by encouraging sympathy with unknown people, and with generations to come.[61]

Marian Evans's view of knowledge was more complex when she considered the work of Carlyle. She and Lewes were in touch with Carlyle upon their return to England; her collaboration on *The Life of Goethe* placed Carlyle's ideas in the forefront of her mind once more. She was acutely aware of the revolutionary effect Carlyle had had upon a whole generation of English thinkers, and she sprang to his defence when he was criticised. Her interest in Idealism which Carlyle's writings had stimulated was apparent in her journalism when she analysed the intellectual framework of the age.[62] Carlyle continued to influence Marian Evans's thought, for he had introduced her to that form of speculation which merged modes of perception and was orientated towards human issues: her view of Carlyle's significance was defined in relation to the origins and function of knowledge. Carlyle's rejection of any single way of viewing the world made him, for Marian Evans as well as Lewes, 'a sceptic yet a prophet'. She deployed the terminology which Carlyle had coined to describe originality of perception in reference to Heine and to Thoreau's *Walden*, a book which owed much to Carlyle.[63] She saw Carlyle as meriting the designation 'philosopher' in a carefully-defined fashion, for she admired the varied modes of perception which he combined to produce the writer's vision, which she saw as superior to the vision of the philosopher who deployed one single method. She commended the way in which he united a metaphysical and generalising tendency with an empirical capacity to observe the specific, for he 'seizes grand generalizations, and traces them in the particular with wonderful acumen'. She praised his psychological insight, for he 'glances deep down into human nature, and shows the causes of human actions'. She noted the various moods which fused to form his unique vision, his piercing insight, his sense of the mystery of existence, his satire and humour, his detachment and subjectivity, all of which made him 'a wonderful paradox of wisdom and wilfulness'. The end result of Carlyle's method was a commanding power to create pictures of extreme vividness; his works were notable for their 'concrete presentation'.[64] In writing of historiography and biography Marian Evans often referred to Carlyle's methods as an ideal against which other writers could be measured. Not only did she commend the mode of perception whereby Carlyle reproduced the complexity of reality, she also praised the kinds of subject he dealt with, for his concern with history and the individual life was congruous with her interest in Comtism. Carlyle's notion of the hero who was at once ludicrous and exceptional and who existed in a *milieu* often unremarkable surfaced in the articles which stemmed from her stay in Germany. She also applied this ideal to the novel, commending Ashford Owen's *A Lost Love*, because it described the heroism of an unpretentious woman in such a way as to constitute an ideal of which Carlyle would have approved, 'a real picture of a woman's life'.[65] She saw Carlyle as applying the artist's complex perception to history and character to evolve pictures capable of inspiring ethical idealism. An art which embodied such an eclectic method of attaining knowledge, and which represented, but did not propagandise, and which yet performed ethical functions in relation to human subjects, represented, for Marian Evans, knowledge valid in genesis, expression, content and function. Her appreciation of these facets of Carlyle's art, and her general concern to define the nature of knowledge, also prompted her interest in Ruskin.

III. RUSKIN

The *Westminster Review*'s contributors frequently championed pioneer works and defended misunderstood innovators. *Modern Painters* attracted Marian Evans's attention on both scores, for it expounded a new theory of art, and helped stem the abuse of Turner's paintings. She wrote to Sara on 19 February 1856, 'We are delighting ourselves with Ruskin's 3d. volume, which contains some of the finest writing I have read for a long time (among recent books)'. Her enthusiasm was reflected in her reviews of Volumes 3 and 4 which appeared in the following April and July. Barbara Smith visited her in Tenby that July, and Marian Evans was delighted to hear that Ruskin was encouraging Barbara's painting, describing him to her as 'the finest writer living'.[66] Ruskin was, in many respects, Carlyle's heir, and received from the grudging Carlyle more praise than any other contemporary writer. Marian Evans, in her review of Volume 3, noted that Ruskin was an eager student of Carlyle, and she sensed an affinity between Ruskin and Carlyle in 'the point of view from which he [Ruskin] looks at a subject.'[67] Carlyle's work was inspired by a desire to arbitrate between rationalism and post-rationalism, and his early writings had discriminatingly extracted from German romanticism those insights which countered the sombre implications of Enlightenment philosophy. Ruskin's work similarly assessed romanticism for, like Carlyle, he sympathised with the philosophical viewpoint and sensibilities of the romantics. To Marian Evans, this seemed an important task. At school, and at Griff, she had read widely in romantic literature, and had encountered the debate about rationalism and romanticism in the works of Coleridge and Carlyle. She had collaborated on *The Life of Goethe*, and Lewes had carefully scrutinised the German romantic school, seeing it as 'brilliant' but also, in some senses, as an 'error'.[68] The romantics engaged in a dialogue with the eighteenth-century philosophers about whether truth was best attained by the exercise of reason, about the nature of reality, and about the respective values of literary and philosophical modes of discourse. Ruskin continued this debate by propounding a theory of the imagination, by defining his own view of reality, and by discussing the role of the artist and function of art.

Ruskin echoed the views of romantic writers, but also elaborated upon them. In *Modern Painters*, he referred to the writings of

Shelley and Keats, but the influences of Wordsworth and Coleridge were the most pervasive. Wordsworth praised Volume 1; Ruskin re-read the works of Wordsworth and Coleridge before he wrote Volume 2.[69] The Preface to *The Lyrical Ballads* (1800) informed Ruskin's ideas on the workings of the imagination, and the material to which it should apply itself; implicit in Wordsworth's treatment of the latter theme was a view of the nature of reality. Wordsworth aimed to 'look steadily at my subject'; Ruskin commented that the imagination must be 'faithful and earnest . . . in the contemplation of the subject-matter'. Wordsworth desired to 'keep the Reader in the company of flesh and blood'; according to Ruskin, the inferior imagination took refuge in German sensationalism via a 'departure from natural forms to give fearfulness'.[70] The Wordsworthian ideal of an imagination which contemplated lovingly the beauty of the everyday lay behind Ruskin's argument that it was an inferior imagination whose vision 'surprises by its brilliancy, or attracts by its singularity'. The idiosyncrasy of perspective and the attention to the mundane detail of the actual, which combined in Wordsworth's way of viewing the world, commended themselves to Ruskin because of a seeming resemblance between Turner's and Wordsworth's mode of vision. Ruskin also argued that the apparently subjective ways of viewing the world, such as those of Shelley and Wordsworth, the least photographic of poets, provided truthful records of light effects.[71] Ruskin, like Wordsworth, adopted a dismissive attitude towards metaphysics. He criticised its terminology, and asserted that the discipline was of little use in formulating a definition of the imagination. Yet Ruskin, like Wordsworth, in attempting to reconcile opposites in his definition of the imaginative process, frequently utilised the method of the synthetic logic which was so prominent in the works of Coleridge and Carlyle. His definition of the theoretic and imaginative faculties drew upon Coleridge's distinction between Fancy and Imagination.[72] Ruskin's youthful absorption in Scottish Puritanism gave him an important point of contact with Carlyle, whose own Scottish Puritanism had encouraged his moralistic bias. Ruskin considered that the way in which the imagination worked allowed it to synthesise direct and indirect modes of instruction. Like Carlyle, he argued that the imagination's visions were of ethical significance, stating that a 'true Thinker, who has practical purpose in his thinking, and is sincere . . . becomes in some sort a seer, and must always be of infinite use in his genera-

tion'. The verb 'to see', as Ruskin used it, had a resonance akin to
that found in *The French Revolution* and like Carlyle Ruskin argued
that the visions of the imagination educated the reader's
perception.[73] In echoing Coleridge's and Carlyle's notions about
the workings of the imagination, Ruskin commended two of the
writers who had influenced Marian Evans's youthful thinking and
who had argued that knowledge was to be gained via a union of
seemingly opposed methods. Carlyle and Coleridge had also suggested that the literary mind was often more able to gain valid
knowledge than the philosophical intellect. Scott, another of Marian Evans's enthusiasms, was termed by Ruskin 'the great representative of the mind of the age in literature'. He praised Scott
for the way in which his imagination balanced opposed modes of
perception; echoing, for instance, the opening chapter in *Waverley*,
Ruskin noted how Scott showed 'under the old armour, the everlasting human nature'.[74]

In his analysis of the workings of the romantic imagination,
Ruskin focused critically upon the relationship between feeling
and knowledge. He considered the state of *rêverie* amidst nature,
so prominent in the work of Rousseau, as 'characteristic of persons
not of the first order of intellect'. Invoking Carlyle, and also
perhaps George Sand's critique of solitude, he noted, 'when we
glance broadly along the starry crowd of benefactors to the human
race, and guides of human thought, we shall find that this dreaming love of natural beauty – or at least its expression – has been
more or less checked by them all, and subordinated either to hard
work or watching of *human* nature'. Ruskin valued the mind which
apportioned feeling discriminatingly: he noted of Turner's imagination that the *'affections* of it clung . . . to humble scenery and
gentle wildness of pastoral life. But the *admiration* of it . . . was
fastened on largeness of scale'. Ruskin's ideal imagination steered
a middle course between dispassionate observation and egotistic
feelings. In the second volume of *Modern Painters*, he emphasised
the importance of subjectivity, and his contemplation of the rational disciplines as a counterbalancing force was characteristically
judicious: 'It is in raising us from the first state of inactive reverie to
the second of useful thought, that scientific pursuits are to be
chiefly praised. But in restraining us at this second stage, and
checking the impulses towards higher contemplation, they are to
be feared or blamed'.[75]

Ruskin criticised, moreover, the limited view of reality presented by the romantic literature which centred thematically upon feeling. Sentimental literature such as Byron's poetry 'is altogether of lower rank than the literature which merely describes what it saw. The true Seer always feels as intensely as anyone else; but he does not much describe his feelings'. Describing the literature of sensibility, he noted the 'use and value of passion is not as a subject for contemplation in itself, but as it breaks up the fountains of the great deep of the human mind'.[76] Ruskin responded favourably, rather, to that aspect of romanticism which premissed a complex reality, and his exegesis of that theme would have interested Marian Evans, for *The Life of Goethe* had presented a complex view of reality, and the subject was a constant theme of the *Westminster Review*'s literary articles. Wordsworth's sense of the miraculous quality of the ordinary, and Coleridge's philosophical pondering of the relationship between the finite and the infinite, initially spoke to Ruskin's view that there was a dimension in reality beyond the visible truth of material objects. In Ruskin's case, this view originated, like Carlyle's, from within a Christian tradition. The world, Ruskin said, was at once 'never distinct and never vacant, she is always mysterious, but always abundant'. This synthetic paradox was elaborated in Volume 4, where, he noted, there was 'a continual mystery throughout *all* spaces, caused by absolute infinity of all things'. This perception of duality was apparent when Ruskin defined 'realism' in art, for he commented, 'we may be quite sure that what is not infinite cannot be true . . .the moment we see in a work of any kind whatsoever the expression of infinity, we may be certain that the workman has gone to nature for it'.[77]

In other respects, however, Ruskin saw great art as revealing a reality even more complex than that unveiled by romantic literature. He praised Turner's depiction of a windmill, for Turner revealed the beauty of human life by emphasising the imperfection of his subject. Great art loved beauty, but could place it in an unlovely context, for art 'accepts Nature as she is, but directs the eyes and thoughts to what is most perfect in her; false art saves itself the trouble of direction by removing or altering whatever it thinks objectionable'.[78] Ruskin suggested that the senses alone could not grasp the nature of reality, and he enlarged the romantic notion of the imagination as synthesising contrary processes into the concept of the imagination as fusing a variety of mental processes. He was sceptical about any theory of the imagination which ignored the mysteriousness of the creative process. Perception was based upon knowledge, for the 'most imaginative men always study the hardest, and are the most thirsty for new knowledge'. Knowledge must also be fused with feeling, which could be itself a valuable route to knowledge. Ruskin catalogued a wide variety of feelings of which the imaginative process availed itself. He emphasised the importance of 'watchfulness, experience, affection, and trust in nature', and showed how the moral feelings and the sense of beauty also contributed to the act of perception. The imagination could reach, 'by intuition and intensity of gaze (not by reasoning, but by its authoritative opening and revealing power), a more essential truth than is seen at the surface of things'. Individuality of vision was also an essential component of the process whereby truth was found: the best imagination was 'like a glass of sweet and strange colour, that gives new tones to what we see through it; and a glass of rare strength and clearness too, to let us see more than we could ourselves'. Ruskin also stressed the importance of humility as regards the powers of human insight, noting that 'our happiness as thinking beings must depend on our being content to accept only partial knowledge'.[79] Because the artist marshalled a range of modes of perception in order to grasp the complexity of reality, Ruskin propounded an elevated view of the artist as being engaged in the serious pursuit of truth: art 'properly so called, is no recreation; it cannot be learned in spare moments'. Ruskin thus evolved theories of the kind of truth art could, and should, represent. Truth 'has reference to statements both of the qualities of material things, and of emotions, impressions, and thoughts'. Yet, once more, Ruskin moved beyond a mere synthesis of opposites: he wanted 'a definition of art wide enough to include all its varieties of aim . . .the art is the greatest which conveys to the mind of the spectator, by any means whatsoever, the greatest number of the greatest ideas'. He rejected as meaningless the presentation of beauty without moral content; he also scorned 'copyism', 'a simple transcript from nature'. Art could be concerned with 'the simple unencumbered rendering of the specific character of the given subject' whilst simultaneously seeing the subject as an ideal type. He criticised distinctions which led 'people to imagine the Ideal opposed to the Real, and therefore *false*'. The imagination, whilst 'pre-eminently a beholder of things, *as* they *are* . . .is, in its creative function . . .a seer . . .delighting to dwell on that which is not tangibly present'. Art was subjective in vision, yet accurately rendered reality, although it was not coloured by personal obsessions. An artist 'becomes great when he becomes invisible', for 'we see as he sees, but we see not him'. The artist's capacity to present a complex reality was seen by Ruskin as one of his most important functions, for the visions of the artist increased the sum of truth, and were thus divine in nature. Yet such visions might also have practical ends, just as 'the step between practical and theoretic science is the step between the miner and geologist'.[80]

Ruskin extended his consideration of art in three other directions. Firstly, he considered the way in which there was an inseparable link between style and the artist's ability to convey his vision of reality. This organicism owed much to Carlyle's innovative use of language, upon which Marian Evans commented.[81] Ruskin criticised any technique which was an end in itself, distinguishing, in literature, between 'what is language, and what is thought', and in painting, between 'the finish of work*manship*, which is done for vanity's sake, and . . . the finish of *work*, which is done for truth's sake'. Ruskin also considered that language could legitimately be ambiguous, and that seeming obscurity was often a sign of accurate vision: 'there is in every word set down by the imaginative mind an awful under-current of meaning, and evidence and shadow upon it of the deep places out of which it has come. It is often obscure, often half-told'. He championed experiment, defining good style as 'nothing but the best means of getting at the particular truth which the artist wanted', dependent upon 'consistency with itself, – the perfect fidelity . . . to the truths it has chosen'.[82] This assigned to the act of evolving a style a mental stringency akin to that found in the formation of a philosophical language. The end result was, once more, to endow the literary task with high intellectual status. Secondly, Ruskin's theory of art gave prominence to the historical viewpoint which Marian Evans had valued since her early reading of Scott. In viewing Calais Church, Ruskin saw objects as time incarnate: he considered those truths 'are always most valuable which are most historical; that is, which tell us most about the past and future states of the object to which they belong'. He castigated 'looking back, in a romantic and passionate idleness', and advocated an historical negative capability, whereby the artist derived his presentational power from 'losing sight and feeling of his own existence, and becoming a mere witness and mirror of truth, and a scribe of visions'. He also asserted that attention to historical fact paradoxically produced art which was 'always universal . . . because it is *complete* portrait down to the heart, which is the same in all ages'.[83] Such had been

Scott's view: George Eliot, in her novels, was to harness historical erudition to a sympathetic psychological imagination, which revealed the recurrence, in all eras, of unchanging human needs, responses and dilemmas.

Thirdly, Ruskin defined the ethical and social functions of art. The historical imagination had an important role to play: not only did it enlarge the imaginative capacity by quickening 'our conception of the dead', it also checked any exaggerated sense of the importance of self and contemporary society. In Volume 2 of *Modern Painters*, Ruskin extended his idea that art might show the unity of all things in God, to an argument that perception of that unity fostered a reverence for life, and human brotherhood. In Volumes 3 and 4 Ruskin shifted his primary focus away from a discussion of the value of art in relation to the psychology of vision; his Christian bias became less evident, and his preparatory reading list showed how he broadened the scope of his work. These volumes were written when Ruskin was involved with F. D. Maurice's Working Men's College, and his views on art were now related to his heightened awareness of the problems of the working class. He deemed a dimension of political truth to be a necessary constituent of artistic vision, and censured those who portrayed peasant life as picturesque. Ruskin criticised 'the casting about for sources of interest in senseless fiction, instead of the real human histories of the people round us . . . the pleasures taken in fanciful portraits of rural or romantic life in poetry and on the stage, without the smallest effort to rescue the rural population of the world from its ignorance or misery'.[84]

Despite his scepticism about the technicalities and terminology of metaphysics, Ruskin's notions of the imagination, reality, and the function of the artist, constantly reconciled opposites by utilising the methods of the Idealist logic. He noted that 'the more I see of useful truths, the more I find that, like human beings, they are eminently biped', and he criticised the contemporary English mind for its 'usual inability to grasp the connection between any two ideas which have elements of opposition in them, as well as of connection'.[85] He did, however, extend the synthetic method beyond a conquest of polarities to multi-facetedness. He praised the imagination as a mode of gaining knowledge because it was not tied to any single form of perception, and was commended by Lewes in 1850 for showing 'the old truth, that empiricism is as idle and pernicious in Art as in Philosophy'.[86] His view of reality gave weight to the existence of non-material dimensions; this spoke to Marian Evans's 'aesthetic mysticism' which recognised the element of beauty in the universe, and in human character.[87] It is ironic that the OED (inaccurately) cites the first use of 'realism' as being Ruskin's in *Modern Painters* in 1856: Ruskin's realism was far removed from the materialist view of the universe with which the term has come to be associated. In outlining the function of art, Ruskin showed, as had Carlyle, that the presentation of an unbiased vision of reality performed an important task in educating perception, and Ruskin demanded that style be tailored to render accurately this vision. Attention to historical truths also revealed universal human truths; the striving for a truthful vision served purposes not only intellectual and moral, but also social and political. Ruskin thus endowed art and the imaginative process of the artist with strenuous seriousness, and art itself with elevated functions. His evolution of such doctrines stemmed, moreover, from a contemplation of the literary critique of Enlightenment philosophy. The initial dynamic impulse of his work was a reaction against the methods, world-view and uses of rationalist speculation: he corroborated, in this respect also, Marian Evans's slowly-evolving decision to relinquish philosophy for literature.

20

Perception and the Medium: The Vindication of Art

an issue which the novel raises more sharply than any other literary form – the problem of the correspondence between the literary work and the reality which it imitates. This is essentially an epistemological problem, and it . . . seems likely that the nature of the novel's realism . . . can best be clarified by the help of . . . the philosophers.

I

In 1838 and 1840 J. S. Mill suggested that Bentham and Coleridge demonstrated the urgent centrality of the question of logical method for all disciplines. Yet Bentham and Coleridge were also seen as having established the sterile sectarianism of the philosophical debate, because of what later writers interpreted as the intractability of their positions. Increasingly, a later generation followed Coleridge's precedent, and looked to other disciplines for answers to the problems of how human perception best operated in the search for truth, how reality could be characterised, and what was the optimum genre for articulating perception and describing the world. The dialogue between empiricism and literary romanticism preoccupied Mill, Carlyle, Lewes and Ruskin as they attempted to define the ideal form of perception, and their definition of that perception was often associated with a recast view of the outer world. They exalted a mode of perception which fused logical methods; their view of reality incorporated reference to the intangible dimensions of actuality, and was far removed from deterministic materialism. They insisted that this mode of perception and view of reality were potentially instructive, and an aid to social reform, and they raised the status of those non-philosophical, and especially literary, forms of expression which embodied such a mode of perception and view of reality. In Marian Evans's journals, letters and journalism written in the period immediately before she embarked upon her career as a novelist, a similar movement of thought was discernible. She continued to refer to those romantic writers she had read in her youth who were implicitly engaged in a dialogue with rationalism. Wordsworth was arguably her favourite poet; she used the early nineteenth-century poets as a yardstick of comparison. She explored the link between romanticism, and religious and political movements, and she considered the value of feeling in a discriminating fashion. In Young's poetic expression of sorrow, she detected 'the unmistakeable cry of pain, which makes us tolerant of egoism and hyperbole', but was critical of Murger's absurd treatment of the same theme in fiction.[1] In reading Rousseau and George Sand, she had encountered writers who perceived and described the outside world both impressionistically and with a neo-scientific attention to detail. Lewes and Ruskin had emphasised that close observation of phenomena promoted a response of wonder at the universe. In writing of nature, Marian Evans emulated this romantic and post-romantic ideal of flexible perception. She echoed Ruskin's view that an appreciation of nature was enhanced by a knowledge of science, and by close inspection of nature's workings. She spoke of the need for 'the eye to be educated by objects as well as ideas' and her letters from Devon incorporated descriptions of flowers, rock forms and shells, and such descriptions were often low-key and consciously loaded with concrete detail, for she rejected the imposition upon reality of preconceived notions of the sublime and the picturesque.[2] Yet she was also aware of the subjectivity of vision, of how reality literally presented itself in different lights, and the transforming effects of a change of light stimulated her imagination. A light effect might be transitory but, while it existed, it presented a vision whose truth was not diminished by its instantaneousness. In the Berlin Journal, she recorded her feeling for the romance of a night-time street scene, but added: 'the next day under the light of the sun, it was perfectly prosaic'. Seeing women gathering cockles on the Swansea seashore, she described them in a way which recalled Wordsworth's descriptions of mysterious and monumental solitaries.[3]

The romantics' criticism of that rationalism which was viewed as the cause of bloody revolution in late eighteenth-century France gave birth to the idea that future reforms could only be initiated by an enlargement of the way in which men viewed the world. Such had been the assumptions and aims of Saint-Simon, Comte, Mill and Carlyle, and their view that social reform was consequent only upon the reform of man's perception of reality continued a tradition established by the visions of Wordsworth, Coleridge, Byron and Shelley in their treatment of political themes. The free dissemination of ideas was deemed essential to the well-being of society. Marian Evans thus championed views which were at odds with philosophical and religious orthodoxy. As the translator of Strauss, Feuerbach and Spinoza, and also in her review of Mackay, she was concerned to present new ideas to the world, and to defend their social utility. Under Chapman's and Marian Evans's editorship, the *Westminster Review* echoed the Comtean notion of progress as dependent upon intellectual reform. She criticised Austrian censorship in two separate articles; she demonstrated how Young curbed his freedom of expression for economic gain. She also welcomed, conversely, works which revealed new perspectives on reality, and praised experimenters such as Wagner, Browning and Meredith. American literature also won her enthusiastic attention, because it expressed the sensibility of a new world.[4] Romanticism had necessitated the evolution of innovative forms to embody its complex mode of perception, and had exalted literature above philosophy as a flexible vehicle for the expression of truth. Lewes and Chapman, the inheritors of romanticism, saw the novel as a form with unexploited powers of expression. If the romantic sensibility had been able to transform poetry by the infusion of new modes of vision, the same might be done in the Victorian period for the novel by the mind earnestly in pursuit of truth. The novel might thus also resemble romantic poetry by serving as a corrective of sectarian philosophical trends, and thereby aiding the cause of social reform.

A phenomenon which may also have given Marian Evans confidence to consider literature as a form of expression was the growing prominence of women in English life, and particularly in literature. From the late 1840s onwards, there were moves to remedy women's legal and educational disadvantages. Marian Evans's reading revealed an interest in the position of women. She supported a petition, to which Harriet Martineau and Mrs Gaskell were also signatories, asking that women should have a legal right to their earnings. She praised Stendhal's support for the idea of equal education for women.[5] Her views on female emancipation reflected her intellectual position: like Carlyle and Lewes, she scorned theories of reform which simplified actuality. Reform, she said, could only be based upon full apprehension of the female lot; it confused the issue simply to see women as innately morally superior, or as inevitably victims. She commended Mary Wollstonecraft and Margaret Fuller, because 'Their ardent hopes of what women may become do not prevent them from seeing and painting women as they are'. The reconciling impulse of the synthetic logic also showed itself when she remarked that improvement in women's position could come only via the 'perpetual action and reaction between individuals and institutions'.[6] Comte's writings vindicated the distinctive contribution female perception could make, and Feuerbach had argued that gender helped to determine vision. Such arguments may have encouraged Marian Evans to abandon her role as a disseminator of others' ideas as translator and journalist. Writing to Charles Bray on 26 March 1856, she asked him not to mention her work on the *Ethics* as she did not wish to be known as the translator of Spinoza. Lewes had long championed women writers, and, as a reviewer, Marian Evans had examples of female writing constantly before her. She reviewed *Histoire de ma vie* by George Sand, and works by Mrs Stowe, Charlotte Brontë and Mrs Gaskell, which had done much to establish women as a force in fiction.[7]

She particularly admired Mrs Browning's *Aurora Leigh* (1856).[8] The central character had much in common with a George Sand heroine; Aurora was passionate, sensitive and intellectual, simultaneously alienated from society, and committed to its improvement. Her character and attitudes, as well as her solitary life as a writer in London, presented a new female type who somewhat resembled the Marian Evans who had settled at 142 Strand in 1851. In that *Aurora Leigh* was vitally concerned with ideas, it also recalled George Sand's and Froude's innovative fictional models which Marian Evans had praised in the 1840s. By considering the ideas of Fourier, Cabet, Comte and Christian Socialists, and ending with the vision of a society regenerated by non-sectarian Christianity, *Aurora Leigh* suggested that art could make use of speculation.[9] The work sceptically proposed, however, the inadequacy of speculation, by showing how its conclusions were not validated by experience. Mrs Browning argued that life did not confirm the separation between intellect and emotions; generalising theories of social reform were also criticised.[10] *Aurora Leigh* was also reminiscent of the post-Romantic tradition represented by Carlyle and Ruskin when it discussed doctrines of art. The true artist possessed a duality of vision whereby he 'Holds firmly by the natural, to reach/The spiritual beyond it', and he,

> . . . should have eyes
> To see things near as comprehensively
> As if afar they took their point of sight
> And distant things, as intimately deep
> As if they touched them . . .

Art should also reflect the complexity of life: French writers were criticised because they distorted reality, being,

> . . . logical
> To austerity in the application of
> The special theory – not a soul content
> To paint a crooked pollard and an ass,
> As the English will because they find it's so
> And like it somehow . . .

Mrs Browning's definition of the function of art was based upon this notion of the eclectic perception. By unveiling the non-material dimension in reality, art, like religion, acted as a counterbalance to the limited visions of desiccated theorising and materialism. It provided the true knowledge of reality necessary for social reform, and fostered that reverence for life which alone could change the world. Mrs Browning suggested, as had Ruskin, that art should not look back with nostalgia, but should concern itself with present realities. She wrote a novel in verse, and considered that literature must evolve new forms, which would be complementary to content. This echoed the organicism of both Carlyle and Ruskin, which opened the way for stringent uses of experimental literary forms.[11]

Marian Evans also contemplated the specific problems of women's writings. She acknowledged the existence of prejudice against women, telling Charles Bray in 1855 that the impact of her article on Cumming 'would be a little counteracted if the author were known to be a *woman*'. In 1856 both she and Lewes advised

Sara Hennell against putting her Christian name on the title page of her prize essay.[12] Marian Evans censured, however, any 'exceptional indulgence towards the productions of literary women'. She lamented the fact that novels by women too often showed their ignorance 'both of science and of life'. She saw women's meagre education, personal vanity about getting into print, and restricted existence, as no excuses for their lack of the qualities she deemed essential for any writer: 'patient diligence, a sense of the responsibility involved in publication, and an appreciation of the sacredness of the writer's art'.[13]

II

The high ideal of art which Mrs Browning proposed, and to which few women writers adhered, was echoed in the definition of the writer's role which emerged from Marian Evans's writings during this period. Reviewing volume 3 of *Modern Painters*, she observed that 'the fundamental principles of all just thought and beautiful action or creation are the same',[14] and her evolution of a doctrine of art was informed by her awareness of the conclusions which had been reached by philosophical thinkers about the nature of perception and truth. In the Hegelian sense which Engels so well described, she saw truth as process and, like Lewes, valued writers who contributed to the evolution of a method which that process should follow. She considered that it was Carlyle's achievement to have taught how 'to obtain not *results* but *powers*, not particular solutions, but the means by which endless solutions may be wrought'.[15] The conclusions of the philosophical debate about logic were also crucial for influencing the way in which men viewed the world and, ultimately, the way in which art expressed that vision. Marian Evans gave assent to Bentham's influential comment that the dry science of logic had implications for 'life and everything else that man holds dear to him'. She noted of philosophy, 'in its function of determining logic or method, it is still the centre and heart of human knowledge, and it has to apply this method to the investigation of Psychology, with its subordinate department, Aesthetics'. Lewes, similarly, considered that the method of philosophical and scientific inquiry applied also to artistic inquiry.[16]

Marian Evans praised Gruppe because he validated a complex mode of perception by insisting that the distinction between empiricism and idealism was not an absolute one. His bias was towards empiricism, but he retained a sense of wonder not usually associated with philosophical method which drew its material from the senses and was seen to have materialistic implications for a view of the world. She noted that modified empiricism might 'lead, not indeed to heaven, but to an eminence whence we may see very bright and blessed things on earth'.[17] Her view of how the imagination worked was tied to her general view of the thought process. A notebook she kept in the 1870s elaborated her view of the mental processes which produced art. She commented, 'Imagination which used to be in high repute for its immensity, is seen nowadays to be no more than a worker in mosaics, owing every one of its glinting fragments & every type of its impossible vastnesses to the small realm of experience'.[18] She agreed that art was rooted in necessarily limited experience, but her metaphor of the imagination as a worker in mosaics, assembling glinting fragments to suggest vastness, showed that she gave weight to the individual's aesthetic impulse which shaped experience into art. She saw the imagination as capable of suggesting by such aesthetic assembly dimensions in reality which were more mysterious than the empirically acquired raw material of art might imply. The vision projected by the work of art was thus the product of empirical experience and subjective impulse, of a complicatedly eclectic process. Marian Evans's realism was consequently distinctive and idiosyncratic; it was defined both by the manner in which her mind confronted an external reality and by the assumptions about the nature of that reality implicit in her approach to it. In neither respect did her realism manifest the detached perception and materialist view of the world with which realism came to be associated after the example of writers such as Zola. Marian Evans decried the narrowness of Balzac's sordid naturalism.[19]

In some respects, a bias towards certain implications of empiricism was apparent in her view of the imagination and the outside world. She spoke of the importance of careful observation. Ruskin's writings, as well as the example of Lewes's scientific research methods, inspired passages in her Devon Journal which were meticulous in their recording of details. She also praised impartiality of observation in Meredith's *The Shaving of Shagpat*, and in a volume of recollections of Heine. She commended Riehl's method because he 'began his observations with no party prepossessions, and his present views were evolved entirely from his own gradually amassed observations'. Young was criticised because his 'muse never stood face to face with a genuine, living human being'.[20] Her own imagination as a novelist annexed to itself the methods of the empirically-based sciences of sociology and psychology. She valued the observation which empiricism might encourage because observation promoted an appreciation of the complexity of life. She criticised wilful distortion of reality: for Marian Evans, as for Carlyle and Lewes, distortion meant over-simplification, viewing reality in the light of theories or preoccupations, in a way akin to that of sectarian logicians. In the realm of moral action she was especially aware of the intricate issues involved, a view often expressed when she discussed her decision to live with Lewes. She was rightly resentful of those who made snap judgments of her actions, as she was of those who hastily condemned Byron or Liszt.[21] The contemporary novel came in for much criticism from Marian Evans because of its oversimplification of reality. She castigated Geraldine Jewsbury because she tried 'to make out that this tangled wilderness of life has a plan as easy to trace as that of a Dutch garden'. She attacked the use of the novel as propaganda, and considered that characterisation was vitiated if the author imposed his own views on the characters. Like Carlyle, she praised *Wilhelm Meister* despite its lack of moralising in the presentation of a seemingly immoral hero, noting that 'we question whether the direct exhibition of a moral bias in the writer will make a book really moral in its influence'. She was ambivalent in her evaluation of *Westward Ho!* because although Kingsley 'sees, feels, and paints vividly . . . he theorizes illogically and moralizes absurdly'.[22]

Yet although she was critical of the deliberate misrepresentation of reality, she admitted 'how inevitably subjective art is, even when it professes to be purely imitative . . . the most active perception gives us rather a reflex of what we think and feel, than the real sum of objects before us'. Everyone 'sees things not as they are, but as they appear through his peculiar mental media'.[23] She suggested that the mind could not operate exclusively with the objectivity empiricism might be seen to presuppose, yet she argued the value of perception's apparently limiting subjectivity in a way which showed her inheritance of romantic presuppositions. She also steered a middle course between views of reality as material or as mysteriously intangible; she merged the objective and subjective elements in perception to provide an accurate index of that reality. Marian Evans praised Wagner for his perception of the natural and supernatural, and admired Browning because his sensibility was 'as thorougly alive to the outward as the inward'. Similar criteria informed her discussion of Frederika Bremer's novels.[24] Whilst Marian Evans insisted upon the 'veracity' of great art, her vindication of eclectic perception suggested that the subjective element within perception would lead the artist to suggest aesthetic and moral notions. Because her ideal of the representational aesthetic incorporated reference to the mind's subjectivity, she saw that aesthetic as legitimately ethical in intent and effect; Lewes was likewise to insist that even science, with its objective quest for knowledge, nevertheless had moral concerns.[25] Marian Evans praised writers whose faithful observation of reality was combined with a deliberate directing of the reader's attention to those facets of existence which were not morally neutral, for she considered that such writers could encourage desirable moral qualities in their audience. She praised those works of art which pointed, in Wordsworthian fashion, to the inspiring beauty of everyday life, and heightened the reader's perception of such loveliness. Browning's 'Fra Lippo Lippi' was better than 'an essay on Realism in Art': the speaker in that poem suggested that the artist's representation fostered a reverence for life, for:

> . . . we're made so that we love
> First when we see them painted, things we have passed
> Perhaps a hundred times, nor cared to see.

Reviewing a book by Kenelm Digby, she noted that 'In teaching us very forcibly that we should quicken our perception of the good and the lovely by being constantly on the watch for it in common things, the author points to one of Dickens's greatest qualities'. Ruskin's ideas on this subject particularly interested her. She discussed how his 'naturalism' made possible a perception of the beautiful and the ideal. Reviewing Volume 3 of *Modern Painters*, she singled out his idea of Grand Style which proposed the valuable subjectivity of art. Ruskin considered that the artist should select noble subjects, and significant truths, and should introduce into his work 'as much beauty as is possible, consistently with truth' and produce 'an inventive combination of distinctly known objects'.[26]

Lewes shared her views on the kind of truth art presented. In 1846; he commented, 'by truth we do not mean *literality*; few tales are as false as those "founded upon facts"'.[27] Jowett was to commend George Eliot's capacity as a novelist for indirect ethical teaching. The ideas Marian Evans evolved in the 1850s about art's presentation of the beautiful remained with the mature novelist. In 1869 she suggested that ideally the novel reconciled veracious objectivity and beneficial subjectivity; she 'was eager to explain the difference between prosaic and poetical fiction – that what is prosaic in ordinary novels is not the presence of the realistic element, without which the tragedy cannot be given – she herself is obliged to see and feel every minutest detail – but in the absence of anything suggesting the ideal, the higher life'. The 1870 notebook suggested that her pondering of the link between objective and subjective, real and ideal, owed much to *Modern Painters*; she also continued to echo Carlyle's notion of the flawed hero.[28]

She also considered that art could have an even more obviously ethical function in encouraging specific moral qualities. She praised *Rachel Gray* because of its attempt to 'impress us with the every-day sorrows of our commonplace fellow-men, and so to widen our sympathies'. The study of art, as proposed in *Modern Painters*, 'according to the mental attitude and external life of that age' led to the author's 'widening our sympathy and deepening the basis of our tolerance and charity'. Conversely, she criticised Heine's 'contempt for the reverent feelings of other men'.[29] Moral idealism underpinned her assertion of the existence of 'disinterested elements of human feeling' in the face of Benthamite and Christian philosophies of self-interest. She rooted virtue in correct feeling such as an author's aesthetic could foster, and disassociated it from codes of belief. Her letters spoke of the need to reverence good qualities in others, and to respect all sincerely-held opinions. She manifested charity and tolerance in her attempt to reconcile Lewes and Harriet Martineau, who were rival expounders of Comte. Harriet had also spread gossip about Marian Evans and Lewes, yet Marian Evans commented generously on her character and achievements. Imaginative sympathy was explicitly commended, and intellectual arrogance and moral and emotional egoism were criticised in Marian Evan's letters.[30]

Yet although she thought that the subjective element in the imagination could suggest ethical truths, Marian Evans also saw literature as even more obliquely moral in intent and effect, because literature contributed to the open-ended process by which truth might be found. She viewed participation in this process as a

moral obligation. Carlyle and Ruskin had assigned great significance to the verb 'to see', and their emphatic use of that verb was
echoed by Marian Evans for she too considered the very presentation of a vision of life as a moral act. In her opposition to fixed
truths, she revealed again her romantic inheritance. Like Mill and
Carlyle, she considered there was a need for the individual's vision
of life to be continually modified and extended: the imagination's
presentation of its visions could play a crucial part in this educative
process. She criticised Michelet's 'oracular style' and generalisations, but praised his 'sober delineation' of facts, wherein 'the
reader may see as in a panoramic view the true significance and
relations of men and events'.[31] Experimental art, she said, presented 'protests which it is wiser to accept as strictures than to hiss
down as absurdities'. The idiosyncratic vision also educated the
reader's perception, the artist presented his 'higher sensibility as a
medium, a delicate acoustic or optical instrument, bringing home
to our coarser senses what would otherwise be unperceived by us'.
She thus saw the meaning of a work, as in her concept of 'involuntary symbol', as often implicit: Lewes, likewise, argued that art
'requires intellectual substance; but when thought assumes the
dominant role, it is a sign of the decay of art. Art is different from
philosophy and its symbols have beauty independent of their
philosophic significance'.[32] Marian Evans, like Ruskin, was much
concerned with the arduous pursuit of a style which would express
a truthful vision of existence. She sought accuracy and appropri-
ateness of expression in a way which recalled Bentham's search for
an ideal language, the linguistic inventiveness of Coleridge, the
stylistic experiments of Feuerbach. Her work as a translator had
fostered her sense of the need for a precise use of words, and she
castigated careless use of language, whether by Chapman, Dr
Cumming or female novelists. She wrote sympathetically to Sara
Hennell about stylistic problems. Significantly emphasising her
words, Marian Evans told Chapman to dismiss from his mind 'all
efforts after any other qualities than precision and force – any other
result than *complete presentation* of your idea'. Her ideal perception
operated in a variety of ways and demanded a flexible medium to
describe the complex reality it apprehended. She commended
Stahr's style for its mingling of 'philosophic insight, picturesque
narration, and poetic enthusiasm'. She defended Young and Carlyle as they strove to mould language to their vision. Yet she
asserted, as an admirer of Carlyle and Ruskin, that language was

appropriately equivocal: even if an unambiguous language existed, it would be 'a perfect medium of expression to science, but will never express *life*'.[33]

Concerns akin to those of thinkers involved in the crucial philosophical debate about mental processes, the nature of reality and the modes and functions of expression, permeated her letters, journals and journalism. That she often explored such topics in relation to literature is not surprising, for romantic literature had offered a powerful critique of philosophical rationalism. Carlyle, Mill and Lewes had learnt from literature in their contemplation of philosophical problems, and had deployed non-philosophical forms of expression. Like many of her associates, Marian Evans came to value literature because it utilised a mode of perception, and embodied a view of reality, in ways which demonstrated the inadequacies of the perceptual and expressive modes and conclusions of philosophical speculation. Much of her writing before she started *Scenes of Clerical Life* emphasised the seriousness of the writer's task; she criticised those who, like Brougham, practised literature frivolously, and insisted that the writer, whether translator or novelist, must possess the moral qualities of patience, diligence, responsibility, honesty. She noted that anyone 'who publishes writings inevitably assumes the office of teacher or influencer of the public mind', and she regarded her work as a novelist 'in the light of a priesthood'.[34] Her high estimation of literature was based upon her notion that the writer inevitably entered into his work, presenting a view of the world which would have a moral effect on his audience. In line with the German romantic tradition described by Carlyle and Lewes, she saw art as assuming the interpretative and instructive functions of religion, but as being free from the sectarianism which vitiated the perception and visions of both Christians and philosophers.

Marian Evans came to fiction from the obviously substantial and erudite disciplines of theology, philosophy, history and science, and, moreover, at a time when the novel was often seen as a frivolous genre. She thus also considered the relationship between art and knowledge. Lewes viewed all disciplines as means of extending man's knowledge of the world, and based this view upon his notion that truth was evolved by a specific mental process: art, science and philosophy could all attain truth if they deployed the correct methods. Of the special contribution the novel had to make, he asked rhetorically, 'Is knowledge of the human heart not information?'[35] Marian Evans considered *The Life of Goethe* as of interest not just from a literary point of view, but also 'to the psychological student'. Art also employed the material of other disciplines. Marian Evans realised that the same phenomena were capable of yielding material to varying kinds of intellectual endeavour. In Ilfracombe, she found 'hills and valleys to employ painters for a life time, and rock pools to make every naturalist's heart thrill with expectation'. She saw great writers as utilising a wide range of knowledge, and followed Ruskin in suggesting that the study of any great subject 'carries the student into many fields'. The 'sphere of art extends wherever there is beauty either in form, or thought, or feeling'.[36] Marian Evans also considered that art had a distinctive form of knowledge to offer and, once more, she evaluated art by reference to a philosophical position. She criticised *a priori* logic because it isolated sensuously-derived generalisations and tried to 'operate with them apart from experience . . . to make them a standing point higher than all experience'. The great Victorian novelists triumphantly challenged the interpretative generalisations and the resultant social and moral nostra of their age. Marian Evans was unique, however, in founding her defiantly anti-doctrinaire aesthetic of representation upon a sceptical eclecticism which was rooted in an awareness of the philosophical debate about associationism and intuitionism. In discussing various writers, she emphasised the extent to which they possessed the capacity to refute generalisations by providing a detailed knowledge of actuality. She commented that ignorance 'both of science and of life' led inept female novelists to produce facile interpretations of existence, and to offer vacuous solutions to its problems. Conversely, she praised Riehl's provision of detailed information, and the 'sympathetic and impartial spirit' of some recollections of Heine. 'Art' she argued, 'is the nearest thing to life; it is a mode of amplifying experience and extending our contact with our fellowmen beyond the bounds of our personal lot.' In fiction, she commended a proximity of the reading experience and the experience of life's immediacy and complexity. She criticised fictional scenes which were 'merely described, not *presented*'.[37]

Rationalism had been tested, and found wanting, in the cataclysmic trauma of the 1789 French Revolution: the nineteenth-century critique of empiricism was haunted and spurred on, as Lewes's and Carlyle's work showed, by the ghost of Robespierre and memories of the Terror. During the first half of the nineteenth century, such a critique was given yet greater urgency by the prospect of actual revolution on the European mainland, and a potentially revolutionary situation in England. Carlyle, Mill and Comte were but three of those thinkers who considered that the reform of society would not occur until men changed the way in which they viewed the world. The earlier generations of post-rationalist thinkers fervently believed that philosophy had important implications for both the individual's perception of the world and for man's social fate. But the political consequences of rationalism led the post-revolutionary generation to mistrust philosophical dogmatism. Flexible modes of perception, a view of reality which conceded its ultimately unfathomable complexity, and an anti-dogmatic concentration upon specifics became associated with the literary sensibility, which was seen as a desirable corrective to the over-simplified philosophical vision which had had such terrifying social consequences. Lewes saw art as springing from social needs and modifying man's life in society.[38] Given Marian Evans's familiarity with the post-Enlightenment philosophical tradition, it is not surprising that she vindicated literature by viewing it as a potential instrument for social reform. The reforming impulse of the Victorian novelists was widely apparent by the middle of the century; Mrs Gaskell and Disraeli had tackled the theme of emergent industrial capitalism, and Dickens had written of a variety of social abuses. But Marian Evans, by her representational aesthetic, attempted first to reform her readers by correcting the way in which they viewed reality, as had Carlyle in *The French Revolution*. Reviewing works of literature just before she started to write her first novel, she welcomed widely differing ways of viewing the world as contributions to the enlargement of her own view of reality. She was as pleased by Browning's complicated intellectuality as she was by Longfellow's simplicity. She insisted that art should not be propaganda, which confined the reader's vision, but should teach a way of looking at the world, 'a reverent contemplation of great facts and a wise application of great principles'. She was also critical of the art which simply promoted knowledge, which remained mere 'acquisition'. She saw knowledge as valuable in so far as it fostered mental attitudes; the worthwhile female novelist 'does not give you information, which is the raw material of culture, – she gives you sympathy, which is its subtlest essence'. Hence emerged Marian Evans's paradox that the writer taught by foreswearing didacticism. When Marian Evans asserted that the acceptance of Ruskin's realism 'would remould our life',[39] her definition of art's social function drew upon a tradition of thinking about perception and social reform which went back to the generation of Wordsworth and Coleridge. The aims of the logical debate informed Marian Evans's view of the social function of art, for a desire to foster understanding of reality, by urging reconciliation of opposed ideas, rather than engagement in partisan controversy, motivated the move towards an eclectic logic. Her contemporaries recalled appropriate qualities in her character. Spencer noted that her 'natural feeling' was 'a longing to agree as far as possible'; she was known as a good listener, a sought-out confidante, and sympathy and careful thought characterised her conversation.[40]

Marian Evans's decision to write novels which should represent, but not schematise, reality was congruous with the novel's origins, and a distinctive English tradition. The novel owed its origins to a rebellion against the fantasies of romance. The English novel, by the end of the nineteenth century, was also remarkable for its opposition to the unrealities of the *roman à thèse*; it was 'specially objective, positive, concrete'. 'We have', noted Mrs Humphry Ward, 'always taken more delight in the mere spectacle of life than our neighbours.'[41] Yet art was also, according to Lewes, not simply the creation of the individual mind, but the expression of a nation's intellectual life.[42] Lewes, in three novels and two biographies, had been concerned with philosophical issues, and had proposed a representational aesthetic which derived from, and was framed as a corrective to, intellectual dogmatism. Marian Evans's decision to write novels, and the nature of her aims in fiction issued also from the contemporary philosophical debate, because she envisaged the presentation of life's 'mere spectacle' as a way in which the literary mind could contribute to that debate. Literature embodied a complex mode of perception and presented a complicated reality: the imaginative process and the literary vision both challenged epistemological dogmatism. Moreover, in amplifying the way in which society was viewed, literature also served a social function. Her arguments claimed much for literature at a time when fiction, her chosen form, was still regarded as lacking in seriousness of intent. Yet Carlyle, for reasons akin to those suggested by Marian Evans, had taken the novel seriously in his criticisms of Scott, his translation of *Wilhelm Meister*, in *German Romance*, and in his abortive attempts at fiction. In the 1850s, because of her contact with Chapman and Lewes, Marian Evans was also in touch with those who considered that the potential of the novel as a vehicle for the expression of a strenuously evolved view of reality, and as a force for social reform, remained virtually unexplored. Reviewing *Modern Painters*, Marian Evans noted Ruskin's comment that great art demanded the exercise of all human faculties. She praised da Vinci as possessing the ideal sensibility, 'at once observant and speculative, practical and theoretic, artistic and reflective, grand in intellect, grand in feeling'.[43] By 1856, when she started to write *Amos Barton*, she was familiar with the notion that art could uniquely express the entire resources of the well-trained mind in which all modes of perception were integrated. It was no accident that Marian Evans's mind, which had been honed on philosophy, ultimately turned from it. Those of the post-enlightenment generation who were concerned with philosophical issues had constantly argued the superiority of the imagination to the reason. They had sought to learn from the literary sensibility, and had profited from the light it shed upon the vexed questions of the workings of perception and the nature of reality. Comte and Feuerbach had also suggested explicitly that which others implied: philosophy should ultimately concern itself with humanity, which was to vindicate the novel's traditional area of concern. Marian Evans's quest to express truth in fictions partook of the strenuousness of philosophical inquiry, but her novels were to contemplate the complexity of reality from a flexible viewpoint, and the reality she described was to reflect her sense of wonder and beauty. Her generalisations and judgments were to be ever-tentative, rooted in a sense of the many-coloured, multi-faceted qualities of social, sensuous and psychological reality. In her rejection of any one mode of literary perception, be it scientific naturalism, escapist fantasy, or moralising propaganda, in her proposal of the complex mystery of the world, she ratified the conclusions of those who were dissatisfied with the speculative discipline. Yet her varied modes of perception, and her representational vision derived from the sceptical eclecticism of much of the philosophy of her age, and were literary counterparts of it.

On her travels in Devon, it was pictures that she found everywhere, and which she recorded in her letters and journals. Her novels, pictures of life as she wanted them to be, implicitly engaged in a critical dialogue with philosophical dogmatism, and followed the path taken by thinkers such as Mill and Carlyle as they attempted to extricate themselves from the agonising implications of sectarian logic. Hence, the one great Victorian novelist who was well-versed in philosophy rejected that discipline because the discipline itself evolved reasons for its rejection. It was, perhaps most importantly, in this sense that philosophy vindicated her choice of the novel as a genre to which she could devote her mind. It was also in this sense that her very rejection of philosophy meant that, as a novelist, she was so deeply indebted to it, continued to engage in dialogue with it, and ratified its conclusions about the inadequacies of the merely rational process as a way of contemplating the mysterious phenomena of mind and life.

Notes and References

ABBREVIATIONS

AM	*Atlantic Monthly*
BEM	*Blackwood's Edinburgh Magazine*
BHP	*A Biographical History of Philosophy* by George Henry Lewes
BQR	*British Quarterly Review*
CM	*Century Magazine*
CR	*Contemporary Review*
DR	*Dublin Review*
ER	*Edinburgh Review*
EngR	*English Review*
FQR	*Foreign and Quarterly Review*
FR	*Fortnightly Review*
FM	*Fraser's Magazine for Town and Country*
GEL	*George Eliot Letters*, edited by Gordon Haight
HM	*Hood's Magazine and Comic Miscellany*
LR	*London Review*
LQR	*London and Quarterly Review*
LWR	*London and Westminster Review*
MC	*Monthly Chronicle*
MLR	*Modern Language Review*
MM	*Monthly Magazine*
MR	*Monthly Repository*
NC	*Nineteenth Century*
NCF	*Nineteenth-Century Fiction*
NQ	*New Quarterly*
PMG	*Pall Mall Gazette*
QR	*Quarterly Review*
SR	*Saturday Review*
VCH	*Victoria History of the Counties of England* (Warwickshire) Vols I–VIII (1904–69)
WFQR	*Westminster and Foreign Quarterly Review*
WR	*Westminster Review*
YULG	*Yale University Library Gazette*
n.s.	new series
n.d.	no date

INTRODUCTION

1. Quoted from David Masson, *The British Novelists and Their Styles* (1859), pp. 269–301 in Richard Stang, *The Theory of the Novel in England 1850–70* (1959) p. 87.
2. F. W. H. Myers, 'George Eliot', *CM* XXIII (November 1881) 61; Oscar Browning, *Life of George Eliot* (1890) p. 139.
3. Mrs Linton, *My Literary Life* (1899) pp. 89, 99.
4. Joseph Mazzini, *Essays* (n.d.) p. 262.
5. John Ruskin, 39 vols, (1903–12) V, 322. Hereafter cited as Ruskin, *Works*.
6. Stang, *The Theory of the Novel*, p. 23.
7. *GEL*, IX, 213.
8. Amy Cruse, *The Victorians and Their Books* (1935) p. 283; Anthony Trollope, *An Autobiography* (Oxford, 1950) p. 246, quoted in J. A. Sutherland, *Victorian Novelists and Publishers* (1976) p. 188.
9. J. B. Tomlinson, *The English Middle-Class Novel* (1976) p. 11.
10. See e.g. K. K. Collins, 'Questions of Method: Some Unpublished Late Essays', *NCF* XXXV (December 1980) 385–405; Valerie A. Dodd, 'A George Eliot Notebook', *Studies in Bibliography* XXXIV (1981) 258–62; Daniel Waley, *George Eliot's Blotter* (1980).
11. Browning, *Life of George Eliot* p. 145; [Frederic Harrison], 'The Life of George Eliot', *FR* XXVII (March 1885) 312–13.
12. Signed 'Y', 'Thomas Carlyle and George Eliot', *Nation* XXXII (24 March 1881) 201; [unsigned review], 'George Eliot: Her Life and Writings', *WR* n.s. LX (July 1881) 187; Mathilde Blind, *George Eliot*, p. 106; Françoise Basch, *Relative Creatures* (1974) pp. xvii, 252; Neil Roberts, *George Eliot* (1975) p. 10; Josiah Royce, *Fugitive* Essays (1920; Freeport N.Y., 1968) p. 272; Ferdinand Brunetière, *Le Roman naturaliste* (11e edition, Paris, n.d.), pp. 248–9 This list is by no means exhaustive.
13. Virginia Woolf, *A Room of One's Own* (1929); (London, 1977); p. 67; Gerald Bullett, *George Eliot* (1947) p. 14; George Moore, *Conversations in Ebury Street* (1924) p. 68.
14. *GEL*, VIII, 14; Linton, *My Literary Life*, p. 36; John Stuart Mill, *The Subjection of Women* (1869; 1929) p. 232.
15. Ruskin, *Sesame and Lilies* (1865; 13th edition, 1892) pp. 138–9.
16. F. A. von Hayek, *John Stuart Mill and Harriet Taylor* (1951) p. 63.
17. Mary Wollstonecraft, *Vindication of the Rights of Woman* (1792; 1975) p. 242; Noel Annan *et al.*, *Ideas and Beliefs of the Victorians* (1949) p. 256.
18. Dorothy Gardiner, *English Girlhood at School* (1929) pp. 446, 462–3.
19. Mary Wollstonecraft, *Mary* (1788; Oxford, 1980) [p. xxxi]; idem, *The Wrongs of Woman* (1798; Oxford, 1980) p. 166.
20. George Henry Lewes, *Ranthorpe* (1847) pp. 188–9.
21. Kathleen Adams, *Those of Us who Loved Her* (Warwick, 1980) p. 109; Blind, *George Eliot*, p. 5.
22. Quoted in Sara Delamont and Lorna Duffin, *The Nineteenth-Century Woman* (London and New York, 1978) p. 48.
23. Thus I dispute the psychological interpretation of Laura C. Emery in

George Eliot's Creative Conflict (Los Angeles and London, 1976). Compare Ian Milner, *The Structure of Values in George Eliot* (Prague, 1968) p. 123.

24. Blind, *George Eliot*, p. 102.
25. Quoted in Gordon S. Haight, 'A New George Eliot Letter', *YULG* XLVI (July 1971) 24.
26. See e.g. Gordon S. Haight, *George Eliot and John Chapman* (1940) p. 19; Margaret Crompton, *George Eliot* (1960) p. 25.
27. See e.g. Henry James, '*Daniel Deronda*: A Conversation', *AM* XXXVIII (December 1876) 686; Leslie Stephen, *George Eliot* (1902) p. 200; David Cecil, *Early Victorian Novelists* (1934) pp. 327–8.
28. George Levine, 'Determinism and Responsibility in the Works of George Eliot', *PMLA* LXXVII (June 1962) 268–79; Bernard J. Paris, *Experiments in Life: George Eliot's Quest for Values* (Detroit 1965); 'George Eliot and Comtism', *LQR* XLVII (January 1877) 446–71; Martha S. Vogeler, 'George Eliot and the Positivists', *NCF* XXXV (December 1980) 406–31.
29. Stephen, *George Eliot*, p. 179; Barbara Hardy (ed.), *Middlemarch: Critical Approaches to the Novel* (1967) p. 13.
30. See her poem, 'Brother and Sister'; *GEL*, III, 145, 148; VIII, 466.
31. E. S. Haldane, *George Eliot and Her Times* (1927) pp. 24–5; Mary H. Deakin, *The Early Life of George Eliot* (Manchester, 1913) pp. 27–8; George Eliot, *Quarry for Middlemarch*, edited by Anna Kitchel, to accompany *NCF* IV (March 1950).
32. J. G. Lockhart, *The Life of Sir Walter Scott* Abridged edition (1848; 1906) p. 233.
33. *GEL*, I, 277–8. I elaborate upon this point later.
34. Henry James, 'George Eliot's Life', *AM* CCCXXXI, Boston LV (May 1885) 678. The mysteriousness of the process which turned George Eliot from philosopher to novelist is also touched upon in Royce, *Fugitive Essays*, pp. 262–4; R. V. Redinger, *The Emergent Self* (1976) p. 4.
35. *GEL*, I, 11–12, 24, 71, 104, 310.

1. INTUITION AND EXPERIENCE

1. Brunetière, *Le Roman naturaliste*, p. 294.
2. Annan, *Ideas and Beliefs*, p. 444.
3. John Stuart Mill, *Autobiography* (1874; Jack Stillinger (ed.), New York, 1969; Oxford, 1971) p. 162. Hereafter cited as Mill, *Autobiography*.
4. In J. S. Mill, *An Examination of Sir William Hamilton's Philosophy*; Andrew Seth, *Scottish Philosophy* (1885; 3rd edn 1899) examines this in detail.
5. John H. Muirhead, *The Platonic Tradition in Anglo-Saxon Philosophy* (1931) pp. 149–50; [Thomas Brown]. 'Villers, *Philosophie de Kant ER*' I (January 1803) 256–7; Seth, *Scottish Philosophy*, p. 194.
6. See René Wellek, *Immanuel Kant in England* (1931); Leslie Stephen, 'The Importation of German' in *Studies of a Biographer*, 4 vols (1898–1902) II, 38–75.

7. Michael St John Packe, *The Life of John Stuart Mill* (1954) p. 178.
8. Hippolyte Taine, *Notes on England* (1872), translated with an Introduction by Edward Hyams (1957) p. 192.
9. Léon Faucher, *Etudes sur L'Angleterre* 2 vols (Brussels, 1845) I, [7]
10. Wellek, *Kant*, p. 5; Malcolm I. Thomis and Peter Holt, *Threats of Revolution in Britain 1789–1848* (1977); Madame de Staël, *Ten Years of Exile* (1904; New York, 1972) p. 69.
11. Mark Pattison, *Essays*, 2 vols (1889) I, 417.
12. *Collected Letters of Samuel Taylor Coleridge*, edited by E. L. Griggs, 6 vols (1956–71) I, 210.
13. *Biographia Literaria* (1817; 1907) 2 vols, edited by J. Shawcross, I, 9, hereafter cited as *Biographia*; Basil Willey, *Samuel Taylor Coleridge* (1972) p. 14; Charles Lamb, *The Essays of Elia and the Last Essays of Elia* (1901) p. 31; Ralph Waldo Emerson, *English Traits* (1856) p. 5; J. B. Beer, *Coleridge the Visionary*, p. 299, reprints Coleridge's Greek Ode, written in 1793, which praised Newton as 'Priest of Nature' and 'King among kings'.
14. Coleridge, *Lay Sermons*, edited by R. J. White (1972) p. 18 note; hereafter cited as *Sermons*.
15. Ibid., p. 114.
16. Coleridge, *Biographia*, I, 187.
17. Coleridge, *Aids to Reflection* (1825; 1913) with a Preface by Dr Marsh, p. 44.
18. Coleridge, *Confessions of an Inquiring Spirit* (1840; 1913) p. 335, hereafter cited as *Confessions*; *Sermons*, pp. 21–2, 95–6, 196–7; *Biographia*, I, 59, II, 256.
19. Coleridge, *Biographia*, II, 8.
20. Coleridge, *Sermons*, p. 170.
21. Ibid., p. 174; Beer, *Coleridge the Visionary*, pp. 13–14, 287; *The Table Talk and Omniana of Samuel Taylor Coleridge* (1917) p. 157.
22. Coleridge, *Biographia*, I, 172–3.
23. Ibid., II, 218; *Confessions*, p. 326; *Biographia*, I, 135.
24. Compare the sixth stanza of *Dejection* to *Biographia*, I, 10.
25. Coleridge, *Biographia*, I, 98; *Letters*, I, 279.
26. Leigh Hunt, *Autobiography* (rev. edn 1860; 1891) p. 254; Lord Byron, Dedication to *Don Juan* (1819); Wellek, *Kant*, p. 172.
27. Coleridge, *Biographia*, I, 104.
28. Frederick Engels, *Ludwig Feuerbach and the Outcome of Classical German Philosophy* (1888; London, n.d.) p. 55.
29. Mill, *Autobiography*, pp. 60, 162–3.
30. David Hume, *Enquiry Concerning Human Understanding* (1748), quoted by Seth, *Scottish Philosophy*, p. 55.
31. Mary P. Mack, *Jeremy Bentham* (1962) pp. 48–9, 66–7.
32. Ibid., pp. 254–7, 273; Mill, *Autobiography*, p. 31.
33. Leslie Stephen, *The English Utilitarians*, 3 vols (1900) I, 231.
34. Arnold Toynbee, *An Historian's Approach to Religion* (1956) p. 281.
35. See Thomis and Holt, *Threats of Revolution*: Edward Royle, *Victorian Infidels* (Manchester, 1974) for their remoteness from the concerns of the working class.
36. Taine, *Notes on England*, p. 247.

37. Coleridge, *Sermons* p. 114.
38. Quoted in Mack, *Jeremy Bentham*, p. 23.

2. MILL AND CARLYLE TO 1828

1. Seth, *Scottish Philosophy*, p. 8.
2. Taine, *Le positivisme anglais* (Paris, 1864) p. 5.
3. Mill, *Autobiography*, p. 132.
4. Ibid., pp. 31–2; *Last Words of Thomas Carlyle* (1892) p. 15.
5. Emerson, *English Traits*, p. 47; Taine, *Notes on England*, p. 248.
6. K. M. Newton, *George Eliot: Romantic Humanist* (1981) puts forward a convincing view of the novels.
7. J. A. Froude, *Thomas Carlyle: A History of the First Forty Years of His Life, 1795–1835* (4 vols, 1882–4; 2 vols, 1882) I, 11. Hereafter referred to as Froude, *Forty Years*.
8. *The Works of Thomas Carlyle* (30 vols, 1897–9) XXVI, 79; XXVII, 64–5. Hereafter cited as Carlyle, *Works*.
9. Wellek, *Kant*, p. 31.
10. C. F. Harrold, *Carlyle and German Thought 1819–34* (1934) pp. 32–6; Charles Richard Saunders, *Carlyle's Friendships and Other Studies* (Durham N.C., 1977) p. 37; Froude, *Forty Years*, I, 63, 69, 130; Richard Herne Shepherd (ed.), *Memoirs of the Life and Writings of Thomas Carlyle* 2 vols (1881) I, 14–17.
11. Froude, *Forty Years*, I, 66–7.
12. Ibid., I, 101; Carlyle, *Works*, I, 133.
13. Carlyle, *Works*, I, 131.
14. Froude, *Forty Years*, I, 173; Andrew James Symington, *Some Personal Reminiscences of Carlyle* (1886) p. 11.
15. On Carlyle's failure to record his debt to Coleridge, compare Carlyle's *Reminiscences*, 2 vols (1881) I, 230–1, 310–11 and Carlyle, *Works*, XI, 52–62, with the opinions of Wellek, *Kant*, p. [139] and Harrold, *Carlyle and German Thought*, pp. 50–4. On the meeting with Hamilton, see Shepherd, *Memoirs*, I, 31.
16. Froude, *Forty Years*, I, 361.
17. R. W. Emerson, *Representative Men* (1850) pp. 209–10; Royce, *Fugitive Essays*, p. [41].
18. Carlyle, *Last Words*, pp. 3, 22–3, 53–4, 62, 69–73, 99.
19. Carlyle, *Works*, XXVI, 30–1, 52, Froude, *Forty Years*, I, 212.
20. Carlyle, *Lectures on the History of Literature* (1892) p. 260; Harrold, *Carlyle and German Thought*, p. 4; Shepherd, *Memoirs*, II, 558; Carlyle, *Works*, XXVI, 81.
21. Carlyle, *Works*, I, 121.
22. Wellek, *Kant*, p. 200; see also Herbert L. Stewart, 'Carlyle's Place in Philosophy', *Monist*, XXIX (April 1919) 164, 170.
23. Carlyle, *Works* XXVI, 66.
24. Ibid., XXV, 195; XXI, 264; XXVI, 22; Carlyle, *Reminiscences*, I, 288.
25. Carlyle, *Works*, XXV, 101–3, 110–13; XXVI, 80–81.

26. Ibid., XXVI, 258, 260, 270–3.
27. Ibid., XXVI, 295.
28. Carlyle, *Reminiscences*, I, 288; Mazzini, *Essays*, p. 111.
29. Charles Taylor, *Hegel* (Cambridge, 1975) p. 21.
30. Wellek, *Kant*, pp. 201–2.
31. R. P. Anschutz, *The Philosophy of J. S. Mill* (1953) p. 59.
32. 'Bentham', *LWR* XXIX (August 1838) 467. See also Mill's discussion of this article in *Autobiography*, pp. 130–1.
33. W. L. Courtney, *Life of John Stuart Mill*, p. 20.
34. Mill, *Autobiography*, pp. 5–11, 13, 20, 25–8, 32, 68; Michael St John Packe, *The Life of John Stuart Mill*, p. 25.
35. Mill, *Autobiography*, pp. 37, 48; Packe, *The Life of John Stuart Mill*, p. 44.
36. Mill, *Autobiography*, pp. 39–43; on the prejudice against the French at this time, see e.g. *Mark Rutherford's Deliverance* (1885) pp. 39–60.
37. Thomis and Holt, *Threats of Revolution in Britain*, p. 123.
38. Mill, *Autobiography*, pp. 47–8, 50, 63, 74–9; Packe, *The Life of John Stuart Mill*, pp. 84–5.
39. Mill, *Autobiography* pp. 30–1, 69, 80–1.
40. Mary Wollstonecraft, *The Rights of Woman*, John Stuart Mill, *The Subjection of Women*, Introduction by Pamela Frankau (1929) p. 221.
41. Mill, *Autobiography*, p. 83.
42. Packe, *The Life of John Stuart Mill*, p. 81.
43. Mill, *Autobiography*, pp. 86–7.
44. Quoted by Packe, *The Life of John Stuart Mill*, p. 214, from *The Letters of John Stuart Mill*, ed Hugh S. R. Elliot (2 vols, 1910) I, 103–6.

3. SAINT-SIMONIANISM

1. [J. S. Mill], *Examiner*, 2 February 1834, quoted by Richard K. P. Pankhurst, *The Saint-Simonians, Mill and Carlyle* [1957] p. 100, hereafter cited as Pankhurst, *The Saint-Simonians*.
2. Engels, *Feuerbach*, pp. 21–2.
3. Quoted in Courtney, *Life of John Stuart Mill*, p. 125.
4. Claude Henri de Saint-Simon, *Social Organization, The Science of Man and Other Writings*, edited and translated with an Introduction by Felix Markham (1964) p. 1, hereafter cited as Markham, *Social Organisation*; Emile Durkheim, *Socialism* 1928, translated by Charlotte Sattler, edited with an Introduction by Alvin W. Gouldner, (1962) p. 142, hereafter cited as Durkheim, *Socialism*.
5. James Joll, *The Anarchists* (1964) p. 53; Markham, *Social Organisation*, p. 40.
6. Charles Gide and Charles Rist, *Histoire des doctrines économiques depuis les physiocrates jusqu'à nos jours* (Paris, 1922) p. 264.
7. Markham, *Social Organisation*, pp. 9,18, 24–5, 29–30, 90.
8. John Bowle, *Politics and Opinion in the Nineteenth Century* (1954) pp. 102–3; Joll, *The Anarchists*, p. 57.
9. J. L. and Barbara Hammond, *The Age of the Chartists* (1930; Hamden,

Connecticut, 1962) p. 359.

10. Owen Chadwick, *The Secularization of the European Mind in the Nineteenth Century* (Cambridge, 1975) p. 76.

11. Markham, *Social Organisation*, pp. 19–20.

12. Ibid., p. 82; Pankhurst, *The Saint-Simonians*, p. x.

13. Thackeray, *The Paris Sketch Book* 1840, in *Works* (12 vols, 1879) VII, 94.

14. Pankhurst, *The Saint-Simonians* 78–80, 89–95; George Sand, *Indiana* (1831; Paris, 1869) p. 2. George Sand's comment on the gossip the movement attracted was made in a Notice to the 1852 edition.

15. Pankhurst, *The Saint-Simonians*, pp. 2, 5; [Robert Southey], 'New Distribution of Property', *QR* XLV (July 1831) 407 (Carlyle called this 'an altogether miserable article' (Froude, *Forty Years*) II, 200); 'Saint-Simonianism &c', *WR* XVI (April 1832) 287; Thackeray, *Works*, VII, 144–5; 'FAIR PLAY', 'Letter on the Doctrine of St. Simon', *FM* V [July 1832] 667; 'Reminiscences', *FM* XXVII (May 1843) 609–14.

16. Pankhurst, *The Saint-Simonians*, p. 52; *QR* XLV (July 1831) 447. In 1838 an informative and fair-minded article appeared in the *DR* IV (January 1838) 138–79.

17. Robert Owen, *The Life of Robert Owen by Himself* 1857–8 (1920) pp. 230, 322; R. K. Webb, *Harriet Martineau* (1960) p. 180; Carlyle, *Reminiscences*, I, 338; Pankhurst, *The Saint-Simonians*, chs 9–12.

18. Carlyle, *Works*, XXVI 115–7, 168–79, 208, 214–5; XXVII, 62, 64, 66–7, 73, 77–80.

19. Hill Shine, *Carlyle's Early Reading to 1834* (Lexington, 1953) pp. 53–4, 148–9; Pankhurst, *The Saint-Simonians*, pp. 35, [79].

20. Froude, *Forty Years*, II, 83; Shine, *Carlyle and the Saint-Simonians* (Baltimore, 1941) p. 58; [unsigned article], 'Letters from Thomas Carlyle to the Socialists of 1830', *NQ* II (April 1909) 280.

21. Carlyle, *Works* XXVI, 131, 143, 208, 235–42; Froude, *Forty Years*, II, 4, 80.

22. Shine, *Saint-Simonians*, discusses this in detail; Froude, *Forty Years*, II, 72.

23. Froude, *Forty Years*, II, 78–9, 82, 133–7, 172; Carlyle, *Reminiscences*, I, 309–10.

24. Carlyle, *Works*, XVII, 83, 86, 89.

25. Ibid., I, 40; Froude, *Forty Years*, II, 131, 195, 347–8; Mazzini, *Essays*, p. 112.

26. Carlyle, *Works*, I, 3, 21–4, 52, 90, 121, 146, 203–4.

27. Ibid., I, 54–5, 137.

28. Ibid., I, 3–4, 16, 57, 170–3.

29. Ibid., I, 92–3, 150–1, 190–1; Shine, *Saint-Simonians*, pp. 13, 74–5.

30. Carlyle, *Works*, I, 237, 223–9; Pankhurst, *The Saint-Simonians*, p. 34, 69.

31. Mazzini, *Essays*, pp. 124, 156, 286.

32. Carlyle, *Works*, I, 126, 156.

33. Mill, *Autobiography*, pp. 88; Coleridge, *Biographia Literaria*, I, 59.

34. Mill, *Autobiography*, pp. 89, 92–3; on Sterling, see Carlyle, *Works*, XI, 51–2.

35. Mill, *Autobiography*, pp. 94, 97.

36. The speech is reprinted in Harold J. Laski's edition of Mill's *Autobio-

graphy (1924) pp. 288–9, 296.

37. Packe, *The Life of John Stuart Mill*, pp. 41, 91–6; Pankhurst, *The Saint-Simonians*, p. [72].
38. Mill, *Autobiography*, pp. 94–5, 99–101.
39. Durkheim, *Socialism*, p. 75.
40. Mill, *Autobiography*, pp. 100–101, 142; Packe, *The Life of John Stuart Mill*, p. 96.
41. Mill, *Autobiography*, p. 98; Pankhurst, *The Saint-Simonians*, p. 88.
42. Mill, 'The Right and Wrong of State Interference with Corporation and Church Property', *The Jurist* (February 1833) reprinted in *Dissertations and Discussions*, 3 vols (1859–67) I, 37; Quoted by F. A. von Hayek, in his introductory essay to Mill's *The Spirit of the Age* (1942) p. xxi.
43. Hayek, *Spirit of the Age*, pp. 1, 4, 6, 12–13.
44. Ibid., pp. 25–6, 35–6, 47, 49, 75–80.
45. Ibid., pp. 12, 18, 60–74, 85.
46. Coleridge, *Aids to Reflection*, p. 44.
47. Hayek, *Spirit of the Age*, p. 15.

4. THE PERSONAL DEBATE

1. Packe, *The Life of John Stuart Mill*, p. 265; *Letters of Thomas Carlyle to John Stuart Mill, John Sterling, and Robert Browning*, edited by Alexander Carlyle (1923) p. 176; 'The Hero as Prophet', reprinted in *On Heroes, Hero-Worship and the Heroic in Literature* (1841).
2. Froude, *Forty Years*, II, 187–8, 190, 241.
3. Carlyle, *Letters*, p. 55; Froude, *Forty Years*, II, 273; Emerson, *English Traits*, p. 8.
4. Mill, *Autobiography*, p. 104; Carlyle, *Letters*, pp. 17, 33, 71.
5. Carlyle, *Letters*, pp. 54, 57; Froude, *Forty Years*, II, 278–9.
6. Carlyle, *Letters*, pp. 9, 19, 41, 45, 51–2, 57, 67, 82; idem. *Works*, XXV, 101–2; Mill, *Autobiography*, pp. 102, 138; Pankhurst, *The Saint-Simonians*, p. 96.
7. Mill, *Autobiography*, p. 102; Froude, *Forty Years*, II, 285–6.
8. Carlyle, *Letters*, p. 49; Mill, *Autobiography*, pp. 103, 116; Froude, *Forty Years*, II, 298–9, 308; Packe, *The Life of John Stuart Mill*, pp. 102–3; Engels, *Feuerbach*, pp. 21–2.
9. Carlyle, *Letters*, pp. 26, 67, 70, 80; Froude, *Forty Years*, II, 325, 330–1; Mill's *Three Essays on Religion*, (1874) shows his closeness to an old-fashioned Deism associated with more traditional forms of Unitarian belief.
10. 'Alison's History of the French Revolution', *MR* VII (August 1833) 507–16; Mill, 'The Right and Wrong of State Interference with Corporation and Church Property', *Dissertations and Discussions*.
11. Froude, *Forty Years*, II, 259–60; Mill, *Autobiography*, pp. 107–9; Packe, *The Life of John Stuart Mill*, p. 271.
12. Mill, *Autobiography*, pp. 104–6.
13. Alison's 'History', 507–8, 513; Carlyle, *Works*, XXVIII, 169, 175–6.

14. 'What is Poetry?', *MR* VII (January 1833) 60; 'The Two Kinds of Poetry', *MR* VII (October 1833) 715.
15. 'The Two Kinds of Poetry', 715, 722–3, 'What is Poetry?', 62.

5. J. S. MILL (1834–1837): LOGIC AND POLITICS

1. Nathaniel Hawthorne, *The Blithedale Romance* 1852 (1899) p. 167.
2. Cited by William Thomas, *The Philosophic Radicals* (Oxford, 1979), p. 171.
3. Thomas, *Philosophical Radicals*, p. 145; David Cecil, *Melbourne*, (1955), p. 199.
4. Earl of Ilchester (ed.), *Elizabeth, Lady Holland to her Son, 1821–1845* (1946) pp. 7, 23, 192.
5. Hammond, *The Age of the Chartists*, p. 219.
6. Quoted in F.E. Mineka, *The Dissidence of Dissent* (1944) p. 279, from H. S. R. Elliott (ed.), *Letters of John Stuart Mill*, I, 56–7; Bolton King, *The Life of Mazzini* (revised 1912) p. 259.
7. Mill, *Autobiography*, pp. 117–118 and note. Mill's first draft recorded his subsequent bitter disappointment in strong language.
8. Mineka, *The Dissidence of Dissent*, pp. vii, 101–2, 214–5, 251–2, 256, 299–300.
9. Mill, *Autobiography*, pp. 119–120.
10. Mill: 'Notes on Some of the More Popular Dialogues of Plato: No. 2 The Phaedrus', *MR* VIII (June 1834) 404, 409; 'Notes . . . No. I: The Protagoras', *MR* VIII (March 1834) 204–5; *Autobiography*, p. 15.
11. Mill: 'Notes . . . No 1: The Protagoras', *MR* VIII (February 1834) 89, 97; 'Notes . . . No III: The Gorgias', *MR* VIII (December 1834) 829, 840, 842; 'Notes . . . No. I: The Protagoras', *MR* VIII (March 1834) 208, 211; 'Notes . . . No. III: The Gorgias', *MR* VIII (September 1834) 707; 'Notes . . . No. III: The Gorgias', *MR* VIII (November 1834) 804, 808.
12. Mill: 'Notes on the Newspapers', *MR* VIII (March 1834) 168, 175; 'Notes on the Newspapers', *MR* VIII (May 1834) 363, 365; 'Notes on the Newspapers', *MR* VIII (July 1834) 527–8.
13. Mill: 'Notes on the Newspapers' *MR* VIII (March 1834) 163–4. 'Notes on the Newspapers' *MR* VIII (May 1834) 368–70; 'Notes on the Newspapers' *MR* VIII (June 1834) 439, 441, 455; 'Notes on the Newspapers' *MR* VIII (July 1834) 522, 525–7; 'Notes on the Newspapers' *MR* VIII (August 1834) 592, 594–5, 589–90.
14. Mill: 'On Miss Martineau's Summary of Political Economy', *MR* VIII (May 1834) 319; 'Letter from an Englishman to a Frenchman', *MR* VIII (June 1834) 385, 391–2.
15. *MR* VIII (September 1834) 606–9.
16. Cecil, *Melbourne*, pp. 234, 236.
17. Mill, 'Notes . . . No IV: The Apology of Socrates', *MR* IX (March 1835) 171.
18. Mill: 'Postscript', *LR* II (April 1835) 255; 'Postscript: The Close of the Session' *LR* II (October 1835) 275; 'Parliamentary Proceedings of the

Session', *LR* II (July 1835) 512, 519, 522; 'The Monster Trial', *MR* IX (June 1835) 393–6.
19. Mill: 'The Monster Trial', 514; 'Postscript: The Close of the Session', *LR* II (October 1835) 270, 273.
20. Mill, 'Tennyson's Poems' *LR* II (July 1835) 403.
21. Mill: 'Parliamentary Proceedings of the Session' *LR* II (July 1835) 519; 'Rationale of Political Representation', *LR* II (July 1835) 343, 347–8.
22. Mill: 'De Tocqueville on Democracy in America' *LR* II (October 1835) 87, 93, 118.
23. Mill: *Autobiography*, pp. 120–1; 'Professor Sedgwick's Discourse on the Studies of the University of Cambridge', *LR* II (April 1835) 95, 103, 108, 114–5, 118, 122.
24. Mill, *Autobiography*, pp. 123–4, 128; Packe, *The Life of John Stuart Mill*, p. 221.
25. Mill: 'State of Politics in 1836', *LWR* III (April 1836) 271, 276.
26. Mill: 'Sir John Walsh's Contemporary History', *LWR* III (July 1836) 281–2, 293–4, 298–99, 375.
27. Mill: 'State of Society in America', *LR* II (January 1836) 371, 375.
28. Mill: 'Civilization', *LWR* III (April 1836), reprinted in *DD*, I, 162, 165, 180, 182–7, 202, 204.

6. MILL (JULY 1837–1840): THE LIMITATIONS OF LOGIC

1. Mill, *Autobiography*, p. 132.
2. Charles Bray, *The Philosophy of Necessity*, II, 341; Charles Kingsley, *Alton Locke*, 1850 (1889) p. 80.
3. Hammond, *The Age of the Chartists*, p. 274.
4. Courtney, *Life of John Stuart Mill*, p. 86; Mill, *Autobiography*, p. 132.
5. Mill, *Autobiography*, pp. 99–100.
6. Ibid., p. 126.
7. G. H. Lewes, *Comte's Philosophy of the Sciences* (1853) p. 2; Frederic Harrison, *Autobiographic Memoirs* (2 vols, 1911) I, 87.
8. Faucher, *Etudes sur L'Angleterre*, II, 160–1.
9. W. H. Simon, *European Positivism in the Nineteenth Century* (Ithaca, 1963) p. 180.
10. Mill (with George Grote), 'The Statesman', *LWR* V (April 1837) 22.
11. Mill, 'Reorganization of the Reform Party', *LWR* XXXII (April 1839) 496, 500.
12. Ibid., 486; Mill: 'Fonblanque's England Under Seven Administrations', *LWR* VI (April 1837) 67; 'Parties and the Ministry', *LWR* VI (October 1837) 16.
13. Mill: 'Reorganization of the Reform Party', 494; 'Fonblanque's England Under Seven Administrations', 67.
14. Mill: 'Parties and the Ministry', 4, 25; 'Reorganization of the Reform Party', 476; 'Lord Durham and the Canadians', *LWR* VI (January 1838) 509; 'Lord Durham's Return', *LWR* XXXII (December 1838) 242–3.
15. Mill, *Autobiography*, pp. 130–1.

16. Mill: 'The French Revolution', *LWR* V (July 1837) 47, 49, 50.
17. Mill: 'Coleridge', *LWR* XXXIII (March 1840) 297–8, 302; 'The French Revolution', 22, 50.
18. Mill: 'Bentham', *LWR* XXIX (August 1838) 467, 473, 482, 488–9; 'The Statesman', 25; 'Coleridge', 267–8.
19. Mill: 'Armand Carrel', *LWR* VI (October 1837) 66, 68, 81, 100; 'Bentham', 496; 'Coleridge', 278.
20. Mill: 'Armand Carrel', 111; 'Bentham', 503.
21. Courtney, *Life of John Stuart Mill*, pp. 20, 25.
22. Mill: 'Bentham', 482, 484–5; 'Coleridge', 280; 'The French Revolution', 48; 'Armand Carrel', 71; 'The Statesman', 27.
23. G. W. F. Hegel, *Early Theological Writings*, trans. T. M. Knox, with an Introduction and Fragments trans. Richard Kroner (Chicago, 1948) p. 312; Engels, *Feuerbach*, pp. 55.
24. Mill: 'Writings of Alfred de Vigny', *LWR* XXIX (April 1838) 2, 31.
25. [Marian Evans], 'The Future of German Philosophy'; *Leader* VI (28 July 1855) 723–4.

7. CARLYLE (1834–1840): ALTERNATIVE REVOLUTIONS

1. Royce, *Fugitive Essays*, p. 81.
2. Carlyle, *Reminiscences*, II, 221.
3. Ibid., I, 69, 83, 189, 300–302.
4. Carlyle, *Works* XXVIII, 319–20.
5. J. A. Froude, *Thomas Carlyle: A History of his Life in London*, 2 vols (1884; rev. edn 2 vols, 1890) I, 14, hereafter cited as Froude, *Carlyle in London*; Carlyle, *Reminiscences*, II, 163–4; Henry Graham, *The Social Life of Scotland in the Eighteenth Century* (2nd revised edition, 2 vols, 1900; 1 vol. 1901) pp. 365–6, 374.
6. Froude, *Forty Years*, II, 437; Carlyle, *Reminiscences*, II, 186.
7. Froude, *Forty Years*, II, 459–61; Carlyle, *Letters* p. 205.
8. Froude, *Carlyle in London*, I, 25, 39, 78–9, 115, 185–6; Carlyle, *Reminiscences*, II, 163.
9. Froude, *Carlyle in London*, I, 56–7.
10. Ibid., I, 10, 45–6, 62–3; Froude, *Forty Years*, II, 471.
11. Froude, *Carlyle in London*, I, 115; John Nichol, *Thomas Carlyle* (1892; 1902) p. 173; Carlyle, *Last Words*, p. 198.
12. Mazzini, *Essays*, p. 173.
13. Froude, *Carlyle in London*, I, 46; Carlyle, *Last Words*, p. 15; Shepherd, *Memoirs of the Life and Writings of Thomas Carlyle*, I, 7.
14. Froude, *Forty Years*, II, 476; Taine, *L'Idéalisme anglais* (Paris 1864) p. 8.
15. Carlyle, *Letters*, pp. 134, 203.
16. Ibid., p. 224; Carlyle, *Works*, XXVII, 89; IV, 121.
17. J. C. Morris, 'Carlyle's Translation of J. P. F. Richter's Novels', University of Bristol thesis (1967) p. 92.
18. Thomas Carlyle, 'Christopher North', *The Nineteenth Century and After* LXXXVII (January 1920) 107–8, 112.

19. Carlyle, *Forty Years*, II, 369; Shine, *Carlyle's Early Reading to 1834*, pp. 12–13.
20. Carlyle, *Works*, XXVIII, 329, 348, 352, 427; XXIX, 2, 10.
21. Froude, *Forty Years*, II, 456; idem., *Carlyle in London*, I, 80.
22. Wilson, *Carlyle to 'The French Revolution'* (1924) p. 423.
23. Ibid., p. 397; Carlyle, *Works* IV, 2, 312.
24. Carlyle, *Works* IV, 137, 259–60; II, 140.
25. Ibid., IV, 55, 205.
26. Mazzini, *Essays*, pp. [150], 176.
27. Carlyle, *Works*, II, 5, 214.
28. Ibid., II, 7, 10; III, 201.
29. Ibid., II, 147; IV, 274.
30. Georg Lukács, *The Historical Novel* (1962; Harmondsworth, 1969) p. 208; Gooch, *History and Historians in the Nineteenth Century*, pp. 78, 174.
31. Carlyle, *Works*, II, 151–2; III, 112; IV, 14–15, 70, 206–7; see especially *The French Revolution*, Part I, Books 5 and 7.
32. Courtney, *Life of John Stuart Mill*, p. 24.
33. Carlyle, *Works*, II, 27–9; III, 64–5, 105, 187; IV, 26, 172, 314.
34. Ibid., IV, 138, 323.
35. Engels, *Feuerbach*, p. 21.
36. Carlyle, *Works*, IV, 138.
37. Mill, 'The Writings of Alfred de Vigny', *LWR* XXIX (April 1938) 31; Mazzini, *Essays*, p. 119.
38. Froude, *Carlyle in London*, I, 90.
39. Carlyle, *Works*, IV, 299.

PART TWO

8. MARIAN EVANS (1819–1840)

1. Owen Chadwick, *The Secularization of the European Mind in the Nineteenth Century* (1975) p. 13; J. S. Mill, *The Subjection of Women*, p. 286.
2. George Sarson, 'George Eliot and Thomas Carlyle', *MR* II (April 1881) [399]; [Frederic Harrison], 'The Life of George Eliot', *FR* XXXVII (March 1885) 314.
3. [Harrison], 'The Life of George Eliot', 313; George Eliot, *Impressions of Theophrastus Such* (1879) p. 205; *GEL*, I, 23.
4. John Prest, *The Industrial Revolution in Coventry* (Oxford, 1960) p. [64] p. 68, 70–71.
5. Henry James, *English Hours* (1905; 1962) p. 124.
6. Mathilde Blind, *George Eliot*, p. 17; K. A. McKenzie, *Edith Simcox and George Eliot* (Oxford, 1961) p. 129; *GEL*, VIII, 260, 261.
7. Hammond, *The Age of the Chartists*, (Hampden, Connecticut: 1931; 1962) p. 131; Kathleen Adams, *Those of Us Who Loved Her* (Warwick, 1980) pp. 5–8.
8. Claude T. Bissell, 'Social Analysis in the Novels of George Eliot', *ELH* XVIII (September 1951) 226.

9. J. W. Cross, *George Eliot's Life*, pp. 8, 10; Blind, *George Eliot*, p. 12.
10. *GEL*, VIII, 409.
11. Taine, *Notes on England*, pp. 72–82; Cross, *George Eliot's Life*, p. 13; *GEL*, VIII, 260.
12. 'Dorothea Casaubon and George Eliot', *CR* LXV (February 1894) 208; Haldane, *George Eliot and Her Times*, pp. 22–3; Eliot, *Theophrastus Such*, p. 205.
13. G. M. Young, *Victorian England* (1953) p. 109.
14. [W. J. Conybeare] 'Church Parties', *ER* XCVIII (October 1853) 275, 281; J. H. Newman, *Apologia pro vita sua* (1865; 1913) p. 196.
15. [unsigned review], 'George Eliot: Her Life and Writings', *WR* n.s. LX (July 1881) 156; Mary Deakin, *The Early Life of George Eliot* (Manchester, 1913) p. 24.
16. Baker, *The George Eliot–George Henry Lewes Library* (London and New York, 1977) p. 231; 'Authorship', edited by Thomas Pinney in *Essays of George Eliot* (1963) p. 441.
17. Sir Walter Scott: *Tales of a Grandfather* 1828 (2 vols, 1898) I, 387 note; *The Antiquary* p. [ix]; *The Abbot*, p. [1]; *Rob Roy* pp. [xi]–xii; *St. Ronan's Well*, p. [vii] my italics; *Woodstock*, p. 170. All page references are to *The Waverley Novels of Sir Walter Scott*, 24 vols, 1912.
18. Scott: *Old Mortality*, p. 356; *Waverley*, p. 4.
19. Scott: *Woodstock*, p. 170; *Tales of a Grandfather*, II, 640.
20. Scott: *Tales of a Grandfather*, I, 342, 365–8; *Guy Mannering*, pp. 110–113; *Old Mortality*, pp. 373–4; *Kenilworth*, pp. 345–6; *Rob Roy*, pp. 453–4; *The Abbot*, pp. 94–6.
21. *GEL*, I, 35.
22. Scott: *Guy Mannering*, pp. xviii, 252–3; *The Bride of Lammermoor*, p. 396; *Waverley*, p. 526; *Tales of a Grandfather*, II, 1162.
23. Scott: *The Bride of Lammermoor*, p. 30; *The Antiquary*, pp. 100–111.
24. Scott: *The Abbot*, pp. 11–12; *The Fortunes of Nigel*, pp. 148–9; *Guy Mannering*, pp. 149, 164; *Old Mortality*, p. 417; *Rob Roy*, p. 415.
25. Scott: *Woodstock*, p. 112; *Waverley*, p. 33; *Old Mortality*, pp. 202–4, 222.
26. Scott: *The Bridge of Lammermoor*, p. 247; *Woodstock*, p. 23; *Tales of Grandfather*, I, 448; *Old Mortality*, pp. 46, 128, 200.
27. Lockhart, *Memoirs of the Life of Sir Walter Scott* (1837–8) new edition 1850, p. 749.
28. Scott, *Waverley*, p. 266.
29. McKenzie, *Edith Simcox and George Eliot*, pp. 126–7; *GEL*, VIII, 5.
30. Eliot, *Impressions of Theophrastus Such*, p. 302.
31. See the essay, 'Looking Backward', in *Impressions of Theophrastus Such*; *GEL*, VIII, 383, 465.
32. Bullett, *George Eliot*, p. 24; *GEL*, I, 11, 28–9.
33. *GEL*, I, 5–6, 15, 21, 24, 29.
34. John Ruskin, *Sesame and Lilies*, pp. 146–8.
35. *GEL*, I, 7, 11–12, 18, 34, 38, 45–6.
36. Ibid., I, 25, 41, 45.
37. Ibid., I, 4, 9, 14.
38. Ibid., I, 17, 19, 32, 42, 46, 59.
39. McKenzie, *Edith Simcox and George Eliot*, p. 126; Signed 'Y', 'Thomas

Carlyle and George Eliot', *Nation* XXXII (24 March 1881) 201; Linton, *My Literary Life*, p. 86.

40. *GEL*, I, 11–12, 71.
41. Ibid., I, 24; Carlyle, *Works*, XXIX, 26, 35, 72. Carlyle's article appeared in *LWR* in 1838.
42. *GEL*, I, 43, 69.
43. Ibid., I, 12, 36, 72, 122–3.
44. Ibid., I, 66, 70.
45. Faucher, *Études sur l'Angleterre*, II, 177; Engels, *The Condition of the Working-Class in England* (1969) pp. 122–3.
46. *GEL*, I, 71–2.
47. Ibid., VIII, 5.
48. Chapman's unsigned article appeared as 'George Eliot', *WR* LXVIII (July 1885) 173; Harrison, 'The Life of George Eliot', 319.
49. *GEL*, I, 86.

9. MARIAN EVANS (1841–1843): COVENTRY

1. Mary Wollstonecraft, *Vindication of the Rights of Woman*, p. 107.
2. *Victoria History of the Countries of England: Warwickshire*, VIII, 66–7.
3. In this section I have drawn upon information to be found in John Prest, *The Industrial Revolution in Coventry* (Oxford 1960); Royle, *Victorian Infidels*, 181, 295, 299; *Victoria History of Warwickshire*, VIII, 228.
4. Blind, *George Eliot*, pp. 23–4; *GEL*, VIII, 128, IX, 265.
5. *GEL*, I, 29–30, 102, 107, 110, 122–3, VIII, 8.
6. Ibid., I, 92, 101, 104, 106–8, 118, 122–3.
7. Ibid., VIII, 27; McKenzie, *Edith Simcox and George Eliot*, p. 130.
8. David de Guistino, *Conquest of Mind* (London and Totowa N.J., 1975) pp. 87–8, 90, 99; Royle, *Victorian Infidels*, 62–3.
9. *GEL*, VIII, 27, 74; Prest, *The Industrial Revolution in Coventry*, pp. 39–40, 44, 62, 107.
10. Baker, *The George Eliot–George Henry Lewes Library*, pp. 93–4; *GEL*, VIII, 276.
11. Ibid., VIII, 466.
12. Mill, *The Subjection of Women*, pp. 260–1; Wollstonecraft, *Vindication of the Rights of Woman*, pp. 264–72.
13. Royle, *Victorian Infidels*, p. 1; Annan, *Ideas and Beliefs of the Victorians*, pp. 335–7; Mark Rutherford, *Mark Rutherford's Deliverance* (1885) p. 45; [unsigned article], 'The Critical and Miscellaneous Writings of Theodore Parker', *Christian Teacher* n.s. VI (no month) 212; Newman, *Apologia pro vita sua*, p. 284; [unsigned review], 'George Eliot: Her Life and Writings', *WR* n.s. LX (July 1881) 158.
14. Carlyle, *Reminiscences*, I, 245–60; Webb, *Harriet Martineau*, pp. 52–3; *The Life and Correspondence of John Foster*, ed. J. E. Ryland, (2 vols, 1846) I, 12, 31; J. D. Y. Peel, *Herbert Spencer: The Evolution of a Sociologist* (1971) p. 33.
15. Alice Lynes, *George Eliot's Coventry*, p. 27; Haight, *George Eliot*, p. 46;

Briggs, *Victorian Cities*, p. 196.

16. [John Chapman], 'George Eliot', *WR* LXVIII (July 1885) 172; *GEL*, I, 124; Charles Bray, *Phases of Opinion and Experience during a Long Life: An Autobiography* [1885], pp. 73–6.
17. Charles Bray, *Philosophy of Necessity*, I, vi; Bray, *Phases*, pp. 3, 116–7.
18. Bray, *Phases*, p. 56 note; De Guistino, *Conquest of Mind*, p. 22; Bray, *Philosophy of Necessity*, I, 51–2.
19. Bray, *Philosophy of Necessity*, I, 36, 67–8, 169.
20. Ibid., I, 240–5; Bray, *Phases*, p. 47.
21. Bray, *Phases* pp. 3–4, 7–8; Bray, *Philosophy of Necessity*, I, 216, 276–7.
22. Bray, *Phases*, pp. 10–12; James Drummond and C. B. Upton, *The Life and Letters of James Martineau* (2 vols, 1902) I, 97.
23. Bray, *Philosophy of Necessity*, I, 298, II, 372.
24. *GEL*, I, 218 and note, 133; Ms Herford's remarks were made in a letter to the *Guardian*, in June 1980.
25. Bray, *Phases*, p. 91; Bray, *Philosophy of Necessity*, I, 245, II, 548–64.
26. Bray, *Philosophy of Necessity*, I, 1–2.
27. Baker, *The George Eliot–George Henry Lewes Library*, pp. xxiv, xxix, xxxvi, 93, 163, 195; Bray, *Phases, GEL*, I, 38, 41, 142.
28. See Valerie A. Dodd, 'Strauss's English Propagandists and the Politics of Unitarianism: 1841–5', *Church History* L (December 1981) 415–35.
29. William Thomas, *The Philosophical Radicals*, pp. [244]–5, 301–2.
30. [unsigned review], 'George Eliot: Her Life and Writings', 160; Haldane, *George Eliot and Her Times*, pp. 55–6.
31. I wish to record my thanks to the late Dr R. L. Eakins for discussion of this subject.
32. Quoted in Reardon, *From Coleridge to Gore*, (1971), p. 57; Pattison, *Essays* (2 vols, 1889) II, 210; Mrs Humphry Ward, *The History of David Grieve* (1892; 1894) p. 454; Engels, *Condition of the Working Class in England*, p. 265; Charles Kingsley, *Alton Locke*, p. 227; *GEL*, VIII, 34.
33. Engels, *Feuerbach*, pp. 26–7 and note; Eduard Zeller, *David Friedrich Strauss in His Life and Writings* (authorized translation 1874) p. 3; Horton Harris, *David Friedrich Strauss and His Theology* (Cambridge, 1973) p. 41.
34. Zeller, *Strauss*, pp. 33–8, 47; Schweitzer, *The Quest of the Historical Jesus*, pp. 68–70.
35. Richard Garnett, *The Life of W. J. Fox* (London and New York, 1910) p. 215.
36. Henry Gow, *The Unitarians*, p. 107.
37. Ibid., pp. 114, 178.
38. Charles Hennell, *An Inquiry Concerning the Origin of Christianity* (1838) p. 145 note; *The Life of Jesus, Critically Examined by Dr. David Friedrich Strauss*, translated from the fourth German Edition [by Marian Evans] (3 vols, 1846) II, 397.
39. Philip Harwood, *German Anti-Supernaturalism* (1841) pp. [v]–vi; Hennell, *Inquiry*, pp. vii; Strauss, *Life of Jesus*, I, vii, xi; Schweitzer, *Quest*, p. 76.
40. Schweitzer, *Quest*, pp. 80–1; Strauss, *A New Life of Jesus* (2 vols, 1865) I, xv; Hennell, *Inquiry*, pp. vii–viii.

41. Hennell, *Inquiry*, pp. 23, 63, 299–301, 334–56; Strauss, *Life of Jesus*, II, 22–5, 59–66.
42. Strauss, *Life of Jesus*, I, 70–2, 88, 224–6, 322–3; Hennell, *Inquiry*, 23, 63, 108–11.
43. Hennell, *Inquiry*, pp. 344–56.
44. Zeller, *Strauss*, p. 108; Philip Harwood, *German Anti-Supernaturalism*, p. 3; Schweitzer, *Quest*, pp. 10, 78; Strauss, *Life of Jesus*, I, 65–87, 179–93, II, 72, III, 11–21.
45. Strauss, *Life of Jesus*, II, 140, III, 430–32; Hennell, *Inquiry*, pp. 151–2.
46. Hennell, *Inquiry*, p. 332.
47. *GEL*, I, 120–1 and note, 135, 148–9, 153.
48. Ibid., I, 122–3, 136, 141–2, 158.
49. Taylor, *Hegel*, p. 16; Lewes, 'Spinoza', *Fortnightly Review* IV (1 April 1866) 387.
50. *The Chief Works of Benedict de Spinoza*, translated from the Latin with an Introduction by R. M. H. Elwes. The *Tractatus* is contained in Vol. 1. All page references are to this edition, pp. 8, 99, 101, 103, Chs VIII–X.
51. [J. A. Froude], 'Spinoza', *WR* n.s. VIII (1 July 1855) 17; Frederick Copleston, *Descartes to Leibniz* (1858) pp. 206–9, 223, 230–7; Spinoza, *Tractatus Theologico-Politicus*, pp. 8, 78, 81, 154.
52. Spinoza, *Tractatus*, pp. 27, 162, 237.
53. Ibid., Chs XVI–XVIII, pp. 5–6, 73–4, 179–81, 183, 185, 188–9, 204–5, 246.
54. Ibid., pp. 69, 75, 118, 257.
55. Lewes, 'Spinoza', *FR* IV (1 April 1866) 405.
56. Quoted by Haldane, *George Eliot and Her Times*, p. 52.
57. *GEL*, I, 125, 143, 162.
58. Strauss, *Life of Jesus*, III, 444; *GEL*, VIII, 466.
59. *GEL*, I, 125–6, 128, 133–4, 143–4, 151.
60. McKenzie, *Edith Simcox and George Eliot*, pp. 131–2; Bessie Rayner Belloc, 'Dorothea Casaubon and George Eliot', *Contemporary Review* LXV (February 1894) 208; *GEL*, I, 125–6, 162–3.
61. *GEL*, I, 143–4; Deakin, *The Early Life of George Eliot*, p. 44.
62. *Gel*, I, 120–121, 125.

10. MARIAN EVANS (1844–1850) FOSTER AND ROUSSEAU

1. George Henry Lewes, 'The Apprenticeship of Life', *Leader* (6 April 1850) 43; [unsigned review], 'George Eliot: Her Life and Writings', *WR* LX (July 1881) 188.
2. Haight, *George Eliot*, pp. 71, 79; *GEL*, III, 321; Faucher, *Études sur l'Angleterre*, I, 181–94; Briggs, *Victorian Cities*, 89, 93.
3. McKenzie, *Edith Simcox and George Eliot*, p. 130.
4. *GEL*, IX, 134; Mary Wollstonecraft, *Vindication of the Rights of Woman*, p. 157.
5. *GEL*, IX, 9.
6. *GEL*, I, 193, 218, 227, 237, 242, 248, 260–1, 265, 275, 280, 318.

7. J. E. Ryland (ed.), *The Life and Correspondence of John Foster*, I, 29, 377, II, 60.
8. Ibid., I, 5, 42, 114, 139, 159–60, 188, 213–4, 223, 343–4, 410, 444, II, 224.
9. Ibid., I, vi, 64–5, 243, 260, 400, 432–3, II, 123–4, 274, 277, 346.
10. Ibid., I, 114; GEL, I, xv–xvi, 271 note; Haight, *George Eliot*, p. 59.
11. *GEL*, I, xv; De Staël, *Ten Years in Exile*, p. 69; Baker, *The George Eliot–George Henry Lewes Library*, p. 175.
12. I have used Rousseau's *Oeuvres Complètes* I (Paris, 1959), IV (Paris, 1969) and *Les Rêveries du promeneur solitaire*, texte établi avec Introduction et relevé de variants par Henri Roddier, (Paris, 1960). All translations are my own. *Oeuvres Complètes*, I, 402, 650, IV, 446, 530, 535, 577, 826.
13. Rousseau, *Rêveries* (ed. Roddier), p. xix; *Oeuvres Complètes*, I, [5], 529, [995]–9, [1002]–4, 1073, IV, 250–1, 324, 493.
14. Ibid., IV, 248, 284, 345.
15. Ibid., I, 1021; IV, 370, 481, 559, 743.
16. Ibid., IV, 524, 528, 571; Rousseau, *Rêveries* (ed. Roddier), p. lix I, 1013.
17. Rousseau, *Oeuvres Complètes*, IV, 599, 607.
18. Rousseau: *Oeuvres Complètes*, I, 392, 422, 567–8, 581, 606, 632, 642, 1028, 1030, 1038; *Rêveries* (ed. Roddier), p. xxii.
19. *GEL*, I, 277.
20. Ibid., I, 251, 253, 256–6, 265, 282, 318.
21. Rousseau, *Oeuvres Complètes*, IV, 599, 607.
22. *GEL*, I, 177, 223, 228, 230–1, 242, 247–8, 255, 264, 302, 329; Haight, *George Eliot*, p. 76.
23. *GEL*, I, 251–2, 276, 291, 295–7, 313–4, 321.
24. Ibid., I, 240, 243 and note, 260, 294, 314–5, 330–1.
25. Ibid., I, 307, 309, 328, 333, VIII, 19.
26. Ibid., I, 203, 271 note; Carlyle, *Works*, I, 156.
27. As in Arnold, *Culture and Anarchy* (1869).

11. PHILOSOPHY, POLITICS AND HISTORY

1. *GEL*, I, 247.
2. Chadwick, *The Secularization of the European Mind in the Nineteenth Century* (Cambridge, 1975), p. 143–161; Royle, *Victorian Infidels*, p. 107.
3. *Dictionnaire Philosophique*, (1764) texte établi par Raymond Naves, notes par Julien Benda (Paris, 1967) pp. xl, 16–18, 31–3, 73, 82, 142, 162–7, 236–50, 288, 328–9, 413–4. All translations are my own.
4. Ibid., 85–9, 109–34, 182, 195–6, 203, 212–25, 251, 304–20, 367.
5. Ibid., pp. 43–4, 99, 150, 167–71, [235]–6, 391.
6. *GEL*, I, 161.
7. Von Hayek, *John Stuart Mill and Harriet Taylor*, pp. 148–9.
8. Prest, *The Industrial Revolution in Coventry*, pp. 38–9; *VCH*, VIII, 227; *GEL*, VIII, 333–4, 347.
9. *GEL*, I, 172–3 and note, 179, 189, VIII, 11–12; Lynes, *George Eliot's Coventry*, p. 32.

10. *GEL*, I, 290, 293, 296, 319. Cross, *George Eliot's Life* (new edition) p. 310.
11. *GEL*, VIII, 18; Read, *The English Provinces*, p. 153.
12. Charles Pouthas, 'The Revolutions of 1848', *New Cambridge History*, X, 389–90, 394; Lukács, *The Historical Novel*, p. 202; Chadwick, *Secularization*, p. 154; Baker, *The George Eliot–George Henry Lewes Library*, p. 113.
13. *GEL*, I, 196, 253, 262, 267, VIII, 359–60; on Blanc, see Gide and Rist, *Histoire des doctrines economiques*, pp. 299–307; on the National Workshops, see Pouthas, 'Revolutions of 1848', p. 399.
14. T. R. Wright, 'George Eliot and Positivism: A Reassessment', *MLR* LXXVI Part 2 (April 1981) 268; *Middlemarch*, Chapter XV.
15. I refute the views of Bourl'honne, *George Eliot*, p. 146, Simon, *European Positivism in the Nineteenth Century*, p. 207 and Alice R. Kaminsky, 'George Eliot, George Henry Lewes and the Novel', *PMLA* LXX (December 1955) who place this interest in the 1850s; Courtney, *Life of John Stuart Mill*, pp. 76–7; I discuss George Eliot's article in Chapter 14.
16. *GEL*, VIII, 44; Packe, *The Life of John Stuart Mill*, pp. 297–8.
17. Durkheim, *Socialism*, p. 11 note; Mill, *Autobiography*, p. 99; [unsigned article] 'Saint-Simonism', *DR* IV (January 1838) 140.
18. Carlyle, *Works*, I, 13–14; F. W. H. Myers, *Essays Modern*, (1883) p. 254; Preface to Comte's *Catéchisme positiviste* 1852 (Paris, 1966) Chronologie, Introduction et notes par Pierre Arnaud, p. 44. All translations from this text are my own.
19. [unsigned article] 'George Eliot and Comtism', *LQR* XLVII (January 1877) 446–71; Stephen, *George Eliot*, p. 43.
20. [David Brewster], 'M. Comte's *Course of Positive Philosophy*' *ER* LXVII (July 1838) 274; Mill, *Autobiography*, p. 164; Harrison, *Autobiographic Memoirs*, I, 87; Morell, *Philosophical Tendencies*, p. 48.
21. [unsigned article], 'Auguste Comte – His Religion and Philosophy', *BQR* XIX (1 April 1854) 303–4; Taine, *Notes on England*, p. 194; Beatrice Webb, *My Apprenticeship* (1926; Harmondsworth, 1971) p. 161; Rudyard Kipling, *Plain Tales from the Hills* (1888; 1913) p. 86.
22. [unsigned article], 'Saint Simonianism &c', *WR* XVI (April 1832) 293; [Signed 'FAIR PLAY'], 'Letter on the Doctrine of St. Simon', *FM* V (July 1832) 667.
23. Comte, *Catéchisme Positiviste*, pp. 70–71, 76–7, 82, 84–5, 99, 103, 107, [122]–3, 132–3, 158.
24. Ibid., pp. [151], 168.
25. Ibid., pp. 162, 165, [222].
26. Ibid., pp. 170–1, 186–90.
27. Ibid., pp. [201]–3, 206–7.
28. Ibid., pp. 224, 227, [237]–8, 243–4.
29. Ibid., p. [261].
30. Church, *The Oxford Movement*, p. 69; Newman, *Apologia*, p. 232.
31. À Kempis, *The Imitation of Christ*, preface by the late H. D. Litton [1889] pp. 5, 9.
32. Comte, *Catéchisme Positiviste*, p. 298.
33. Quoted in Durkheim, *Socialism*, p. 131.
34. Condorcet, *Sketch for a Historical Picture of the Progress of the Human*

Mind (1795).

35. Mill, *Autobiography*, p. 127.
36. K. K. Collins, 'Questions of Method: Some Unpublished Late Essays' *NCF* XXXV (December 1980) 386.
37. Werner Blumenberg, *Karl Marx* (1962; translated by Douglas Scott 1972) p. 77.
38. George Eliot, *Impressions of Theophrastus Such*, pp. 36–40; Annan, *Ideas and Beliefs*, p. 56.
39. Erskine Perry, 'A Morning with Auguste Comte', *NC* II (November 1877) 631.
40. Harrison, 'The Life of George Eliot', 320.
41. Morell, *Historical View*, II, 473–4, 532–6; Lewes, *Biographical History*, IV, 198–230.
42. *GEL*, I, 247, II, 511, V, 118, 122, 169, VIII, 152–3; Pattison, *Memoirs*, p. 210; George Eliot, *Middlemarch*, I, 318.
43. Lovejoy, *Essays in the History of Ideas*, p. xiv.
44. George Sand, *Spiridion*, 1838–9 (Paris, 1954) p. 147.
45. Rousseau, *Oeuvres Complètes*, I, 1020–3, IV, 446, 524; Rousseau, *Rêveries* (ed. Roddier), p. xix; G. R. G. Mure, *An Introduction to Hegel* (Oxford, 1940) pp. viii–ix; Lewes, *Comte's Philosophy*, p. 9.
46. James, Joll, *The Anarchist*, p. 53.
47. Morell, *Historical View*, I, xiv.
48. Comte, *Catéchisme Positiviste*, p. [270]; Seth, *Scottish Philosophy*, p. 207.
49. *GEL*, I, 107–8; Wellek, *The Romantic Age*, p. 44; Hallam, *Introduction to the Literature of Europe* (4 vols, 1837–9) I, 9.
50. G. W. F. Hegel, *Lectures on the Philosophy of History*, translated from the 3rd German Edition by J. Sibree 1849 (1888) pp. xi, 15; Hegel, *Early Theological Writings*, p. 21.
51. Seth, *Scottish Philosophy*, p. 217; *GEL*, I, 71.
52. Hegel, *Lectures*, pp. iv, 10, 16, 414, 464.
53. Ibid., pp. 17–18, 27, 145–7, 155–7, 250, 392–3, 458, 462 note.
54. Ibid., pp. 21–4, 75–9, 121–5, 170, 398–405, 465.
55. Engels, *Feuerbach*, p. 97.
56. Mure, *Introduction to Hegel*, p. 135; Hegel, *Lectures*, pp. ix, 55–6, 77–9, 82, 180, 232–4, 290–1, 333–41, 433.
57. Hegel, *Lectures*, pp. ix, 53, 348, 461, 472. Compare his *Early Theological Writings*, pp. 168–9.
58. Hegel: *Early Theological Writings*, p. 97; *Lectures*, pp. iv–v, ix, 25–6, 43.
59. Engels, *Feuerbach*, pp. 21–22, 54–5; Mure, *Introduction to Hegel*, pp. 65–6; Seth, *Scottish Philosophy*, pp. 190–1.
60. Hegel, *Early Theological Writings*, pp. 15, 31, 53, 58.
61. Harrison, *Autobiographic Memoirs*, I, 56; Gaskell, *Mary Barton* (1848; Knutsford Edition, 8 vols, 1906) p. lxxiv.
62. Comte, *Catéchisme Positiviste*, pp. [51]–5.
63. *GEL*, I, 187; Edward Gibbon, *Autobiography* 1796 (with an Introduction by J. B. Bury 1907) pp. [1], 31–3, 179–80.
64. Hayek, *John Stuart Mill and Harriet Taylor*, pp. 132–3, 223; Thomas Babington Macaulay, *History of England: Volumes One and Two* (1848; 2 vols, 1906) I, 19, 315, 596, II, 175.

65. Macaulay, *History*, I, vi–vii; Stephen, *Studies of a Biographer*, III, 224.
66. Macaulay, *History*, I, 19, 120–1, II, 56–7; *GEL*, III, 191.

12. PHILOSOPHY AND THE NOVEL (1844–1850)

1. Thackeray, *Paris Sketch Book*, p. 192.
2. Watt, *The Rise of the Novel*, pp. 15, 23–7.
3. *GEL*, I, 192–3, 240, 245–6, 260, 265, VI, 223, IX, 282; Rousseau, *Oeuvres Complètes*, I, 546–7.
4. Disraeli: *Tancred*, pp. 45–57, 112–14, 151–4, 300; *Coningsby*, pp. 430–433; *Sybil*, pp. 290, 490–492; *Vivian Gray*, pp. 88–94, 112–114, 144–7, 151–4, 422–4.
5. Disraeli, *Sybil*, pp. 50–51; *GEL*, I, 234–5, 245.
6. Rosemary Ashton, *The German Idea*, p. 155; *Bray-Hennell Extracts*, quoted by Haight, *George Eliot*, p. 69.
7. Winifred Gérin, *Elizabeth Gaskell* (Oxford, 1976) pp. 245–6.
8. Ashton, *The German Idea*, pp. 22–3.
9. Quoted in Haight, *George Eliot*, p. [68].
10. J. A. Froude, *The Nemesis of Faith*, 1849 (second edn 1849) pp. [iii], 81. The second edition contained Froude's explanatory Preface.
11. Froude, *The Nemesis of Faith*, pp. 79, 92, 134, 140.
12. Ibid., pp. 24–5, 101–3, 118, 197–202.
13. Ibid., pp. vii, 26, 35, 43, 49, 114, 126, 132, 156, 184–5, 220.
14. Ibid., pp. v, ix, xiv, 17–19, 25, 41, 51, 56, 63, 226–7.
15. Ibid., pp. 180–1, 197, 162–3.
16. Patricia Thomson, *George Sand and the Victorians* (1977) p. 22; [Mazzini], 'George Sand', *MC IV* (no month 1839) 24; Thackeray, *Paris Sketch Book*, pp. 174–5; [Margaret Oliphant], 'Two Cities – Two Books', *BEM* CXVI (July 1874) 91; McKenzie, *Edith Simcox and George Eliot*, p. 6; Basch, *Relative Creatures*, p. xiii; King, *Life of Mazzini*, p. 91; Mrs Humphry Ward, *David Grieve*, p. 239; Stang, *The Theory of the Novel in England 1850–1870*, pp. 215–7.
17. Nathaniel Hawthorne, *The Blithedale Romance* (1852; 1899) p. 58.
18. *GEL*, III, 374, 416, V, 8–9, VI, 223; Blind, *George Eliot*, pp. 6–7, 147; Linton, *My Literary Life*, p. 100.
19. *GEL*, I, 241, 243, 250, 275, 267, II, 67, VI, 99, 197 note, IX, 221; George Sand: *Spiridion*, pp. 67, 177; *Lettres d'un voyageur* (1834; Paris 1869) pp. 206–9; *Mauprat* (1836; Paris, n.d.) p. 470. All translations from George Sand's novels are my own.
20. *GEL*, I, 243, 250, 277–8, II, 91, 171.
21. Courtney, *Life of John Stuart Mill*, p. 125.
22. The novels referred to are *Spiridion*, *Lélia*, *Lettres d'un voyageur*, *Le meunier d'Angibault*, *Jacques* and *François le champi*; She also read *Indiana*, *Mauprat* and *Consuelo*. All translations are my own. *GEL*, I, 203, 241, 243, 250–1, 270, 275, 277–8, 330; Haight, *George Eliot*, p. 59. I also make reference to George Sand, *Winter in Majorca* (1855; trans. Robert Graves, Mallorca, 1956) and Bartomeu Ferra, *Chopin and George Sand in*

Majorca (trans. R. D. F. Pring-Mill, Palma de Mallora, 1974). *Winter in Majorca*, p. 11; George Sand: *Mauprat*, pp. 43–4, 147; *Spiridion*, p. 114; *Consuelo*, I, 10, 297, II, 149, 292–3; Blind, *George Eliot*, p. 7.

23. Sand: *Consuelo*, I, 1; Quoted in Ruth Jordan, *George Sand* (1976) p. 317.
24. Sand: *Lélia* (1833; 2 vols, Paris, n.d.) I, 9; *Lettres d'un voyageur*, pp. v, 186, 299–302; *Spiridion*, pp. 145, 258–9, 288; *Indiana*, p. 5.
25. Sand: *Indiana*, p. 1; *Lélia*, I, 9; *Le Meunier d'Angibault*, p. 1; *François le champi* 1850 (Paris, 1898) p. 11.
26. Thackeray, *Paris Sketch Book*, p. 184.
27. Sand: *Le Meunier d'Angibault*, p. 183; *Lettres d'un voyageur*, pp. 165, 339; *Indiana*, pp. 107–9, 205–6, 250; *Jacques*, p. 36; *Spiridion*, pp. 302–3; *Mauprat*, pp. 214, 255, 366–7, 470–2.
28. Sand: *Lettres d'un voyageur*, pp. 213, 329; *François le champi*, pp. 9, 129; *Lélia*, I, 132; *Spiridion*, pp. 153, 212–22, 227, 272; *Consuelo*, I, 169, II, 41, III, 260.
29. Sand: *Mauprat*, pp. 148, 236; *Lettres d'un voyageur*, pp. 84, 197; *Lélia*, I, 213; *Spiridion*, pp. 136, 148, 294; *Consuelo*, II, 240.
30. [Mazzini], 'George Sand', *Monthly Chronicle*, 28.
31. Sand: *Lettres d'un voyageur*, p. iv; *Mauprat*, p. 251.
32. Sand: *Lettres d'un voyageur*, pp. 168, 181, 285; *Indiana*, p. 333; *Lélia*, I, 148–9; *François le champi*, pp. [5]–6; *Winter in Majorca*, pp. 165–6.
33. Sand: *Spiridion*, p. 39; *Lettres d'un voyageur*, pp. 103, 267; *Indiana*, pp. 7–9; *Lélia*, I, 4; *Jacques*, p. 201; cf. Rousseau, *O.C.* I [995], [1002].
34. Sand, *Indiana*, p. [10].
35. Sand: *Indiana*, p. 12; *Lettres d'un voyageur*, p. 143; *Spiridion* p. 272.
36. R. H. Super (ed.), *The Complete Prose Works of Matthew Arnold*, 10 vols, Ann Arbor 1960–74 VIII, 220; [Mazzini], 'George Sand', *MC* 23, 25; [Margaret Oliphant], 'Two Cities – Two Books', *BEM* 73; King, *Life of Mazzini*, p. 91.
37. Sand, *Winter in Majorca*, p. 41.
38. Sand, *Lélia*, II, 72.
39. Thackeray, *Paris Sketch Book*, p. 185; Sand, *Indiana*, p. 2.
40. Sand, *Winter in Majorca*, p. 100; Thackeray, *Paris Sketch Book*, p. 175; Sand, *Spiridion*, p. 295.
41. [G. H. Lewes], 'Continental Literati. No. III – George Sand', *MM* XCV (June 1842) 590.
42. Sand: *Lettres d'un voyageur*, p. 183; *Winter in Majorca*, pp. 121–2, 165–6; Mazzini, *Essays*, p. 82; Quoted in Pailleron, *George Sand*, p. 160.
43. Sand: *Winter in Majorca*, p. 108; *Spiridion*, p. 5; Pailleron, *George Sand*, p. 305; Thackeray, *Paris Sketch Book*, p. 185; Ferra, *Chopin and George Sand in Majorca*, p. [55]; *GEL*, II, 5, IX, 218.
44. Sand: *Mauprat*, p. 472; *Consuelo*, II, 138; *Le Meunier d'Angibault*, pp. 119–20, 142, 215.
45. *GEL*, I, 243, 250–1, II, 171; Sand, *Lettres d'un voyageur*, pp. 163–8, 254–5, 297–8.
46. [Mazzini], 'George Sand', *MC* 24.
47. Jordan, *George Sand*, p. 92; [Lewes], 'Continental Literati. No. III – George Sand', *MM* 589.

13. THE RELEVANCE OF IDEAS (1844–1850)

1. Royce, *Fugitive Essays*, p. [261].
2. Faucher, *Études sur L' Angleterre*, II, 162; Prest, *The Industrial Revolution in Coventry*, pp. 38–9, [43], 92–3, 96–7; *VCH*, VIII, 228–9.
3. *GEL*, I, 162 note, 274, II, 414–5, III, 23, IV, 65, V, 422, VIII, 11.
4. Carlyle, *Works*, X, 39, 47, 239, 286; Thomis and Holt, pp. 5–6.
5. Carlyle, *Works*, X, 38, 57–8,46.
6. Ibid., X, 60, 117, 136–7, 225–32.
7. Ibid., X, 23–4, 217–21, 226, 264–5, 268–9.
8. Ibid., X, 227, 241–2, 293.
9. *GEL*, I, 253.
10. Shepherd, *Memoirs of the Life and Writings of Thomas Carlyle*, II, 365–8. The articles contained in Shepherd's Appendix are not in the Centenary Edition. They are, (1) 'Louis Phillipe', *Examiner*, (4 March 1848), (2) 'Repeal of the Union', *Examiner* (29 April 1848), (3) 'Legislation for Ireland', *Examiner* (13 May 1848), (4) 'Ireland and the British Chief Governor', *Spectator* (13 May 1848), (5) 'Irish Regiments of the New Era', *Spectator* (13 May 1848), (6) 'Trees of Liberty', *The Nation* Dublin (1 December 1849).
11. Shepherd, *Memoirs of Carlyle*, II, 390, 394–5, 398.
12. *GEL*, I, 244, 255, 308, 310.
13. [Mazzini] 'George Sand', *MC* (no month 1839) 23.
14. McKenzie, *Edith Simcox and George Eliot*, p. 12.
15. *GEL*, I, 244.
16. Ibid., I, 292–3, 304.
17. Ibid., I, 192, 216, 237, 242, 264, 282, 315.
18. Ibid., I, 254, 267, 329, VII, 47.
19. Ibid., I, 235, 242, 252–4; Rousseau, *Oeuvres Complètes*, IV, 524.
20. *GEL*, I, 173, 230–1, 261, 297, 330–1.
21. Ibid., I, 254–5, 269, 270–1.
22. T. R. Wright, 'George Eliot and Positivism', *MLR* LXXVI (April 1981) 269.
23. *GEL*, I, 189, 228, 239, 241, 248, 303, 313–4, 322, 334.
24. Ibid., I, 195, 241, 251, 263–6, 310, 316.
25. Ibid., I, 217, 234, 265, 307, 309, 318, 323, 328, 333.
26. Ibid., I, 234, 259, 280.
27. Carlyle, *Works*, X, 293.
28. Taylor, *Hegel*, p. 82; *GEL* I, 321.
29. *GEL*, I, 247–8.
30. Ibid., I, 247, VIII, 201; Baker, *The George Eliot–George Henry Lewes Library*, p. 91.
31. Sand, *Lélia*, I, 83; Blind, *George Eliot*, p. 6.
32. [G. H. Lewes], 'Balzac and George Sand', *Foreign Quarterly Review* XXXIII (July 1844) 276.
33. *GEL* I, 223 note, 252, 255, 272–3, 279, 322, 334.
34. Comte, *Catéchisme positiviste*, p. [222].
35. Sand, *Spiridion*, p. 135.

14. LONDON (1851–1854.)

1. Mary Wollstonecraft, *Vindication of the Rights of Woman*, p. 148.
2. *GEL*, I, 358, 362.
3. Ibid., I, 338 note, 343 note.
4. Ibid., I, 338 note; [Marian Evans], 'The Progress of the Intellect', *WR* LIV (January 1851) 353–68.
5. 'Progress' 353, 355–6, 361, 365–8.
6. Ibid., 363, 365, *GEL*, VIII, 26.
7. 'Progress', 362, 364–5.
8. Ibid., 353–5, 358, 365–8.
9. *GEL* VIII, 45.
10. 'Progress', 355, 357–8.
11. Ibid., 354–5.
12. Ibid., 354, 360, 367.
13. [unsigned review], 'George Eliot: Her Life and Writings', *LWR* n.s. LX (July 1881) 162; Haldane, *George Eliot and Her Times*, p. 69.
14. *GEL*, VIII, 131.
15. Prest, *The Industrial Revolution in Coventry*, pp. 81–2; Valerie A. Dodd, 'Strauss's Propagandists', 432–3.
16. Hayek, *John Stuart Mill and Harriet Taylor*, p. 203; *GEL*, VIII, 54, 62, 118.
17. *GEL* VIII, 52.
18. George Henry Lewes, 'The Apprenticeship of Life', *Leader* (27 April 1850) 114.
19. Quoted in Halévy, *The Age of Peel and Cobden*, p. 349.
20. See the unsigned review, 'Tendencies towards the Subversion of Faith' in *Eng R* X (December 1848) 427; Pattison, *Memoirs*, p. 317.
21. Carlyle, *Letters to Mill* p. 288; Altick, *The English Common Reader*, pp. [381]–390; Haight, *George Eliot and John Chapman*, p. 131.
22. Altick, *The English Common Reader*, pp. 318–64.
23. Mill, *Autobiography*, pp. 56, 58–9, 79; Thomson, *George Sand and The Victorians*, p. 19.
24. *GEL*, I, 351, VIII, 38; Haight, *George Eliot and John Chapman*, pp. 32–3.
25. Blind, *George Eliot* p. 59; Hayek, *John Stuart Mill and Harriet Taylor*, p. 188; Adams, *Those of Us Who Loved Her*, p. 91; *GEL*, II 55 note VIII, 33; Herbert Spencer, *An Autobiography* (2 vols, 1904) I, 421.
26. *GEL*, II, 163; VIII, 29, 54, 56 note, 59.
27. Ibid., II, 54, 57, 63, 110, VIII, 37, 59.
28. Ibid., II, 74–5, 90, 112; VIII, 68.
29. *Essays of George Eliot*, edited by Thomas Pinney (1968) p. 441; *GEL*, I, 346, 349.
30. Basch, *Relative Creatures*, p. 10.
31. Linton, *My Literary Life*, pp. 94–5.
32. Delamont and Duffin, *The Nineteenth-Century Woman*, p. 48.
33. *GEL*, VIII, 28.
34. Bessie Rayner Belloc, 'Dorothea Casaubon and George Eliot', *CR* LXV (February 1894) 203, 207–8, 213–14; *GEL*, IX, 185.
35. *GEL* I, 368, II, 9 note, 44, 87, 111.
36. Ibid., I, 344, II, 9, 20, 28, 59, 94.

37. Ibid., II, 38.
38. Ibid., II, 45, IX, 325–6; M. C. Bradbrook, *Barbara Bodichon, George Eliot and the Limits of Feminism* (Oxford, 1975) pp. 3, 8; Virginia Woolf, *Three Guineas* (1938; Harmondsworth, 1977) pp. 155–6.
39. *GEL*, II, 7; Mackenzie, *Edith Simcox and George Eliot*, p. 10; Sir Edward Cook, *The Life of Florence Nightingale* (2 vols, 1913) I, 96–7, 118.
40. *GEL*, I, 361, 363–4, II, 4–5 32, 62, VIII, 64; George Eliot, *Middlemarch*, Chapters 3, 84.
41. *GEL*, II, 59, 69.
42. Ibid., I, 356, II, 5, 105; Thomson, *George Sand and the Victorians* p. 18; King, *Life of Mazzini*, pp. 11, 152–3, 222, 267; Mazzini, *Essays*, pp. 41, 101–2; Read, *The English Provinces*, p. 153.
43. Pouthas, 'The Revolutions of 1848', *New Cambridge Modern History*, X, pp. 411–14.
44. *GEL*, II, 21, 59, 69.
45. Ibid., II, 5.

15. DOGMATISM AND TRUTH (1851–1854)

1. *GEL*, II, 11, 18, 22–3; Herbert Spencer, *An Autobiography* (2 vols, 1904) I, 392–3.
2. Delamont and Duffin, *The Nineteenth-Century Woman*, pp. 62–3, 66.
3. *GEL*, II, 22, 29, 65, 118, 126, VIII, 50, 56–7; Baker, *The George Eliot–George Henry Lewes Library*, p. 191–2.
4. Spencer, *Autobiography*, I, 11–13, 42, 151–2, 200–3, 208, 217–21, [225]–8, 415.
5. Ibid., I, 230–1, 242–3, 252–3, 265–6; David Duncan, *The Life and Letters of Herbert Spencer* (1908) pp. 539, 541; [George Eliot], 'A Word for the Germans', *Pall Mall Gazette* I (7 March 1865) 201; Herbert Spencer, *Essays; Scientific, Political and Speculative* (1858) pp. 168–71, [262].
6. Spencer, *Autobiography*, I, 81, 335, 338, 403.
7. Beatrice Webb, *My Apprenticeship*, pp. 48, 53.
8. Spencer, *Autobiography*, I, 399; *GEL*, II, 40, 119.
9. *GEL*, II, 128; Spencer, *Autobiography*, I, 184, 381.
10. Duncan, *The Life and Letters of Herbert Spencer*, pp. 512, 535, 547, 562; Spencer, *Essays*, pp. 180–1, 414–5; Peel, *Herbert Spencer*, p. 83.
11. Albert Sorel, *Europe and the French Revolution* (1885; translated and edited by Alfred Cobban and J. W. Hunt, 1969) p. 211.
12. Duncan, *The Life and Letters of Herbert Spencer*, p. 554; Spencer, *Autobiography*, I, 346, 419; Spencer *Essays*, pp. 27–9, 53–4.
13. Spencer, *Essays*, pp. 260–1.
14. R. K. Webb, *Harriet Martineau*, p. 245; *GEL*, II, 140.
15. Spencer, *Autobiography*, I, 241, 445; Duncan, *The Life and Letters of Herbert Spencer*, p. 545.
16. Duncan, *The Life and Letters of Herbert Spencer*, pp. 112–3, 131, 376; Spencer, *Autobiography*, I 444.
17. *GEL*, II, 165; Spencer, *Essays*, pp. 171, 215, 255.
18. Spencer, *Autobiography*, I, 444–5; Spencer, 'Auguste Comte – His

Religion and Philosophy', *BQR* XIX (1 April 1854) 305–7, 324, 327, 332 note; Duncan *The Life and Letters of Herbert Spencer*, p. 542; Spencer, *Autobiography*, I, 407, 458.

19. Spencer, *Essays*, pp. 7–8, 29, 51–2, 400, 432.
20. *GEL*, II, 145, 165; Spencer, *Essays*, pp. 281, 300; Duncan, *The Life and Letters of Herbert Spencer*, p. 567.
21. Spencer, *Essays*, pp. [158], 223–4.
22. Harrison, *Autobiographic Memoirs*, I, 79, 240.
23. Sir Erskine Perry, 'A Morning with Auguste Comte', *NC* II (November 1877) 629–30.
24. Spencer, *Essays*, pp. 54.
25. Spencer, 'Auguste Comte', 327.
26. Baker, *The George Eliot–George Henry Lewes Library*, p. 64; *GEL*, I, 142, 177 and note, 247, II, 144 and note.
27. *GEL*, II, 90, 159.
28. Zeller, *David Friedrich Strauss in His Life and Writings*, p. 106; Engels, *Feuerbach*, pp. 26–7; Quoted in Eugene Kamenka, *The Philosophy of Ludwig Feuerbach* (1970) p. [35].
29. Kamenka, *The Philosophy of Ludwig Feuerbach*, p. 27.
30. *GEL*, II, 137.
31. Engels, *Feuerbach*, p. 29; Kamenka, *The Philosophy of Ludwig Feuerbach*, p. 38; Karl Barth's Introduction to George Eliot's translation of *The Essence of Christianity* (New York, 1975) p. xi.
32. Feuerbach, *The Essence of Christianity* (1854) pp. ix–x.
33. Hegel, *Early Theological Writings*, pp. 56–7, 291; Feuerbach, *Essence*, pp. 5, 74, 180, 332–7.
34. Feuerbach made these comments in a letter to C. Riedel, quoted in Kamenka, *The Philosophy of Ludwig Feuerbach*, p. 93; Feuerbach, *Essence*, pp. vi, 93; Hegel, *Lectures on the Philosophy of History*, p. 27.
35. Feuerbach, *Essence*, p. 80.
36. K. K. Collins, 'Questions of Method: Some Unpublished Late Essays', *Nineteenth Century Fiction* XXXV (December 1980) 392; Feuerbach, *Essence*, pp. 59–60, 198 note, 203, 228.
37. De Guistino, *Conquest of Mind*, p. 110; Engels, *Feuerbach*, p. 27; Feuerbach, *Essence*, p. 62.
38. Feuerbach, *Essence*, pp. 20–22, 45–8, 56–7, 156, 183, 260, 270.
39. Ibid., pp. 22, 145, 174.
40. Carlyle, *Works*, XXV, 101–2; Feuerbach, *Essence*, pp. 64–8, 80, 82, 156, 195.
41. Feuerbach, *Essence*, pp. vi, 47–8, 72, 91–2, 151, 169, 268 note; Engels notes the superficiality of Feuerbach's historical sense compared to Hegel's (*Feuerbach*, p. 46).
42. Feuerbach, *Essence*, pp. 12, 101–2, 115, 181, 192, 194–5, 273–4, 281, 316–8.
43. Ibid., pp. 13, 25, 101–2, 196–7; ibid., Barth edition, p. xi.
44. Feuerbach, *Essence*, pp. 40–42, 66, 231, 244, 278, 282 note, 337.
45. *GEL*, II, 152, 165 note, 173 note, 187 note, III, 320, 359, VII, 358–64, IX, 205 note.
46. *GEL* II, 137, 153; Feuerbach, *Essence*, p. xvii.

47. See *Middlemarch*, Ch. 42; *Felix Holt*, Ch. 1; *Daniel Deronda*, Ch. 69.
48. Engels, *Feuerbach*, p. 27.
49. Feuerbach, *Essence*, pp. 115, 195, 282.
50. Kamenka, *The Philosophy of Ludwig Feuerbach*, p. [vii].
51. Spencer, *Autobiography*, I, 397–8; *GEL*, I, 365, II, 15, 19–20, 48, 69.
52. *GEL*, II, 156, 166. She quotes from John Keble's '24th Sunday after Trinity', in *The Christian Year*.
53. *GEL*, I, 376–7, 369, 371–2, 374, II, 69.
54. [Marian Evans], 'Contemporary Literature of England', *Westminster Review* LVII (January 1852) 247–51.
55. *GEL*, I, 247.
56. [Marian Evans], 'Contemporary Literature of England', 249–51.
57. *GEL*, I, 359, II, 49, 127, 134, 156.
58. Ibid., I, 367, 370; Royle, *Victorian Infidels*, pp. 174–5, 216.
59. *GEL*, I, 363, II, 49, 61, 68.
60. *GEL*, I, 360–1, II, 17, 54, 127, 132–3.
61. Ibid., I, 341–3.
62. Ibid., I, 354, 365, 372, II, 3, 33, 43, 88, 102, 121, 126.
63. Ibid., I, 354, 372, II, 111.
64. [Marian Evans], 'The Creed of Christendom', *Leader* II (September 20 1851) 897–9.
65. Ibid., 898; *GEL*, I, 347, II, 120, 125–6; Royle, *Victorian Infidels*, p. 157.
66. Quoted in Haight, *George Eliot and John Chapman*, p. 33–44; *GEL*, VIII, 25, 27.
67. *GEL*, I, 342, 375, II, 12, 18, 52, 67–8, 86, 145, VIII, 26.
68. Adams, *Those of Us Who Loved Her*, p. 90; Haldane, *George Eliot and Her Times*, p. 74; Quoted in Haight, *George Eliot and John Chapman*, p. 33; *Collected Works of John Stuart Mill* (20 vols, 1963–)XIV, 72, 79, XVI, 1007, [1226]; Haight, *George Eliot*, p. 98.
69. *GEL*, I, 359, 366, II, 23 and note, 33, 49, 95, 137.
70. *GEL*, I, 365, II, 11, 21, 25, 31, 47–50, 55–6, 66–7, 91–3, 96–7, 149.
71. Ibid., I, 370, II, 21, 29, 43–4, 48, 83–4, 141, VIII, 23–4, 92.
72. Ibid., II, 88, 127, VIII, 90, 105.

16. GEORGE HENRY LEWES TO 1850

1. George Henry Lewes, *The Life of Goethe* (2 vols, 1855) I, 147.
2. *GEL*, IX, 316.
3. Thomson, *George Sand and the Victorians*, p. [137].
4. George Henry Lewes, 'Spinoza', *FR* IV (1 April 1866) [385]–7, 398; Baker, *The George Eliot–George Henry Lewes Library*, p. 193.
5. Moncure D. Conway, *History of the South Place Society* (1894) p. 113.
6. *GEL*, IX, 280.
7. Engels, *Feuerbach*, pp. 19, 25; Baker, *The George Eliot–George Henry Lewes Library*, pp. 34, 91.
8. G. H. Lewes, 'A Word to Young Authors on their True Position', *Hood's Magazine and Comic Miscellany* III (April 1845) 366, 368, 370–1, 374–6.

9. Ibid., 370–1; *GEL*, IX, 272; Anna T. Kitchel, *George Lewes and George Eliot*, pp. 56–60; G. H. Lewes, 'The Condition of Authors in England, Germany, and France', *FM* XXXV (March 1847) 292.
10. *GEL*, VIII, 148–9, 357, 386, 484.
11. Courtney, *Life of John Stuart Mill*, p. 92; Mill, *Works*, XVII, 1913.
12. Morell, *A Historical and Critical View of the Speculative Philosophy of Europe in the Nineteenth Century* (1846) II, [519]; Lewes, *A Biographical History of Philosophy* (4 vols, 1845–6) I, 182–3, II, 28–101.
13. Hock Guan Tjoa, *George Henry Lewes. A Victorian Mind* (Cambridge Mass. and London, 1977) p. 104.
14. Morell, *Historical and Critical View*, II [519].
15. Lewes, *BHP*, I, 6, 11–12.
16. Ibid., I, 11–12, 15–16, 18, 22, 216; IV, 130–1.
17. Ibid., I, 9, II, 209, IV, 89–230; [George Eliot], 'A Word for the Germans', *PMG* I (7 March 1865) 201.
18. Lewes: *BHP* I, 15, 91 note, II, 119, 121, III, 6, 37, 138 note, IV, 45, 203–3; 'A Word to young Authors', 370.
19. Lewes, *BHP*, I, 23, IV, 234–8.
20. Tjoa, *George Henry Lewes*, p. 64.
21. Lewes, *BHP*, I, 21 note, 60 note, 69 note, 99, 131, II, 150–1, IV, 243, 248.
22. [George Henry Lewes], *Ranthorpe*, pp. 14, 127, 37, Ch. 5.
23. Ibid., pp. 120, 197, 350; Ashton, *The German Idea*, pp. 22, 110.
24. [Lewes], *Ranthorpe*, pp. 13, 34, 113–4, 165, 170–1, 234, 314, 350.
25. *GEL*, VIII, 51.
26. George Henry Lewes, *Rose, Blanche and Violet* (3 vols, 1848), I, 66, 95–6, II, 136–51, III, 54–5.
27. Ibid., II, 122–3, 166–9, 219, III, 4.
28. Ibid., I, v–vi.
29. Ibid., I, 228, [Lewes], *Ranthorpe*, pp. 85, 96, 203–4, 271–2.
30. [Lewes], *Ranthorpe*, pp. 181, 188; Lewes, *Rose, Blanche and Violet*, I, 161, 168, II, 81, 229–30, 256–7, 264.
31. Ibid., I, vii–ix, 2–3, 169, II, 35, 80, III, 14–15, 81, 150.
32. Ibid., II, 38–9, 56, 214, III, 11–12, 16, 18, 175–7, 256–9.
33. Lewes, 'Condition of Authors', 290.
34. [G. H. Lewes], 'Recent Novels: French and English', *FM* XXVI (December 1847) 686; 'G. H. L.', 'Historical Romance: "The Foster Brother", and "Whitehall"', *WR* XLV (March 1846) 35.
35. [Lewes] 'Recent Novels', 687, 692, 694–5.
36. Ibid., 691, 695; Lewes, 'Jane Eyre', *WFQR* XLVIII (January 1848) 581; *GEL*, IX, 287.
37. Quoted in Thomson, *George Sand and The Victorians*, p. [137].
38. 'G. H. L.', 'Historical Romance', 46; [G. H. Lewes], 'Ruth and Villette', *WFQR* n.s. III (April 1853) 490; Lewes: 'Balzac and George Sand', *FQR* XXXIII (July 1844) 296–7; 'Continental Literati. No. III. – George Sand', *MM* XCV (June 1842) 578.
39. Lewes: 'Balzac and George Sand', 274; 'Continental Literati', 578–80, 584, 587, 589.
40. Lewes: 'Balzac and George Sand', 266–9, 271; 'Continental Literati', 582–3; 'Ruth and Villette', 475; *GEL*, I, 247.

41. See Kaminsky's bibliography, *George Henry Lewes as Literary Critic*; [G. H. Lewes], 'George Sand's Recent Novels', *FQR* XXXVII (April 1846) 22, 24–6, 28–31, 35–6.
42. [G. H. Lewes], 'Lessing', *ER* LXXXII (October 1845) 454, 456, 461, 465, 470.
43. Lewes, 'Strauss's Political Pamphlet', *ER* LXXXVIII (July 1848) 94.
44. Lewes, 'Condition of Authors', 285–95.
45. Baker, *The George Eliot–George Henry Lewes Library*, p. xlii; Lewes: 'Democracy in France', *Athenaeum* No. 1108 (20 January 1849) 67–8; *The Line of Maximilien Robespierre* (3rd edn 1899) Ch. 3, pp. 27 and note, 169, 337.
46. Lewes, *Robespierre*, pp. vi–vii; Baker, *The George Eliot–George Henry Lewes Library*, p. 74.
47. Lewes, *Robespierre*, pp. vi, 178–9, 280.
48. Ibid., pp. viii, 4, 261, 394.
49. Ibid., pp. [v], 279, 342 note.
50. Ibid., pp. [1], 64, 178–9, 287.
51. Ibid., pp. 58, 105, 309, 313.
52. Ibid., pp. 4, 58–9, 190, 394, 395–6.
53. Ibid., p. 28.

17. GEORGE HENRY LEWES AND MARIAN EVANS
(1850–1854)

1. G. H. Lewes *Rose, Blanche, and Violet*, I, 95; Wollstonecraft, *Vindication of the Rights of Woman*, p. 241.
2. Linton, *My Literary Life*, pp. 19, 26.
3. Spencer, *Autobiography*, I, 377; *GEL*, IX, 249, 296; [unsigned article], 'George Eliot: Her Life and Writings', *WR*, n.s. LX (July 1881) 162.
4. Belloc, 'Dorothea Casaubon and George Eliot', 216; *GEL*, IX, 288.
5. Spencer, *Autobiography*, I, 377; Blind, *George Eliot*, pp. 83–4; Linton, *My Literary Life*, p. 26.
6. Quoted in Royle, *Victorian Infidels*, p. 157.
7. E. C. Gaskell, *The Life of Charlotte Brontë* 1857 (Oxford 1919) p. 356.
8. Bray, *Phases of Opinion and Experience During A Long Life: An Autobiography* [1885], p. 82; Francis Espinasse, *Literary Recollections and Sketches* (1893) p. 284; Lewes, *A Biographical History of Philosophy*, III, 116–7.
9. Linton, *My Literary Life*, pp. 22–3; Hayek, *John Stuart Mill and Harriet Taylor*, pp. 76–7, 136, 168; Spencer, *Autobiography* I, 268.
10. Linton, *My Literary Life*, 23, 25–6; [G. H. Lewes], 'Ruth and Villette', 476–7, 484–5; Lewes, *Rose, Blanche, and Violet* II, 278–9.
11. *GHL Journal* 28 January 1859, cited in Haight, *George Eliot*, p. 133.
12. [G. H. Lewes], 'Currer Bell's "Shirley"', *ER* XCI (January 1850) 159–60.
13. Ibid., 154–5, 160, 165.
14. Linton, *My Literary Life*, pp. 22–3.
15. Ibid., p. 32; Lewes, 'Condition of Authors', 289; Spencer, *Autobiography* I, 386; Tjoa, *George Henry Lewes*, pp. 15, 46–7, 53–4.

16. *GEL*, I, 352.
17. George Henry Lewes, *The Apprenticeship of Life*, serialised in ten parts in the *Leader*. 1 June 1850, p. 236.
18. Ibid., pp. 43, 114, 164, 212.
19. Ibid., pp. 17, 42–3, 139, 163, 211.
20. [Lewes], *Ranthorpe*, p. 34; Lewes, *Apprenticeship of Life*, pp. 17, 140.
21. Lewes, *Apprenticeship of Life*, pp. 18, 44, 68, 163, 212.
22. [Lewes], 'Ruth and Villette', 476.
23. Lewes, 'Recent Novels, French and English', *FM* XXXVI (December 1847) 694.
24. Lewes, *Rose, Blanche, and Violet*, III, 255; GE MS Journal, 19 June 1861; *GEL*, VIII, 128.
25. *GEL*, I, 376–7, II, 13, 37, 56, 68, 83, 94, 98, 104, VIII, 36, 42–3 and note, 63.
26. Lewes, *Apprenticeship of Life*, p. 163.
27. Wollstonecraft, *Vindication*, pp. 165, 247; Gail Cunningham, *The New Woman and the Victorian Novel* (1978) pp. 21, 43–4.
28. Gérin, *Elizabeth Gaskell*, pp. 254–6; *GEL*, VIII, xvii, 123, 126, IX, 313.
29. Belloc, 'Dorothea Casaubon and George Eliot', 214–5.
30. *GEL*, VIII, 129; G. M. Young, *Victorian England* (1936) p. 36; Arnold Bennett, *The Old Wives' Tale* (1908; 2 vols, 1931) I, 152; Kaminsky, *George Henry Lewes as Literary Critic*, p. 7.
31. Lewes, 'Balzac and George Sand', 269; *GEL*, II, 46, 118; [unsigned article], 'George Eliot: Her Life and Writings', *WR* n.s. LX (July 1881) 162, 188; Stephen, *George Eliot*, p. 48.
32. *GEL*, 1X, 266; Lewes, *BHP*, III, 116–7.
33. Baker, *The George Eliot–George Henry Lewes Library*, p. xlix.
34. Spencer, *Autobiography*, I, 348, 380, 415; *GEL*, VIII, 52, 70.
35. [G. H. Lewes], 'The Lady Novelists', *WR* n.s. II (July 1852) 129, 141.
36. *GEL*, II, 18–19, 25, 31 and note, 115, 126, 148, VIII, 73; Haight, *George Eliot*, p. 143.
37. [John Chapman] 'George Eliot', *WR* LXVIII (July 1885) 207; Kitchel, *George Lewes and George Eliot*, p. 206; *GEL*, II, 50, 93, 130.
38. *GEL*, VIII, 44, 91 and note.
39. Royle, *Victorian Infidels*, p. 156; *GEL*, I, 370 and note; Simon, *European Positivism in the Nineteenth Century*, p. 197; Morell, *Historical View* II, 520; Spencer, *Autobiography* I, 445; Duncan, *The Life and Letters of Herbert Spencer*, p. 545; Kitchel, *George Lewes and George Eliot*, p. 84.
40. Bray, *Phases*, p. 186.
41. Lewes, *BHP*, III, 174–5; Harrison, *Memoirs*, I, 82.
42. Baker, *The George Eliot–George Henry Lewes Library*, p. xx; Tjoa, *George Henry Lewes* p. 63.
43. G. H. Lewes, *Auguste Comte's Philosophy of the Sciences* (1853) pp. iii, [1]–2; Harrison, *Memoirs*, I, 22–3, 134–5.
44. Harrison, *Memoirs*, I, 22–3, 134–5.
45. Ibid., pp. 8–9, 48–9, 265, 332–3; Durkheim, *Socialism*, p. 142.
46. Quoted in Kitchel, *George Lewes and George Eliot*, p. 81; Mill, *Autobiography*, p. 92.
47. Lewes, *Comte's Philosophy of The Sciences*, pp. 92, 142, 161–2, 164, 339–40.

48. Ibid., pp. 6–7.
49. Ibid., pp. 5–6, 90, 226, 259, 268, 389.
50. 'The Natural History of German Life', *Westminster Review* LXVI (July 1856) 51–79.
51. Lewes, *Comte's Philosophy of The Sciences*, pp. 165, 244–5, 252–5, 328, 330–1, 337–8, 341.
52. Ibid., pp. [iii], 2, 56, 110–11, 131, 197, 210, 232; Baker, *The George Eliot–George Henry Lewes Library*, p. xx; Sir Erskine Perry, 'A Morning with Auguste Comte', 630.
53. *GEL*, I, 56; Kitchel, *George Henry Lewes and George Eliot*, p. 85; Lewes, *CS*, pp. 10, 105–6, 170–1, 213–32, 246–7, 319, 327.
54. Durkheim, *Socialism*, pp. 234, 271; Lewes, *Comte's Philosophy of The Sciences*, pp. 88, 92, 113, 320, 322–6, 342.
55. Lewes, *Comte's Philosophy of The Sciences*, pp. 235, 237–40, 339, 343–4.
56. [unsigned review], 'Contemporary Literature. Science', *WFQR* n.s. V (January 1854) 255–7.

18. GERMANY (1854–1855)

1. *GEL*, II, 213–14; Lewes, *Comte's Philosophy of the Sciences*, p. 260.
2. *GEL*, II, 176, VIII, 64, 129; Haight, *George Eliot*, p. 168.
3. Lewes, *The Life of Goethe*, II, 62; quoted in Haight, *George Eliot*, p. 162.
4. Lewes, 'Condition of Authors in England, Germany and France', *FM* XXXV (March 1847) 287.
5. *GEJ* (Yale microfilm) n.p.; George Eliot, 'Three Months in Weimar', *FM* LI (June 1855) 700.
6. *GEL*, VIII, 132, 134; [G. H. Lewes], 'Weimar and Jena', *SR* II (7 June 1856) 137.
7. *GEL*, II, 180, 183, VIII, 119; [Marian Evans], *Berlin Journal*, p. 28; Haight, *George Eliot*, p. 168.
8. [Marian Evans], *Weimar Journal*, pp. 12, 18; *GEL*, II, 170–1, 173–4, 186, 190; [Lewes], *Ranthorpe*, p. 271; Lewes, *Rose, Blanche, and Violet*, II, 150.
9. *GEL*, II, 170, 172–3, 175–6, 178–9, 184, 187–9, VIII, 123, 129.
10. Ibid., II, 169–71, 173–4, 185–6, 190; [Marian Evans], 'Three Months in Weimar', 706; [Marian Evans], 'Liszt, Wagner and Weimar', *FM* LII (July 1855) 59.
11. *GEL*, II, 169, 171–2 and note, VIII, 116–7; Lewes, *Life of Goethe*, II, 446.
12. *Recollections of Berlin*, 1854–5, MS Journal, p. 29; *GEL*, VIII, 486–7.
13. *GEL*, II, 190; [Marian Evans], *Berlin Journal*, pp. 42–3; Cross, *George Eliot's Life*, p. 190.
14. *Recollections of Berlin*, p. 45; *GEL*, II, 169, 171–3, 185, 189, 192–3; Cross, *George Eliot's Life*, pp. 189–91.
15. Cross, *George Eliot's Life*, II, 186, 188–9.
16. [Marian Evans with G. H. Lewes], 'The Romantic School of Music', *Leader* V (28 October 1854), 1027–8.
17. [Marian Evans], 'The Art of the Ancients', *Leader* VI (17 March 1855) 257.
18. [Marian Evans], 'Memoirs of the Court of Austria', *WR* LXIII (April

1855) [303]–.

19. *GEL*, II, 86, 174.
20. [Marian Evans], 'Woman in France: Madame de Sablé', *WR* LXII (October 1854) 450.
21. *GEL*, II, 187, VIII, 116.
22. Ibid., II, 190; [Marian Evans], 'Woman in France', 450–5, 472–3.
23. [Marian Evans], 'Woman in France', 470.
24. Ibid., 449, 453, 456, 468, 472–3.
25. [Marian Evans], 'Liszt, Wagner and Weimar', 49, 51.
26. [Marian Evans] 'Three Months in Weimar', 702–3; *Recollections of Berlin*, p. 43.
27. [Marian Evans] 'Three Months in Weimar', 699–700; 'Liszt, Wagner and Weimar', 48–9, 61.
28. [Marian Evans]: 'Liszt, Wagner and Weimar', 48; 'Three Months in Weimar', 699–700.
29. Haight, *George Eliot*, pp. 158, 172.
30. *GEL*, VIII, 52.
31. Ibid., I, 107; Baker, *The George Eliot–George Henry Lewes Library*, pp. 85–6; Lewes, *BHP*, III, 112, 124–5, 133–43, 148, 152, 154.
32. Bray, *Phases*, pp. 18, 101–3, 189; Spinoza, *Works*, II, 129.
33. Spinoza, *Works*, II, 147.
34. Froude, 'Spinoza', 27; Spinoza, *Works*, II, 80–81, 135–7, 162, 195.
35. Spinoza, *Works*, II, 120, 134, 187, 235–6.
36. Ibid., II, 78–9, 126–7, 211, 219, 239, 250, 252–3; Arnold, *Works*, III, 177.
37. The manuscript of the translation is in Yale University Library; Haight, *George Eliot*, pp. 199–200; *GEL*, VIII, 156 and note, 159.
38. Mill, *The Subjection of Women*, p. 275.
39. Lewes, *Life of Goethe*, I, 275–6, 280–3; [G. H. Lewes], 'Goethe as a Man of Science', *WR* n.s. II (1 October 1852) 487; Haight, *George Eliot*, p. 170; Baker, *The George Eliot–George Henry Lewes Library*, p. lviii; Cross, *George Eliot's Life*, p. 190.
40. *GEL*, VIII, 125, 131.
41. Ibid., II, 172, 185–6, 189; Waley, *George Eliot's Blotter*, pp. 19–20; [Marian Evans]: 'Three Months in Weimar', 701, 703–5; 'Liszt, Wagner and Weimar', 50, 60–1; *Weimar Journal*, pp. 14, 16, 21; *Recollections of Berlin*, p. 39.
42. *GEL*, VIII, 140; Mineka, *The Dissidence of Dissent*, pp. 104, 115–6, 318–20; Lewes, *Life of Goethe*, II, 419 note.
43. Lewes's wording appeared before the text of the First Edition; Carlyle: *Works*, IV, 55, XXIII, 23, 25, 31; XXVI, 203, 208, 210, XXIX, 472–6; 481–2; *Last Words*, p. 199; *Lectures on the History of Literature*, p. 205; *Reminiscences*, I, 288.
44. Mill, *Autobiography*, p. 98.
45. Kitchel, *George Lewes and George Eliot*, p. 27; Lewes: *BHP*, IV, 44; *Apprenticeship of Life*, p. 114; 'Recent Novels', 693; 'A Word to Authors', 373; 'George Sand's Recent Novels', 21; 'Lessing', 457.
46. Tjoa, *George Henry Lewes*, p. 14; Lewes: 'Continental Literati. No. III – George Sand', 584; 'The Lady Novelists', 135; Carlyle, *Reminiscences*, II, 250.

47. Lewes, 'Goethe as a Man of Science', 487.
48. Ibid., 485–6, 497.
49. Ibid., 479, 483–4, 486, 490–1, 505–6.
50. Blind, *George Eliot*, p. 82; GEL, VIII, 204, IX, 246, 273; the best biography was Boswell's *Life of Samuel Johnson*.
51. Baker, *The George Eliot–George Henry Lewes Library*, pp. 74–7; Haight, *George Eliot*, p. 171; GEL, II, 170, 178 note, 180, 184–5, 192 and note, 193, VIII, 120.
52. *Recollections of Berlin*, p. 29; GEL, II, 176–8, 185, VIII, 141, 145; Lewes, *Life of Goethe*, I, 222, 355; II, 179, 396 note, 409, 432–3, 436, 440–2.
53. Lewes, *Life of Goethe*, I, 295–6, 322, 342, 410, II, [351]–2, 374.
54. Ibid., I, 393; Lewes, 'Goethe as a Man of Science', 481–2.
55. Ibid., 498.
56. Lewes, *Life of Goethe*, II, 49, 394, 437.
57. Mazzini, *Essays*, p. 175 note.
58. Lewes, *Life of Goethe*, II, 63, 135, 150, 163–81, 250, 378, 435.
59. Ibid., I, 4, 15, 48, 378, 396–7; GEL, I, 318; Mazzini, *Essays*, pp. 94–5, 102, 119, 174; [Lewes], *Ranthorpe*, pp. 170–1; Carlyle, *Works*, XXVI, 208.
60. Lewes, *Life of Goethe*, I, 114–5, II, 31–3, 46, 140; Spencer, *Autobiography*, I, 419–20.
61. Lewes, *Life of Goethe*, II, 190, 391–3; GEL, I, 315.
62. Lewes: *Life of Goethe*, II, 54–5; 'Weimar and Jena', 137.
63. Lewes: *Life of Goethe*, I, [29]–30, II, [3]–4, 321.
64. Ibid., II, 216; Tjoa, *George Henry Lewes*, pp. 67–8.
65. Lewes, *Life of Goethe*, I, 158, 194–6, 389, II, 283, 440.
66. *Recollections of Berlin*, P. 43.
67. Kaminsky, *George Henry Lewes as Literary Critic*, pp. 45–6, 83; Taylor, *Hegel*, p. 472; LG, II, 388–90.
68. Ibid., I, 74, 173, 222, II, 187–9, 248, 376, 395; (1864 edition) p. 403.
69. GEL, I, 247–8.
70. Lewes, *Life of Goethe*, I, 210, 222, II, 5, 235, 302, 316, 334, 425.
71. [Lewes], 'Ruth and Villette', 474–5.
72. Lewes, *Life of Goethe*, II, 210–11, 228, 339, 426; George Sand, *François le champi*, p. 11.
73. Lewes, *Life of Goethe*, II, 280, 375.
74. Ibid., I, 171, II, 375, 390; Lewes, 'Goethe as a Man of Science', 485.
75. Lewes, *Life of Goethe*, I, xi, 396, II, 90, 206, 286–7, 411, 423–8; (1864 edition) pp. xi, 517.
76. [G. H. Lewes], 'T. B. Macaulay – History of England', *BQR* IX (February 1849) 3; [G. H. Lewes], 'Influence of Science on Literature', I (12 April 1856) 482; Lewes, *Life of Goethe*, (1864) pp. 51–2.
77. Lewes, *Life of Goethe*, II, 339–40.
78. Ibid., II, 189.
79. King, *The Life of Mazzini*, p. 317; Taylor, *Hegel*, p. 21.

19. PLANS FOR A NOVEL (1855–1856)

1. *GEL*, IX, 197. Lewes made these remarks in conversation with Lady Holland. She recorded them on 7 October 1877.
2. Oscar Browning, *Life of George Eliot*, p. 145; Belloc, 'Dorothea Casaubon and George Eliot', 214.
3. Haight, *George Eliot*, p. 61.
4. *GEL*, II, 199, 202–3, 220, 231–2, 238.
5. Lewes, *Apprenticeship of Life*, p. 163.
6. Cited in Adams, *Those of Us Who Loved Her*, p. 186.
7. *GEL*, II, 194, 196, 202, 276; [Marian Evans]: 'Margaret Fuller's Letters from Italy', *Leader* VII (17 May 1856) 475; 'Recollections of Heine', *Leader* VII (23 August 1856) 811; 'Worldliness and Other Worldliness: The Poet Young', *WR* LXVII (January 1857) 10.
8. *GEL*, VIII, 147, IX, 267; Adams, *Those of Us Who Loved Her*, pp. 125; Haight, *George Eliot*, p. 199.
9. Haight, *George Eliot*, pp. 177, 188–9; *GEL*, II, 197, 202, 204, 213–14, 216, 223, 230–231, 235–7, 254.
10. *GEL*, II, 216, 219 note, 223, 237, 256, 263, 271 and note; Spencer, *Autobiography*, I, 350, 398, 492.
11. *GEL*, II, 212–3, 219; [G. H. Lewes], 'Herbert Spencer's Principles of Psychology', *SR* I (1 March 1856) 352–3.
12. *GEL*, II, 196–8, 200, 217, 228, 255.
13. Quoted in Haight, *George Eliot and John Chapman*, p. 203.
14. [unsigned article], 'The Progress of Fiction as Art', *LWR* n.s. IV, (October 1853) 343–4, 346, 352–3, 355, 358–61, 370, 372–4.
15. 'Contemporary Literature of England' n.s. I (January 1852) 255, 287. The articles are hereafter cited as 'CL' with month and year only. 'CL' (April 1852) 625–6, 629–30, 635; 'CL' (July 1852) 552; 'CL' (October 1852) 262, 551; 'CL' (January 1853) 264–7, 280, 285; 'CL' (April 1853) 587–8; 'CL' (July 1853) 246–8, 251–2.
16. 'CL' (January 1852) 284; 'CL' (April 1852) 654, 656–8; 'CL' (October 1852) 268, 271–2.
17. 'CL' (July 1852) 567–8; Harriet Martineau, 'The Political Life and Sentiments of Niebuhr', *LWR*, n.s. II (July 1852) 145, 157, 172.
18. 'CL' (July 1852) 247.
19. 'CL' (January 1852) 286; 'CL' (April 1852) 656–7 'CL' (July 1852) 255; 'CL' (January 1853) 281; 'CL' (July 1853) 273.
20. Lewes, *The Life of Goethe*, II, 5.
21. Lewes: 'Continental Literati. No. III. – George Sand', 584; 'Balzac and George Sand', [265], 276, 291.
22. Lewes, 'The Lady Novelists', 130–4, 138, 141; Haight, *George Eliot and John Chapman*, pp. 80–81.
23. *GEL*, II, 210, 220, 264, VIII, 143–5; Bray, *Phases*, pp. 34–5.
24. *GEL*, II, 264 and note, 268, VIII, 148; Haight, *George Eliot*, p. 198.
25. Haight, *George Eliot*, p. 192; McKenzie, *Edith Simcox and George Eliot*, p. 120.
26. Cross, *George Eliot's Life*, pp. 192–4, 197.
27. Eliot, *Impressions of Theophrastus Such*, p. 208; Oscar Browning, *Life of*

George Eliot, p. 32; *GEL*, II, 198, 201, 212, 228, 240–1, 258, 260–1, VIII, 384, 466.

28. [Marian Evans]: 'The Future of German Philosophy', *Leader* VI (28 July 1855) 723; 'Art and Belles Lettres', *WR* LXV (April 1856) 626; 'German Wit: Heinrich Heine', *WR* LXV (January 1856) 1–3.

29. [Marian Evans]: 'The Natural History of German Life', *WR* LXVI (July 1856); 'Belles Lettres', *WR* LXVI (October 1856) 572; 'The Art and Artists of Greece', *SR* II (31 May 1856) 109; 'German Mythology and Legend', *Leader* VI (22 September 1855) 918.

30. [Marian Evans]: 'Evangelical Teaching: Dr. Cumming', *WR* LXIV (October 1855) 449; 'Lord Brougham's Literature', *Leader* VI (7 July 1855) 653; 'German Wit', 14–15; 'Worldliness and Other-Worldliness', 32, 40.

31. [Marian Evans]: 'Belles Lettres', *WR* LXIV (July 1855) 306; 'German Wit', 16–19.

32. *GEL*, II, 197.

33. [Marian Evans], 'Sight-seeing in Germany and the Tyrol', *Saturday Review* II (6 September 1856) 424–5.

34. *GEL* II, 229; [Marian Evans]: 'German Wit', 30; 'The Shaving of Shagpat', *Leader* VII (5 January 1856) 16; 'Natural History of German Life', 77; 'Belles Lettres and Art', *WR* LXVI (July 1856) 264; 'Belles Lettres', (July 1855) 307; 'Belles Lettres', *WR* LXIV (October 1855) 613; 'The Antigone and Its Moral', *Leader* VII (29 March 1856) 306; 'Belles Lettres', (October 1856) 566.

35. [Marian Evans]: 'German Wit', 6; 'The Art and Artists of Greece', 109; 'Menander and Greek Comedy', *Leader* VI (June 16 1855) 578.

36. [Marian Evans]: 'Belles Lettres', (July 1855) 302; 'Belles Lettres', (October 1855) 602–3; 'German Wit', 1–6; 'Menander and Greek Comedy', 578–9; 'Memoirs of the Court of Austria', LXIII (April 1855) 304; Love in the Drama' *Leader* VI (25 August 1855) 820–1; 'Heine's Poems', *Leader* VI (1 September 1855) 843.

37. *GEL*, II, 200, 215; 'George Eliot: Her Life and Writings', n.s. LX (July 1881) 157; [Marian Evans]: 'Who wrote the Waverley Novels?', *Leader* VII (19 April 1856) 375; 'Three Months in Weimar'', LI (June 1855) 705; 'Love in the Drama', 821; 'Art and Belles Lettres', (April 1856) 632–3; 'Margaret Fuller's Letters from Italy', *Leader* VII (17 May 1856) 475.

38. J. G. Lockhart, *The Life of Sir Walter Scott*, 1837–38, (London 1906) p. 233.

39. [Marian Evans]: 'Belles Lettres', (July 1855) 290; 'Belles Lettres', (October 1855) 612; 'Belles Lettres', *WR* LXV (January 1856) 300; 'Silly Novels by Lady Novelists', *WR* LXVI (October 1856) 458.

40. Lukács, *The Historical Novel*, p. 161.

41. [Marian Evans]: 'Natural History of German Life', 54, 56; 'Belles Lettres', (October 1856) 572.

42. Lewes, 'The Lady Novelists', 130; [Marian Evans], [Worldliness and Other-Worldliness', [1].

43. *GEL*, II, 203, 205; Spencer, *Autobiography*, I, 396–7; [Marian Evans]: 'Belles Lettres', (July 1855) 293–4; 'Who wrote the Waverley Novels?', 375–6; 'Evangelical Teaching', 451–3.

44. Pattison, *Essays*, I, 450; Lewes, *BHP*, IV, 237–8; [Marian Evans], 'The

Future of German Philosophy', 723.

45. *GEL*, II, 220, 228, 243–4, 247.
46. Ibid., II, 253, 278; [Marian Evans]: 'Margaret Fuller and Mary Wollstonecraft', *Leader* VI (13 October 1855) 989; 'Translations and Translators', *Leader*, VI (20 October 1855) 1015; 'Belles Lettres', (January 1856) 312; 'Lord Brougham's Literature', 653; 'German Wit', 7, 16–17, 21.
47. *GEL*, II, 238; Durkheim, *Socialism*, p. 24 note.
48. 'CL' (July 1852) 264; 'CL' (January 1853) 271; 'CL' (April 1853) 598; [Marian Evans]: 'Margaret Fuller's Letters from Italy', 475; 'Felice Orsini', *Leader* VII (August 30 1856) 835; 'Belles Lettres', (October 1855) 559; 'Lord Brougham's Literature', 653; *GEL*, II, 225, 236.
49. [Marian Evans]: 'Margaret Fuller and Mary Wollstonecraft', 989; 'Life and Opinions of Milton', *Leader* VI (4 August 1855) 750; 'The Antigone and Its Moral', 306; 'Natural History of German Life', 69.
50. [Marian Evans], 'Natural History of German Life', 55–6, 63–5, 69.
51. Ibid., 63–7.
52. [William Palmer], 'On Tendencies Towards the Subversion of Faith', *Eng R* X (December 1848) 426–7.
53. Haight, *George Eliot*, p. 203; *GEL*, II, 265, 271.
54. [Marian Evans]: 'Introduction to Genesis', *Leader* VII (12 January 1856) 41–2; 'Memoirs of the Court of Austria', 306; 'Evangelical Teaching', 446.
55. [Marian Evans]: 'History of German Protestantism', *Leader* VII (9 February 1856) 140; 'Church History of the Nineteenth Century', *Leader* VII (5 April 1856) 331–2, 332; 'Life and Opinions of Milton', 750; 'Evangelical Teaching', 437–9; 'German Wit', 22; 'Worldliness and Other-Worldliness', 18–19.
56. *GEL*, IX, 227 c.f. ibid., IX, 217.
57. [Marian Evans]: 'Rachel Gray', *Leader* VII (5 January 1856) 19; 'The Lover's Seat', *Leader* VII (2 August 1856) 736; 'Evangelical Teaching', 441–2, 461.
58. [Marian Evans]: 'Evangelical Teaching', 437; 'The Future of German Philosophy', 724.
59. [Marian Evans]: 'Worldliness and Other-Worldliness', 32–3; 'German Wit', [1]–2; 'German Mythology and Legend', 918; 'The Natural History of German Life', 71–2, 75; 'Belles Lettres', (October 1855) 603; Prest, *The Industrial Revolution in Coventry*, p. 18.
60. [Marian Evans]: 'Love in the Drama', 820; 'The Natural History of German Life', 75; Baker, *The George Eliot–George Henry Lewes Library*, pp. 170–1.
61. [Marian Evans]: 'Worldliness and Other-Worldliness', 33, 37; 'Evangelical Teaching', 442.
62. [Marian Evans]: 'Thomas Carlyle', *Leader* VI (27 October 1855) 1034–5; 'Belles Lettres', (July 1856) 261; 'Belles Lettres', (October 1856) 579–81; 'Translations and Translators', 1014–15; 'German Wit', 12–13, 32.
63. [George Henry Lewes], 'T. B. Macaulay. – History of England', 7; [Marian Evans]: 'German Wit', 6; 'Belles Lettres', (January 1856) 302.
64. [Marian Evans]: 'Belles Lettres', (July 1855) 289; 'Thomas Carlyle', 1035.

65. [Marian Evans]: 'Michelet on the Reformation', *Leader* VI (15 September 1855); 'Church History of the Nineteenth Century', 331; 'Belles Lettres', (July 1856) 267; 'Lord Brougham's Literature', 652; 'Belles Lettres', (October 1855) 610–11.
66. *GEL*, II, 228, 255.
67. [Marian Evans], 'Belles Lettres', (April 1856) 627.
68. Lewes, *Life of Goethe*, II, 216.
69. Ruskin, *Works*, III, xxxvii, IV, 293, 390.
70. Ibid., III, 582–3; IV, 139, 200, 298; VI, 398–9; Wordsworth, *Lyrical Ballads, 1800 Preface*, in *Nineteenth-Century English Critical Essays*, selected and edited by Edmund D. Jones (Oxford, 1916) pp. 7–8.
71. Ruskin, *Works*, III, 353, 364, 405; IV, 98–9.
72. Ibid., IV, 224; V, 201, 334–5.
73. Ibid., IV, 52–3, 348; V, 334–5, 427–8, VI, 438.
74. Ibid., V, 330, 337.
75. Ibid., V, 334, 359–60, 386; VI, 303.
76. Ibid., IV, 204; V, 334.
77. Ibid., III, 329, 387; VI, 75.
78. Ibid., V, 57, 111, 117; VI, 18–19.
79. Ibid., III, 12, 37, 110, 137, 143, 509; IV, 52–3, 284, 288; VI, xxi, 89.
80. Ibid., III, 22, 25, 48, 92, 104, 470, 611, 624; IV, 26, 32–3, 164, 211; V, 58, 181, 188–9.
81. [Marian Evans]: 'Thomas Carlyle', 1035.
82. Ruskin, *Works*, III, 90–91; IV, 252; V, 151; VI, 62–3, 81, 96.
83. Ibid., III, 163; V, 124, 127–8, 336–7; VI, 12–13.
84. Ibid., III, 203; IV, 92, 148; V, xlix, 100–1; VI, 132–3, 391.
85. Ibid., V, 169; VI, 482.
86. Tjoa, *George Henry Lewes*, p. 63, quoting from the *Leader* (13 April 1850).
87. 'George Eliot: Her Life and Writings', *WR* LX (July 1881) 193.

20. PERCEPTION AND THE MEDIUM: THE VINDICATION OF ART

1. [epigraph] Watt, *The Rise of the Novel*, p. 11; Waley, *George Eliot's Blotter*, p. 21; [Marian Evans]: 'Belles Lettres', *WR* LXV (July 1855) 298; 'Church History of the Nineteenth Century', *Leader* VII (5 April 1856) 331; 'Worldliness and Other-Worldliness: The Poet Young', LXVII (January 1857) 26; 'Pictures of Life in French Novels', *SR* II (17 May 1856) 69–70.
2. [Marian Evans]: 'Belles Lettres', *WR* LXVI (October 1856) 578; 'Worldliness and Other-Worldliness', 30–1; 'Ferny Combes', *Leader* VII (16 August 1856) 787; *GEL*, II, 238–9, 241–5, 250–251, 254; [Marian Evans], 'Three Months in Weimar', *FM* LI (June 1855), 699–702.
3. [Marian Evans], *Recollections of Berlin*, p. 47; *GEL*, II, 241, 247–8, 251–2.
4. *GEL*, II, 52, 85; [Marian Evans]: 'Memoirs of the Court of Austria', *WR* LXIII (April 1855) [303]; 'The Court of Austria', *Leader* VII (12 April

1856) 352; 'Worldliness and Other-Worldliness', 4–5; 'Liszt, Wagner, and Weimar', *FM* LII (July 1855) 49; 'Belles Lettres', *WR* (January 1856) 290–1, 297; 'The Shaving of Shagpat' *Leader* VII (5 January 1856) 15–17; 'The Poets and Poetry of America', *Leader* VII (1 March 1856) 210.

5. *GEL*, II, 205, 218, 225, 227, 229, 282; [Marian Evans]: 'Art and Belles Lettres', *Westminster Review* LXV (April 1856) 642–3; 'Liszt, Wagner and Weimar', 59.

6. [Marian Evans]: 'Belles Lettres' (July 1855) 296; 'Margaret Fuller and Mary Wollstonecraft' *Leader* VI (13 October 1855) 989.

7. Cross, *George Eliot's life*, p. 199; [Marian Evans]: 'Belles Lettres' (January 1856) 301; *GEL*, I, 355; II, 86–7, 92.

8. *GEL*, II, 278, 282; [Marian Evans]: 'Belles Lettres', *WR* LXVII (January 1857), 307.

9. Elizabeth Barrett Browning, *Aurora Leigh* (1856) pp. 60, 110, 139–40, 207, 209, 399, 402.

10. Ibid., pp. 48, 60, 116, 352.

11. Ibid., pp. 187, 189, 232–3, 302, 305, 343, 346–7.

12. *GEL*, II, 218, 282.

13. [Marian Evans], 'Silly Novels by Lady Novelists', *WR* LXVI (October 1856) 449, 460.

14. [Marian Evans], 'Belles Lettres' (April 1856) 626.

15. Engels, *Feuerbach*, pp. 21–2; [Marian Evans], 'Thomas Carlyle', *Leader* VI (27 October 1855) 1034.

16. [Marian Evans], 'The Future of German Philosophy' *Leader* VI (28 July 1855) 724; Kaminsky, *George Henry Lewes As Literary Critic*, p. 186; cited in Mack, *Jeremy Bentham*, p. 23 – cf. Mill's comment in 'Bentham', *London and Westminster Review* XXIX (August 1838) 467.

17. [Marian Evans], 'The Future of German Philosophy', 724.

18. Quoted in K. K. Collins, 'Questions of Method: Some Unpublished Late Essays', 387.

19. [Marian Evans]: 'The Morality of Wilhelm Meister', *Leader* VI (21 July 1855) 703.

20. [Marian Evans]: 'The Shaving of Shagpat', 16; 'Recollections of Heine', *Leader* VII (23 August 1856) 811; 'The Natural History of German Life', *WR* LXVI (July 1856) 68; 'Worldliness and Other-Worldliness', 11.

21. *GEL*, II, 214, 278; [Marian Evans]: 'Evangelical Teaching', *WR* LXIV (October 1855) 444–5; 'Liszt, Wagner, and Weimar', 48.

22. [Marian Evans]: 'The Morality of Wilhelm Meister', 703; 'Silly Novels by Lady Novelists', 449; 'Belles Lettres' (October 1856) 576; 'Belles Lettres and Art', *WR* LXVI (July 1856) 258; 'A Tragic Story', *Leader* VII (19 July 1856) 691; 'Belles Lettres', LXIV (October 1855) 612; 'Belles Lettres' (July 1855) 29, 78, 295; 'The Antigone and Its Moral', *Leader* VII (29 March 1856) 306; 'Belles Lettres' (July 1855) 289.

23. [Marian Evans]: 'Belles Lettres' (July 1856) 272; 'Three Months in Weimar', 703; 'Worldliness and Other-Worldliness', 18–19.

24. [Marian Evans]: 'Lizst, Wagner and Weimar', 52–9; 'Belles Lettres' (January 1856) 290–1; 'Belles Lettres' (October 1856) 576.

25. Tjoa, *George Henry Lewes*, p. 84.

26. [Marian Evans]: 'Belles Lettres' (April 1856) 627–31; 'Belles Lettres' (January 1856) 296; 'The Lover's Seat', *Leader* VII (2 August 1856) 736.
27. Lewes, 'Historical Romance', *WR* XLV (March 1846) 36.
28. K. K. Collins, 'Questions of Method', 391, 401; *GEL*, VIII, 466; IX, 284.
29. [Marian Evans]: 'Rachel Gray', *Leader* VII (5 January 1856) 19; 'Belles Lettres' (October 1856) 574; 'German Wit: Heinrich Heine', *Westminster Review* LXV (January 1856) 7; 'Art and Belles Lettres' (April 1856) 626.
30. *GEL*, II, 122, 160, 199, 214–5, 229–30, 237, 254, 257–8, 260, 278; [Marian Evans]: 'Evangelical Teaching', 459–60; 'Worldliness and Other-Worldliness', 19; 'Belles Lettres and Art' (July 1856) 261.
31. [Marian Evans]: 'Sightseeing in Germany and the Tyrol', *Saturday Review* II (6 September 1856) 425; 'Michelet on the Reformation', 892.
32. [Marian Evans]: 'Belles Lettres' (July 1855) 289; 'Worldliness and Other-Worldliness', 40; 'Liszt, Wagner and Weimar', 51; Kaminsky, *George Henry Lewes as Literary Critic*, pp. 73–4.
33. *GEL*, II, 147, 206, 208, 259; [Marian Evans]: 'Evangelical Teaching', 440; 'Silly Novels by Lady Novelists', 449–51; 'The Natural History of German Life', 69; 'The Art and Artists of Greece', *Saturday Review* II (31 May 1856) 109; 'Worldliness and Other-Worldliness', 1–3; 'Thomas Carlyle', 1035; 'Lord Brougham's Literature', *Leader* VI (7 July 1855) 652–3.
34. [John Chapman], 'George Eliot', *WR* (July 1885) 171; George Eliot: *Works* XXI, 290–1; [Marian Evans]: 'Lord Brougham's Literature'; 'Translations and Translators', *Leader* VI (20 October 1855) 1015; 'Heine's Book of Songs', *Saturday Review* I (26 April 1856) 523; 'Silly Novels by Lady Novelists', 460.
35. Kaminsky, *George Henry Lewes as Literary Critic* pp. 41, 186; Lewes, 'Historical Romance', 36.
36. *GEL*, VIII 154; [Marian Evans]: 'Belles Lettres' (April 1856) 626; 'The Morality of Wilhelm Meister', 703; 'Life of Goethe', *Leader* VI (3 November 1855) 1060.
37. [Marian Evans]: 'The Future of German Philosophy', 724; 'Silly Novels by Lady Novelists', 449; 'The Natural History of German Life', 54; 'Belles Lettres' (July 1856) 260.
38. Kaminsky, *George Henry Lewes as Literary Critic*, p. 31.
39. [Marian Evans]: 'Belles Lettres' (April 1856) 626–7; 'Evangelical Teaching', 455; 'Silly Novels by Lady Novelists', 454–5.
40. Spencer, *Autobiography*, I, 396; [unsigned article], 'George Eliot', *WR* n.s. LX (July 1881) 157.
41. Mrs Humphry Ward, *The History of David Grieve* (10th editions 1893) p. xv.
42. Tjoa, *George Henry Lewes*, p. 60.
43. [Marian Evans]: 'Belles Lettres' (April 1856) 629; 'Belles Lettres' (January 1856) 305.

Bibliography

This is arranged as follows:
I. George Eliot
(a) Books and documents
(b) Articles in periodicals
II. George Henry Lewes
(a) Books
(b) Articles in periodicals
III. Thomas Carlyle
IV. John Stuart Mill
(a) Books
(b) Articles in periodicals
V. Secondary sources
(a) Books
(b) Articles
(i) Those of known authorship
(ii) Those of unknown authorship
Unless otherwise stated, the place of publication is London.
I have given the first edition date, and where an alternative edition is
    used, the date of this is also given.
A note on abbreviations used can be found on p. 316.
Matter enclosed in square brackets is inferred by me but not explicit in the
    text cited.

I GEORGE ELIOT

(a) Books and Documents

The Novels of George Eliot, Illustrated Copyright Edition, 21 volumes
    [1908–1913].
The George Eliot Letters, edited by Gordon S. Haight, 9 volumes (New
    haven, 1954–1978), cited as *GEL*.
*The Life of Jesus, Critically Examined by Dr. David Friedrich Strauss: Translated
    from the Fourth German Edition*, 3 volumes (1846).
The Essence of Christianity, by Ludwig Feuerbach, translated from the
    second German edition by Marian Evans, 1 volume (1854).
    I have also used the edition of George Eliot's translation of Feuerbach
    published in New York in 1957, which has an Introductory Essay by
    Karl Barth and a Foreword by Richard Niebuhr.
Quarry for 'Middlemarch', edited with an Introduction and Notes by Anna
    Theresa Kitchel, to accompany *Nineteenth-Century Fiction* IV (March
    1950).

'George Eliot's Notebook', Document in Nuneaton Library. *Diaries and Journals*, Yale University Library Microfilm of George Eliot MSS 1–12. These include the *Berlin Journal, Recollections of Berlin* and the *Weimar Journal*.
Essays of George Eliot, edited by Thomas Pinney (1963).

(b) Articles in Periodicals

1851
'The Progress of the Intellect', *WR* LIV (January 1851) 353–68.
'The Creed of Christendom', *Leader* II (29 September 1851) 897–99.
1852
Review of Carlyle's *Life of John Sterling*, in 'Contemporary Literature of England', *WR* LVII (January 1852) 247–51.
1854
'Woman in France: Madame de Sablé', *WR* LXII (October 1854) 448–73.
[With Lewes], 'The Romantic School of Music', *Leader* V (28 October 1854), pp. 1027–8.
1855
'The Art of the Ancients', *Leader* VI (17 March 1855) 257–8.
'Memoirs of the Court of Austria', *WR* LXIII (April 1855) 303–35.
'Westward Ho!', *Leader* VI (19 May 1855) 474–5.
'Three Months in Weimar', *FM* LI (June 1855) 699–706.
'Menander and Greek Comedy', *Leader* VI (16 June 1855) 578–9.
'Liszt, Wagner and Weimar', *FM* LII (July 1855) 48–62.
'Belles Lettres', *WR* LXIV (July 1855) 288–307.
'Lord Brougham's Literature', *Leader* VI (7 July 1855) 652–3.
'The Morality of Wilhelm Meister', *Leader* VI (21 July 1855) 703.
'The Future of German Philosophy', *Leader* VI (28 July 1855) 723–4.
'Life and Opinions of Milton', *Leader* VI (4 August 1855) 750.
'Love in the Drama', *Leader* VI (25 August 1855) 820–1.
'Heine's Poems', *Leader* VI (1 September 1855) 843–4.
'Michelet on the Reformation', *Leader* VI, (15 September 1855) 892.
'German Mythology and Legend', *Leader* VI (22 September 1855) 917–8.
'Evangelical Teaching: Dr. Cumming', *WR* LXIV (October 1855) 436–62.
'Belles Lettres', *WR* LXIV (October 1855) 596–615.
'Margaret Fuller and Mary Wollstonecraft', *Leader* VI (13 October 1855) 988–9.
'Translations and Translators', *Leader* VI (20 October 1855) 1014–5.
'Thomas Carlyle', *Leader* VI (27 October 1855) 1034–5.
'Life of Goethe', *Leader* VI (3 November 1855) 1058–61.
1856
'German Wit: Heinrich Heine', *WR* LXV (January 1856) 1–33.
'Belles Lettres', *WR* LXV (January 1856 290–312.
'The Shaving of Shagpat', *Leader* VII (5 January 1856) 15–7.
'Rachel Gray', *Leader* VII (5 January 1856) 19.
'Introduction to Genesis', *Leader* VII (12 January 1856) 41–2.
'History of German Protestantism', *Leader* VII (9 February 1856) 140.
'The Poets and Poetry of America', *Leader* VII (1 March 1856) 210.

'The Antigone and its Moral', *Leader* VII (29 March 1856) 306.
'Art and Belles Lettres', *WR* LXV (April 1856) 625–50.
'Church History of the Nineteenth Century', *Leader*, VII (5 April 1856) 331–2.
'The Court of Austria', *Leader* VII (12 April 1856) 352–3.
'Who wrote the Waverley Novels?', *Leader* VII (19 April 1856) 375–6.
'Story of a Blue Bottle', *Leader* VII (26 April 1856) 401–2.
'Heine's Book of Songs', *SR* I (26 April 1856) 523–4.
'Margaret Fuller's Letters from Italy', *Leader* VII (17 May 1856) 475.
'Pictures of Life in French Novels', *SR* II (17 May 1856) 69–70.
'The Art and Artists of Greece', *SR* II (31 May 1856) 109–10.
'The Natural History of German Life', *WR* LXVI (July 1856) 51–79.
'Belles Lettres and Art', *WR* LXVI (July 1856) 257–8.
'A Tragic Story', *Leader* VII (19 July 1856) 691.
'The Lover's Seat', *Leader* VII (2 August 1856) 735–6.
'Ferny Combes', *Leader* VII (16 August 1856) 787.
'Recollections of Heine', *Leader* VII (23 August 1856) 811–2.
'Felice Orsini', *Leader* VII (30 August 1856) 835.
'Sight-seeing in Germany and the Tyrol', *SR* II (6 September 1856) 424–5.
'Silly Novels by Lady Novelists', *WR* LXVI (October 1856) 442–61.
'Belles Lettres', *WR* LXVI (October 1856) 556–82.
1857
'Worldliness and Other-Worldliness: The Poet Young', *WR* LXVII (January 1857) 1–42.
'History, Biography, Voyages and Travels', *WR* LXVII (January 1857) 288–306.
'Belles Lettres', *WR* LXVII (January 1857) 306–26.
1865
'A Word for the Germans', *Pall Mall Gazette* I (7 March 1865) 201.

II GEORGE HENRY LEWES

(a) Books

A Biographical History of Philosophy, 4 vols (1845–46).
Ranthorpe, 1847.
Rose, Blanche and Violet, 3 vols (1848).
The Life of Maximilien Robespierre (1849; 3rd edition, 1899).
Comte's Philosophy of the Sciences (1853).
The Life and Works of Goethe, 2 vol (1855).
The Life of Goethe (2nd edition, partly rewritten, 1864).

(b) Articles in Periodicals

'Continental Literati. No. III. – George Sand', *MM* XCV (June 1842) 578–91.
'Balzac and George Sand', *FQR* XXXIII (July 1844) [265]–98.

'A Word to Young Authors on their True Position', *HM* III (April 1845) 366–76.
'Lessing', *ER* LXXXII (October 1845) 451–70.
'Historical Romance: "The Foster Brother", "Whitehall"', *WR* XLV (March 1846) 34–55.
'George Sand's Recent Novels', *FQR* LXXII (April 1846) 21–36.
'Morell's History of Modern Philosophy', *FM* XXXIV (October 1846) 407–15.
'The Condition of Authors in England, Germany and France', *FM* XXXV (March 1847) 285–95.
'Recent Novels: French and English', *FM* XXXVI (December 1847) 686–95.
'Jane Eyre', *WFQR* XLVIII (January 1848) 581–84.
'Strauss's Political Pamphlet: Julian the Apostate and Frederick William IV', *ER* LXXXVIII (July 1848) 94–104.
'Democracy in France', *Athenaeum* No. 1108 (20 January 1849) 67–8.
'T. B. Macaulay–History of England', *BQR* IX (February 1849) [1]–41.
'The Aesthetic and Miscellaneous Works of Frederick von Schlegel', *Athenaeum* No 117 (24 March 1849) 295–6.
'The Caxtons', *WFQR* LII (January 1850) 407–19.
'Currer Bell's "Shirley"', *ER* XCI (January 1850) 153–73.
'Apprenticeship of Life'(1), *Leader* (30 March 1850) 17–18.
'Apprenticeship of Life'(2), *Leader* (6 April 1850) 42–4.
'Apprenticeship of Life'(3), *Leader* (13 April 1850) 67–8.
'Apprenticeship of Life'(4), *Leader* (27 April 1850) 114–15.
'Apprenticeship of Life'(5), *Leader* (4 May 1850) 139–41.
'Apprenticeship of Life'(6), *Leader* (11 May 1850) 163–5.
'Apprenticeship of Life'(7), *Leader* (18 May 1850) 187–9.
'Apprenticeship of Life'(8), *Leader* (25 May 1850) 211–13.
'Apprenticeship of Life'(9), *Leader* (1 June 1850) 236–7.
'Apprenticeship of Life'(10), *Leader* (8 June 1850) 260–1.
'The Lady Novelists', *WR* n.s. II (July 1852) 129–41.
'Goethe as a Man of Science', *WR* n.s. II (1 October 1852) 479–506.
'Ruth and Villette', *WFQR* n.s. III (April 1853) 474–91.
'Herbert Spencer's Principles of Psychology', *SR* I (1 March 1856) 352–3.
'Influence of Science on Literature', *SR* I (12 April 1856) 482–3.
'Weimar and Jena', *SR* II (7 June 1856) 137.
'Spinoza', *FR* IV (1 April 1866) [385]–406.

III. THOMAS CARLYLE

The Works of Thomas Carlyle, Centenary Edition, 30 volumes (1897–99).
Lectures on the History of Literature, edited with Preface and Notes by Professor J. Reay Greene (1892).
Letters of Thomas Carlyle to John Stuart Mill, John Sterling and Robert Browning, edited by Alexander Carlyle (1923).
Last Words of Thomas Carlyle (1892).
Carlyle's Reminiscences'. The first edition by J. A. Froude, 2 volumes (1881), contained certain errors which were corrected in Charles Eliot Norton's edition, 2 volumes (1887). Neither Froude nor Norton include the

section entitled 'Christopher North', first printed in the *Nineteenth Century and After* LXXXVII (January 1920) 103–17.

IV JOHN STUART MILL

(a) Books

Collected Works of John Stuart Mill, 20 volumes (Toronto, Buffalo and London)
A System of Logic, 2 volumes (1843).
Dissertations and Discussions, 3 volumes (vols I and II, 1859; vol. III, 1867).
Utilitarianism (1863).
The Subjection of Women (1869; 1929).
Autobiography (1874). The definitive edition of the text is that which I have cited throughout: *Autobiography*, edited with an Introduction and Notes by Jack Stillinger (New York, 1969; Oxford, 1971). I have also used Harold J. Laski's edition (Oxford, 1924) which has an Appendix of Mill's speeches.
Three Essays on Religion (1874).
The Spirit of the Age, with an Introductory Essay by Frederick A. von Hayek (Chicago, 1942).

(b) Articles in Periodicals

1833
'Alison's History of the French Revolution', *MR* VII (August 1833) 507–16.
'What is Poetry?', *MR* VII (January 1833) 60–70.
'The Two Kinds of Poetry', *MR* VII (October 1833) 714–22.
1834
'Notes on some of the More Popular Dialogues of Plato. No. 1. The Protagoras', *MR* VIII (February 1834) 88–9.
'Notes on the Newspapers', *MR* VIII (March 1834) 161–76.
'Notes on Some of the More Popular Dialogues of Plato. No. I The Protagoras', *MR* VIII (March 1834) 203–11.
'On Miss Martineau's Summary of Political Economy', *MR* VIII (May 1834) 318–22.
'Notes on the Newspapers', *MR* VIII (May 1834) 354–75.
'Notes on the Newspapers', *MR* VIII (June 1834) 435–56.
'Letters from an Englishman to a Frenchman', *MR* VIII (June 1834) 385–95.
'Notes on some of the More Popular Dialogues of Plato. No. II. The Phaedrus', *MR* VIII (June 1834) 404–20.
'Notes on the Newspapers', *MR* VIII (July 1834) 521–8.
'Notes on the Newspapers', *MR* VIII (August 1834) 589–90.
'Notes on Some of the More Popular Dialogues of Plato. No. III. The Gorgias', *MR* VIII (September 1834) 691–710.
'The Close of the Session', *MR* VIII (September 1834) 605–9.
'Notes on Some of the More Popular Dialogues of Plato. No. II. The Phaedrus', *MR* VIII (September 1834) 633–46.

'Notes on the Newspapers', *MR* VIII (September 1834) 656–65.
'On Punishment', *MR* VIII (October 1834) 734–6.
'Notes on Some of the More Popular Dialogues of Plato. No. III. The Gorgias', *MR* VIII (November 1834) 802–15.
'Notes on Some of the More Popular Dialogues of Plato. No. III. The Gorgias', *MR* VIII (December 1834) 829–42.
1835
'Notes on Some of the More Popular Dialogues of Plato. No. IV. The Apology of Socrates', *MR* IX (February 1835) 112–21.
'Notes on some of the More Popular Dialogues of Plato. No. IV. The Apology of Socrates', *MR* IX (March 1835) 169–78.
'Postscript', *LR* II (April 1835) 254–6.
'Professor Sedgwick's Discourse on the Studies of the University of Cambridge', *LR* II (April 1835) 94–135.
'The Monster Trial', *MR* IX (June 1835) 393–96.
'Parliamentary Proceedings of the Session', *LR* II (July 1835) 512–24.
'Tennyson's Poems', *LR* II (July 1835) 402–24.
'De Tocqueville on Democracy in America', *LR* II (October 1835) 85–129.
'Rationale of Political Representation', *LR* II (July 1835; 341–71.
'Postscript: The Close of the Session', *LR* II, (October, 1835) 270–7.
1836
'State of Society in America', *LR* II (January 1836) 365–89.
'State of Politics in 1836', *LWR* III (April 1836) 271–8.
'Sir John Walsh's Contemporary History', *LWR* III (July 1836) [281]–300.
1837
[With George Grote], 'The Statesman', *LWR* V (April 1837) [1]–32.
'Fonblanque's England Under Seven Administrations', *LWR* V (April 1837) 65–98.
'The French Revolution', *LWR* V (July 1837) 17–53.
'Parties and the Ministry', *LWR* VI (October 1837) [1]–26.
'Armand Carrel', *LWR* VI (October 1837) 66–111.
1838
'Lord Durham and the Canadians', *LWR* VI (January 1838) 502–33.
'Writings of Alfred de Vigny', *LWR* XXIX (April 1838) 1–44.
'Bentham', *LWR* XXIX (August 1838) 467–507.
'Lord Durham's Return', *LWR* XXXII (December 1838) 241–60.
1839
'Reorganization of the Reform Party', *LWR* XXXII (April 1839) 475–508.
1840
'Coleridge', *LWR* XXXIII (March 1840) 257–302.

V SECONDARY SOURCES

(a) Books

Adams, Kathleen, *Those of Us Who Loved Her* (Warwick, 1980).
Altick, Richard D., *The English Common Reader* (1957; Chicago and London, 1963).

Altick, Richard D., *Victorian People and Ideas*, (1st UK edn, 1974).
Annan, Noel, *et al.*, *Ideas and Beliefs of the Victorians* (1949) p. 256.
Anschutz, R. P., *The Philosophy of J. S. Mill* (Oxford, 1953).
Arnold, Matthew, *The Complete Prose Works*, edited by R. J. Super, 10 volumes (Ann Arbor, 1960–74).
Ashton, Rosemary, *The German Idea* (Cambridge, 1980).
Baker, William, *The George Eliot–George Henry Lewes Library* (London and New York, 1977)
Basch, Françoise, *Relative Creatures* (1974).
Bayley, John, *The Characters of Love* (1960).
Beard, Rev. J. R., *Strauss, Hegel and Their Opinions* (London and Manchester, 1844).
Beer, J. B., *Coleridge the Visionary* (1959).
Bennett, Arnold, *The Old Wives' Tale* (1908); 2 volumes, 1931).
Bennett, Joan, *George Eliot* (Cambridge, 1948).
Blind, Mathilde, *George Eliot*, (5th edn), 1890).
Blumenberg, Werner, *Karl Marx* (1962; translated by Douglas Scott, 1972).
Blunden, Edmund, and Griggs, Earl Leslie, *Coleridge: Studies by Several Hands on the Hundredth Anniversary of His Death*. (1934).
Bourl'honne, Pierre, *George Eliot* (Paris, 1933).
Bowle, John, *Politics and Opinion in the Nineteenth Century* (1954).
Bradbrook, M. C., *Barbara Bodichon, George Eliot and the Limits of Feminism* (Oxford, 1975).
Bray, Charles, *Phases of Opinion and Experience During a Long Life: An Autobiography* [1885].
————, *The Philosophy of Necessity* (2 volumes, 1841).
Briggs, Asa, *Victorian Cities* (revised edn, Harmondsworth, 1968).
Browning, Elizabeth Barret, *Aurora Leigh* (1856).
Browning, Oscar, *Life of George Eliot* (1890).
Brunetière Ferdinand, *Le roman naturaliste* (11th edn, Paris, n.d.).
Buchan, John, *The Life of Sir Walter Scott* (1932).
Buckland, Anna J., *The Life of Hannah More* (n.d.).
Buckley, J. M., *The Victorian Temper* (1952).
Bullett, Gerald, *George Eliot* (1947).
Cazamion, Louis, *Le Roman Social en Angleterre: 1830–1850* (Paris, 1903).
Cazamion, Madeleine L., *Le Roman et les idées en Angleterre* (Strasbourg, Paris and Oxford, 1923).
Cecil, David, *Early Victorian Novelists* (1934).
————, *Melbourne* (1955).
Chadwick, Owen, *The Secularization of the European Mind in the Nineteenth Century* (Cambridge, 1975).
Church, R. W., *The Oxford Movement* (1891; 3rd edn, 1892).
Clark, G. Kitson, *The Making of Victorian England* (1962).
Coleridge, Samuel Taylor, *Aids to Reflection and the Confessions of an Inquiring Spirit to Which are Added His Essay on Faith and Notes on the Book of Common Prayer* (1913).
————, *Lay Sermons*, edited by R. J. White (London and Princeton, 1972).
————, *Biographia Literaria* (1817); edited by J. Shawcross, 2 volumes, 1907).

——————, *The Table Talk and Omniana of Samuel Taylor Coleridge* (Oxford, 1917).

——————, *Collected Letters of Samuel Taylor Coleridge*, edited by Earl Leslie Griggs, 6 vols (Oxford, 1956–71).

Collingwood, R. G., *An Autobiography* (1939; Oxford, 1970).

Comte, Auguste, *Catéchisme Positiviste* (1852; Chronologie, Introduction et Notes par Pierre Arnaud, Paris, 1966).

Condorcet, Antoine Nicolas de, *Sketch for a Historical Picture of the Progress of the Human Mind*, trans. June Barraclough (1955).

Conway, Moncure D., *History of the South Place Society* (1894).

Cook, Sir Edward, *The Life of Florence Nightingale*, 2 vol (1913).

Copleston, Frederick, *A History of Philosophy* (8 vols, 1944–66) vol. 4, *Descartes to Leibniz* (1958; 4th impression, 1965).

Courtney, W. L., *Life of John Stuart Mill* (1889).

Crompton, Margaret, *George Eliot*, (1960).

Cross, J. W., *George Eliot's Life* (1885; new edn, 1 vol., Edinburgh and London, [1887]).

Cruse Amy, *The Englishman and His Books in the Early Nineteenth Century* (1930).

——————, *The Victorians and Their Books* (1935).

Cunningham, Gail, *The New Woman and the Victorian Novel* (1978).

Cunningham, Valentine, *Everywhere Spoken Against* (Oxford, 1975).

Davie, Donald, *A Gathered Church* (London and Henley 1978).

Deakin, Mary H., *The Early Life of George Eliot* (Manchester, 1913).

De Guistino, David, *Conquest of Mind* (London and Totowa N.J., 1975).

Delamont, Sara, and Duffin, Lorna, *The Nineteenth-Century Woman* (London and New York, 1978).

De Staël, *Ten Years of Exile* (1904; New York, 1972).

——————, *Germany*, translated from the French, 3 vols (1813).

The Novels and Tales of Benjamin Disraeli, Bradenham edn, 12 vols (1926–27).

Drummond, James and Upton, C. B., *The Life and Letters of James Martineau*, 2 vols (1902).

Duncan, David, *The Life and Letters of Herbert Spencer* (1908).

Durkheim, Emile, *Socialism* (1928; translated by Charlotte Sattler, edited with an Introduction by Alvin W. Gouldner, from the edition originally edited, and with a Preface by Marcel Mauss, London and New York, 1962).

Elek, Peter, *Humanism in the English Novel* (1975).

Emerson, Ralph Waldo, *Representative Men* (1850).

——————, *English Traits* (1856).

Emery, Laura Comer, *George Eliot's Creative Conflict* (Los Angeles and London, 1976).

Engels, Frederick, *Ludwig Feuerbach and the Outcome of Classical German Philosophy* (n.p., n.d.).

——————, *The Condition of the Working Class in England* (1st German) edition, 1845; 1st English edition, 1892; 1969).

Espinasse, Francis, *Literary Recollections and Sketches* (1893).

Essays Mainly on the Nineteenth Century Presented to Sir Humphrey Milford. (1948).

Faber, Geoffrey, *Oxford Apostles* (1933).

Faucher, Léon, *Etudes sur l'Angleterre*, 2 vols (Bruxelles, 1845).

Ferra, Bartomeu, *Chopin and George Sand in Majorca*, translated by R. D. F. Pring-Mill (Palma de Mallorca, 1974).

Froude, J. A. *The Nemesis of Faith* (1849; 2nd edn, 1849).

——————, *Thomas Carlyle: A History of the First Forty Years of His Life*, 2 vols (1882).

——————, *Thomas Carlyle: A History of His Life in London* (1884; 2 vols, 1890).

——————, *My Relations with Carlyle* (1903).

Gardiner, Dorothy, *English Girlhood at school* (1929).

Garnett, Richard, *The Life of W. J. Fox* (London and New York, 1910).

Gaskell, Elizabeth C., *The Works of Mrs. Gaskell*, 8 vols (1906).

——————, *The Life of Charlotte Brontë* (1857; Oxford, 1919).

Gérin, Winifred, *Elizabeth Gaskell* (Oxford, 1976).

Gibbon, Edward, *Autobiography* (1796; with an Introduction by J. B. Bury, 1907).

Gide, Charles and Rist, Charles, *Histoire des doctrines économiques depuis les physiocrates jusqu'à nos jours* (4th edn revue et corrigée, Paris, 1922).

Gooch, G. P. *History and Historians in the Nineteenth Century* (1913).

Gow, Henry, *The Unitarians* (1928).

Graham, Henry Gray, *The Social Life of Scotland in the Eighteenth Century* (2nd revised edn, 2 vols, 1900; 1 vol., 1901).

Haight, Gordon S., *George Eliot and John Chapman* (London and New Haven, 1940).

—————— (ed.), *A Century of George Eliot Criticism* (1966).

——————, *George Eliot* (Oxford, 1968).

Haldane, Elizabeth, *George Eliot and Her Times* (1927).

Halévy, Elie, *The Triumph of Reform* (1923; translated by E. I. Watkin, 2nd revised edn, 1950).

——————, *The Growth of Philosophic Radicalism* (1928; translated by Mary Morris, 1934).

——————, *The Age of Peel and Cobden* (1946; translated by E. I. Watkin, 1947).

Hallam, Henry, *Introduction to the Literature of Europe*, 4 vols (1837–39).

Hammond, J. L. and Hammond, Barbara, *The Age of the Chartists* (1930; Hamden, Connecticut, 1962).

Hanson, Lawrence and Elisabeth, *Marian Evans and George Eliot* (1952).

Hardy, Barbara, *The Novels of George Eliot* (1959).

—————— (ed.), *Middlemarch: Critical Approaches to the Novel* (1967).

Harris, Horton, *David Friedrich Strauss and His Theology* (Cambridge, 1973).

Harrison, Frederic, *Autobiographic Memoirs*, 2 vols (1911).

Harrold, Charles Frederick, *Carlyle and German Thought: 1819–34* (New Haven and London, 1934).

Harvey, W. J., *The Art of George Eliot* (1961).

Harwood, Philip, *German Anti-Supernaturalism* (1841).

Hawthorne, Nathaniel, *The Blithedale Romance* (1852; with an Introduction by Moncure D. Conway, 1899).

Hayek, F. A. von, *John Stuart Mill and Harriet Taylor* (1951).

Hegel, G. W. F., *Lectures on the Philosophy of History*, translated from the 3rd German edition by J. Sibree (1849, 1888).

——————, *Early Theological Writings*, translated by T. M. Knox, with an Introduction and Fragments translated by Richard Kroner (Chicago, 1948).

Hennell, Charles C., *An Inquiry Concerning the Origin of Christianity* (1838).

Holloway, John, *The Victorian Sage*, (1953).

Houghton, Walter E., *The Victorian Frame of Mind* (New Haven and London, 1957).

Howe, P. P., *The Life of Hazlitt* (1922; Harmondsworth, 1949).

Hunt, James Leigh, *The Autobiography of Leigh Hunt* (revised edn, 1860; 1891).

Ilchester, The Earl of (ed.), *Elizabeth, Lady Holland to her Son, 1821–1845* (1946).

Inglis, K. S., *Churches and the Working Class in Victorian England* (1963).

Jacobs, Joseph, *George Eliot, Matthew Arnold, Browning, Newman* (1891).

James, Henry, *English Hours* (1905; 1962).

——————, *The House of Fiction*, edited with an Introduction by Leon Edel (1957).

Johnson, R. Brimley (ed.), *The Letters of Hannah More* (1925).

Joll, James, *The Anarchists* (1964).

Jones, Peter, *Philosophy and the Novel* (1975).

Jordan, Ruth, *George Sand* (1976).

Kamenka, Eugene, *The Philosophy of Ludwig Feuerbach* (1970).

Kaminsky, Alice R., *George Henry Lewes as Literary Critic* (Syracuse, N.Y., 1968).

Keble, John, *The Christian Year* (1827; Oxford and London, 1860).

Á Kempis, Thomas, *The Imitation of Christ*, preface by the late H. P. Liddon ([1889]).

Kent, Christopher, *Brains and Numbers* (Toronto, Buffalo and London, 1978).

King, Bolton, *The Life of Mazzini*, revised edn (1912).

Kingsley, Charles, *Alton Locke* (1850; 1889).

——————, *Glaucus* (1885; 1890).

Kipling, Rudyard, *Plain Tales from the Hills* (1888; 1913).

Kitchel, Anna T., *George Lewes and George Eliot* (New York, 1933).

Knoepflmacher, U. C., *Religious Humanism and the Victorian Novel* (Princeton, 1965).

Knox, R. A. *Enthusiasm* (Oxford, 1950).

Lamb, Charles, *The Essays of Elia and the Last Essays of Elia* (1901).

Larkin, Maurice, *Man and Society in Nineteenth-Century Realism* (1977).

Leavis, F. R., *The Great Tradition* (1948).

Lerner, Laurence, *The Truthtellers* (1967).

Linton, Mrs Eliza Lynn, *My Literary Life* (1899).

Lockhart, J. G., *The Life of Sir Walter Scott* (1837–38; new edn, 1 vol, 1850).

——————, *The Life of Sir Walter Scott* (abridged edn 1848; 1906).

Lovejoy, Arthur O., *Essays in the History of Ideas* (1948; Baltimore and London, 1970).

Lucas, John (ed.), *Literature and Politics in the Nineteenth Century* (1971).

Lukács, Georg, *The Historical Novel* (1st UK edn, 1962; Harmondsworth, 1969).

Lynes, Alice, *George Eliot's Coventry* (Coventry, 1970).

Macaulay, Thomas Babington, *History of England*, vol 1 and 2 (1848; 1906).

Mack, Mary P., *Jeremy Bentham* (1962).

Mckenzie, K. A., *Edith Simcox and George Eliot* (Oxford, 1961).

Martineau Harriet, *The Positive Philosophy of Auguste Comte*, 2 vols (1853).

Mazzini, Joseph, *Essays*, edited with an Introduction by William Clarke (n.d.).

Milner, Ian, *The Structure of Values in George Eliot* (Prague, 1968).

Mineka, Francis E., *The Dissidence of Dissent* (Chapel Hill, 1944).

Moore, George, *Conversations in Ebury Street* (1924).

Morell, J. D., *An Historical and Critical View of the Speculative Philosophy of Europe in the Nineteenth Century*, 2 vols (1846).

——————, *On the Philosophical Tendencies of the Age* (1848).

Morris, J. C., *Carlyle's Translation of J. P. F. Richter's Novels* (University of Bristol Thesis, March 1967).

Mozley, Rev. T., *Reminiscences Chiefly of Oriel College and the Oxford Movement*, 2 vols (1882).

Muirhead, John H., *Coleridge as Philosopher* (1930).

——————, *The Platonic Tradition in Anglo-Saxon Philosophy* (1931).

Mure, G. R. G., *An Introduction to Hegel* (Oxford, 1940).

Myers, F. W. H., *Essays Modern* (1883).

Newman, J. H., *Apologia pro Vita Sua* (1864, 1865; the two versions of 1864 and 1865, prefaced by Newman's and Kingsley's Pamphlets, with an Introduction by Wilfrid Ward, Oxford, 1913).

Newton, K. M., *George Eliot: Romantic Humanist* (London and Totowa, N.J., 1981).

Nichol, John, *Thomas Carlyle* (1892; 1902).

Noble, Thomas A., *George Eliot's 'Scenes of Clerical Life'* (New Haven, 1965).

Orsini, G. N. G., *Coleridge and German Idealism* (Carbondale and Edwardsville, 1969).

Owen, Robert, *The Life of Robert Owen by Himself* (1857–58); with an Introduction by M. Beer, 1920).

Packe, Michael St John, *The Life of John Stuart Mill* (1954).

Pailleron, Marie-Louise, *George Sand* (Paris, 1938).

Pankhurst, Richard K. P., *The Saint-Simonians, Mill and Carlyle* ([1957]).

Paris, Bernard J., *Experiments in Life: George Eliot's Quest for Values* (Detroit, 1965).

Pattison, Mark, *Memoirs* (1885; Introduction by Jo Manton, Fontwell, Sussex, 1969).

——————, *Essays*, 2 vols (Oxford, 1889).

Peel, J. D. Y., *Herbert Spencer* (1971).

Pelling, Henry, *The Origins of the Labour Party* (1954).

Prest, John, *The Industrial Revolution in Coventry* (Oxford, 1960).

Read, Donald, *The English Provinces* (1964).

Reardon, B. M. G., *From Coleridge to Gore* (1971).

Redinger, Ruby V., *The Emergent Self* (1976).

Roberts, Neil, *George Eliot* (1975).

Rousseau, Jean-Jacques, *Oeuvres complètes: Vol. I: Les Confessions: Autres textes autobiographiques* (Paris, 1959); *Vol. IV: Emile: Education – Morale – Botanique* (Paris, 1969).

—————, *Les Rêveries du promeneur solitaire*, texte établi avec Introduction, Notes et relevé de variants par Henri Roddier (Paris, 1960).

—————, *Emile*, translated by Barbara Foxley (1911).

Royce, Josiah, *Fugitive Essays* (1920; with an Introduction by J. Loewenberg, Freeport, N.Y., 1968).

Royle, Edward, *Victorian Infidel* (Manchester, 1974).

Ruskin, John, *Works* edited by E. T. Cook and Alexander Weddenburn, 39 volumes (1902–12).

—————, *Sesame and Lilies* (1865; 13th edition with new Preface, 1892).

Rutherford, Mark, *Mark Rutherford's Deliverance* (1885).

Ryland, J. E. (ed.), *The Life and Correspondence of John Foster*, 2 vols (1846).

Saint-Simon, Claude Henri de, *Social Organization, the Science of Man and Other Writings*, edited and translated with an Introduction by Felix Markham (1952; New York, 1964).

Sand, George, *Indiana* (1831; Oeuvres complètes, Calmann-Lévy, Editeurs, 3 Rue Auber, Paris, n.d.).

—————, *Lélia* (1833; 2 volumes, Oeuvres Complètes, Calmann-Lévy, Editeurs, 3 Rue Auber, Paris, n.d.).

—————, *Jacques* (1834; Calmann-Lévy Editeurs, 3 Rue Auber, Paris, 1928).

—————, *Lettres d'un voyageur* (1834; Oeuvres complètes, nouvelle édition, Michel Lévy Frères, Paris, 1869).

—————, *Mauprat* (1836; Nelson and Calmann-Lévy Editeurs, Paris, n.d.).

—————, *Spiridion* (1838–39; avec une Introduction de Charles Moulin, Les Belles Lectures, Paris, 1854).

—————, *Winter in Majorca* (1841; translated by Robert Graves, Mallorca, 1956).

—————, *Consuelo* (1842; 3 vols, Oeuvres complètes, nouvelle édition, Calmann-Lévy Editeurs, 3 Rue Auber, Paris, 1897–98).

—————, *Le Meunier d'Angibault* (1845; Oeuvres complètes, Calmann-Lévy Editeurs, 3 Rue Auber, Paris, n.d.).

—————, *François le champi* (Oeuvres complètes, nouvelle édition, Calmann-Lévy Editeurs, Paris, 1898).

Saunders, Charles Richard, *Carlyle's Friendships and Other Studies* (Durham, N.C., 1977).

Schweitzer, Albert, *The Quest of the Historical Jesus* (1906; translated by W. Montgomery, 1910).

Scott, Sir Walter, *The Waverley Novels* 24 vols (1912).

—————, *Tales of a Grandfather* (1828; 2 vols, 1898).

Seth, Andrew, *Scottish Philosophy* (1885; 3rd revised edn., 1899).

Shepherd, Richard Herne (ed.), *Memoirs of the Life and Writings of Thomas Carlyle*, 2 vols (1881).

Shine, Hill, *Carlyle and the Saint-Simonians* (Baltimore, 1941).

—————, *Carlyle's Early Reading to 1834* (Lexington, 1953).

Simmons, James C., *The Novelist as Historian* (The Hague/Paris, 1973).

Simon, W. H., *European Positivism in the Nineteenth Century* (Ithaca, N.Y., 1963).

Smith, Anne (ed.), *George Eliot: Centenary Essays and an Unpublished*

Notebook (1980).

Sorel, Albert, *Europe and the French Revolution* (1885; translated and edited by Alfred Cobban and J. W. Hunt, 1969).

Speare, M. E., *The Political Novel* (New York, 1924).

Spencer, Herbert, *Essays* (1858).

—————, *An Autobiography*, 2 vols (1904).

Spinoza, Benedict de, *The Chief Works*, translated from the Latin, with an Introduction by R. M. H. Elwes (Vol. I, 1908; Vol. II, revised edn, 1909).

Stang, Richard, *The Theory of the Novel in England 1850–1870* (1959).

Stephen, Leslie, *Studies of a Biographer*, 4 vols (1898–1902).

—————, *The English Utilitarians*, 3 vols (1900).

—————, *George Eliot* (1902).

Strauss, David Friedrich, *A New Life of Jesus* (1864; Authorized translation, 2 vols, 1865).

Sutherland, J. A., *Victorian Novelists and Publishers* (1976).

Symington, Andrew James, *Some Personal Reminiscences of Carlyle* (Paisley and London, 1886).

Taine, Hippolyte, *Le Positivisme anglais* (Paris, 1864).

—————, *L'idéalisme anglais* (Paris, 1864).

—————, *Notes on England* (1872; translated with an Introduction by Edward Hyams, 1957).

Tannahil, Reay, *Paris in the Revolution* (1966).

Taylor, Charles, *Hegel* (Cambridge, 1975).

Tennyson, Alfred Lord, *The Princess* (1847).

Thackeray, William, *Works*, 12 vols (1879).

Thale, Jerome, *The Novels of George Eliot* (New York, 1959).

Thomas, William, *The Philosophic Radicals* (Oxford, 1979).

Thomis, Malcolm I. and Holt, Peter, *Threats of Revolution in Britain 1789–1848* (1977).

Thomson, Patricia, *George Sand and the Victorians* (1977).

Thoreau, Henry David, *Walden or, Life in the Woods, and On the Duty of Civil Disobedience* (New York, 1961).

Tjoa, Hock Guan, *George Henry Lewes* (Cambridge, Mass., and London, 1977).

Tomlinson, J. B., *The English Middle-Class Novel* (London and Basingstoke, 1976).

Toynbee, Arnold, *An Historian's Approach to Religion* (1956).

Victoria History of the Counties of England. Warwickshire, Vols I–VIII (1904–69).

Voltaire, *Dictionnaire philosophique* (1764; texte établi par Raymond Naves, notes par Julien Benda, Paris, 1967).

Ward, Mrs. Humphry, *Robert Elsmere*, 3 vols (1888).

—————, *The History of David Grieve* (1892).

Waley, Daniel, *George Eliot's Blotter* (1980).

Warren, Alba H., *English Poetic Theory: 1825–1865* (Princeton, 1950).

Watt, Ian, *The Rise of the Novel* (1957).

Webb, Beatrice, *My Apprenticeship* (1926; Harmondsworth, 1971).

Webb, R. K., *Harriet Martineau* (1960).

Wellek, René, *Immanuel Kant in England: 1793–1838* (Princeton, 1931).

——————, *A History of Modern Criticism: 1750–1950: The Romantic Age* (1955).

Whittaker, Thomas, *Comte and Mill* (1908).

Wiley, Basil, *Nineteenth Century Studies* (1949).

——————, *Samuel Taylor Coleridge* (1972).

Williams, Raymond, *Culture and Society 1780–1950* (1958).

Wilson, David Alec, *Carlyle to 'The French Revolution'* (1924).

——————, *Carlyle on Cromwell and Others* (1925).

Wollstonecraft, Mary, *Mary* and *The Wrongs of Woman* (1788, 1798; edited by Gary Kelly, Oxford, 1976).

——————, *Vindication of the Rights of Woman* (1792; edited with an Introduction by Miriam Kramnick, Harmondsworth, 1975).

Woodward, W. L., *The Age of Reform*, corrected edn (Oxford, 1946).

Woolf, Virginia, *A Room of One's Own* (1929; 1977).

——————, *Three Guineas* (1938; Harmondsworth, 1977).

Young, G. M., *Victorian England; Portrait of an Age*, 2nd edn (Oxford, 1953).

Zeller, Eduard, *David Friedrich Strauss in His Life and Writings* (authorised translation, 1874).

Zola, Emile, *Le Roman expérimental* (1880; Paris 1933).

(b) Articles

(i) Those of Known Authorship

Acton, H. B., 'Comte's Positivism and the Science of Society', *Philosophy* XXVI (October 1951) 291–310.

Allot, Miriam, 'George Eliot in the 1860s', *Victorian Studies* V (December 1961) [93]–108.

Baumgarten, Henry, 'From Realism to Expressionism: Towards a History of the Novel', *New Literary History* VI (Winter 1975) [415]–27.

Belloc, Bessie Rayner, 'Dorothea Casaubon and George Eliot', *CR* LXV (February 1894) [207]–16.

Bissell, Claude T., 'Social Analysis in the Novels of George Eliot', *ELH* XVIII (September 1951) 221–39.

[Brewster, David], 'M. Comte's Course of Positive Philosophy', *ER* LXVIII (July1838) [271]–308.

[Brown, Thomas], 'Villers, *Philosophie de Kant*', *ER* I (January 1803) [253]–80.

[Chapman, John], 'George Eliot', *WR* LXVIII (July 1885) 161–208.

Collins, K. K. 'Questions of Method: Some Unpublished Late Essays', *NCF* XXXV (December 1980) 385–405.

[Conybeare, W. J.], 'Church Parties', *ER* XCVIII (October 1853) [273]–342.

Dodd, Valerie A., 'Strauss's English Propagandists and the Politics of Unitarianism: 1841–5', *Church History* L (December 1981) 415–35.

——————, 'A George Eliot Notebook', *Studies in Bibliography* XXXIV (1981) 258–62.

[Froude, J. A.], 'Spinoza', *WR* n.s. VIII (1 July 1855). [1]–37.

Haight, Gordon S., 'The Tinker Collection of George Eliot Manuscripts', *YULG* XXIX (April 1955) 148–50.

Haight, Gordon S., 'Cross's Biography of George Eliot', *YULG* XXV (July 1950) [1]–9.

───────, 'The George Eliot and George Henry Lewes Collection', *YULG* XXXV (July 1960) 170–1.

───────, 'The George Eliot and George Henry Lewes Collection', *YULG* XLVI (July 1971) 20–3.

───────, 'A New George Eliot Letter' *YULG* XLVI (July 1971) 24–8.

[Harrison, Frederic], 'The Life of George Eliot', *FR* XXVII (March 1885) [309]–22.

Harrold, Charles Frederick, 'The Mystical Element in Carlyle (1827–34)', *Modern Philology* XXIX (May 1932) 459–75.

Hough, Graham, 'Novelist-philosophers.–XII George Eliot', *Horizon* XVII (January 1948) 50–62.

[Huxley, T. H.], 'Contemporary Literature. Science.', *WR* n.s. V (January 1854) 254–70.

Hyde, William J., 'George Eliot and the Climate of Realism', *PMLA* LXXII (March 1957) 147–64.

James, Henry, 'Daniel Deronda: A conversation', *AM* Boston XXXVIII (December 1876) 684–94.

───────, 'George Eliot's Life', *AM* CCCXXXI, Boston LV (May 1885) 668–78.

Kaminsky, Alice R., 'George Eliot, George Henry Lewes, and the Novel', *PMLA* LXX (December 1955, 997–1013.

Kendrick, Walter M., 'Balzac and British Realism: Mid-Victorian Theories of the Novel', *Victorian Studies* XX (Autumm 1976) [5]–25.

Knoepflmacher, U. C., 'George Eliot, Feuerbach and the Question of Criticism', *Victorian Studies* VII (March 1964) [306]–9.

Levin, Harry, 'What is Realism?', *Comparative Literature* III (Summer 1951) 193–9.

Levine, George, 'Determinism and Responsibility in the Works of George Eliot', *PMLA* LXXVII (June 1962) 268–79.

───────, 'Intelligence as Deception: *The Mill on the Floss*', *PMLA* LXXX (September 1965) 402–9.

[Linton, Eliza Lynn], 'George Eliot', *Temple Bar* LXXIII (April 1885) 512–24.

Mansell, Darrell Jnr., 'A Note on Hegel and George Eliot', *Victorian Newsletter* 27 (Spring 1965) 12–15.

───────, 'Ruskin and George Eliot's "Realism"', *Criticism* III (Summer 1965) 203–16.

[Martineau, Harriet], 'The Political Life and Sentiments of Niebuhr', *LWR* n.s. II (July 1852) 142–73.

[Mazzini, Joseph], 'George Sand' *MC* (no month 1839) 23–40.

Merle, Gibbons, 'The Social System of Fourier', *Chamber's Edinburgh Journal* VIII (14 September 1839) 268–69.

Myers, Frederick W. H., 'George Eliot', *CM* XXIII (November 1881) 57–64.

[Oliphant, Margaret], 'Two Cities – Two Books', *BEM* CXVI (July 1874) 72–91.

[Palmer, William], 'On Tendencies Towards the Subversion of Faith', *EngR* X (December 1848) 399–444.

Paris, Bernard J., 'George Eliot and the Higher Criticism', *Anglia* LXXXIV (1966) [59]–73.

Perry, Sir Erskine, ' A Morning with Auguste Comte', *Nineteenth Century* II (November 1877) 621–31.

Pouthas, Charles, 'The Revolutions of 1848', *New Cambridge Modern History* edited by J. P. T. Bury (Cambridge, 1960) X, 389–415.

Robinson, Carole, '*Romola*: A Reading of the Novel', *Victorian Studies* VI (September 1962) [29]–42.

——————, 'The Severe Angel: A Study of *Daniel Deronda*', ELH XXXI (September 1964) 278–300.

Rust, James D., 'The Art of Fiction in George Eliot's Reviews', *The Review of English Studies* n.s. VII (1956) 164–72.

Salvan, Albert J., 'L'essence du réalisme français', *Comparative Literature* III (Summer 1951) 218–33.

Sarson, George, 'George Eliot and Thomas Carlyle', *Modern Review* II (April 1881) [399]–413.

[Southey, Robert], 'New Distribution of Property', QR XLV (July 1831) 407–50.

[Spencer, Herbert], 'The Universal Postulate', LWR n.s. IV (October 1853) 513–50.

——————, 'Auguste Comte – His Religion and Philosophy', BQR XIX (1 April 1854) [296]–376.

Stewart, Herbert L., 'Carlyle's Place in Philosophy', *Monist* (Chicago and London) XXIX (April 1919) [161]–89.

Svaglic, M. J. 'Religion in the Novels of George Eliot', *Journal of English and Germanic Philology* LIII (April 1954) 145–59.

Vogeler, Martha S., 'George Eliot and the Positivists', NCF XXXV (December 1980) 406–31.

Wright, T. R., 'George Eliot and Positivism: A Reassessment', MLR LXXVI Part 2 (April 1981) [257]–72.

Those of Unknown Authorship

'Coleridge as a Theologian', BAR XIX (1 January 1854) 112–59.

'The Critical and Miscellaneous Writings of Theodore Parker', *Christian Teacher* n.s. VI (no month) 212.

'Saint Simonism', *Dublin Review* IV (January 1838) 138–79.

(Signed 'FAIR-PLAY'), 'Letter on the doctrine of St. Simon, To the Editor of *Fraser's Magazine*', FM V (July 1832) 666–9.

'Reminiscences of Men and Things, By One who has a Good Memory. No. VI. The History and Mystery of St. Simonianism', FM XXVII (May 1843) 609–14.

'George Eliot and Comtism', LQR XLVII (January 1877) 446–71.

'George Eliot's Opinions about Religion', *Month* LIII (April 1855) [473]–82.

'Notes on the Press: A Catholic View of George Eliot', *Month and Catholic Review* XXIII and XLII (June 1881) [272]–78.

(Signed 'Y') 'Thomas Carlyle and George Eliot', *Nation* XXXII (24 March 1881) 201–2.

'Letters from Thomas Carlyle to the Socialists of 1830, *New Quarterly* II (April 1909) 277–88.

'Saint-Simonianism &c', WR XVI (April 1832) [279]–321.

'Contemporary Literature of England', LWR n.s. I (January 1852) 247–88.

'Contemporary Literature of England' LWR n.s. II (April 1852) 625–62.

'Contemporary Literature of England', *LWR* n.s. II (July 1852) 550–83.
'Contemporary Literature of England', *LWR* n.s. II (October 1852) 247–72.
'Contemporary Literature of England', *LWR* n.s. III (January 1852) 264–87.
'Contemporary Literature of England', *LWR* n.s. III (April 1852) 585–605.
'Contemporary Literature of England', *LWR* n.s. IV (July 1853) 246–74.
'The Progress of Fiction as an Art', *LWR* n.s. IV (October 1853) 342–74.
'George Eliot as a Novelist', *WR* n.s. LIV (1 July 1878) 105–35.
'Illusion and Delusion: The Writings of Charles Bray', *WR* n.s. LV (1 April 1879) 488–506.
'George Eliot: Her Life and Writings', *WR* n.s. LX (July 1881) 154–98.

Index

Cobden, Richard, 84, 197; *see also*
  Anti-Corn Law League
Cohen, 202, 204
Coleridge, Samuel Taylor, on Idealism,
  10f; on Locke, 10; influence on
  ME, 81, 86f, 93f; influence on
  Lewes, 203f; 18f, 41, 49f, 90, 97,
  100f, 105, 109, 113f, 118, 120, 122,
  147, 156f, 174, 176, 183, 191, 225,
  229, 233, 247, 250, 259, 266, 281,
  289, 291ff, 299, 301, 313 *passim*
  Biographia Literaria, 10, 11, 37, 94,
    250
  Confessions, 11
  Lay Sermons, 11
Combe, George, 81f, 84, 159ff, 163f,
  166, 198f, 228, 240, 242
Communism, 111, 119, 222
Comte, Auguste, 115–20; influence on
  Mill, 47; and the Unknown, 122;
  influence on ME, 6, 148ff, 156,
  193f, 288ff; influence on Spencer,
  177ff; influence on Lewes, 204ff,
  236–7, 238–9, 260; influence on
  WR, 273, 274–5ff; 4, 33f, 107, 110,
  112ff, 127f, 131, 142f, 145, 152f,
  159, 163, 170, 190, 195, 207f, 214,
  218, 226, 229–30ff, 245f, 250, 254f,
  256ff, 271, 281, 284, 286, 301f, 308,
  312, 314 *passim*
  Bibliothèque prolétaire, 127, 205
  Catéchisme des industriels, 113
  Cours de philosophie positive, 47, 113,
    118, 178, 208
  Système de politique positive, 180, 236
Condillac, Étienne, 22, 49
'Condition of England' Question, 46
Condorcet, Jean Antoine, Marquis de,
  119, 180, 215, 235, 288
Confessions, see Rousseau
Congreve, Maria [*née* Bury], 74, 146
Congreve, Richard, 114, 146
'Contemporary Literature' series, 199,
  274; *see also Westminster Review*
Conybeare, William John, 195
Coventry, 68, 79f, 82ff, 100, 111, 121,
  143–4, 147, 156, 159f, 160, 164ff,
  170, 173, 213, 227, 246
Coventry Herald, 82, 130, 159
Crimean War, 241
Critic, The, 163
Cross, John Walter, 4, 70, 99, 167, 201,
  228
Cumming, Dr John, 280, 287, 303, 309

Cuvier, 258; *see also* St Hilaire

D'Albert Durade, Alexandre François,
  99, 100, 105
D'Alembert, Jean le Rond, 12, 18, 26,
  40
Daniel Deronda, see Eliot, George
Darwin, Charles, 81, 112
  Origin of Species, 233
Das Leben Jesu, see Strauss, David
  Friedrich
Dawson, George, 84, 106, 111
D'Eichtal, Gustave, 26, 28–9, 30, 39,
  43f
Defence of Poetry, 37; *see also* Shelley,
  Percy Bysshe
Descartes, René, 182, 235
Dessoir, Ludwig, 243
Dickens, Charles, 2, 10, 13, 129, 197,
  199, 204, 210, 268, 307, 312
  Dombey and Son, 129
  Martin Chuzzlewit, 129
  A Tale of Two Cities, 10
Diderot, Denis, 18, 129
Digby, Sir Kenelm, 288, 307
Disraeli, Benjamin, 129, 130, 143, 149,
  169, 269, 312
Dissent, 17, 19, 21, 40, 45, 53f, 56, 63,
  70, 85, 88, 101, 148, 154, 160, 173,
  194, 236
Divorce
  reform, 41
  commissioners, 167, 227
Dublin Review, 113
Dumas, Alexander, 215, 263
Dumont, Pierre, 12, 22
Durade, M. D'Albert, *see* D'Albert
  Durade, Alexandre François

Eckerman, J.P., 256
Eclecticism, 39, 44, 49, 56, 120
Economist, 174
Edgeworth, Mrs Maria, 3
Edinburgh Review, 12, 54, 221
Eichhorn, Johann Gottfried, 89
Eliot, George, at the Priory, 2; and
  ideals of womanhood, 3; and
  Comte, 4, 109–28, 193; interest in
  George Sand, 5, 132–42; influence
  of Carlyle and Mill, 6, 16, 20, 67,
  76; at Griff, 6, 31, 69, 74, 81;
  early reading, 6, 68, 74–5;
  urban/rural background, 69;
  education, 70, 71; and Scott, 72;